Noble Firs

By Jayne Menard

Noble Firs

By Jayne Menard

www.jaynemenard.com

International Standard Book Number ISBN: 978-0-9975373-2-1

Also by Jayne Menard

The Spook Hills Trilogy
Book 1: Old Growth & Ivy
Book 2: New Growth

Author's Note

In *Noble Firs* Brian Tovey and Moll O'Leary are former FBI Agents who left the Bureau to found a startup company aimed at protecting banks from illicit money laundering schemes. Each of the men wants to define new lives for themselves, meet their individual expectations and keep up with the meteoric growth in demand for their company's services. Tall and slender, Brian is often likened to an Italian male fashion model. Equally tall and thin with silvery curled hair, Moll hides his brains and his talents behind a somewhat goofy demeanor.

With one man cautious and meticulous and the other laid back and casual, they find themselves challenged by their psychological and emotional barriers as they work to expand their lives. Even as they rise to these challenges, younger leaders in the underworld organize to strike back after Brian and Moll uncover a money laundering scheme leading to the arrests of several senior mobsters. Will Brian and Moll survive to see the futures they each want?

Noble Firs is the third book of the Spook Hills Trilogy. While the story stands alone, the roots of its characters and plot are in *Old Growth & Ivy* and *New Growth*, the first novels in the trilogy. Over the course of the three books, the stories of FBI agent extraordinaire, Steve Nielsen, and his three top agents are told as each one struggles to define a new life for himself away from the FBI. At 60 years old Steve meets the love of his life and continues to transform himself into a broader man. Steve's story is in the first book of the trilogy.

Mathew Heylen, Steve's friend, best agent and now business partner, also seeks to find his life-long love while founding a vineyard in the Oregon wine country, which they jokingly dubbed Spook Hills. *New Growth* is about Mathew and his desire to find someone to share his life. Handsome Mathew finds his childhood fear of rejection stands in his way while old and new business with the FBI disrupts his life. Even so he is drawn to his neighbor's niece who visits occasionally but is married and living in California.

I invite you to curl up by the fire or stretch out in the shade and enjoy a good read with *Noble Firs* as we follow the challenges and personal growth of Brian Tovey and Moll O'Leary.

Dedication

Noble Firs is dedicated to my faithful furry friends who served as my supporters. Even when my corgi, Missy, would rather be out in the garden with me or my cat Pagan would have preferred cuddling, each one helped me find the fortitude to write and edit. Sadly Pagan is no longer with me, but his memory is an inspiration of feistiness and purring loyalty. May sweet yet cheeky Missy encourage me in future endeavors for many years.

Acknowledgements

My heartfelt appreciation to my wonderful preview readers -- Cindy Gelezinsky, Marilee Haase, Sandy Pfaff and Jane Siebert. Their support, comments and edits have meant more to me than they know.

Part I: Deluded

May-August, 2016

Chapter 1

Brian

In London Brian Tovey came awake with his face buried in a sweet-smelling fluffy pillow. Although cozy in the warmth of the bed, a wave on unease slid over him. The lithe body of his lover, Emma, lay on his left under his arm. A hand glided down his back. Larger than her hand but almost as silken soft. Gathering himself, he tossed off the covers and sprang backward, landing on his knees at the foot of the bed. Emma continued sleeping on his left. A man smiled at him on his right.

"Who the hell are you?" Brian hissed through his teeth.

"Peter – Emma's husband," the man said in an upper-crust voice. "You are her lover-of-the-night, I presume? As usual her taste is exquisite -- you could have stepped out of a Botticelli painting."

Brian scooted off the bed, hit the floor and rushed to gather his clothes left folded in a neat stack on a chair. He yanked up his boxer shorts, scrambled into his undershirt and pulled on his suit pants.

"No need to go," the man named Peter said. "This could be brilliant."

The scattered wrappers of Brian's used condoms on the nightstand mortified Brian. The man's lack of anger at finding him in bed with his wife was so bizarre the entire scene took on a surreal distortion.

"I don't understand what you're playing at. This is not my game. Emma never indicated she is married." Brian kept his voice low, wanting to slip away before Emma woke up.

"Emma likes variety. I like men. This works for us. Why not stay for the weekend?"

"No way. I am not into threesomes." Brian pulled on his shirt and then

1

scooped up his tie, socks, shoes and blazer.

"You Americans can be so provincial, although I have met the odd adventuresome one," Peter said as he rolled on his back and stretched to show his full manhood. In the dim light from the street, the man appeared blond, thin and not well-hung. His derisive expression might one day become cruel and mocking.

Disgusted with himself for falling into this situation, Brian dashed out of the room, jamming his feet into his socks and shoes, shrugging into his jacket and grabbing his Mac from the sofa. As he headed to the door, soft laughter came from the bedroom followed by the muted tones of Emma's voice.

This past night stood out as the capper on his debauchery of the last eighteen months. Brian needed to stop this uncharacteristic behavior of his now. Stepping out into the middle of the night light of London, he left the chic Mayfair apartment and began walking through a mist of rain and fog, hoping to find the all-night Starbucks he remembered on Berkeley Square.

Once fortified with a hot sweet latte, Brian walked on as he tried to calm the muddle of images flying through his head. Emma hung out with a group he had hooked up with more than a year ago. As a fast-moving crowd of singles, they liked to drink and party. No one paired up for more than a night or two as they moved through their lives. The fluid, easy-going and affluent group turned his head. As a guy from the Italian section of Boston who worked on improving himself every day, being welcomed into their group had captivated Brian and flattered his ego.

A couple of times at his place and once out in the country, he had slept with the temptress Emma. Tall and slender, her strawberry blonde hair fell in waves down her back, giving her a Lady Godiva image when naked. Sometimes she paired off with another guy, while at other times in the city she would leave early without saying goodbye, simply disappearing. Last night marked the first time she ever invited him to her flat.

Heading towards the financial district where he maintained a loft for his weeks in London, Brian walked along the Strand. Passing St. Paul's Cathedral, he slowed and stopped to sit on the damp steps and consider the mess he had let himself drift into. At forty-four and unattached by choice, his current lifestyle verged towards degeneracy.

Suffused in the fog off the Thames, the streets were fairly quiet around him. While Brian liked London, right then he wanted to be back at his adopted home in Oregon, working with his two partners and away from the crowd he had let seduce him.

A year and a half ago the startup of the London office attracted him because he had hoped a European location might put him closer to a woman he had guarded for a few days and never encountered again -- Annetta. In appearance she was as elegant as a Ming vase. Underneath her controlled exterior, she had struck him as almost as fragile. Her startling turquoise eyes reminded him of the aqua seas of the Caribbean. The features in her oval face with her defined chin and cheekbones were edgy like a piece of art. In his mind the perfect tilt of each angle collected into harmonious, alluring beauty.

Annetta's vulnerability had attracted him the most. After the abuse she had suffered as a child, she had disguised herself as a man who bought and sold information in the underworld. Rather than finding a hardened criminal, he had discovered a self-contained woman revealing snippets of a gentle, caring and delicate nature.

Some guys would think him prudish for turning down the threesome invitation, but that failed to matter to him. Finding Emma's husband in bed with them crystallized his perceptions. His drifting lifestyle eroded what he prized in himself. He always aimed to be the worthy man. Careful in his habits, diligent, meticulous at analysis and dedicated to their company, he had taken a detour in his personal life. He would not continue in the same direction. He must stop now and force himself to polish his values and redirect his life. Brian rose and began walking back to his flat wanting to put his resolution into a goal with a list of action steps.

Chapter 2

Moll

Early that evening in Portland Oregon, Moll O'Leary pushed back from his desk and frowned. Everything about their company was clicking along. Business was steadily growing, the financials were in good order and their staff was first rate. Even so a sense of unease lurked on the fringes of his mind as if an issue skulked in the shadows, not a small forgotten item on a checklist, but something major.

Outside spring continued to warm as the long rainy season of a Pacific Northwest winter scuttled haphazardly away to make room for the sun and summer. While the sixth of July could be counted on to signal the start of warm, bright days, May thus far varied widely with showers one minute and sun the next.

When his business partner Terry sounded his familiar rat-tat-tat on the door jamb, Moll turned to greet him. At the sight of Terry's clasped jaw and intense gray eyes peering through his blue-tinted wire glasses, Moll asked, "What's wrong?"

With a quick glance around, Terry walked in and closed the door. "I think everyone is gone for the weekend, but just in case let's talk behind closed doors. Check your inbox. I sent you some files," Terry said. "Start with the first email."

Spinning back to his PC, Moll opened the file, rotating his flat screen to allow them both to view what Terry sent him.

"In reviewing transactions for the bank we signed a week ago in Baltimore, I spied these six."

Moll checked the records, which ranged from five thousand to a million dollars in odd figures. They followed a pattern of money movement from the Baltimore area to Istanbul. "Not seeing the issue."

"Next email. I researched the businesses involved. None appear to be operating entities. Paper companies."

As Terry leaned over and pointed at the screen, Moll caught the familiar minty scent of his long curly blond hair from the shampoo he used. Whether a whiff of a woman's perfume, a heady aroma of Italian herbs or the tang of fresh-cut evergreen boughs, natural fragrances stood out as the first and most memorable to Moll's senses. Color came next in his sensory impressions. He had set the standard in their company to color-code any findings in their analysis to highlight unique characteristics.

Without further discussion, Moll read through the second email. "Smart cross-check on those companies. Interesting."

"Diabolical is more like it," Terry said. "I remembered encountering similar transactions last month in another client's file but they didn't strike me as suspicious at the time. Today I traced them. Same patterns. Same or analogous companies. While the initiating banks are different, the destination accounts are owned by the same companies or by ones named in the same way. So far I didn't find any operating entities. Checked two other banks in the same locale and discovered similar financial transactions."

"Money laundering. We've seen patterns like this before back at the Bureau and here at Noble Firs," Moll said. "We'll need to report them. What put your jeans in a twist?"

"This is my fault, dammit. I missed seeing the problem before when reviewing the transactions. How could I have failed to see the pattern?" The tightening of Terry's cheeks along his jaw pulled his mouth into a thin line of annoyance with himself.

"The sample was too small as if someone counted on keeping the quantities down to throw off scrutiny. Let's not panic," Moll said. "We'll work tonight and through the weekend until we figure out how extensive the concern is."

"This means going back to our clients with corrected reports. They'll freak out. Their compliance filings are reliant on the information we supply."

"We'll worry about client communications after we understand the scope," Moll said. "Com'on Terry – this is one heck of a find. Your unique snapshot memory identified this concern. Only you would recall this pattern of six doubtful transactions in the gazillions of records we process."

From behind his high-tech glasses, Terry regarded him with a doleful expression. "Why aren't you pissed at me?"

"Why would I be? We're like a team. Shit happens, man. Now we're on the cleanup committee." Wanting to ease Terry's anguish, Moll grinned in his lop-sided way.

As former FBI agents, Moll and his partner Brian each aimed to continue fighting crime. Although his experience came from the business sector, Terry shared their commitment to their enterprise. Together they became a potent force, drawing energy from the successes of their activities and from each other. After being shot at in FBI operations, a small finding like this would only unnerve him if the reputation of their company might be put at risk.

As if reading his mind, Terry said, "This could kick us right in the nuts."

"You know what's weird? I've had this bizarre feeling of some skulking issue haunting me. Thought I was getting paranoid, but here it is. Everything has been going so well, then bam -- we get hit on the back of the head with a shovel. Nothing for it, but to scope the problem out. If more findings turn up, we'll call Brian-boy to get his input."

Balling up his fists by his sides, Terry almost vibrated with emotion as he stood in front of him. Sometimes Terry's passion for his work made him lose perspective until he worried himself into a state. His double-edged intensity flashed out both as a strength and a weakness. While they shared the same business goals and values, in disposition they differed. Terry's emotional states pumped him up until he acted as touchy as a teenager with rampant hormones.

"We'll get through this, Terry. First let's scope out how big the problem is."

After a couple of hours of searching through the records for the most recent six banks, Moll accepted the gravity of their situation. He walked out of his office to talk with Terry about a plan to go through more data.

As he approached Terry swiveled his head away from his computer, his face whitening with fury. "Our fucking database administrator archived all the earlier files for completed clients."

"What? Tom did that? At least six months' worth of data should be available to us. That is our documented standard."

"He's always quoting rules at us like we didn't write them," Terry hissed through his teeth. "I remember him saying a few weeks ago the servers experienced performance concerns, but I never followed up on the comment. I'm going to find out what the hell's going on."

When Terry reached for his cell phone, Moll grabbed his hand. "Don't."

"Why the hell not? We need the data."

"What if he's covering the tracks for some money launderers?"

"Now you're reverting to an FBI agent, suspicious of everyone."

"Terry, think about this. Did we ever experience any performance slowdowns? No one here or in London mentioned any. Let's restore the databases ourselves to a separate server and keep this contained for now."

Since Terry set his jaw in the way he did when he became determined, Moll waited for a continued argument, but Terry stayed silent. He sat hunched over his phone in his standard Portland casual – hiking boots, plaid shirt with the sleeves rolled up and blue jeans – all pressed and tidy with his shirt-tail tucked in. Neatness for Terry sprang from his obsession with having control, whereas Moll struggled to maintain the tidy appearance and work habits he had learned from his chief mentor in the FBI.

While Moll admired Terry's passion about their work, he lacked his adamant assurance when he perceived himself to be in the right. On the flip side, Moll listened to what others said with a more open mind than Terry. In creativity they were brain-twinners.

Reaching into the back pocket of his jeans, Moll pulled out his wallet, "Hundred bucks if you're right and I'm a suspicious ex-agent."

"Easy money," Terry said, visibly relaxing a little. "I think you may be turning paranoid, but if you arrange space at the server farm, I'll start the restore procedures."

"Turn off the audit trail while they're running."

Terry pushed his glasses up a little higher and began clicking around on his PC. "Gotta find my notes on how to disable the logging feature."

Moll searched for the 24-hour technical service line for their outsourced server farm and dialed, listening to the ring as he returned to his office. Despite the circumstances, he smiled a little. Using a bet to sway Terry from one of his pig-headed stances proved an effective way to deflect his stubbornness. They ran about fifty-fifty on who won.

He completed the call, emailed the technical IP address of the server to Terry, pushed back from his desk, rose and stared out the window. If this find of Terry's proved extensive, the reputation of their business would be tarnished and even irreparably damaged. Everything they had worked for over the past three years could be put at risk. Would this be a fatal blow or would their business survive and thrive? Financial data investigation and identifying suspect transactions were what he and Brian carried from their FBI careers into the business world. This type of data analysis work was all Terry had ever done. Their hearts, their livelihoods and their dreams were all here at Noble Firs.

Moll stood slouched over with his hands in his pockets. He had learned early on that life can kick a person in painful ways, but he rarely let himself worry about it. His nature was to look ahead and hope for the best. He stood up straighter. None of them were quitters. They would find a way through this. No matter how dark the outlook might appear, he had to focus on the best way to continued success.

A half hour later Terry was back in his office doorway. "Restore routine is running with logging off. Will take a few hours to complete the restore and rebuilding the indices."

"Let's update Brian, grab dinner and check back on status. We should catch some shut-eye and hit the analysis fresh in the morning."

"We're expected for dinner down at Spook Hills Sunday night – let's reschedule. One glance from your old mentor Steve, and you'll spew out the details of this problem faster than a sinner in a confessional," Terry said, shaking his head and making his long blond curls bob back and forth.

Moll jumped up, ready to get some food even though Terry blocked the doorway. Since they stood about the same height, when Moll confronted Terry's intent gaze, their eyes met on the same plane.

"And if Ivy senses anything," Moll said, to help Terry keep his perspective, "she will pry the specifics out of you."

"This is our business. If we identify a concern, we should handle it. Only then should we communicate the results to our board when necessary."

"They are not only on our board of directors. They are investors. Most important they are buddies. Any one of them would put their own priorities aside to help us. You don't exclude your friends."

"You might be into the rah-rah team stuff from your days playing secret agent man with the FBI. I'm not. I stand on my own." Terry stepped forward in an aggressive stance, almost shouting in Moll's face. "This isn't the damn FBI. This is a business, and we aren't under gunfire."

Even as Terry glared at him, Moll understood his friend well enough to know that his anger came from annoyance with himself for not having seen the problem earlier as well as from a fear of how much this issue could hurt their business.

"Still best buds?" Moll said, holding out his arm for a fist bump.

Tucking his hair behind one ear, Terry regarded Moll with a pained expression, tapped his fist and said in a softened tone, "Too much alike not to be friends."

Moll turned to grab his jacket when he realized he scheduled a date this weekend. "Oh, crap. Made a date for tomorrow night. Yikes."

"With the screwy gal?" Terry asked, peering at Moll over his glasses.

"She's quirky. She'll blow if I cancel."

"So cancel. Might be to your benefit to find someone less volatile."

Moll nodded. "Dating is depressing, you know? Like, why can't I stick with anyone?"

"You're asking me? Mr. Gay-but-Stranded? No wonder we work so much. What the heck, let's go for a burger and fries over at the Veritable Quandary before they close."

"Now you're talking. I'll give Brian a jingle after we order. Some ale, a decent meal and a few hours of sleep will let us hit the analysis tomorrow with a refreshed perspective."

As they left the office suite, Moll pondered his dating situation. He wanted a wife and a family but he tended to date women who were idiosyncratic. Maybe he was too hard to please or expected too much or maybe he simply related to guys better. Even as obsessive as Terry could sometimes be, they remained best buddies. He always felt as sure of Terry as he did about his legacy FBI friends. Their strong bonds transcended minor disagreements or even heated arguments. He wanted love with that same strong bond as a foundation.

Chapter 3
Brian

As he finished the action list at the desk in his apartment, Brian's cell phone gave the ring sound he reserved for his two business partners. A glance at the number told him the call came from Moll.

"Moll?" Brian said into the phone, glad of the distraction. It would be almost nine Friday night in Portland but still an unusual hour for his partner and friend to call given that it was nearing four a.m. in London. Moll would be in his Friday casual attire, slightly disheveled, but with a glow of concentration in his eyes.

"Hey man. Gnarly problem here. This afternoon Terry happened across a few transactions ringing the proverbial bell with him. Same format and content as he remembered in another bank's files. Might be a new pattern of money laundering."

"What's the issue? We research the extent of its impact and go back to both clients."

"Like this may be a problem we didn't detect before. The suspect records are showing up in data from other banks too."

"You're thinking of our liability for not reporting the issue earlier?"

"This has the potential to ruin us."

Brian's gut tightened making the coffee churn around inside him. Their Noble Firs Company formed the center of his life. In their third year as a successful startup, their growth continued to be spectacular. Sometimes they careened along as if on a roller coaster with no end in sight, going faster and faster as more banks contracted for their services.

Did they miss identifying problems in their clients' records? With their state-of-the-art software, they reviewed hundreds of millions of transactions each year, checking for patterns in the data representing illegal operations or monetary transfers.

"Let's not panic," Brian said to Moll. "We'll review all the original client files processed in the last three months. How many suspect records are we talking about?"

"Around six per client, running between one and three million smackeroos."

"Six? Out of how many millions of records reviewed? You're lucky to find them at all."

"Our clients might not share your perspective. Remarkable that Terry discovered this issue. Only he possesses such a super ability to recall this pattern in so few records."

Making a quick decision, Brian said, "I'll hop on a flight out today. Text you my arrival time. Nothing happening here I can't work on from Portland."

"We're supposed to go to dinner down at Steve and Ivy's on Sunday night. I better cancel."

"We'll need to brief them anyway. May as well communicate with them while we're at Spook Hills."

"Terry wants to keep this contained," Moll said.

"Steve, Ivy, and Mathew are on our board. They invested money in our company, for chrissakes. No way can we avoid telling them."

"You don't have to tell me. They're like family to us, but Terry is adamant."

"We'll discuss disclosure when I see you. Reload the databases and grab some sleep. We're in for some hard days."

"Thanks, Brian-boy. Better knowing you're on your way across the pond."

"We'll make our way through this crisis. Ivy can help us with the communications to our clients. She likely ran into something similar during her executive life."

"Excellent point. Later, guy," Moll said and ended the call.

Brian selected Delta Airlines in his list of contacts, listening to the voice response system. At least this crisis would take his mind off his screwy personal life. He would use this break to find his way back from this mudslide he had slipped into.

Chapter 4

Terry

On Sunday evening down at the Spook Hills vineyard, the four former agents plus Terry sat in the living room at Steve and Ivy's house. Tantalizing aromas of roasting chickens filled the air making Terry's stomach rumble despite his worries. While examining the data with Moll and Brian on Saturday and all day Sunday, they found similar transactions for four more clients worked on during the last six months. Now they faced going back in three-month blocks of time until no similar transactions turned up.

"Something is going on with you three. May as well tell us," Steve said in his blunt way to Brian, Moll and Terry. He leaned forward in his chair, his eyes warm but penetrating.

Brian exchanged a glance with Moll who nodded at him, while Terry pressed his lips together and shook his head in the negative. Although he still did not agree with disclosing their issue, Brian and Moll remained convinced they needed help. While he was closer to Moll from working with him every day, Brian was more of the businessman. He was polished and as handsome as an actor, yet he was painstakingly careful when doing analysis work. What Brian might lack in creativity, he made up for in diligence. Brian had the coolest head of the three of them, but Terry never doubted his commitment.

"While we don't want to raise an alarm, you're on our board, you're our investors and most importantly, you're our friends," Brian began. "On Friday we found an issue which might prove ruinous to our business."

Moving from the doorway to the kitchen, Ivy stepped forward and rested her hip on the arm of Steve's chair.

Brian waited until she was settled. "Terry, you identified this issue. Would you explain what you found?"

After an annoyed glare at his partner for drawing him into this disclosure, Terry shifted his eyes over to Ivy. Before joining Noble Firs, he had worked for her until her retirement. Ivy had always been his supporter. Often a demanding and sometimes fiery boss when needing results in a hurry, with him she was direct but supportive.

With her knack for sensing his deepest troubles, Ivy held his eyes with her clear gaze. Never did she let him down. She had helped him work through frustrating times at the office, celebrated victories in his career and assisted him through personal struggles after a past relationship floundered. If he did not speak now, he risked tarnishing Ivy's regard for him.

"Certain transactions – six to be exact – appeared familiar in a new client's files," Terry began. "Standalone they did not jump out as suspicious. However they resembled records we encountered in another bank. Since they appeared in the transactions from two banks, those six raised a red flag."

"What alarmed you about them?"

"Money flowing from east coast cities to Istanbul. Significant sums, though never more than a million at a time. Similar business names on the originating and destination companies. In researching the corporations, nothing about them indicated they are operating entities. As we kept digging, Moll and I found the same sort of transactions in two more clients. Never more than six in any one bank's data."

"Today we unearthed additional comparable records in another four sets of files handled in the last three months," Moll said with a glance at him. "Only Terry possesses the keen memory to realize the same types of transactions appeared last month in another client's data."

Observing Moll as he spoke, Terry noticed the smooth flow of his voice. As soon as Moll focused on business, he dropped the colorful expressions often peppering his speech. He used a mishmash of jargon from pop language as far back as the seventies. If such things existed as soulmates, Moll was his.

"How much in total?" Mathew asked.

"Across the eight clients? A little short of ten million."

"Now you need to go back further in time," Steve said, arching an eyebrow at Ivy. "If you need us, we can start tomorrow to help with the analysis. Mathew will be tied up here."

"Since we didn't find them before, we're worried about our liability," Terry said.

Every person in the room contemplated Terry's words, but all eyes focused on Ivy. Her long history of business experience gave her the best perspective.

"Easy to explain," Ivy said, although she spoke without her characteristic smile. "In such small quantities as these, only experts of your caliber would have spotted them at all. If you handle this right, you could appear as heroes. By presenting the facts clearly, you will be perceived as so on top of things you keep researching a client's data even after you finished a project for them."

"Besides," Mathew said, "you're protected by those hedge-words in your contract terms about only certifying the results based on the state-of-the-art at the time and reliance on the files provided."

Brian said, "Although we have the clause, I would hate to quarrel over a technicality. Wouldn't reliance on our contract make us appear defensive?"

Mathew nodded. "Right. If you want to retain your client base, better to own up to the oversight, however minuscule your chances were of finding the potentially bogus financial records."

"Ivy, will you work with us on the communication to our clients?" Brian asked.

"Sure will."

Mathew's wife, Callie, said, "I'm not in classes now. I can help if you show me what to do. Perhaps I could document the research process and the results."

"Definitely," Terry said. He had taken a liking to Callie from the first time he met her. "We need someone to be meticulous in logging our actions for each client and in documenting our findings."

"You appreciate you have to report these results, right?" Steve said, his eyes turning the icy blue Terry remembered from the first time he encountered the big agent before he retired from the FBI.

"To the Treasury Department or the Bureau?" Brian asked. "First we must scope the problem out in full. Make sure our analysis is performed with care, and our findings are confirmed. Once we are confident we defined the extent of the problem, we will inform our clients and discuss taking the facts to the responsible government entity."

Steve frowned and peered up at Ivy who nodded her confirmation. "Since this impacts multiple banks, Brian's approach is acceptable. Speed is of the essence, however."

"Not more than accuracy," Terry said with a sharp edge in his voice. "We don't want to compound our dilemma with any false or incomplete findings.

"Agreed," Steve said, his eyes softening to a warmer gray-blue. "Terry, you haven't worked much with the FBI. In a matter such as this without a ticking time-bomb, the FBI proceeds in a planned, deliberate manner. While in all probability some underworld characters are laundering money, if the FBI acted with undue haste, they would risk losing their case. Back with the Bureau, I moved as fast as possible on cases. Nevertheless as Brian, Moll and Mathew will attest, we never moved ahead without conclusive evidence."

When each of the three former agents nodded their heads in agreement, Mathew said, "We had to have painstakingly acquired and documented facts."

"Furthermore when a company stepped forward and owned up to an issue without being forced to do so, their forthrightness earned them leniency. The same should be true for your banks under contract."

Terry glanced over at Brian and Moll. "A review procedure of the findings must be established. We want four sets of eyes on each client's files. Two of us will do the analysis with a different two people reviewing the results. By working from here, we run less risk of alarming our employees. Moll will return to Portland to keep projects running in the office."

"Let's eat dinner and make this an early night. Do you want to stay here?" Ivy asked. "Guest rooms are made up."

"Thanks," Terry said. "I brought my Firewire cat on the assumption we could stay here. Hope that's okay."

Ivy nodded, and Steve said, "Sure. As a side thought, all the detail from your clients should be fed into a repository to run comparatives against accumulated history."

"They might not like having their data co-mingled with other banks," Brian said, his brow furrowing with concern.

"Agree with each of you," Terry said. "Been on my list, but other priorities kept coming up. Brian, we can devise our own confidential pseudo-keys which will hide any direct links to the individual client. By handling the information in such a manner, I believe the banks working with us would agree."

Followed by Callie and Mathew, Ivy slipped back out to the kitchen leaving the other four to map out specific plans for the next few days. Now at ease with bringing in Steve, Terry realized how much he had misread him. The big man projected a dominant image, yet he offered to roll up his sleeves and work with them under their direction.

His thoughts drifted to his partner. Moll had attracted him right from the first time they worked together. The excitement of finding another guy who thought the way he did had appealed to him. Each of them commanded the quickness to focus on possibilities outside of the norm, yet possessed the discipline to ascertain the facts. He liked Moll's appearance with his gray eyes and corkscrew silvery brown hair topping his six-foot lanky frame.

About eighteen months later when Moll had called him and asked him to join Noble Firs, he had accepted the job with alacrity. In a few months Brian and Moll had offered him a partnership. Working with Moll had deepened his initial attraction, yet he continued to hold back from telling Moll his feelings. The barrier between straight men and gay men remained too high, and he feared placing his friendship with Moll at risk.

Late in the afternoon the next day when Steve and Brian walked out in the vineyard to speak with Mathew, Terry decided to talk with Ivy because he remained closer to her than anyone else besides his two business partners.

"Hey Terry," Ivy said when he walked into the kitchen. "Right about now, I think you might like a cold mug of ale."

"Nothing would be better," Terry answered as he went to the overstuffed chair to pick up his bright gold Firewire cat who always received a warm welcome here at Spook Hills.

"Let's sit by the fire. The rain makes the house chilly." Ivy scooped up her own cat, an old grey-striped ball of purr named Druid. After a day of hunting out in the young grapevines, the cats now appeared to want only companionable sleep, cuddling and dinner in whatever order those comforts were offered.

Sitting in silence in the living room across from Ivy, Terry took a long drink from the frosty mug of ale. In front of them, the fireplace flickered and glowed between the living room and the dining area. Its blue-gray stacked stone gave the oversized room solidity. When he had first seen the house, the dimensions had overwhelmed him since he preferred smaller, more intimate spaces. After coming here several times, the home's warmth now enfolded him in its comforts.

Ivy took a sip from a glass of white wine and asked, "Is this about Moll?" She tended to be as direct as Steve. While the question surprised him, he also appreciated Ivy's sharp perceptivity.

"Yes," Terry said. Now confronted by Ivy he hesitated to discuss his most heartfelt emotions. She held his gaze with the same penetrating expression she used to give him in the office, prompting him to continue. "Right from the start, Moll attracted me. Working with him every day made those initial feelings crystallize. I love him."

"Is Moll aware of your affection for him?"

"No, he treats me like I'm one of the guys. Sure he likes me as a friend, but he's straight, right?"

"Thought so," Ivy said. "On the other hand Moll dates and yet he never becomes involved with anyone."

"He likes the nut cases."

"Perhaps he wants an excuse not to form a relationship?"

"Wishful thinking on my part." Terry said. "So frustrating to work with Moll, knowing he will never view me as more than his business partner and friend. Brian and Moll may need to buy me out."

"Terry never is a long time."

"Besides he wouldn't want to disappoint Steve or you or Brian or Mathew."

"Each of us accepts you, don't we? Your sexual orientation makes no difference to the person you are."

"As one of their FBI gang, would Steve support Moll in a relationship with me?"

"Put your concern aside. This is between you and Moll. Since Steve wants the best for each of you, I think he would accept you and Moll as a couple."

Wanting time to think over Ivy's words, Terry jumped up to add a log to the lazy fire.

"Moll is changing," Terry said as he sat back down and finished his ale. "In the last couple of days, he grew up. He is becoming more distant from me."

"Stepping up to the responsibility of the downside of business leadership is a challenge without reward. Taking on such accountability rattles a sensitive guy like him. Stress and duty weigh on kind hearts."

"Did on you, right?"

"Not sure anyone would call me a kind person in business."

"You came across as caring and supportive to the high performers and staff members with personal issues, especially with me."

Rising from her chair, Ivy took Terry's mug and went to the kitchen, coming back with a second icy-cold ale. She curled up in the oversized fireside chair, as much as her six-foot frame would allow.

"I'm beginning to understand how narrow and rigid I can be," Terry said. "Moll is more open-minded, and he can peer around an issue to take in a broader field."

"Awareness of our limitations is the first stage of taking our next growth step."

"My focus is my best strength."

Ivy stayed silent for a few moments, staring into the fire before she spoke.

"Steve can be extraordinarily stubborn. His obstinacy can be a strength for him when he needs to accomplish a goal, pursue a criminal, whatever. Nonetheless he became aware of how his closed mindedness can limit the possibilities he may grasp. This explains why he is so into team contributions, brainstorming and developing scenarios. Listening to others helps Steve to work around his initial position. One day you should talk with him about how he used teamwork to broaden his perceptions.

"Change isn't easy for any of us. Capitalizing on the times when we need to make a shift in our lives is vital for continuing personal growth. As part of the process, a person can turn the stress associated with fundamental changes into excitement about the achievable potential."

Although he admired Steve and understood he functioned both as an excellent problem-solver and leader, Terry found him hard to talk with. His own prejudices about the big man and his upright ways might be preventing him from comprehending his nature. He would consider this new perspective. For now, he needed to figure out what his next step should be with Moll.

"Should I approach Moll?" Terry asked.

"My advice would be to wait a few more months. Let things smooth out at Noble Firs. If you still love him, sit down with him and tell him."

"Not sure how waiting will help."

"How long have you been business partners? Less than eighteen months? Not so long."

"Over the years you never steered me wrong, and you always supported me. You wouldn't tell me to wait to put me off. Is this one of your gut feelings?"

She took a sip of wine, frowned and said, "Something says waiting is right. How about helping me prepare dinner? Is Moll on his way down?"

"Got one of his texts. Standard Moll, something like 'BRF 6; CHW DWN 7.' I confirmed those times back to him. Ivy, would you not talk about my love for Moll with Steve or anyone?"

"Not a word until you give me the go ahead."

Steve yelled hello from the back door. "Be right in. Got to brush off my shoes. Brian will be here with Mathew by six."

When he first met Steve while working for Ivy, the big agent had treated him in the same direct way he acted towards his regular agents. Perhaps talking with Steve might not be so difficult. Although he might not be an easy man to like, he garnered respect which meant more to Terry.

Chapter 5

Nicola

Annetta Fuentes, now living under the name of Nicola Machado, sat facing her psychiatrist in the eighth story office suite in Barcelona. During this third appointment with the doctor, Nicola's tension rose as the minutes ticked by. After years of debating she had finally found the courage to seek professional help for the childhood abuse issues still haunting her.

"By talking about what your father did to you, you are making progress," her psychiatrist said. "To advance further you should contemplate forgiving him."

While by practice she contained her emotions, Nicola glared at the woman. Some acts a person committed were too monstrous to be forgivable. Her father had sexually abused her for more than ten years, doing nasty, painful things to her to make her cooperate.

"I will never forgive him. When actions are so heinous, the person committing them should never be absolved from those sins."

"You can never be free until you let your hardened feelings soften."

"Should the world exonerate Hitler? Should we absolve terrorists? My father got less than he deserved when he was killed in a drive-by shooting. He should have suffered more. A disgusting, mean and selfish man."

"If you do not forgive, you will never heal. You are Catholic, yes?"

"Raised in the faith. No longer believe in the fairy tale."

"You might find comfort in the church, perhaps through confession and absolution."

"Even while she was aware of what went on in my house, my mother went to mass every day. She did not care about me. What did Catholicism do for her?

Grant her a pardon for her own role of neglect and avoidance in this travesty?" Nicola struggled to control her annoyance and keep her voice in her usual mid-range tone. "You fail to appreciate how my father made me suffer."

"By not forgiving your parents, you are letting them still control you."

Nicola sucked her breath in, picked up her purse and stood. She tilted up her chin. "No one controls me. Not now. Not ever again. If you cannot see me as I am today, you are one lousy doctor."

Without waiting for a response, Nicola walked across the room to the door.

"When will you stop running?" the psychiatrist said to her.

Nicola spun around. "I define my own life."

Without bothering to close the door behind her, she marched out of the doctor's office in an uncharacteristic fit of temper. Forgiveness should be earned. She wanted to open up as a person, but she would never absolve her parents for their treatment of her.

Riding the elevator down, Nicola breathed deeply several times, glad to be alone to regain her composure before leaving the office building and hailing a taxi. A peaceful place would help her regain some inner harmony. After giving instructions to the driver, Nicola settled back in her seat. The sweet *Parc de Cervantes* with its fragrant roses would soothe her ruffled spirits, calm her anger and push away the memories of her father.

Her extensive reading had broadened her knowledge of victimization, child abuse and the emotional, mental and physical impacts on people subjected to extended periods of trauma. Not allowing herself to become close to anyone sprang from a deep-rooted fear of betrayal, traceable to what her father did to her. Thoughts of intimacy remained abhorrent, and yet she wanted to love and be loved. After escaping her father's perverse clutches, Nicola had spent her life alone. For over two decades she had lived, if not in contentment, at least free of harassment. Now matured into her forties, escape and hiding failed to be enough.

Returning later to her condo overlooking the Mediterranean in Barcelona, Nicola continued to grapple with retaining an inner sense of calm. Strolling along through the beds of roses, letting their sweet perfumes quiet the memory of her aborted session with the doctor, her visit to the *Parc de Cervantes* soothed her nerves, but her mind remained unsettled.

Some crimes should not be pardoned, including those inflicted on a child or teenager by the people who should be trustworthy. Revenge, justice and punishment remained unachievable since her parents were dead. Nicola wanted to place her horrid childhood in the past. Those events had happened more than twenty-five years ago. Now she must define a new freedom for herself.

She walked into her study where she worked each day on the script for her animation of a good guy/bad guy action series. So far Nicola had drawn sketches of the major characters. While she had typed out an outline of the plot and developed scripts for the first vignettes, she now tussled with converting the action to animated characters. Brian Tovey had given her the Adobe Tool Suite for Christmas in 2014, the year she and her cousin Maxim had bartered for and bought their freedom from their lives of crime. The learning curve for the software was high, and the work was tedious. Each step of skill development showed the need for more knowledge, overwhelming her as she failed to make progress.

Reaching out, she touched the photograph of Brian she had downloaded from the website of the company he ran with his two partners. Tall and slender, Brian's warm brown eyes shone with kindness. Even from the photograph, his smile reached into her heart. Since he had helped liberate her and her cousin while he consulted with the FBI, she had not seen him or heard from him except for his gift of the software. Did he ever think about her?

For now she must put her concerns with her history and her attraction for Brian aside. A glance at her wristwatch told her she needed to jump on Skype with the man whose Twitter handle was Bentlight. In her past life he had assisted her in learning technology which allowed her communications with various underworld figures to be secure when she sold information for huge facilitation fees. Other than an exchange of texts to set up this Skype session, she had not communicated with Bentlight in nearly three years.

After rushing to key in her password, Nicola adjusted the camera and went into the scheduled Skype meeting where Bentlight waited for her.

Nicola and Bentlight sat staring at each other. Whenever they spoke before, Bentlight appeared carefree and vibrant with health.

"Vexen. Is that you? What the hell?" Bentlight said.

"Hi. Been a long time."

"I'm confused. You're now a woman?"

"Always a woman," Nicola said. "You saw the cover I used in my former life. But you, what happened?"

"What do you mean? Same old Bentlight here."

"You're in a wheelchair."

"Didn't move into my desk chair. I've used a wheelchair since turning fourteen. Lost my feet after falling through the ice when I snuck off to skate by myself in one of the fjords. Advanced frostbite does nasty things."

"I wasn't aware."

"Nicola, think of me as lucky. I am ambulatory, and my brain is terrific. My life is a super one, if not entirely mobile. No pity. Not for me, understand?"

Bentlight smiled in his bright, likable way. His pale face with a sprinkling of freckles became a beacon of hope to her. She thought of him as a man untouched by tragedy. Yet he had been damaged. Bentlight reached up and lifted his thick chestnut hair off his forehead and pushed it back out of his face.

"What made you revert?" he asked.

"To myself, you mean? Let's say I paid for my many sins and now I can live in relative freedom."

"You scammed people before?"

"Only criminals. Be assured my life in the shadows is over and behind me. The consulting you did kept me safe, but you did nothing wrong. A non-disclosure agreement with the FBI in the United States prevents me from telling you more. However I can introduce myself. I am Nicola Machado, and I live in Barcelona."

"No more Vexen?"

"To you and only to you, Vexen is my handle."

"Cool. A man/woman of mystery. Always liked Vexen, but now better understand the wordplay on vexation and on vixen. My name is Mikael Sigurdsson, and I live in Akureyri which is the northern-most city of Iceland, sitting at the end of its leading fjord." He typed his name and city into a panel on Skype.

Nicola listened to the unfamiliar Icelandic pronunciations, thinking the names sounded like *Mee-kel Si-gourd-son* and the city *Ak-kur-ray-vi.* "Hi Mee-kel."

"Nicola, I want your assurance we are not engaging in anything illegal. I don't knowingly work for criminals, I won't work in the greedy financial sector, and I don't support terrorists."

"Once I dealt in the underworld. All that is behind me now. If you are concerned, I can put you in touch with a former FBI agent who assisted me."

Mikael stared at her with a chilliness she had not seen before.

"Someday I would like to understand your story, Nicola. Although I always feared you dabbled in crime, I perceived a worthy if tortured soul hid away inside your sleek metrosexual exterior. Your vulnerability made me want to help you."

His face softened, and he said, "Back to the now and your texted request about help with animation. Although I can't assist you, I can find someone to coach you in using the software."

"I want to learn the basics so I can sketch things out. A production company will be hired to do the actual animation."

"Give me a few days. Let's Skype again on Friday. What's your edge going to be? What will set you apart from the many other wannabes writing the same type of fiction?"

Nicola thought for a few moments and murmured, "The bad guys are often one-dimensional. My desire is to show their complexities and reveal some who are lost souls, trapped by family allegiances or frozen in place by insufficient confidence to break away, or held in the underworld by threats or force."

Mikael nodded. "Make sure you go deep enough inside them. How about throwing in a wheelchair-bound charismatic man from Iceland as a relentless detective?"

While he said the last part with a mocking laugh, he would make a fascinating detective. They talked for a few more minutes before ending their session. Bentlight. Did his name carry a high-tech meaning as she used to think or did he take the moniker from the way the light slanted in the extreme north?

Although Mikael possessed superior intelligence, he explained complex technical subjects using terms she understood. Companies and governments paid him a remarkable rate to solve the most challenging technological issues in telecommunications. In her past life she had always turned to him for guidance with a complex technology problem and she was glad to find that she could still get help from him.

Bentlight or Mikael with his pleasant ways, his generosity with his knowledge and his brainpower, had suffered in his youth, leaving him confined to a restricted life. Tears of sadness for the excellent man came into her eyes. He should not be a man with a severe disability, and yet he was facing the world, pursuing a career and making himself esteemed in his field. He conquered pain, limitations and loss of mobility.

The image of Mikael shone with more brightness in her mind. A shift occurred inside of herself as some of her own pain from her perverse and cruel father became, if not less sharp, at least easier to thrust away. She resolved to remember Mikael's words, 'No Pity, Not for Me.'

Studying the pages of the Noble Firs website cycling by on a display screen, Nicola longed for a more complete life. While Nicola derived comfort from her new existence in Barcelona, inside of herself she stayed uneasy within herself. For the first time in her life, she wanted a loving relationship with a man. At forty-four she struggled to find a way to begin.

Most of her adulthood had been spent in hiding under her pseudo-male persona, Julio. When young, men had found her attractive and now as a woman again she still turned heads here in Barcelona. However with her criminal past preceded by the sexual abuse of her childhood, how could she allow herself to date much less pursue a relationship?

Brian, who she had only known for a few days, and never so much as kissed, had understood her history. In spite of his years in the FBI spent hunting people like her, he had endured as a kind and gentle man. Had she developed the equivalent of a teenage crush on him? At love and at dating, her inexperience made her doubt her judgment and her attraction for him. Should she seek him out? Should she attempt to make contact? In all probability she lay buried in his stack of memories. Why would he be interested? She wore a weighty serape striped with the vivid, ugly colors of her past and yet the longing in her heart wanted more.

Nicola sighed and pushed herself out of her chair, hating her mood of discontent. She decided to head to Old Town to buy fruit and cheese. Tonight she would sip champagne out on her terrace and devise a plan for her next steps in the morning.

Seeing Mikael reminded her that life gave only so many years and a limited number of chances. He had moved on from a dark tragedy marring him for life. Would she ever be able to leave her past behind?

Chapter 6
Arielle

At their three-person summit to define the future of their spheres of influence, Arielle Moreau acted as the host at the posh Four Seasons George V hotel in central Paris. She completed her opening remarks for the meeting with her counterparts in the United States and Eastern Europe. As men and women in their thirties, they represented the new generation in the underworld with each of them planning to take over a family business in drugs, prostitution, fraud and money laundering when their parents decided to step down or were forced out.

Taking more time than usual with her short dark hair and makeup, Arielle had dressed with care in a stylish navy suit and printed blouse aiming to present the image of a woman-in-charge. Of medium height and with a curvier body than she wanted, Arielle had set ambitious goals for her life where career success meant more than marriage and children.

"Are we agreed our meetings over this afternoon and tomorrow will focus first on short-term tactical issues and second on laying out our long-term strategies?" Arielle asked, regarding first the American, Carlos Ochoa, as he rose to refill his coffee. When he nodded confirmation, she turned her gaze to Kazimír Horak.

"Only if we function as a triumvirate," Kazimír replied, his intense almost black eyes never leaving hers. "None of us more equal than the others."

Carlos swung back to the meeting table, sloshing some coffee on the carpet. "For now."

"Now is what we are discussing," Arielle said. "How can we springboard from the businesses our fathers built and move forward to push out our competitors and gain market share?"

Carlos set his coffee down on the glass table and paused to check his image in the mirrored wall on the far side of the room. A handsome man with dark skin, eyes and hair, he managed to keep his physique toned even with his playboy lifestyle and nights of decadence.

"Let's give our situation reports," Carlos said, "starting with Eastern Europe as our primary source of products for now."

His "for now" was not lost of Arielle and Kazimír as they exchanged a glance, each aware of their surreptitious plans to find additional outlets for their products. For the present they were dependent on the drug empire Carlos would one day control on the eastern seaboard of the United States. Even as they jointly planned their futures together as a triad, they each planned to form other alliances and business interests to expand the scope of their fathers' empires.

Kazimír displayed a document from his laptop on the white wall using a little high-tech projector he carried with him. The image showed a map of the Middle East, Turkey, Eastern and Western Europe. He reached up and tucked some locks of curly shoulder-length hair behind one ear, revealing a large diamond stud in his earlobe, his only concession to vanity. Unlike tall, buff Carlos, Kazimír was of middle height, thin and wiry. Arielle suspected he was the more agile of the two men.

"As this map shows, we continue to use three channels to bring our opium products out of Turkey and neighboring countries. The bulk of the drugs still come through Silvengrad. After this meeting I will visit the area to consider a shift to using the Black Sea port towns of Burgas, Sunny Beach and Varna.

"My plan is to also explore a route or two through the mountains of northeastern Greece and from there into Bulgaria. With the Bulgarian government working with representatives from the American Drug Enforcement Agency to improve border control, I need to select routes with extra care." Kazimír stared at each of them in turn. His eyes were piercing, and many people had trouble keeping eye contact with him. Arielle forced herself to hold his gaze while Carlos began fidgeting with his cell phone.

"What about the supply chain for the upscale prostitutes?" Carlos asked without looking up.

"Secure holds in boats, train cars and private jets, packed under luggage and legitimate goods such as produce. Our routes will migrate to border crossings with lighter staffing where we can facilitate the ease of inspections," Kazimír responded.

"Bribes, you mean?"

"Bribes, threats, the usual incentives," Kazimír said with a tone of impatience. "Same as in the States."

Kazimír had done his undergraduate work at Cornell and taken an advanced technical degree at the University of Birmingham in the United Kingdom. Although his English carried a mild Czech accent, he had studied languages and demonstrated fluency in half a dozen. Arielle perceived Kazimír as having the most brainpower of the three of them and as proceeding with the most caution.

"What about the exit points into Western Europe?" Arielle asked.

"Shifting some to the Baltic States. However these Eastern Europe/Western Europe distinctions carry little meaning now with the European Union. Only Albania, Montenegro, Serbia, Bosnia and some minor states are not in the EU."

"Turkey is not," Carlos said, baiting Kazimír, knowing those old political grudges went deep.

"Segments of Turkey aspire to be more European, but the country remains a crossroads of East and West."

"And Russia?"

Kazimír made a "PFFT" sound of disgust, as a sour expression came over his face.

"Russia and its former satellites are not EU, but a cross between over-controlled and lawless," Kazimír spat out in disdain, the muscle in his left cheek pulsing the way it did whenever he became very annoyed. "They can be as foreign to Europeans, as Muslims are to Christians. Do not goad me, Carlos. I am proud to be Bohemian and to be part of *Czechia*."

"Let's not bicker," Arielle interjected, regarding each man with severity. "We agreed not to be like our fathers, always squabbling among themselves. When they work together, they do it in a grudging, mistrustful manner. Our education stressed a culture of collaboration. The best way to achieve our individual goals is by working as a team."

Arielle paused to sip some Perrier. "Doors remain open to the United Kingdom; however the vote may go against continuing in the EU. If the UK does decide to exit the EU, the process will take many months if not years to complete. During the interim period, we can expect an increased tightening of the UK borders. Coming back to our product flow, how about moving more product through the Mediterranean and the Baltic? Do less overland. Let's work on this together,

Kazimír."

Arielle said the last to keep Kazimír engaged. While fiercely proud of his heritage, Kazimír functioned in a careful, rational manner and was unlike Carlos who tended to be hot-headed, arrogant and at times cruel. With his family dominating drug trafficking on the Eastern Seaboard, they needed the market share Carlos would one day possess in the United States, even though Carlos himself was untrustworthy. Back when they played together as children, he had wanted to dominate and would cheat to win.

One summer she had a brief affair with Carlos when he bummed around Europe during college. While she had enjoyed being seen with him, the fling never deepened into a relationship. Even as Carlos pumped her rhythmically in bed, she had suspected his mind sped ahead to his next conquest.

"Carlos, what changes are you recommending in your area?"

"Most of the street people will remain the same. I want to shake up the intermediate structure by promoting the best in the middle layer on the East Coast and sweeping out the older guys. They have become slow. They take on a 'you-owe-me' outlook. Without my father their loyalties will be uncertain. Better to put my own crowd in place, but my old man resists every change."

"Anything else in the current situation?"

"That I am allowed to touch? No, let's move on to planning our future. Ever wonder when we can make our plans a reality? Will the future open up for us with a bang all at once or piecemeal? So damn frustrating how little my old man lets me do."

After completing two days of discussions with Carlos and Kazimír, Arielle sat down for lunch with her father at their country estate in the Loire Valley, a couple of hours drive from Paris. They ate out on the terrace with her mother absenting herself to work in her art studio, as she did when any business discussions came up. While her mother enjoyed the comforts of their lifestyle, she avoided facing the way her father made much of his money.

Across from her at the table, her father sipped his white Burgundy. Of medium height, his burliness had softened into bourgeois rotundness as he aged.

Even though he worked out on a regular schedule in the gym, he no longer stayed ahead of his thickening waistline. From the time she was a child sitting on his lap until now, Arielle had wanted to spend time with him. Although she pursued other interests, she still gloried in the hours they spent together.

After serving their fish, the aging maid walked back to the kitchen, knowing better than to linger and eavesdrop. As they listened to her retreating footsteps, Arielle breathed in the clean country air. The vineyard ran away from the house in several directions of green rows contouring to the land. Between two fields an old orchard grew where the apples were harvested each autumn to distill calvados. While more of a Parisian than a provincial person, on early summer days like today, Arielle found the chateau a divine place to be.

"The near-term modifications are all right," her father said taking another sip of wine. "How are you doing with Carlos these days?"

"Carlos is hot-headed like his father."

"Which means he will become vengeful. Are you two still involved?"

"You heard about us?" Arielle asked in surprise.

"Not much I don't know about you," her father said. He lifted his left hand the way he did and rocked it back and forth. "You like men, you like women. You don't like anyone for long."

"The fling with Carlos lasted less than a summer. Definitely *passé*."

"I understand about variety. Stability is needed too."

"Like having *Maman* and your various *affaire passionnées*?"

He grunted and shrugged his shoulders. "Your mother has them too. This is our way. Back to your grand plans."

"One topic we spent much time on are the changes technology is bringing. We want to participate in this new NadirNet. Unlike our current communications for phones, texts and emails which are by public networks, NadirNet is a private network developed solely for us, except part of the capacity is sold to fund our activities."

"Go on."

"NadirNet will be used for discussions between the leaders in our areas of influence. At the beginning much of our communications will flow the same as today. However we can ship files around too as we move into more electronic ventures."

"Such as?"

"Personal information, funds manipulation, auctions of goods and so on."

"Auction of goods?"

"Let's say we are offered a chance to buy a block of bulk heroin out of Turkey. We can't move all the product through our regular channels, so we put the excess up for auction."

"Do we have to take what is bid?"

"When we put the product up for auction, we set a minimum price and see where the bidding goes."

Her father stayed quiet as he mopped up the sauce on the fish with a piece of bread. He drank more wine and pushed back from the table.

"This is your education you're applying. You are moving into another world."

"Same world, but a changing one."

"Can you pursue this without too much risk?"

"Kazimír understands the technology much better than I do."

"What about Carlos?"

"Carlos is lazy. He would rather spend time in his playboy lifestyle where he is photographed for flashy magazines or for social media."

"Do not underestimate him. He is crafty like his father."

"Not a man to be trusted."

"Is anyone in business?" Her father let the question hang between them as he stood and moved to the ornate railing of the terrace.

"Pursue this, Arielle. Let me see what you can accomplish and what money you can make. You are a talented manipulator. Pretend to work cooperatively with your buddies, Carlos and Kazimír, while you take over more control."

Chapter 7

Brian

Early Thursday evening Brian walked from Steve's house at Spook Hills over to Mathew's new house, built while engaged to Callie. After marrying they had been living there for about six months. The open yet warm house resembled his friend and former fellow FBI agent, Mathew. Light filled the interior on cloudy days as well as sunny ones. Brian never contemplated designing a home the way Steve did, and now Mathew had. His bachelor digs with Moll in Ivy's former house in the hills above Portland met his needs thus far when he was back from London.

Mathew opened the door and led him back into the kitchen where Callie and her daughter, Susannah, arranged an antipasto on a colorful platter he guessed came from their honeymoon travels in Provence. Perhaps they would talk more about the time they had spent cruising the Mediterranean with Cruze and the divine Annetta, or as they called themselves now, Maxim and Nicola.

Hanging right where the spacious kitchen opened into a great room, a blown-up color photograph of the four of them caught his attention. They were on what he guessed must be Maxim's sailboat. Nicola's life-size face startled him and drew him closer to gaze into those eyes of hers, dramatic in turquoise and different from any other eyes he had encountered. From the photo, they pierced his soul with their intensity. Her expression carried sadness, belying her smile.

The last time he had seen her, back when she still masqueraded as a man named Julio, she had worn her hair much shorter. In the photograph, mid-length dark waves blew behind her in a tumbled way with streaks of copper and aged brass near her face catching the sunlight. Her power over him failed to diminish. He still wanted this remarkable woman with the troubled past.

"Still think about our terrific trip," Mathew said, handing him a glass of vintage Argyle champagne. Callie walked in from the verandah, having placed the appetizers and wine outside where Susannah played on the lawn with a half-grown golden retriever. When Mathew encircled Callie in his left arm, they smiled at each other, but Brian perceived a hint of anxiety in each of their faces.

"Nicola and Maxim look happy, like their new lives agree with them," he said. "During the days I spent with them, I never saw Maxim smile. Here he appears not to carry a care in the world."

"Proud as he can be of his sailboat -- calls her *Segunda Oportunidad* or Second Chance. Maxim likes us, you know? You, me, Moll, Callie, Steve and Ivy. His heart is loyal, and he views us as his new family."

"Any signs of trouble?"

"Not so far. And I pray each night for them to remain safe."

"Annetta, um, Nicola looks well."

"She is a dear," Callie said. "She could be my sister. Nicola remains so worldly and controlled, and yet I find a certain artlessness about her. I'm not sure she ever formed friendships before. We email a couple of times a week and talk now and then. Sometimes when she finds something I might like, she texts me or sends a photo. The carved antique chest by the wall is from Barcelona. After I had told her we needed a piece of furniture for that spot, she came across the chest in a shop and snapped some photos. Of course what she found looked perfect. Mathew and I bought the chest and arranged to have it shipped here."

"She inquired about you and Moll. I'd say she developed a little crush on you, old charmer," Mathew said and poked him in the ribs.

With his face heating up in a blush, Brian turned away, snuck another glance at the photo and followed Callie and Mathew outside. Susannah came over to share a lounge chair with him as they dipped crusty pieces of baguette into a local, pressed olive oil from nearby Red Ridge Farms. Putting olives on the tips of her pinkies, Susannah held them up to her eyes and waggled them at him. Despite his worries about their business issues and his personal problems, Brian found himself laughing at her antics.

"Better," she said leaning over to him. "You needed cheering up. Why don't you roll down the hill? The grass is soft and finally dry enough. Always makes me laugh."

"Your Uncle Brian isn't the rolling down the hill type," Callie said.

Except for those rare times when he had escaped his mother's watchful eye, Brian had never been allowed to be a carefree little boy. In those few instances of boyhood freedom, he did fall into a scrape or two. In defiance of his staid image, he kicked away his shoes, tore off his socks, jumped up and peered down at Susannah.

"Race you to the top," she yelled and took off at a run.

Brian gulped down some champagne and chased after her. A fast little runner, Susannah spurted ahead making him push himself up the hill to catch her. Near the crest he slowed a little to let her win.

"Show me how to go about this rolling thing," he said.

"You go to the left of the fountain. I'll take the right side." Susannah flopped down on the grass. She put her arms down tight to her sides and began rolling, gaining speed and laughing as she went downhill. Where the land flattened by the fountain, she slowed and came to a stop before the brick patio. She flipped on her side and taunted him. "Com'on slowpoke. Are you chicken?"

Brian laid down, aiming towards the other side of the fountain and hoping not to crash into the stone or the herb bed on the side. After a hefty push, he started rolling. Grass, clouds and sun swirled across his eyes until he stopped, feet in a rosemary bush and his head thankfully away from the fountain.

He found himself laughing as he brushed blades of grass off. If family life could be this much fun, perhaps he might find his way to enjoying marriage and a family.

After dinner Brian sat in the great room with Mathew while Callie took Susannah upstairs to settle her into bed. Susannah had been kidnapped two summers before when Callie was married to her first husband. After a cousin of her birth father had run up gambling debts in the underworld, the mob boss had wanted them repaid with Susannah's ransom.

"Any lingering after-effects of the kidnapping?" Brian asked.

"She seems well adjusted and feels protected with us. We do worry about when she will need to go to San Francisco to spend time with her father. If she goes, Callie and I will go with her. When he calls her, Susannah becomes upset and clingier. Not sure if memories of the kidnapping haunt her or if being separated from her father bothers her or if she's afraid he might try to take her from us. Although he keeps his alcohol consumption down to evenings and weekends, I suspect her father still drinks to excess. He can be adept at pretending to be sober."

"Susannah is a delightful child. May she never lose her bright laughter. How old is she now?"

"Soon to be thirteen. She acts grown-up sometimes and then at other times, like when she was rolling down the hill tonight, she still seems a child. As she moves into her teenage years, having a stable home where she feels happy and secure is critical. Unfortunately John Henry will not let me adopt her. I can't help thinking he wants to retain a little control of Callie and disappoint me. We will continue the negotiation however slow and frustrating it is."

Mathew paused and took a sip of his brandy, gave a slight smile of approval and set the glass back down. "What about you? How's your data issue going?"

"We found money laundering type transactions in four additional client files. We are now checking files from over a year ago and not finding anything. Terry went up to Portland this afternoon to walk Moll through our findings. Although we will keep probing the data, I think the problem is scoped out. Next we must communicate with our clients and, whether Terry agrees or not, alert the Bureau."

"He'll come to understand the sense of bringing in the FBI."

"Terry possesses one heck of a stubborn streak which doubles as a strength and a weakness. I worry about bringing in the Bureau too. What if we've missed something else?"

The question hung between them, bringing a groundswell of unease into the room.

"How's life in London?" Mathew asked. "Any chance you hooked up with a real girlfriend?"

Brian glanced down at his apple brandy, took a sip and said, "About a year ago, I fell in with a fast group -- the first time the so-called in-crowd found me worth including. Fluid, no partnering up, companions for a night. Very quickly I became caught up in their fashionable life in London and out on country estates."

"And?"

"Sometimes I spent the night with a beauty. A week ago I discovered she's married and her husband wanted in on our intimacy. I scarpered."

"Holyshmoley."

"Made me feel lousy. I should have sensed an oddness to the situation, but my head got turned."

"So no one you want to be with in a relationship?"

To avoid revealing how much Nicola attracted him, he shook his head in the negative. "What about you and Callie? Will you start a family of your own?"

"We're trying. Been trying since we got married, but so far nothing. Callie blames her years on the pill, while I worry something's wrong with me."

"You been to a doctor?"

"Not yet. Guess we are each afraid to face the truth."

"Sorry Mathew. You appear to be a guy who has everything."

"I can be content with Callie and Susannah, but we wanted our own children too."

Unsure what to say, Brian nodded. They sat in silence for a long minute before he changed the subject. "Back to the business, would you review the text Ivy is working up as a speaking script for when we contact our clients? We need your attorney's eyes to check the wording. My own are bleary from worrying and from reviewing data."

"Sure. Sorry I've been so busy on the vineyard with planting the vines that arrived late and overseeing the construction of our production facility."

"No need to explain. This is your life here at Spook Hills. Steve and Ivy remain supportive."

"Steve is worried."

"About our issue at Noble Firs, you mean?"

"More about you. Expect him to corner you before you leave."

"Been afraid he might. He's as skilled at reading people as ever. Between his agent's eye and his sixth sense, he can tell when something's off."

"With his marriage to Ivy and his retirement, he is mellower though he remains penetratingly observant."

"Think I'll go talk with him early tomorrow before Ivy is up and about. Does he still jump out of bed at 4:30?"

Mathew chuckled. "You know Steve -- he keeps some of his old habits."

"Better I spill what's wrong than wait for him to corner me."

"Your courage has always been impressive. Facing Steve isn't the easiest. He will hone in with questions until he pries the story out."

With worrying about talking to their clients, the FBI and now Steve, Brian would sleep but little. Best to tackle them one-by-one with Steve first.

Rising before four Brian showered, made coffee in the guest suite and sat down to make a list of the points he wanted to cover with Steve. At 4:45 Steve walked by on his way to the office. As soon as his former boss and mentor settled himself at his desk, Brian strode the few paces down to the office area.

"Steve?" he said, trying to keep his voice steady. "May I talk to you about something?"

The big man arched an eyebrow at him. Pushing his laptop away, he leaned back in his chair and folded his hands over his well-toned abs. At sixty-three Steve still worked out every day, and despite his prodigious appetite, no extra weight accumulated around his middle.

"This isn't about the data issue, is it?" Steve said, his voice coming out in a rumble.

"No, this is about me. Not sure where to begin."

"You brought a list, so let's discuss one point at a time."

"Back in London I became isolated. The guys I hung around with from the year I spent at the London School of Economics had moved into their own lives.

"After a few months I fell into a crowd of affluent Londoners. We met on Friday nights at an upscale pub or bistro -- a fluid group of about twenty of us. Sometimes when one of the folks had access to a family country home, we would organize cars and head out for the weekend."

"You became involved with someone?"

"No one paired off except for a night of tumbling into bed together. The next weekend the deck seemed to get shuffled with different pairings occurring. Not everyone and not every weekend. For the first time in my life, I wasn't the analytical nerd the cool people ignored. They treated me like I fitted in with them."

"But something went haywire."

Brian nodded. "I let myself become entangled with them. Drinking too much. Some of them did coke or smoked a joint, but I stayed clear. Faster life than I was used to."

Steve had experienced a bad time in his life filled with one night stands with women he had picked up in hotel bars. Despite those past practices, Steve remained an upright and sometimes naive man. His nickname at the Bureau had been "The Boy Scout" because of his high ideals and the way he avoided becoming tainted. Brian admired Steve, who over time became more than a mentor – not quite a father but certainly a favorite uncle.

Brian held Steve's eye and asked, "You ever run into quirky stuff back in your hotel pickup days?"

Steve's disgust showed on his face. "Yeah. Women who liked the bondage thing. One woman wanted to bring her friend with us. Other stuff. I would tell them to enjoy plain vanilla sex or nothing. Trust me, I never regretted not going down those paths."

"Glad to hear you say those words because I've been worrying I'm not enough of a playboy. Last Friday night ..."

Brian's cell phone rang with the Moll/Terry ring. Right after he pushed the call to voice mail, Steve's cell phone vibrated on the desk. After checking to see who called, Steve said, "Moll's calling. Sorry but I think we should take this."

Laying his phone on the desk, he put it on speaker and answered the call. "Moll, Brian is here with me. Got you on speaker."

"Right, Terry and I are still at the office. We've been going through databases all night. Spotted something late yesterday."

"What?"

"We decided to compare our working copy of the data with the secure backups Terry keeps."

"Super idea," Brian interjected. "News to me he made those copies."

"Me too. Back when Terry first joined up, he inserted some code into our load routine so if anything should ever happen, a pristine copy was squirreled away on a separate server."

"What turned up?" Steve asked.

"The original files show about three times as many of those funky transactions as what we've been analyzing."

"Holy Shit. Someone is doctoring the data," Brian yelled, jumping up. "But wait, our control totals would be off."

"Ingenious alteration -- the same number of records and the same dollar totals. The originations of the payments and their destinations were changed, taking away our concerns with suspect locations."

"How far back?"

"We've been here all night, but we only reviewed the last three months."

"You guys organize your findings?"

"I'll email you a spreadsheet. We're so tired that we're punchy. Steve we want you and Ivy to check what we found. Make sure we aren't hallucinating or something. We took copies of the files Terry accumulated and put them out on another server where we reserved emergency expansion space. I'll email you the address using your secure email, Steve. You should be able to access the databases. We're going to take cabs home, try to sleep and regroup with you later today. Brian, would you come up to the office today to keep things going here?"

"Come down here around three, and we'll go over our findings today."

"Thanks. We're so freaked out."

They ended the call. Brian sat with his head in his hands. This would ruin them for sure. As he refocused on the business issues, his personal problems diminished.

Reading his mind Steve said, "Let's take the next fifteen minutes so you can tell me the rest of your story."

"I can wait."

"All week you've been struggling with some internal issue. If we go through the rest of it, I may be able to help you put your troubles in perspective."

When Brian told him about Emily and Peter, Steve winced a little as he listened.

"How did I miss the signs? What made them think I would want a threesome?" Brian asked. "Her husband crawled into bed with us like he thought that was normal."

"Perhaps to them threesomes are a frequent occurrence. Sometimes we miss the signals. I sure did in those incidents I mentioned. What are you going to do?"

"Use this break to mend my ways. Work and go to museums and stuff while I'm in London."

"More exists than you are telling me. Something caused you to cruise into this casual life."

When Brian hesitated, Steve waited the way he did if he thought a person might talk.

"Not ready to discuss the rest. I need to reconcile myself to this incident first. How did you walk away from your life of hotel pickups?"

"Cranky as hell for about a month until I adjusted to a monk-like existence. While I wanted a more fulfilling life, I was too empty inside. Back in those days, I could offer a woman little besides sex. I exercised, worked, read a lot, tried to define a different lifestyle. Awkward geek that I am, I couldn't fathom how to make a relationship work. When Ivy walked into my life, I dug deep and found enough inside of me to build a bond with her.

"As for you I advise taking up a hobby you are passionate about – a sport, an activity or a craft -- whatever will give focus to your time away from the office."

Brian pondered what he might be interested in. "My grandfather on my dad's side kept a rose garden in his small backyard. He loved tending those roses, and he let me help him. How rewarding we found seeing a rose nurtured from nothing more than a bare root, leaf out, grow tight buds and then flower. Used to think I wanted a rose garden when I grew up.

"After my Dad moved out, my parents divorced. From then on my mother made up excuses to keep me away from my father and his family. After about five years my grandfather died. I pretended to be sick to stay home from school and snuck out for his funeral. Might be silly, but I want to learn about roses and how to grow them."

"Not silly to me. Working in Ivy's gardens is rewarding. So is caring for the grapevines on the vineyard from planting to harvest. While Mathew likes the growing part well enough, he is more interested in becoming a vintner than a farmer. Pursue your interest in roses. Read, go visit gardens, learn. At some point, plant your own rose garden to putter around in."

Steve paused and said, "Will you tell me more about your issues when you're ready?"

"I need to think for a bit."

At that moment Ivy walked in, the sound of her footsteps hushed by her slippers. "Think about what?" she asked.

Chapter 8
Moll

Over at Spook Hills in mid-afternoon, Ivy briefed the three business partners on their findings from their work that day. She put a summary up on a projector shining on the wall in their office space. Moll admired the way she kept the work organized and summarized their findings into targeted facts.

"We didn't need to go back far," Ivy said, staring at each of them in turn. "The changes stopped nine months ago."

"Who did you hire around August/September of 2015?" Steve asked.

Brian stopped keying into his laptop. "One of our hiring spurts. Emailing you a list to bring up on the screen, Ivy. As you know we remain a small firm. Besides us three partners we employ five analysts in the London office and a dozen in Portland. We also have two admins, three programmers, an accountant and a DBA. Six people had been hired in the two months preceding the date of the first altered data."

When Brian's phone rang he glanced at the screen and said, "International call. I better take it." He jumped up to hastend down the hall away from the meeting.

Ivy, Terry, Steve and Moll turned their attention back to the list of recent hires.

"Tom. Our fucking DBA," Terry said. "Dammit. He is the only one of those six who possesses the access rights to alter the transactions when the files first come in. He archived the databases for completed clients to push the evidence out of our sight. Guess you win our bet Moll."

"A bet I would be happier if I lost," Moll said disturbed that such a valuable member of their staff would betray them.

"Let's step back," Ivy said. "Where did your DBA work before he joined

44

Noble Firs? What did his references say?"

After exchanging an uneasy glance with Terry, Moll said, "Overloaded at the time. When the first reference checked out, we made the offer and Tom joined us within a week. Since he started making contributions so fast, we thought of him as our best hire. Stupid, stupid, stupid."

"Let's pull together a task list." Ivy brought up a spreadsheet and began typing. "We need to call his other references. Tell them we are auditing our HR practices. I'll put my name down for this task."

"Try to find any audit trails revealing when he altered the transactions," Steve said. "While he probably turned the logging off, we should check for gaps in time and compare any you find to your access logs."

"How the hell do we explain this to our clients?" Moll asked as he rubbed his hands over his still-tired eyes and massaged his temples.

"Disable the DBA-rat's access," Terry said.

"Whoa. For now perhaps we don't do either," Steve said. "I think we should call the Bureau. They can try to link the DBA to the perps. Some underworld scum must be paying him to alter data to allow their money laundering to go undetected."

"Too risky for him to continue operating in our system," Terry hissed through his teeth.

"Today is Friday," Moll said and fixed his eyes on Terry in hopes of gaining his agreement. "Call the FBI today. Give them the long Memorial Day weekend. We track everything the DBA does until Tuesday morning when we shut off his access. The Bureau will investigate over the weekend. We can't risk any more time."

Brian walked back in and stood listening, but now he spoke up, "Got a call from the biggest bank in Barcelona. Their internal audit team worked almost through the night and now they want us in the bank's offices next week. This is a follow-up to the bust earlier this year for money laundering in the Spanish unit of the Industrial and Commercial Bank of China. Told them I needed to talk to my partners. Sounds like we can't take on more business now."

"You should go," Steve said with a quick glance at Ivy. "Make the pitch. Understand what their needs are. The servers will be secured before any of their extracts are loaded."

"But ..."

"This could be bigger than these transactions. Some underworld figures might want to discredit Noble Firs as well as turn dirty drug money into clean money. If you stop taking on new clients, you are playing into their hands."

"We need a new DBA," Terry said.

"How about someone out of the Bureau or the Drug Enforcement Agency – the DEA -- to fill the gap?" Steve asked. "Let them track what we are doing by having an agent on the job."

"No way," Terry spat out and set his mouth in a thin line of determination.

Ivy held up her hand in a stop motion. "In a situation like this, the more we open up the proverbial kimono, the more forthcoming we appear. Your clients should applaud having a government agent serve as the DBA to sort this out. You thinking of someone, Steve?"

"One of those guys from the DEA who audited the FBI back in 2013. They found those moles the Fuentes hired to spy for them at the Bureau and at the DEA."

"I want a condition if we bring in the feds," Terry said. "They need to agree not to pursue any action against our clients unless we find conditions of gross negligence in their processes. So far none popped up."

Ivy added tasks to the spreadsheet. When they finished, Steve suggested taking a break and coming back to confirm their proposed action plan.

"And Barcelona?" Brian asked. "Do we all agree I should make the pitch?"

Every person nodded except Terry who sat thinking until Moll bumped his arm.

"Uh, okay. I agree." Each word of Terry's came out at a measured pace. "I can be resistant to sharing control, but you're lifesavers, Steve and Ivy."

"Brian call El Banko de Barcelona or whatever the bank is called," Moll said and pushed himself up straighter in his chair. With Brian due to fly out, he needed to take control and appear to be the assured businessman. "You'll process their data in the London office. If they need us to start work right away, we'll fly a couple of people over to help at our expense."

Turning to Steve he continued, "Would you ask Mathew to join us after the break? I'd like his perspective on this before we agree to our task plan."

Steve nodded and dialed his phone while he opened the sliding door at the end of the room and walked outside.

With Terry now supporting the concept of help never being more than a call away with Steve and Ivy, the friction between Moll and Terry evaporated. The Bureau would assist in bailing them out. Although rough times and uncomfortable client conversations lay ahead of them, Moll now possessed hope their business would survive.

The weekend went by with a bustle of activity. Local agents arrived at their offices Friday evening and others flew in from the New York office early Saturday along with the DEA agent who Steve requested. Between leading the on-site agents through their findings and training the new DBA, Moll and Terry kept busy during the long days. Ivy and Steve came in to relieve them at night as the agents worked round-the-clock, working in shifts. As it turned out their findings at Noble Firs provided the final definitive proof required against several gangsters on the East Coast where the FBI already pursued cases.

On Tuesday morning following the Memorial Day long weekend, Moll unlocked the door to their offices at six where he expected to meet Terry, Steve and Ivy.

Steve came out to greet him, "Morning. Ivy went out for coffee and breakfast sandwiches. We're planning to stay until the arrest is made."

"How late was the team here last night?"

"Left around three this morning. The two East Coast guys got right on a Bureau plane to head back. Arrests are expected to start back east possibly as early as today."

When the door opened again, Terry hustled in. "Hey guys what's the drill today?"

"Same as we discussed last night. The arrest team will be here at seven to charge your DBA when he arrives in the office at his usual time. Should only take a few minutes. He'll be out of here and sequestered at the FBI offices in Portland until the sting happens back east later today or worst case tomorrow."

"Time to disable his access."

"The agent-auditor from the DEA serving as your new DBA will shut his access off at seven. He will monitor activity from his hotel until the arrest is over. No activity from your DBA all weekend, which is lucky. Does he not usually work weekends?"

"If we needed him or if he was backlogged, he would either come in or work from home. He was organized and focused. He worked long hours whenever needed but otherwise he did not tend to work on weekends," Moll said.

"The DEA agent is a sharp guy," Terry said. "Picked up our database and file structures right away when I went through them with him. I'll continue his training this week."

Ivy appeared outside the glass office door carrying a loaded handle bag of food and two cardboard thermoses of coffee. Steve rushed to offload her.

"Nothing like an FBI operation to make a person hungry," Steve said as they laid out the breakfast in the conference room. "I think we should become scarce this morning. Don't want to alarm your DBA. Seeing us might make him bolt."

Striding over to the exterior wall, Moll lowered the window blinds while Terry did the same on the inner glass wall and Steve dimmed the lights. Within minutes the FBI team of three agents arrived and scrambled to grab coffee and breakfast. After a short discussion Moll and Terry exited the conference room to go to their own offices. Moll planned to call Steve when the DBA arrived.

Leaving his breakfast sandwich untouched and tossing his coffee away, Terry's obviously taut nerves sent Moll to grab a ginger ale for him out of the refrigerator in their kitchenette. While he had experience with these types of situations, Terry did not. He walked into Terry's office and handed him the soda.

"Hey man these guys are professionals. Be over in the next half hour."

"Can't be too soon for me. Until this last week I'm not sure I appreciated who you are. Since the day we disagreed over disclosing our issues to Ivy and Steve, you became different."

"Like how different?"

"Don't take this wrong. You started acting more professional especially after Brian departed for Barcelona. Like watching a geeky teenager grow up overnight."

Moll smiled at his friend. "Same old Moll underneath. This issue is weighing heavy on me like a humongous rock tumbled down on my chest. Reached deep to make my way through this nasty time."

The office door opened again, and their DBA walked in with his usual bustle of self-importance. Moll hated the sight of him. What he had thought of as professional confidence in the man's demeanor now appeared as deceitful arrogance. He conjured up a visual of the DBA in a full frame photo with bars in front of him. He gave a surreptitious thumbs-up sign to Terry, walked back into his office and called the team to come out to nab the DBA. According to the FBI's plan, neither Moll nor Terry needed to be present at the actual arrest, although he did intend to step out for the satisfaction of seeing the man taken away in handcuffs.

The DBA occupied a cubicle in front of his office. The damn sneak had made those changes right in front of them. The man possessed cunning and operated deviously.

The three FBI agents came out of the conference room. Moll perceived them from a new perspective -- each one intent on the job ahead, making him appreciate what must have been his own concentrated determination when he went after criminals. One stationed himself at the front door to the suite. The other two split up, each taking a different path to the cubicle opening. Steve headed to the back of the office suite where an emergency exit led to the stairs. Only Ivy remained in the conference room.

The arrest scene unfolded in front of him. When the agents approached and spoke to him, the DBA jumped up out of his chair, his eyes darting around. He went to leap up on the desk to escape, but the agents grabbed him. They pushed him face down and cuffed him in one fast motion. One agent recited his rights. When they moved to lead the criminal away, Terry opened his office door, stepped out and walked over to stand next to Moll.

The DBA stayed quiet with his head down, but he squirmed in the strong grips of the two agents. With the third agent, they left the office space. The elevator dinged and they wrestled the still resistant DBA through the doors. Terry went down to the conference room to alert Ivy.

"The arrest is over," he remarked to Ivy.

"Sure happened quickly. Let's watch them leave."

Standing by the windows facing the front of the building, Steve, Moll, Ivy and Terry observed the foursome below walking out to the street. As they turned towards the waiting car, the DBA gazed up at their office windows. The agents shoved the man into the back of a dark car. Moll observed the action with no remorse. The man's reprehensible activities almost ruined their business.

"Let's hope he will be convicted and spend time in jail," Steve said. "No future in front of him. He will never be trusted in a responsible technical position again."

The car down below pulled away leaving a wave of relief in its wake. Moll hugged Ivy and then Steve and thanked them before pulling Terry into a hug. "You're the best man. And the best come along all too seldom."

"As we can well appreciate after today," Terry said in a grim tone. "You're not bad yourself. Well handled."

Moll nodded and stepped back. "Ivy and Steve, thank you for working through this with us. I think I aged about ten years in the last week."

"You learn what you're made of during extreme stress," Ivy said. "You each did well."

"Different when we made arrests with the FBI. With the crime perpetrated in our business, the action today grabbed me right by the *cojones*. Finding out our own DBA stuck a hunting knife in our guts and twisted the serrated blade around was sure hard to take. Not yet eight o'clock and I need a second shower. You two must be worn out. Why don't you head back to Spook Hills and we'll work our way through the day?"

"Keep us posted," Steve said as he and Ivy moved to leave. "Call the DEA guy. Apprise him of the status."

Terry nodded and pulled out his cell phone.

They must communicate with their staff, hiding the DBA's departure under the guise of a resignation. They would tend to other business until the FBI completed making additional arrests. Once the clearance call came in from the FBI, they planned to contact the clients whose data contained the money laundering transactions. Those conversations would be uncomfortable, but each of their client contacts had developed a relationship with him, Terry or Brian. Since the FBI had agreed not to pursue any action against each bank, the conversations might be a bit smoother.

"KTF," Moll called out as Steve and Ivy went to leave the Noble Firs offices.

Ivy regarded him with a quizzical expression.

"Keep the Faith," Steve murmured as they passed through the doorway.

"Moll used KTF as our motto in our FBI days when we went through trying times – expression is out of the sixties, I think."

Ivy made a peace sign back at Moll through the glass door.

Chapter 9
Nicola

On Wednesday morning the first of June, Nicola found herself discontented and unable to focus. Her restlessness led her to return to Barcelona's rose garden where she hoped to find peace wandering between the rows and patterns of roses, letting the heady perfumes envelop her. After pulling on a pair of lightweight jeans flattering to her figure, she selected a striped white wrap-around blouse tied on the side and walking sandals. Grabbing a chic pair of red sunglasses, she left her condo, took the elevator down to ground level and hailed a taxi.

At the garden Nicola wandered along, remembering an article she had read about the meanings the colors of roses carried in various cultures. In Latvia red roses were for funerals and not for Valentine's Day. While usually yellow roses signified friendship instead of romance, in Germany yellow ones meant your host is cheating.

She stopped to sit on a bench under the long, curving pergola with the Parc de Cervantes cascading below her. Several circular beds with curving paths wove their way down a gentle slope. Trees grew plentifully, supplying needed shade on sultry summer days. Now in early June the moderate temperatures only ranged up in the mid-seventies.

A smattering of visitors strolled around, but the park tended to be quiet on weekday mornings unless busloads of tourists pulled up. On the level down below her, a slender man with his suit jacket folded over his arm strolled around a curved walkway. Nicola sat still as a deer scrutinizing him, telling herself the man might resemble Brian Tovey, but could not possibly be him. He sauntered along, sometimes stopping to cup a rose in his fingers or to lean closer to experience a particular scent. Carrying a little notebook with him, he jotted a few comments as he made his way along at a slow pace.

The man neared the curve to come up to the pergola. As she kept her eyes trained on him, he turned and walked up into the shade of the leafy arcade. He took off his sunglasses to examine the roses blooming above him. When his gaze moved back down, he spotted her sitting down not more than thirty feet away. She jumped up and turned to stare at him.

"Nicola," he called in his resonant yet soft Brian voice.

A part of her had longed for this moment. Another part had feared the time she might run into Brian. Her fantasy crush on him would be tested if she spoke to him. She wanted to spin around and rush away. He called her name again.

Torn by a desire to talk with Brian and fear of where further association with him could lead, Nicola stood frozen in place as Brian jogged towards her. What brought him here? Had he been trying to find her? What else would make him travel to Barcelona? Had he been sent to arrest her? Did something go wrong with their agreement? Did the FBI think someone might be after her and send Brian to warn her?

While she wanted to stay and talk with him, her fears made her want to skitter away from where a direct encounter might lead. These thoughts swirled in her mind like little cyclones blocking a more rational perspective. Her hesitation gave Brian time to reach her, and he stood smiling at her. He possessed the sweetest, most sincere smile of any man she had ever met.

"I can't believe you're here," he said. "I flew in last night to pitch a bank in town. With some free time this morning, I wanted to see this garden. Loved roses since I was a kid working with my grandfather in his backyard. Trying to get back to my roots so to speak. Nicola how are you?"

Nicola struggled to find her normal outward equanimity while her emotions whirled around inside her -- frightened, thrilled and worried all at one time. Flight and avoidance persisted as her preferred methods of self-preservation, yet here she was mesmerized into talking with this man who attracted her like no other. He remained as handsome as before, although he seemed a little more careworn.

"Nicola? Are you okay?"

"Surprised to run into you."

"Amazed at seeing you too. What brings you here?"

"I like to visit parks to regain my composure."

'I have never seen you dis-composed not even in the most extreme circumstances."

"My whole life has been a charade to keep my exterior from reflecting the jumble of thoughts and conflicts of emotion inside."

"I am so happy to see you again. Could we get together later today to catch-up while I'm in town? Like for a glass a wine or dinner?"

"I am leaving within the hour."

"Shucks. Bad timing. Are you living in Europe?"

"Yes."

"I'm in London most weeks. Could we hook up sometime?"

"Brian I don't think that is a good idea."

"You don't like me?"

The sad look in his eyes taunted her. How could she possibly explain that her attraction to him was so potent it scared her? How could she date him given her past?

"I do like you, but you know my history. I don't date. I can't."

He fished a card out of his suit jacket pocket and quickly wrote a phone number on the back. "Here's my work number and my cell phone. Think about having lunch or dinner with me, if not today, then another day. If not here, then London, Paris, or wherever you choose."

"Brian, did you come here to find me? Are you working for the FBI again?"

He reached out and picked up her hand, holding it gently in his. She trembled when he touched her. "I am here on business. Running into you is a total surprise – a wonderful surprise." He lightly placed a second hand over their joined ones and then slowly released her.

"I must get going," Nicola said.

"Call me? At least say you will think about it."

"I will promise that much." Nicola turned and walked towards a nearby exit from the park to the street. She could feel Brian watching her as she moved. Nearing the street she turned and looked back. He held up his cell phone and waved goodbye.

Had Brian come to Barcelona only for business? She could text Callie. A simple text question should not reveal her daydreams about him. The time neared noon but was only 3 a.m. in Oregon. She needed an answer.

Hi Callie. Just saw Brian in Barcelona. Can you confirm he is here on business and not working for the FBI? N.

Nicola's rush of conflicted feelings refused to be calmed. Should she agree to meet him again? Where might that lead? She wished she had not sent the text to Callie. She wanted her message answered. She jumped into a cab and headed home. Once there she would jam her feet into her deck shoes, throw on a broad-brimmed sun hat, grab her boat bag and hurry down to where she kept her boat docked. Out on the water, she would try to make her thoughts settle down.

As Nicola guided her boat back into the marina, the sun lowered to the horizon. The time on the water helped her to regain some inner serenity. Callie sent her a reply text telling her Brian had traveled to Barcelona on a sales call, just as he had said. Remaining undecided about whether she should call him, Nicola resolved to talk with her cousin Maxim first.

As usual she docked with skill and without bumping the mooring. After tying up in the slip, tidying the cabin and stowing the gear away, she picked up her tote and went to step on the dock, but then she stopped. Staying consistent with her habits, she slid her eyes around to check out who might be nearby. The marina rested in dusky quietude. A couple of docks over a woman sat on the deck of her boat. On another craft a couple sipped tall iced drinks.

She sat down on the edge of her boat, took out her iPhone and called her cousin Maxim.

"Hello Nicola. Funny – just about to call you."

"You were?"

"Fancy sailing with me this weekend? Thinking of going up to Eze on the French Riviera to explore the medieval part of the town. Rent a car and drive around the area."

"Perhaps."

"Did something happen?"

"Brian is here in Barcelona."

"Why?"

"He's traveling on business, and I ran into him. He wants to see me again for dinner or lunch or something. Would I be crazy to go?"

Maxim stayed quiet for a few moments. "You should go. Back when we made our escape into our new lives, I noticed you liked Brian. You never regarded a man the way you did him. When you thought no one was looking, the look on your face was filled with longing."

"But how can a relationship between us ever go anywhere?"

Maxim lapsed into silence. Since he tended to be cautious and thoughtful, Nicola waited, afraid of what he might say.

"Brian might be the only man who could share in your future. Not only is he versed in your criminal past, he is aware of your father's horrid abuse. You will encounter hurdles, but you should take this chance."

This time Nicola turned silent.

"Be brave," Maxim said. "Brian would never hurt you. You can do this Nicola. If things work out between you, Brian may help you to push your bad times into your past."

Nicola smiled glad of Maxim's support. "What about you Maxim? You shouldn't always be alone."

"With my past how can I ever allow a woman into my life? You do not understand my complete story. One day I will tell you. Call Brian. Try to have dinner with him. Call me tomorrow."

Nicola ended the call. What Maxim hinted about his past piqued her curiosity, but Maxim would not be hurried. He would tell her on his terms and his timetable. She looked up Brian's cell phone number on his business card and dialed.

After talking with Brian and scheduling dinner with him, Nicola tried to keep her nervousness contained at the prospect of seeing him again so soon. Brian said he was out jogging and had reached the beach. She walked down the dock and glanced up and down the sandy coastline spying a man running towards her who might be Brian. She began walking while keeping her eyes fixed on the man as he waved and sped up into a sprint. Now dressed in baggy shorts and a T-shirt, Brian ran towards her on the sand. Right in front of her, he stopped and wiped the sweat off his face. She dropped her beach bag and stood facing him.

"Nicola," he exclaimed and opened his arms wide.

To her surprise she dove towards him, leaning against his chest. He wrapped his arms around her without holding her tight but continuing to embrace her until she pushed back away from him.

"What changed?" he asked.

"I texted Callie, and she confirmed you came here on business to pitch a prospect. I was worried you were here in an FBI capacity to arrest me or something. Anyway I went out on my boat today, or I would have called you earlier."

He smiled at her and said, "You're different. I found you lovely before Nicola. Now you appear less stressed and almost happy. Your hair is beautiful grown longer."

When he reached out and caressed her hair, she stood very still.

"So lustrous. This wind-blown look becomes you. What time do you want to meet for dinner?" Brian asked.

She glanced down and back up, smiling out of shyness. "I need to wash the salt spray off my skin first."

"Are you familiar with the city?"

"Yes," she said not wanting to reveal too much but not wanting to lie either.

"How about meeting me up on the sidewalk in an hour? Any favorite place you would like to go?"

Nicola frowned for a moment and said, "I'll book a table. One hour will be at nine. A little early to dine out in Barcelona, but I know an accommodating place."

Brian leaned in to kiss her on each cheek as Spaniards liked to do. "You will be here?"

"Yes, and you?"

"Never doubt," he said taking her hand.

As soon as she felt her hand enclosed by his, Nicola tensed and started to pull away, but remembering his kind nature, she let her hand ease back into his. Her fingers rested against his warm skin with the slightest of trembles as she worried about trusting this man.

Chapter 10

Arielle

From the motorboat she kept winter-docked in Barcelona, Arielle pulled out her camera to zoom in on the couple on the beach. Each of them appeared a little familiar. Focusing closer with her lens, their identities did not jump out at her. Perhaps the handsome guy with his slender build acted in some movie. His masculine yet refined facial features and trim body would play well on film or stage. He struck her as reminiscent of an Italian actor.

Like someone from a distant memory, Arielle found the woman hard to place. Her father had taught her to mentally catalog details in her surroundings and in people. The woman's face might belong to a casual acquaintance, and yet no particular identity or memory popped out at her. As they talked she clicked a few shots of them to be downloaded later to her laptop.

The couple walked up the beach, turned and strolled hand-in-hand to the sidewalk, their backs now to her. They exchanged a few more words and parted, each turning after a few steps to gaze at the other. Perhaps they might hook up again soon. Arielle shadowed the woman through her high-powered lens until she walked from view.

Arielle had watched the woman earlier when she had docked and tied up her sleek motor yacht. She had struck her as beautiful even though wind-blown from boating. The feline grace of her thin body appeared to be gifted with more feminine curves than she actually possessed. Arielle found herself attracted and intrigued. Although she stayed clear of relationships, she liked the occasional affair with a man or a woman.

Camera in hand Arielle stepped off the deck, glanced around in case anyone noticed her and followed the mooring to where the woman had tied up her boat. She surveyed the small yacht from the dock and considered boarding, but decided not to take the risk. To find out the name of the owner, she took quick photos of the name on the side of the craft and the license number. The name on the bow read *Hildago* which had been the name of a movie. The woman might be an actress. *Hildago* in Spanish meant a member of the nobility, like *nobleza*.

Tomorrow she planned to journey on to meet Kazimír in Greece and discuss moving more product on the Mediterranean. In need of a break she wanted to use her fast motorboat as transportation for this trip. If she found out the woman lived in Barcelona, perhaps she would return here and try to bump into her.

Right when she boarded her own craft, her cell phone rang and noticing the call came from her mother, Arielle answered quickly.

"*Maman*," she said and turned to sit on the deck.

"Arielle," her mother paused and inhaled, "I have the worst of news. The *gendarmes* killed your father this afternoon."

Although aware this horrible event might one day occur, Arielle had hoped her father would live into retirement and old age. A sigh came from deep in her chest. "Hold on while I walk to where we can have a private conversation."

Stunned by the news she ran into the cabin and closed the small door, then she sank down on the narrow bench and said into the phone, "What happened?"

"An arrest in Paris went wrong, and he is dead. Some of his men too. I stayed away from his business dealings. Now this."

"Where are you?"

"At the chateau of course. You know I seldom go to Paris anymore."

Arielle needed to spring into action before the threatening sadness and panic took hold of her. She had adored her father and was having trouble absorbing the thought that she would never talk with him again. Tears welled up in her eyes, but she forced them back. She must act quickly to take over his business empire. At his insistence she had developed a plan to assume control in case this day ever came. She must review it as she traveled back to Loire.

She and her father had discussed this very possibility. He had said he would not allow himself to be arrested, but he would go down fighting. Now older and slower he likely stood little chance against an aggressive police force.

"I'll drive back tonight and leave my boat docked here."

"Where are you?"

"Barcelona."

"Is it not dangerous for you to come home?"

"However much of a mess things are, I must pick up the pieces. Papa hadn't yet involved me in the actual operations, but I'm acquainted with the key people from gatherings in Paris. He kept me briefed on his dealings with the shops and export businesses – wine distribution, French country antiques, scents and oils and cheeses. Although I will be questioned, don't imagine I can contribute anything. Papa did not want me involved."

Even while she said those words, Arielle was surprised at how naturally the lies to her mother came. While she did not participate in the day-to-day running of her father's underground businesses, she was well-acquainted with the key people, how product moved, what the cash flows were and where the trouble spots tended to occur. Her father kept her mother out of his business dealings. She would as well.

"The authorities are never rational," her mother said.

"No one at the house?"

"They came here to tell me. Questioned me. They will be back. Perhaps you should stay away?"

Her mother's prevarication on whether she should return home told Arielle the degree of her mother's upset. Her mother's demeanor tended to be controlled and remote.

"My place is with you. We must honor my father. I should be by your side at the funeral. If I do not come home, I will appear guilty. They should find no cause to arrest me, but if they do our attorney will be engaged. Nothing will hold up in court as convincing evidence."

"Like your father you are skilled at deceit when you need to be. You know far more about the business than you are letting on. I know you and your father did not discuss fashion or your love life in all the time you spent together."

"*Maman*, let's not argue. I should arrive a little before dawn if I can stay awake enough to drive through the night."

Arielle ended the call and dialed Kazimír to alert him she would not be meeting him. When she reached voicemail she left a quick message about needing to return to Paris.

She was midway through snatching up a few things in the cabin and tossing them into her duffle bag when the news about her father hit her. She stood motionless in the middle of the cabin as the shock of his death sunk in. The tears she had been forcing back slid down her cheeks, and she dropped to the floor and started sobbing. She lost her protector, her mentor and her best friend all in one shootout. For the first time in her life, she understood the meaning of the word alone. From this day forward she would be isolated. Her mother kept herself too distant to be what her father had been to her.

The light in the cabin from the setting sun faded. Rising up on her knees, Arielle finished packing, zipped the duffle shut and then rose to wash off her face. She closed and locked the door and ran up the dock to hail a taxi, thinking the airport the best place to find a rental car at this time of night. As she sank into the cab, her thoughts swirled around in a jumble.

After years of discussion about one day taking over the family business from her father, was she ready? What had the police discovered so far? How much of the network of dealers, pushers and brothel owners remained in place?

Her disposition and orientation were modeled on her father's. Arielle put thoughts of the business first and shoved her sadness over the loss of her favorite parent into the back of her heart. How deeply she would mourn him and how much she would miss him. She choked back a sob which settled at the top of her throat in a constricting lump. Setting her jaw Arielle became determined to be as potent and shrewd as her father, although she would adopt her own style and would modernize their commercial interests. While she would start with their traditional trades, over time she wanted to move away from the street pushing of drugs and prostitutes.

First she must assert her position as the authority figure for the business. Later she would enact the plans concocted during those days in Paris with Carlos and Kazimír. As the future opened before her, she stood on the precipice of a changing world. She teetered there alone without her father to grab her if she started falling. Reality gobsmacked her with its harshness and yet she must step up to the challenge.

Above all Arielle was driven to prove herself. She wanted to run the networks her father established. She wanted to change the businesses, expand them and become an influential figure not just in France but in Europe and perhaps beyond. She was not after the money. She had to demonstrate her capabilities and power. She possessed a natural coldness that she could turn on whenever required and from this point forward she would need both the façade and the calculating, manipulative ability behind it.

Once in the car and driving up to the Loire chateau, she planned to call Carlos to find out if he had heard about the raid in Paris. She would also alert him of her intention to stand in her father's place to block any of Carlos' power-grabbing. That done, she would use the text to audio software on her laptop to listen to her contingency plans for taking over her father's business interests as she drove. In the coming days she would have to be two people, the dutiful daughter who mourned her father and the tough new business leader.

Chapter 11

Brian

Once back in his hotel room, Brian checked the suit he planned to wear if he needed to meet with the bank again the next day. He showered, shaved and dressed in a navy blazer and trousers for his date with Nicola. Just as he was finishing, his cell phone rang.

"Hello," he said without checking the caller's number.

"Brian? Antonio here."

Antonio led the bank auditors he had pitched in the afternoon. "This is Brian. Hi Antonio."

"We make the arrangements for your firm. The contract has the signatures. I will send a copy on the email. We want to make a start now."

Fantastic news but bad timing. Noble Firs needed this client after the debacle in Portland, and yet after running into Nicola and planning to spend the evening with her, Brian was torn. Why did Antonio have to want to start work tonight?

"Is the schedule we make not convenient? Your firm is busy?" Antonio asked.

Brian's mind raced. "Sorry but when I didn't hear from you, I scheduled an appointment for tonight. How about I send you the specs for the data? One of my partners in Portland will be available for any questions, and I can be at your office no later than midnight."

He listened for a response only to receive a long silence. Did he blow the deal?

"Oh *Señor* I understand," Antonio said. "My English is poor. Tomorrow I mean. We are, what is the word, constrained? We are constrained by a small time to run the extracts from our databases. I hesitate to ask so much, but can you arrive at our offices at four in the morning? We will make the extract with you. The program must make the start at six when the night, what do you call them? Batch runs I think. When the batch runs finish, we run the extract we make together."

"Perfect. Your English is terrific. My Spanish is lacking. How about I meet you at the front door to your building at four in the morning?"

"*Si. Buena Noches, Señor Tovey.*"

Brian ended the call. As a precaution against over-sleeping, he set alarms for three-fifteen in the morning and for three-thirty. While he would be short of sleep, he always found bursts of energy when needed. Next he sent a quick text to his partners on landing the client and confirming having two analysts from Portland in London on Thursday. Smoothing down his shirt Brian checked his appearance and hustled out the door in nervous anticipation of spending time with Nicola.

What an emotional few weeks he had been through – the threesome incident, the data issues in Portland, flying to Spain for the sales call, the FBI arrests, running into Nicola and now having a date with her. After eighteen months of torment from not seeing the exquisite woman, he could discover if she might be interested in him. She remained as intriguing as he remembered, and she was splendidly beautiful now that she let herself be a woman again.

When masquerading in the guise of Julio, she still attracted him. Until today he had seen her only once dressed as a woman on the day he met her and Maxim to begin the journey to gain their freedom. In her fashionable suit she might have stepped out of a Chanel ad in Vogue. For the first time in his life, he understood the word smitten. However given her past, did any hope of a relationship exist?

Brian had contented himself with dating, having fun, and moving on. Not until now did he want to become involved with someone. Nicola was not a woman to date with insouciance.

The evening with Nicola had started with an almost teenage awkwardness where each of them struggled to find topics to discuss. Once Brian had begun updating Nicola on Moll, Mathew, Callie, Steve and Ivy, they fell into a comfortable conversation.

Sitting across from him at the table, Nicola had both masked emotions and revealed snippets of them. Brian found himself experiencing feelings of protectiveness and a desire to help this haunted woman find a full life in the present and the future. He wanted to assist her in chasing away the ghosts of her past.

Taking her hand as they left the restaurant, again her fingers trembled in his gentle hold. When they neared the marina, he asked, "May I take you out again?"

Nicola walked in silence before saying in a hesitant voice, "Brian, I don't think ..."

"We're like magic together," he said softly to press his case although unsure how to approach this confident yet distant and cautious woman.

"A little spell comes over me with you," she whispered.

When they stopped at the marina, he asked, "Nicola, do you live here?"

"On the boat, no."

"I mean here in Barcelona."

"Yes."

"May I walk you to your door? You may not need my protection, but I'm the kind of guy who wants to ensure your safety."

She smiled at him and reached out to touch the silvered hair along his cheek. "As you did before. Three blocks up. You may walk me."

They sauntered on in silence. At Nicola's condo building she stopped and asked in an unsure voice. "Would you want to join me for breakfast or lunch tomorrow?"

"I'm booked to fly out early in the afternoon. If you can be flexible on time, I do want to see you again before I go."

"Call me when we can meet tomorrow."

Although Brian desired so much to hold Nicola and discover the thrill of kissing her soft, generous mouth, he feared he might spook her. Instead he raised her hand to his lips, kissing the back, turning it over and kissing the palm in a soft, slow motion he hoped would be memorable.

Chapter 12
Brian

N, sweet spending time with U in B. My town this weekend? Brian texted Nicola Thursday afternoon after landing at Heathrow and jumping on the train to Paddington.

Their reunion in Spain carried a promise of more. Although Nicola was weighted down by a load of troubles, he wanted her to enjoy the fullness of life. Finding himself attracted to a woman with a criminal past seemed inexplicable. If their relationship advanced, he would be making a commitment fraught with issues including a term in her agreement with the FBI which kept her from returning to the United States. To align himself with Nicola would be to give up his life in Portland, and perhaps his business, friends and family.

Only after he stepped out of a cab from Paddington at the Noble Firs offices did his phone buzz with a text message.

BKD Goring Hotel. C U Friday NT? LKNG FWRD, N.

After worrying Nicola would not want to hook up with him again, he now broke into a smile and pumped his fist a couple of times in celebration. In rapid taps he sent a confirmation back.

DNR 8? Wll Bk tbl nr Goring. Can't wait to be with you again. B.

So far they had skirted the issues between them, which one day they must address. For now he wanted them to date like a man and a woman who were attracted to each other and who wanted to understand each other better.

While he would proceed with caution, Nicola struck him as more than worth the wait. He was impressed by her courage in the face of the pain she continued to experience, her commitment to an honest and ethical life as required by the FBI and her donation of a substantial sum of money to a foundation for abused women. Each of these meant more to him than her considerable beauty. Nicola worked to make herself beautiful on the inside, and he found the attraction compelling. With that sighting of her sitting in the rose garden, he had gone from deluded to hopeful.

Brian reread the text exchange and smiled to himself. This first weekend in June he would be with Nicola. The direction of his life had turned upward. His two terrific business partners continued to handle their business back home, allowing him to tackle their expansion in the United Kingdom and now on the continent. His future appeared promising.

Two hours later his office phone rang. Noting the call came from his friend Mathew, Brian answered while debating if he should tell him about running into Nicola.

"Mathew super of you to call. Still busy on the vineyard?"

"Sure am. We solved a drainage issue in the new field, so we are planting more vines. Up early every morning, out in the fields all day or over at the construction site for the production facility. I'll tell you, a rain storm would be a gift, allowing us to take some rest. How did you do in Barcelona?"

"Landed the client. Got their data extracted this morning and we are loading the files now. About to do my duty calls to a couple of East Coast clients to explain the situation to them with the money laundering. Steve called me while I waited at the airport in Barcelona early this afternoon. The FBI arrested a mob boss out of Philadelphia and three of his henchmen and are now working to dismember their drug-based network.

"He talked about the action in Paris turning into a bloodbath and then said the one in Sofia should put another mob boss in jail, provided he survives his bullet wounds. The FBI did a great job of acting quickly to stop the criminal activity represented in the flow of money we found. Our findings matched up with work they had pursued out of the New York and Philadelphia offices."

"This will increase those stats Moll keeps, right?" Mathew asked.

"The success will help shore him up. He loves those numbers. During rough times like the past couple of weeks, the stats help us to focus on our successes. We lost one big client when we told them about the incident, and two more are on the fence. All we can do is keep up a dialogue with them and hope to lure them back while we step up our marketing efforts. Great to land that bank in Barcelona – our first client on the continent."

"You provide top notch services. This was just a nasty bump in the road. It will all work out, you'll see," Mathew said and paused. He took a deep breath and said, "Could we move on to a different topic? I need some advice."

"Sure, I'll help if I can. What's up?"

"We're continuing the battle with Callie's miserable ex-husband to let me adopt Susannah. We already conceded visitation rights for John Henry as well as allowing calls with her. We will pay Susannah's expenses including her college tuition. John Henry will be left with no financial responsibility for his daughter. Susannah must feel assured that this is her home. She needs to be guaranteed we are her parents and no one can take her away."

"What else can John Henry want?"

"The prick wants to be compensated for the loss of his only child. Of course he didn't lose her. His behavior forced Callie to leave with Susannah. He's a bully, an alcoholic and a sexual deviant. We would win the case in Court, but we don't want Susannah to go through a legal proceeding, and I don't want Callie suffering any more grief from the miserable John Henry. Even so I hate to buy a child."

"What's he asking for?"

"A million up front and five grand for every month he doesn't spend time with her. The bastard is still drinking. We don't want him near her."

"The man is outrageous," Brian said. "How can he use his sweet little girl to gain money? So despicable. Didn't Callie's divorce terms contain language about his sobriety?"

Mathew sucked in some air before he said, "As a part of the divorce agreement, Callie is obligated to pay for her husband to dry out from his alcoholism at a treatment center. If he stays sober, he will receive additional money each month for two years. So far he didn't complete a program."

"Why not go back to Callie's divorce terms? On principle you don't want to pay money to adopt Susannah. However you might consider adding to the trust fund for John Henry. The Trust will only disburse money if John Henry goes through an approved sobriety program and remains abstemious, demonstrated through testing each month. Visitation rights and calls with Susannah should be dependent on his achieving these conditions. In exchange John Henry allows you to adopt her."

"Dammit Brian. I shouldn't need to ..." Mathew growled out in protest.

Brian paused to organize his thoughts to sound persuasive. While a strong man, Mathew tended to function rationally. "For Susannah's sake you do. With all the upheaval and changes in her life, she needs stability. She needs the security of living in a settled situation."

When Mathew became quiet, Brian glanced at the display on his phone to make sure the line remained active.

After a prolonged silence Mathew said, "I needed those words from you. Callie and I become so emotional about this situation, we lose perspective. Thanks to my dad the money is available to me. If he remained alive, I think he would agree this is a proper use of his fortune. While my dad lived to make money, he never stinted on spending."

"Glad I helped."

"What's new with you?" Mathew asked.

"You heard I ran into Nicola in Barcelona? We went to dinner together."

"You like her, don't you? You stared at the photo of her here at my house, and your face lights up when we talk about her.

"I like her more than I should. Nicola is coming to London this weekend. She's so skittish that we're taking these first steps with caution."

"Callie and I are both fond of her. She does carry lots of concerns from her past."

"She owns her future," Brian said in defiance.

Mathew began laughing in a deep belly rumble of amusement.

"What's so funny?"

"You. When we talked before, you were upset by finding yourself trapped in a potential threesome. Now you're taking up with a known felon."

"She paid her debt," Brian said surprised by the vehemence in his own tone. "Psychologically she is still paying. What her father did to her haunts her."

"Funny you would wind up attracted to her. The determined playboy is an old softie on the inside. Brian, I wish you and Nicola only the best."

"Don't tell Steve."

"Not a word but if things progress with you two, you must fill him in."

"Take the dreaded walk to his office like we used to do when we encountered an issue on an FBI case? He'll explode when I tell him."

"Steve isn't always predictable, and he's mellower than when we worked for him. Don't leave him ignorant of your situation too long."

After finishing the call Brian called up a picture on his cell phone taken of Nicola when they shared a late breakfast in Barcelona. Sitting on a terrace overlooking the Mediterranean, she wore a sunhat pushed back on her head for the photo, making the yellow straw brim stand up like a crown. Thoughts of Nicola diminished his reservations about her past, allowing him to focus on the possibilities of a shared future.

Chapter 13
Nicola

On Saturday morning Nicola waited in the elegant Goring Hotel lounge for Brian to join her for breakfast and to discuss their plans for the day. Dining with him the previous evening stayed with her as the most fantastic two hours of her life. Her attraction to him and her respect for him grew as she started to get to know him better. They had talked about the fictional action series she had created and now struggled to progress into animation. Before she departed on Monday, he promised to go over her sketches and outline. Their time today would be pure enjoyment even though he needed to work for a few hours at the office.

"*Hola*," Nicola said as she moved towards him when he walked into the lounge. Dressed for a day about town, she blushed when Brian gave her a look of obvious appreciation at the way her dressy jeans showed off her long legs and flared out a bit like sixties bell-bottoms.

"*Hola*," Brian replied and leaned in to kiss her on each cheek. "Did you sleep well?"

Nicola stared at him and shook her head in the negative. "I am embarrassed to say I spent too much time thinking of our time together. Thank you again for a delightful evening. You do appreciate I love to dine well."

"You eat so sparingly that I worry for your health."

"I savor what I choose to eat," she said with a smile.

"Let's order our breakfasts first and plan our day second," Brian said with a smile. He smiled so much that Nicola found herself feeling a little more carefree.

After the waiter departed with their orders, Nicola settled back into her plush seat and said. "London may be my favorite city. Let's be tourists this weekend and go to Buckingham Palace – I've never been, have you?"

"Not visited the queen either. How about I buy tickets for tomorrow? This afternoon I need to be in the office for a couple of hours reviewing the findings in the data from the bank in Barcelona. Same late Sunday afternoon. In between those times, I am yours."

"Gives me time to shop at Harrods. Today until you go to the office, let's visit Westminster Abbey and stroll around the city. How about a sunset ride on the London Eye?"

"Perfect. I booked a table for a late dinner at the Ledbury. Tomorrow morning would you show me your sketches and outline for your action series?" Brian asked.

"Here over breakfast?" Nicola replied. She sat as the waiter poured their coffee. An expression of uncertainty and sadness crossed her face.

"What's troubling you?" Brian asked and covered her hand with his.

As she had become more comfortable with his touch, she didn't withdraw her hand reflexively.

"At some time we must talk about ... my past." Her voice faded and her speech faltered until the last two words came out in a whisper.

"We will at some point. For now let's enjoy each other's company – as friends, as dates, as a couple starting a relationship. This time will only come once to us. We should enjoy each moment. If we are lucky, our affections will deepen and perhaps what haunts you from the past will not remain so important, not to you and not to me."

"Are we starting a relationship?" Nicola asked. She could feel her eyes widen in surprise.

"Sure hope so."

Their breakfasts came with their full English orders appealingly arranged on the plate. Nicola leaned towards him, this time reaching over to take his hand.

"I am afraid at some point you will want more than I can give."

Brian reached out and placed his fingers under her chin. "Nicola, I am old-fashioned enough to believe love can conquer all. I've never been in love, and yet sitting here with you and talking with you fills me with hope."

Nicola smiled at him, her thoughts still clouded with doubt. Nonetheless a bit of sunshine broke into them. "Maxim said you might be the only man I could form an association with."

"No wonder I liked your cousin. I would like to hang out with him again."

Releasing his hand she picked up her fork and lifted a dainty portion of the scrambled eggs to her lips. She tended not to let her mouth widen when she smiled, but the more she saw of Brian, the more happiness broke through her barriers.

Chapter 14
Arielle

Over a month later following harassing conversations with municipal police and the national gendarmes, Arielle surreptitiously picked up the pieces of her father's business. Concealed in his wine cellar in the Loire, her father had kept an emergency list of contact numbers and clearance codes to be used in case of his premature death or incarceration. After the worst of the sessions with the gendarmes had ended, Arielle went down to the cellar on the pretense of bringing up wine for dinner and extracted the list.

Several of his key people remained unidentified by the police or at least not arrested. Moving with care she re-established communications with the remaining middlemen and shored up a significant part of the operations.

After the questioning at her parents' home in the Loire and the follow-up interrogation at the *Gendarmerie Nationale* in Paris, she remained free but under surveillance. Even after a month Arielle remained fearful of having calls monitored. To meet with Carlos and Kazimír by Skype, Arielle acquired a new laptop, checked into a hotel with Wi-Fi in Paris and accessed a secure connection. While they had exchanged information when necessary, most of the activities between them were frozen except for the movement of a reduced amount of drugs.

Following preliminary updates on status in each of their organizations, they began discussions of current business.

"Let's discuss the tally on the payments in transit that the FBI froze. Kazimír and I came to an agreement, and he has been paid the agreed part of my share. You have not made restitution to Kazimír and me," Arielle said.

"You mean for this five million you asked about? We're out five million. I lose, you lose."

"But you kept your profit," Kazimír said. "No more product flows until you pay up."

Carlos shrugged. A glitch in the transmission left his shoulders up a little too long. "Then I go south. Buy drugs from Mexico or Colombia where suppliers will be more accommodating."

"If you work with other suppliers, we will sell to your competitors in the west and south and those dealers will put the squeeze on you. Your territory would be in chaos in six months," Arielle said.

"You would screw me over, wouldn't you? Never trust a Frenchie. My old man understood how you operate. I don't have the cash right now."

"Then sell some of your assets. How many boats and condos do you own?"

"Leave my personal stuff out of it. All right. We'll strike a deal. Let me come up with some terms."

Refusing to be provoked Arielle said, "This will be our first topic tomorrow. What are we going to do about how we move money? Who tipped off the FBI? Most of them are too dumb to figure out evasive tactics in money movement."

"Those fucking consultants as they call themselves. The ex-FBI punks out west. I think whatever brains the FBI employed walked out when those guys left. We thought we had neutralized them with having their data guy disguise our transactions. Now they hired a damn technical Narc to manage the data from the banks."

"We should set up our own financial institution," Kazimír said. "Fund the setup with our legitimate businesses and base the bank in Turkey or some other country not cooperating with foreign government investigations."

"Sounds like a long-term strategy and a worthwhile goal. Let's discuss the idea in the future and stay focused on the issues of today," Arielle said while making a note to follow-up on the bank idea.

"Essential for us to smurf our funds," Carlos said. "Suggest we beef up what we are running through the international charities. Hey, do you remember the mastermind calling himself El Zorro Astuto who turned out to be three brothers? How did they move money around for so long? Those dudes pushed money through the banking system for years before they got nabbed."

"Extensive network of sham companies with many phony officers. The one brother engineered all the money movement routing and rerouting the funds once, twice, three, four or more times. He was a genius holed up in some provincial town. Never went outside," Arielle said.

"Where did you get your info?"

"Amazing what the FBI discloses. Too bad you don't read more, Carlos."

Carlos glared at her. "So those brothers did what we were doing."

"Except faster-paced on changing companies and identities. Plus they let huge wads of money accumulate in various accounts. After some time they shifted the funds around in a sort of shell game. However I believe they are all dead now."

"*Ano*," Kashmir said in Czech, meaning yes. "All three of the brothers plus some cousin or something. Dealt in information. Name of Julio."

Arielle forced herself not to smile. She had tried to seduce Julio once at a party in Miami. He used to be a metrosexual head-turner who could excite her with a glance. They danced a slow version of the wobble with some other couples by the side of a pool. When she turned around Julio had vanished as though he became a shadow and slid away. Damn shame he's dead. She remembered him as a foxy man who only drank the best of champagnes.

"When do we shut down these consultants?" Carlos asked.

"We need photos of them."

"I'll put a guy on them doing surveillance. Photos are on their website. You are the one who should read more, Arielle," Carlos said. "Got an org chart from the stupid DBA we hired. We'll hit them in their hometown – freaking Portland, Oregon. After we kill one or two of them, they will shit in their pants and close-up shop."

"This is my action item. Our goal should be to silence those brains one-by-one and avenge our fathers. Gives us the bonus of leaving the fucking feds as a body with a peanut for a brain. I gotta finish sorting out the East Coast Ops first. Lost six of our middlemen along with my old man and his two musclemen."

Nodding agreement Arielle raised an eyebrow at Kazimír. Those two tasks would keep Carlos busy for the next few weeks giving her and Kazimír more time to consolidate their positions and strengthen their networks. They needed Carlos now, but she wanted to find alternative distribution channels in the United States. His egotistical and volatile ways meant he should not be depended on for long as their sole U.S. distributor.

"Right now we all need to consolidate each of our operations under our new leadership," Kazimír said. "Let's not do anything on the revenge objective until August. Agreed?"

"I'll do some surveillance when I can spare a guy, but I agree. No rush on Operation Payback," Carlos said. "Those stoolies will still be there in one or two months."

Chapter 15
Nicola

A few weeks later as she reclined out on her balcony, Nicola read the text from Brian with a mixture of joy and trepidation.

"Cotswold Sojourn? FDY AM thru SNDY? B."

The weekends Nicola and Brian had spent together in the last month, including a few days of sailing the Mediterranean with her cousin Maxim, were idyllic. Brian had enjoyed Maxim's company and appreciated his soul of an artist. When they drove to visit his home and glass studio high in the arid mountains, Brian had complimented Maxim on the skill and care in his glass work. In his showroom, one shelf showed pieces made since he had begun working with glass, going from thick and somewhat clunky to the more refined pieces of today. He marketed his creations in a shop in the Gràcia district of Barcelona in contemporary galleries. The proceeds went to benefit a monastery higher up in the mountains near his home.

As their bond grew and deepened, Brian was stealing into her heart, transforming her teenage-type dreams about him into reality. They had toured London, Barcelona and the small, charming Bruges to discover the sights and personalities of the cities. Often during the week she replayed in her mind the joy of spending time with Brian on weekends.

Would Brian become frustrated by her fear of feeling passion for him? One day he would want to make love with her. After what her father had put her through, she remained frightened and frigid when she thought about sex. As soon as her passions became aroused with Brian, she pulled away. Although she continued to seek help from a therapist to work through her problems, she remained afraid of having sex. How naïve for her to think love would outweigh the abuse she had experienced as a child and as a teen.

Although she let Brian hold her and they kissed, she would pull away and retreat inside herself as soon as she became aroused. At other times she would gaze at him and shake her head. Each time they parted she feared she would lose him.

After rereading his message she decided to call him.

"Brian," Nicola said by way of greeting him.

"Hello my sweet Nicola. What do you think of a long weekend in the Cotswolds?"

"The country scares me. I'm a city girl."

"Couldn't we go to a quiet spot? Wander country lanes. Visit gardens tumbling with flowers. The Cotswolds should be beautiful this time of year."

"I like cities because I understand them and I am skilled at slipping away in the streets, shops and buildings."

"Are you still fearful one day someone out of the underworld will want revenge, figure out where you live and who you are now? I'll be with you. While I may be a little rusty, I used to be more than a respectable FBI agent."

Again Nicola remained quiet, thinking. "You want to talk, don't you?" she asked in a flat tone.

"I think we've reached the time when you need to share your burdens. Hasn't our relationship progressed far enough for you to trust me with your pain? How about a small city? Edinburgh or Oxford?"

Nicola hesitated only for a moment. "Edinburgh. Been wanting to visit the city. Will you fly to the airport up there or take a train?

"I'll check travel options and email you. Nicola, tell me if you are not ready."

"We can't dodge this forever," Nicola said, keeping her voice carefully modulated. "Every time we are together, I am reminded of my need to face my problems. Yet every time, I want to savor my days with you."

"Darling we can find our way through this," Brian said. "I love you too much not to."

"You love me?" she asked in a voice shaking timorously.

"Yes."

"With your knowledge of my past and my obligations, you love me?"

"When I think of the way you pulled away from your earlier existence to make a new life, how could I not love you?"

"You are handsome, kind, intelligent and so much of a man, while I am nothing. How can you love me?"

"In you I perceive an inner beauty, an indomitable spirit and a desire to become the woman you should be."

"I never experienced a man's love untainted by an evil side."

"Putting physical love to one side, what about your cousins Cruze, Cristo and Eduardo? Did you not all enjoy the love of family? Did you not love their parents?"

"Yes, but ..."

"Can't you place your confidence in me to love you in a kind and gentle way?"

As his words circled around her, she fell silent. If Brian did love her, she must conquer her past and her fears.

"Any chance you might be smiling?" he asked.

"More like glowing. Something inside me wants to come alive."

"Your glow gives us a foundation to build on." Brian asked her to hold on while he talked with one of his staff members. "Nicola my love business calls. Email me your logistics, and I'll find a hotel."

"You're busy at the office. Let me handle making our reservations."

His pushing for a discussion scared her. How long would he be willing to wait for her? What if she never conquered her issues? Would he be repulsed when she related more about her past?

With this conversation darkness tinged their relationship. For reassurance Nicola brought up the photos of Brian on her cell phone. If she began to open up and talk with him about her troubles, could he help her to recover?

Nicola found herself shaken. Brian loved her. As their connection deepened and grew, his words made her dreams move closer to reality. Would she be able to love him physically? Even as he stirred her and made her want him, memories of what her father did to her crowded in.

The way he used to grab her. Those episodes were so perverse, so dirty and so wrong. The foul man had made her unclean. All these years later, his actions left her tainted. Brian failed to understand the pain and fear associated with relating her past. Behind his regard for her, lurked his desires as a man. He stayed kind and tender. Could he turn into a monster like her father?

Never had she sought girlfriends to confide in, not as a child and not as an adult. Callie was the first woman she thought of as a friend. Ivy might be a friend. Each of them did more than endure their husbands. They thrived on their love-making. Could she ever put away her fears, disgust and self-loathing?

Nicola's phone sounded her appointment reminder to meet with her current counselor. This would be a momentous session. While she wanted to trust Brian and she desired his love, she needed to learn how to give more of herself to him. Did she possess the courage?

Her solitary life required self-reliance, but now after experiencing the warmth of Brian's arms around her and the sweetness of the loving expression in his kind brown eyes, she wanted him to share her life. While he freely offered her love, she needed to cast off her reserve and her shame to love him back as a woman should. Did she possess the capacity in her heart, much less in her body, to love Brian?

With these considerations buzzing through her head, Nicola grabbed her purse and keys. Without her habitual once-over in the mirror, she raced out of the apartment to her therapy session.

In talking with her counselor, Nicola had previously skirted the issue of Brian because she did not want her new relationship tarnished by examination.

Halfway through her hour, her counselor said, "Tell me what is on your mind. You are different today. More distracted and yet more assured."

Nicola hesitated, paused and blurted out, "For the first time in my life I am dating. One man, one exceptional man. Today he told me he loved me. I am afraid."

"Of love?"

"Of passion. Of his desires. Of intimacy."

"Two people are in a relationship, Nicola. We have talked about you and the horrible things done to you as a child. When you love someone, you put them before yourself in many ways."

"Are you saying I should endure his demands?" Nicola asked as her fears came closer to the surface.

"What I am saying is you should not compare this man to your father. He is himself, with his own thoughts, emotions and values. What is your perception of him?"

"Always with me he is kind and gentle. I see him as an idealist and a man of character. He and the other FBI agents who helped my cousin and me are like people from another world. They witnessed terrible badness, they solved the most complex FBI cases dealing with criminals of the worst kind – major drug lords, high-stakes smugglers, child prostitution rings. Yet they remain untouched. To say they remained unaffected by the cases they solved would not be valid, but their beliefs in justice are inviolate. Nothing shakes their convictions. Each of them will do anything for each other and for anyone they decide to protect."

"They make you feel what?"

"Unworthy and yet valued."

"If people of their caliber can appreciate you and if this excellent man can love you, why can you not love yourself? What happened was done to you. Did you ask for your father's abuse? No. Don't keep engaging in self-torture. The fault is not yours. This man is aware of your past?"

"While serving with the FBI, he came to be acquainted with my past. Not the details and not my feelings. Now he wants to talk, and I wish to continue dating without considering my past."

"Do you want only friendship from this man?"

"I never dated. Never let anyone touch me. With his gentleness, he bypasses some of my barriers. When he holds my hand, he makes me tremble. When he takes me in his arms and kisses me, I run away inside of myself. I freeze up."

"Ask yourself honestly – do you find his attentions unpleasant?"

Nicola sat thinking. Brian's attentions pleased her and she liked the way he made her tingle. "Not unpleasant, but I am frightened of where they will lead."

"Love-making between a man and a woman should not be hurtful. You kept apart for your entire life, first as a child by hiding what was being done to you and then as an adult when you masqueraded as a man. Aloneness became your normal. Allowing someone to share your life will require you to give. Are you unable to give? Think of this man as well as yourself."

With those words she realized the self-centered nature of her perspective. Brian possessed his own desires, wishes and perhaps issues to deal with too. This constituted a new perspective for her, and she needed time to contemplate this insight.

Though she never thought of herself as selfish, her life did orbit around herself. When she gave to charities and even when she funded a foundation to benefit abused children, she gave nothing of herself. The fund disposed of the money left to her from her parents' estate, gained through her father's drug-running. She had wanted nothing from her parents. The donation of their money to charity gave her a way to retaliate.

With learning Brian loved her, shifts started happening inside of her isolated heart, like geological plates sliding under the ocean floor, moving with a slight tremor. When she found she wanted to share this slight change with Brian, the plates around her heart shifted a little more.

"Where do I summon the courage to tell him and how much should I reveal?"

Her counselor consulted her calendar. "We can schedule a second appointment at the end of my day. Why don't you go home and make notes about what you want to say to this man to help him understand you? Then come back here at five and go over what you want to say. Would this approach help you?"

"Possibly."

"Will you return at five?"

Nicola thought and nodded. "Thank you for making the time for me. I will be here."

As she faced the prospect of talking with Brian, she began to see the benefits of tackling this much-feared obstacle of sharing her past. Perhaps she could anticipate her upcoming time with Brian with a little less trepidation.

Chapter 16
Brian

Late on Friday Brian stepped off the train from London, both anxious and eager to meet Nicola in Edinburgh. A part of him worried she might not fly in to meet him. Another part feared he had asked too much of her when he wanted to discuss her past. Despite those concerns the longer they waited, the harder talking would become. Overriding his apprehensions was the joy that Nicola brought into his life. She had raised his expectations and taught him to notice and value even small objects or events with an exquisite aspect -- the fringe on a lily petal, the fresh splash of water in a fountain, the reflection of the sun in London's tall windowed buildings.

He glanced around the platform. Not spotting Nicola standing there, he headed into the station, bustling alive with students and commuters. After glancing around and starting to fear she was standing him up, he spied her near an exit from the train station, chic yet casual in black slacks and a light cashmere sweater with a long gray shawl draped over her shoulders. Her face lit up when she saw him, although signs of strain showed around her eyes.

"You're here," Brian said, dropping his luggage and encircling her in his arms.

"I confess to moments when I considered canceling. Avoidance and flight are my preferred methods of self-defense, but I must be fair to you."

"The longer we wait the more this issue will grow in our minds. I hope our discussion will be helpful for you and for me."

"I booked a suite at the Nira Caledonia – quiet, walkable, refined – gives us a place to talk."

Holding hands in the back of the taxi, they rode the short distance to the hotel in silence. Each of them felt too apprehensive to talk much or admire the city.

"Shall we walk out for an early lunch?" Brian asked as they stepped out of the taxi.

"Let's go up to my suite and talk before I lose my courage."

He gripped her hand a little tighter, leaned over and whispered, "Your bad memories torture you. Do not fear the loss of my love over them."

The sadness in her eyes deepened, giving his precious Nicola a haunted appearance. Did he ask too much by wanting her to share her burden?

Nicola directed the porter to store Brian's luggage in her suite until his room became available. Once the porter departed Nicola opened the mini-fridge, took out two bottles of water and gave one to Brian. He sat on the love seat while she chose a chair opposite him.

"I need to do this my way, Brian. Let me talk. Best not to touch me during these revelations. Do not interrupt me until I am finished."

He nodded and wished she sat next to him to hold her hand and give her reassurance, but he followed Nicola's directions to avoid making this any harder on her than necessary.

Nicola planted each of her feet on the floor, took a sip of water and clasped one hand with the other. After breathing deeply several times, she began talking in a flat voice. "My father started to abuse me when I was about five years old. For several years, he stayed with making me touch him and stroke him, but always with threats of hurting me or beating me to make me cooperate and then stay silent about these episodes."

Pausing she licked her lips and took another sip of water, coughed and drank again. "When I turned twelve he forced me to give him oral sex. Sturdy and muscular he controlled me through threats, physical punishments and beatings.

She stared at the floor and said in a monotone voice, "The attacks were random. Weeks and sometimes months would go by, and life would appear to be normal. He would talk to me at dinner and treat me with affection. One day without warning he would be after me again. Part of the terror came from not having any forewarnings.

"I tried to tell my mother when he first cornered me. She slapped me and told me not to talk such filth. After giving me a stern lecture, she put me in the car and took me to the Catholic Church where she went every day to pray. She made me pray on my knees to ask for forgiveness for my wicked imagination."

Brian paid attention to her dull voice, absorbing the horror of what she told him. He understood she ran away from home right after her 16th birthday. His lovely Nicola had suffered sexual and physical abuse for eleven years. Her mother must have perceived the truth and failed to step in. Abhorrence of her parents and outrage at the brutality she had endured filled him.

Nicola shifted in her seat and leaned back to stare at the wall.

"Most of the time when my father accosted me, I escaped in my own brain. I would mind-travel to a favorite park or remember a story I had read or think of times with my cousins playing games or talking. The mind-travel allowed me to keep my innermost self separate and secure. I fought him particularly on the days when I found no chance to flee inside myself because he snuck up on me or when I failed to find my mental escape hatch."

Becoming quiet Nicola appeared to shrink within herself. When she spoke again the pitch of her voice rose higher and carried more inflection.

"One day a few weeks before my sixteenth birthday, I returned from school and sat at the desk in my bedroom doing homework. The house was empty except for me. My father seldom hung around during the day, and my mother often went out. I put music on, some rock station or other, and began doing my algebra homework."

Her face changed. All the color drained from her cheeks, and her eyes lost focus. Brian leaned forward in his chair ready to go to her if she needed him.

"There were times when I could bear being in my home – when I was alone. I loved mathematics and doing the complex problems in my homework was fun for me."

She paused again and seemed to shrink inside of herself as if going back in time in her mind gave her the stature of a child. When she spoke again, she no longer spoke in the past tense. She moved back into her mind to relive the memory. Brian wanted to stop her and not cause her more pain, but he had agreed to let her tell her story in her own way.

"I finish three of the problems assigned and start on the fourth."

"Suddenly his hands are on me rubbing my breasts. I squirm and try to break away, but he is strong. He reaches down under my skirt, forces my legs open, rips my underpants, sticks his fingers on me and begins rubbing. I struggle to break away, pushing at the desk. The chair flips sideways, and I fall to the floor on my stomach. I squirm away to free myself. He jumps on me, groping to turn me over. When I resist he punches me in the buttocks once, twice, three times. I scream in agony and grab the leg of the desk trying to pull myself away.

"He grasps me by my shoulders and turns me on my back. His penis is out. He shoves the big hot thing up to my mouth. I bite as hard as I can. He roars in pain. I have an instant. I scramble up and jump on the bed to run away, but he is too fast."

Brian sits transfixed by this woman who he loves, wanting to help her and comfort her, but she has left him to move into her past. Tears flowed down his face as he listened in astonishment to how her father had pinned her to the bed and beat her until she gave him oral sex. When he was satisfied the dastardly man had gone after her with his mouth and hands until her most private parts were raw and painful.

Shocked by how the man had mixed sex and brutality, he wished the bastard lived today. Brian wanted to make him suffer many times. The man's bestial treatment of his daughter appalled him. He suffered from a mental illness Brian failed to understand, or perhaps the devil did exist and had entered human form.

Nicola hesitated, curling over with her hands gripping her abdomen. Her voice sank to a whisper and Brian leaned forward to catch her words.

"When he is finished he sinks back down on top of me, sitting on his knees and staring at me. He reaches up and strokes my face and calls me 'his virgin whore.'

"Those words signify what I am, what he forces me to become. I begin crying. He slaps me across the face. I yelp out loud. I am scared, so scared. Sometimes he wants a second go at me. My mother comes into the house downstairs and turns on the television. He climbs off me, punches me hard between my legs to remind me never to say anything and leaves my room.

"I hurt all over from his brutality. I want to die to end my life of misery. I want to curl up into a ball on my bed and cry, but I must get rid of the foul taste of him and the smells on my body. I crawl off the bed, undress, inspect my bruises and step into the shower where I lather up the soap and scrub and scrub and scrub. No matter how much water runs over me, I still feel dirty. Finally I dry myself off and brush my teeth, but again find no escape from my guilt and shame."

Nicola pauses, sits back up, but stares without seeing him. His tears are flowing down his cheeks. She lets out a deep sigh and gasps in a fresh breath.

"The next day on my dresser I spotted a gold chain necklace with a mermaid charm. He liked to reward me with gifts. Whether pleased with me or filled with guilt, I never figured out. I hated to touch those objects, but if I didn't wear them, the punishments worsened.

"Again he did not come near me for several weeks. Not until my sixteenth birthday. The night he raped me. He attacked me with more brutality than usual, and he kept going at me for hours. No place on my body remained unfouled by his hands, mouth or penis. Everywhere possible, he probed and entered."

Brian choked on a sob and reached for his handkerchief. Bile rose in his throat.

"The next day I ran away to my cousins' mother – my sweet aunt. I hid in her home while I healed. We devised my escape plans. I escaped. I escaped."

After a few moments Nicola straightened and pushed back her shoulders. Her eyes slowly regained focus. She stared at him. Her face changed as compassion replaced fear and hatred. Rising she walked the three steps over to sit next to him, taking him in her arms and letting him cry for her.

"You are sweet to weep for me," she said in a gentle tone.

Brian encircled her with his arms and said, "Never again. No one will ever hurt you again." He pushed back to wipe his damp cheeks. "So sorry this happened to you. Thought I toughened up after my work in the FBI. How did you remain so calm when you related these dreadful events?"

"Sometimes my self-control became all I possessed of myself."

"When you speak of the abuse in general terms, a person cannot fathom the depth of torment and despair in what you endured for all those years. With telling me of the one incident, I can only begin to understand the depth of your misery. Eleven years. Oh Nicola, how horrible for you."

"Talking about my past now, the part of me I protected keeps me grounded.

Over the years I cried about my young life many, many times until I can't weep any more."

"May I ask a question or two now? Don't worry. I won't ask you to relive another of those memories of sadistic horror."

"Ask me anything."

"How did you turn into Julio?"

"I hid at my aunt's – Maxim's mother and father's – for two months. We discovered my father had made me pregnant."

"You went for an abortion, didn't you?"

"How could I bear the bastard's child? My aunt helped me to arrange an abortion. Sorry if I shock you."

"You did what needed to be done. You were so young, and the baby was …"

"The product of incest. A week later I went out during the night and went to my father's legitimate business, a dry-cleaning plant where I knew he kept huge amounts of cash in a safe in his office. I went with him sometimes as a child, and I remembered he kept the combination taped to the bottom of his desktop, inside the middle drawer. After breaking in I packed as much of the money as I could carry into a duffle. Although I took mostly large bills, a few hundred thousand is bulky and cumbersome.

"My uncle helped me to secure the money in a safety deposit box. He booked me on a flight to Venezuela. He was the most honest of men, but for me he had gone underground a week or so before to buy a fake passport and other papers. After arriving in Caracas I rented a tiny apartment. Once there under my false identity, I set up a bank account. My uncle transferred money to me each week. While I continued to be terrified my father might discover where I went and come after me, I felt less frightened than back when I was living in my parents' house.

"Before I left Miami I confided in Cristo. He was young and hot-headed but also my best friend. Although hearing what happened to me made him furious, he agreed to be silent and to go along with the plan for my escape. Some days after I arrived in Caracas, his mother – my aunt -- called me and told me my father had been killed in a drive-by shooting. I realized Cristo must have killed him. At not quite seventeen he had heisted a car, stolen gun and trailed my father until he found his chance.

"After hearing the news I cried from sheer relief to be free of that man. Sadly the killing marked a turning point for Cristo when he took his first step from juvenile delinquent to the gangster he turned into. Always for me he remained my protector and my dear cousin. Over time I also came to perceive him as shallow, money-hungry and egotistical.

"What about Maxim?"

"When all this was happening, he was incarcerated in juvie – the prison for juvenile delinquents. The police had caught him after peddling some drugs. He took the full sentence rather than reveal that Cristo was his partner."

Brian nodded. He remembered reading about the juvenile sentence in the FBI case file on Maxim back when he went by his original name of Cruze. "How did the shooting lead to your life as Julio?"

"Living alone didn't worry me. Only when I went out did I feel scared. I sensed men's eyes on me when I went to the market for food. The way their eyes followed me, alarmed me. In my first tiny apartment, I conceived the plan to live my life as a man. From my initial thought I created Julio and transformed myself into him.

"After moving to another location in Caracas, I tried out my alternate persona. In the years following I took self-defense lessons, learned how to shoot a gun and enrolled in technical college where they trained me in programming, using the Internet and communicating by email. I frequented parties and social scenes popular with the trendy younger set. People from the underworld joined those gathering. When people talked to me as Julio, I listened, made contacts and put together my plan of trading in information.

"Several years later I returned to Miami where I lived as Julio for more than twenty years. Each year my web of connections and insights grew until I charged hundreds of thousands of dollars to disclose information or to obtain secrets and protected data. From my initial base of contacts and knowledge, I built my network until my fees started at a million dollars.

"Only to buy my and Maxim's freedoms did I cease living as Julio. Learning about Cristo's and Eduardo's deaths devastated me. I stopped taking contracts although I stayed in Miami most of the time, waiting for Cruze to contact me. He had left the business a year before, while Cristo and Eduardo stuck with their prized Fuentes Enterprises. With Cristo and Eduardo dead, I lacked any way to reach

Cruze. I feared endangering him by using any underground sources.

"After many months Cruze did call me. We met several times and talked often. Once we decided on our course of action, we did our stupid abduction of Ivy and made the deal with Steve and the FBI. Mathew devised the twist to fake our deaths to give us a better chance of survival. For my transformation I gave up Julio. Only after I settled in Barcelona did I reveal myself as a woman.

"Since the day I met you, when we flew back for our last trip around the United States, you stayed on my mind. You treated me with gentleness. Strange to say you reminded me of the other half of Julio. The decent half."

"You lingered in my thoughts too. And I hold the hope of a future with you close to my heart."

Telling me about your past made you relive those terrors. You must be exhausted. The emotional impact of hearing them drained me. We should take a break. Let's freshen up and I'll call to have a late lunch brought up. Then we can walk around the city, maybe go to the castle, whatever you want to do."

"A long walk would help."

"Then if you will let me, I am going to hold you in my arms until you send me to my room. We can talk more this weekend about you and about me, but today you went through enough trauma."

"So many times as a girl, I wanted to be held and taken away from all the hurt," Nicola whispered. This time tears did glisten in her eyes and Brian gently pulled her closer. Never had she been more beautiful to him than now after revealing the realities of her despair to him.

Chapter 17
Arielle

Late on the second Thursday afternoon in August, Arielle's phone buzzed with a call from Carlos. She walked from the kitchen of her family home in the Loire to the back verandah to be out of her mother's hearing. Her father conducted business this way to leave her mother untroubled by his unattractive drug-based domain.

"Carlos did something happen? I am at my mother's. This is family time."

"Sorry. I got street photos of those consultants. Sending you the ones for the partners. Two of them were former FBI agents. The third one sounds like part of their brain trust, but he worked only in business. Call me back when you've opened the files. I sent two guys out to Oregon. Time to activate Operation Payback."

"Give me about five minutes. Easier to review photos and websites on my laptop. So far our movement of money in smaller amounts and in the new routing is all working, right?"

"Yeah. Totals are confirmed."

Walking into the house she tiptoed past the *conservatoire* where her mother enjoyed tea with a neighbor, sharing gossip along with *pâtisserie*. She had put avenging her father's death on hold in her mind, focusing instead on ensuring the businesses continued to operate and would be profitable. Killing the men who made their money transfer activities more difficult would not bring her father back, but they would gain more freedom in their business operations.

Once upstairs she opened the email from Carlos and followed the link. Three full shots of the principals of the company displayed next to their credentials. She zoomed in on Brian Tovey's face, her eyes widening as she recognized him. With a few rapid clicks, she brought up the photographs she had taken in Barcelona.

Tovey the former FBI agent was the man she saw on the beach in Barcelona. She must have seen a photograph of him, perhaps on the FBI's site, and that made him appear familiar to her. She glanced back at the text about the Noble Firs Company and read about his holding the FBI Medal of Valor, awarded a few years before following an FBI bust of a child prostitution ring in Bulgaria.

Her father had been secretive about the arm of their business dealing in prostitutes. When she had found changes in their cash flow and inquired about them, he had put her off. Three years later when she asked again, he told her about his other sources of income. At first her father's dealings in prostitution had bothered her. He had traded in young women, young men and children, talking about them like they were pedigree dogs to be bought, sold and kenneled. While she had kept those reactions to herself, a couple of years passed before she could think of the venture like any other business.

The *gendarmes* had shut down a few of their set-ups in Paris, Brussels, and Amsterdam, but had failed to trace about two-thirds of their operating sites to her father. The police had searched his regular businesses and kept them under scrutiny, even as she ran them along with the remaining underground operating sites.

She had read about the FBI action where Tovey got his medal. Arielle pushed back in her chair to study his photo. Since he was also the man on the beach in Barcelona with the intriguing woman, she wondered if the woman was a fellow FBI agent or a casual acquaintance of this Brian Tovey?

Picking up her iPhone, Arielle called Carlos back.

"Let's take out this O'Leary guy first. Tovey runs the London office from what I see on their website. If rubbing out O'Leary doesn't force them out of business, we'll hit either Tovey or this Fenwick guy."

"Any insights on them?"

"Saw Tovey with some *petite amie* in Barcelona. A bank there is on their client list."

"Who's the broad?"

"No one significant is my guess. An accidental encounter."

Carlos snickered, "A babe for the night, eh? Would like one of those myself right about now. I'll give the go ahead on the setup to hit O'Leary. Already left a voice mail for Kazimír. Let you know when the deed is done."

"Do the shooting as a drive-by. At night if possible. No ties to you."

"I can run my own ops. Going to do the hit one night when they leave the office late. They often work late, and the city will be quieter then."

The line went dead. By telling him how to run the operation, Arielle had overstepped and riled Carlos and his damn ego. Kazimír would discuss tactics and ask her opinion on the best approach. Carlos always acted like he possessed the best brain of the three of them even though Kazimír was gifted with the most intelligence while she ran second.

Chapter 18
Brian

Over in London on the second Friday evening of August, Brian hung up the phone in his studio apartment from talking with Moll, sharing the pride Moll had communicated over their upcoming employee meeting and the announcement of their new stock program. He would hold a similar meeting on Monday with the staff in the London office.

Nicola joined him after picking up a take-out dinner for the two of them at Fortnum's. Once they had eaten they sat on the couch with the drapes opened to the clear-sky view of the Thames and Southwark on the far side of the river. Brian kissed Nicola, nuzzled her neck and held her close. He never moved too fast with her, fearing she might shut down and pull away. While he became frustrated by being with this beautiful woman and not making love with her, he stuck with his commitment to their relationship.

She surprised him as they cuddled by unbuttoning his shirt and sliding her hands along his back. Moving in slow motions she removed his shirt, followed by his undershirt. Smiling at him she reached to touch his chest, tracing the lines of his collar-bones first with her fingers followed by her lips.

"You're well-toned for a man so slender," she said in a voice coming out as a throaty whisper. "You're like a cat with long, sinewy muscles."

"And you are making me purr," Brian said struggling to keep his desire under control. Did she have any idea how much he wanted her? Before when Nicola kept her distance, he could better keep himself from becoming aroused. Even now when she made advances to him, he had to remain in control. An aggressive move by him could set their progress back. As hard as it might be, he had to suppress his desires as the only way to continue to build a bridge of trust with her.

After pushing herself away and standing up, Nicola untied the top of her billowy cotton peasant blouse and tossed it over her head. From where he lay in a half-reclining position, Brian appreciated the laciness of her camisole and how her small nipples poked against the delicate fabric. Even with the subtle curves of her sleek body enticing him, he sensed she must lead to make any progress towards more closeness.

When she picked up the bottom of her camisole and teased the soft garment over her head, he let himself admire her half-naked form, but he made no move to touch her. She smiled at him, moving closer until she brushed his chest and caressed his nipples with hers in a slow, teasing back and forth motion. Placing his hands lightly on her back, he refrained from holding her tight. Having her so temptingly close aroused him but he forced himself to stay in control.

"This is enjoyable," she said in a whisper. "May we sleep together tonight? Almost naked where I can cuddle next to you? Can you bear only having me close?"

Afraid to trust his voice, Brian nodded and rose, holding out his hand to her. When she grasped his fingers, he raised her wrist to his lips. She led him into the darkened bedroom where she opened the drapes and began to undress until she wore only a pair of pink and white lace panties. They folded down each side of the covers and stood staring at each other, each aware of how the next step marked a momentous change in their liaison. That morning he had changed the sheets as he did each time Nicola arrived in London, in hopes of her sleeping with him one night.

Doing only what Nicola permitted challenged his self-control, but years of discipline as a student, as an agent and as a businessman kept him focused on the long term no matter how enveloped he might be in the present. If he exercised patience, consideration and self-restraint, a chance existed that this enticing woman would become his. No matter how frustrating he may find these times, he would rely on his fortitude in hopes of having her as his lover and one day as his wife.

They snuggled and kissed as their bodies learned to curve around each other. Nicola slid her hand down to stroke his manhood with a tentative caress. Recognizing what a huge step she was taking, Brian let her stroke the part of him modeled on himself, long and slender. All the while he focused on self-control

"Can we try to be closer?" she whispered. "Do not touch me in my, um crotch, with your hands, but tonight I want to experience you inside me."

Reaching down she slid off her panties and climbed on top of him, signifying she wanted control. She glided down and gasped a little as he ever so slowly entered her moist warmth. Neither of them moved. They stayed studying each other until she pressed down and began a slow rocking. He smiled up at her and placed his hands softly on the sides of her thighs.

With slight motions he began to match her pace, wary of spoiling their first love-making, yet enthralled by her. She skimmed across him like silken heaven while they moved together in a mesmerizing motion. She stopped. He waited worrying she was having regrets about this step in their intimacy. Placing her hands on his upper arms, she began rocking again. Slowly at first as she closed her eyes.

The grip on his arms tightened as her pace picked up. Nicola leaned forward, curving her back and gasping as her body lifted and her spasm trembled against him. She pulled back, her eyes wide with surprise.

"All right?" he asked.

She hesitated and ducked her head, then glanced at him almost shyly, "Mmm. Surprising. Delicious. Not ..."

"Forced?"

She sighed and nodded a bit miserably.

"Enough for now," he said with an effort, pulling back and shifting Nicola over to lie by his side. "Our expressions of love should bring you joy."

"What about you?"

"Nicola, pulling away from you is hard for me. While I want you with every fiber of my body, we need to take our intimacy slowly. One step at a time, only as you are comfortable."

"You named your company well. You are noble. And tall like a fir tree." Sliding off him, she snuggled against his side. He pulled his hips back, needing to cool off and maintain his control. This was a new experience for him in bed to shut down his desires, but he wanted Nicola not just for tonight but for a very long time.

"The company appellation comes from a variety of evergreen called Noble Fir which is native to the mountainous regions of California and Oregon. We didn't name the company after ourselves."

"You are each honorable -- you and Moll and perhaps Terry too."

He flipped to his side, gathering her in his arms and whispered close to her ear. "You too are noble. You are finding your potential. My love. My sweet Nicola."

Chapter 19
Moll

At five in the Noble Fir offices in Portland that same day, Moll and Terry hosted their periodic employee update and gathering. Friday was casual day for most of Portland, and everyone was dressed down ready to start the weekend. While lenient about office attire, each person needed to be spick-and-span, not wearing wrinkled or overly worn clothes. Everyone kept a suit in the closet near their amenities room in case a client or prospect came for a visit.

Once everyone settled in their seats, Moll checked the clock. With a half hour before their staff's spouses, partners and dates arrived for the catered buffet, Moll decided to open their remarks.

"Hey, gang. We exceeded our targets again. Like wowser – another record-breaker, based on forecast revenues for the rest of this month. When you signed on to work with us, you might recollect some doubts about this start-up enterprise we call Noble Firs," Moll said and paused. A couple of the employees nodded while another two appeared sheepish.

"Again you should find you made the right decision when bonus checks come out in the fall. As a further reward for your hard work and commitment, Terry will tell you about yet another incentive program at the end of this meeting. First let's go over our financials. We believe in an 'Open Kimono' policy on our company's performance. Noble Firs is prospering because you make us successful."

While Terry walked up near the screen, Moll moved over to the table with the laptop. The Noble Firs logo with its three blue-green trees shone at the front of the room. His partner signaled him with a flip of his hand and Moll brought up the first slide on financials.

"So far this year we are exceeding our target by 15%," Terry said in a tone revealing his pride in their performance. "Remember our objective for this year is 25% higher than our actual numbers last year, making us 40% greater than in 2015. We are driven by the impetus from past successes like a snowball gathering size and momentum as we roll along." Terry's face became intent as his eyes moved from person to person in the room.

"To paraphrase my partner, our growth is like beyond epic."

Moll grinned back at Terry. The growth jazzed up each of them. The travel to sell their services, the pressure to keep a balance between workload and staffing and their drives to succeed were wearying. The issue with their DBA had been a sobering event reinforcing the seriousness of their work. He still hated to think that they had lost a big client over it and might lose a couple more.

The results pumped them back up again. Every time their project load grew, they added staff conservatively. After flipping up a new chart, Moll went to lean against the window, gazing out at the city below and listening to Terry deliver their message.

Down on the sidewalk two men stared up at their building. The warm August day had everyone wandering around in shirt sleeves. Both these guys wore dark shirts and pants, out of sync with the locals in their practical light colored clothes. Some were in shorts. Those guys must be out-of-towners. They gabbed for a few minutes, and when he checked again, the men no longer stood down on the corner. Other folks walked along to cars, buses or the rapid transit Max line as their work days wound down.

He stepped up to take over the meeting for the next discussion. They stewarded a series of non-financial measures of success and Moll walked through them now.

"Crime-fighters – last quarter we contributed to an action where the FBI ended money laundering, drugs and other illicit activities by major crimesters in Boston, New York, Pennsylvania, the D.C. area, right down into Georgia. Thanks to our efforts, over twenty alleged criminals were arrested and are awaiting trial including a crime boss out of Phili. This action led to more arrests in Europe in a cooperative action among the FBI, Interpol and investigative units in France and Hungary. Seven mobsters are listed as killed in the action – including two mob bosses.

"Your efforts are not only helping our clients to detect illegal activities, but you are also supplying the proof required for government forces to take legal actions to end crime. If we can help prevent kids and adults from ruining their lives with drugs or save innocent children and adults from prostitution and slavery, we serve not only a business purpose but an important humanitarian one."

A hand went up in the second circle of chairs. "Yeah, man?" Moll asked.

"What's the story on Tom, our former DBA? I heard he's in jail."

Moll exchanged looks with Terry and their contract DBA on loan from the DEA.

"Information on him is part of an ongoing investigation, and we are bound not to discuss the case. Let's say certain irregularities came to our attention. I can't tell you anything more."

"Anyone else under suspicion?

"No. And we hope never to experience a repeat. Our integrity must be above question. Any other topics for discussion?"

A few other questions came up, but in general spirits in the room kept a casual cheerfulness. The DBA's removal and arrest had made some people apprehensive, but now they accepted the event.

"Next Terry is going to brief you on our announcement," Moll said and walked to the side of the room. Again he lounged by the window.

"We will be offering a stock ownership program for employees to help you to further share in our successes," Terry began. "We are privately held so these are not shares you can trade in the stock market. In high-performing years we plan to pay dividends. A reserve pool of 50,000 shares has been established for this purpose. Commensurate with their contributions each staff member will be awarded the opportunity to buy our stock at a reduced price after a year of service. If anyone should leave the company, the shares revert to this reserve pool and the owner will be compensated for their original investment.

Moll glanced out the window again. The two men in black had returned as if they had taken an exploratory walk around the block. They again stared up at the building, turned and walked away together. Moll found them a bit suspicious if not outright creepy in their dark clothes and sunglasses, almost like street narcotics officers trying to imitate east coast hoodlums. He watched them until they strode out of sight, before turning his attention back to the meeting. Outside of the interior glass wall of the conference room, family members and dates drifted into their office space.

"What happens if you guys sell the company?"

"First we have no plans to sell Noble Firs," Terry said with firmness in his voice. "But if we did or if we did something crazy like go public with an offering, you would profit by those changes by receiving a proportionate share of the proceeds. Starting next quarter, we will steward stock ownership and any dividends paid out. This offering will be beneficial to you, giving you much to gain."

Most of the staff showed enthusiasm. Each one would attend an individual briefing, and Moll hoped for 100% participation in the program.

"Time," Moll said to Terry and nodded towards the group gathered outside the conference room.

"Thank you again for your contributions," Terry said. "Let's party. Food this time is from Elephant's Deli, so enjoy and remember we will offer door prizes including everyone's favorite – a weekend out on the town. Thanks again for making Noble Firs what we are today."

The party went on for over two hours. Moll and Terry wandered around the room to talk with each employee and anyone who joined him or her. Well after eight-thirty they waved away the last employee. Terry poured a little more wine, and the two of them lounged in Moll's office talking about how the evening went.

By the time they left, the long August day was sliding into night. The security guard shift had changed downstairs, and old Alberto was at the reception desk. Moll wished him good night as he and Terry walked out.

Around them the city quieted. Together they walked in the direction of the parking lot eight blocks away. The warm evening air reinforced their buoyancy. Overhead the sky had only a few puffy clouds. A full moon glowed with intensity as if determined to make the most of the clear night. After a productive day and a great evening with their staff, all seemed well in the world they had built as Noble Firs.

Moll glanced around noting how few people were out. After all it was Friday night in the business section of Portland. People had already started the weekend or were home getting ready to go out and party at their favorite hangout. He wanted to go camping this summer up in the mountains -- hike out, set up a tent and let nature work its magic on erasing the stresses of his work. He dealt with people every day, traveled several times a month to see clients and prospects. He needed to recharge. Even so he could appreciate these times in the city when the business was going well, the weather was Portland-perfect, and he could relax after a hard week of work.

In the distance behind them, a car started and rolled down the street. When Moll glanced back, his former agent's eye detected a shiny black town car creeping along the curb. He turned away when Terry said something and he responded, yet a part of his mind stayed on the car behind them. When he looked behind him again, he grew uneasy noting that the car was keeping pace with them, staying a couple of blocks behind.

He stopped to turn fully around wanting to see why the vehicle was moving so slowly. Maybe it had a flat or something. Just then the passenger window slid down, and he could see a man dressed in black start to lean out.

In that instant he twigged those guys who had talked outside the building now pursued them. Even as the car sped up, time slowed for Moll. He gathered himself to act with the car drawing near. Stretching out his arms to grab Terry, in a fast motion he threw himself over him to push him to the pavement.

They fell slowly and he put out his one arm to slow the impact of their fall, jamming his shoulder back into its socket. He could feel Terry resisting. He yelled for him to stay down, pushing him towards the sidewalk as he spread himself out in a protective position over his friend.

Rapid-fire shots from a gun with a silencer sounded. Moll flinched as a bullet hit him in the back and then in the skull. He collapsed on Terry. The car sped away with a screech of tires. Moll tried to look up to see the license plate, but a shadowy grayness began to overcome him. As if from a distance, Terry screamed out. He could feel him start to squirm when darkness and silence ended thought and sensation.

Part II: Mind Tricks

August -- October, 2016

Chapter 20
Terry

With Moll weighing him down like a massive sleeper sofa, Terry tried to squirm his way free, but he failed to dislodge his partner and friend. Shifting enough to move his hands under his shoulders, he pushed them both up a little and wriggled out, taking care to let Moll slowly sink to the pavement. Terry spun back on his knees to check on Moll. Blood seeped from his back and head, pooling dark red on the pavement.

"Moll, oh no, Moll. No. No. This can't be happening. Not to you, Moll," Terry began sobbing and screaming for help, but no one appeared within several blocks.

Realizing he had to help this man who he loved, Terry struggled to regain control and force back his sobs. He scrabbled in his pocket for his cell phone and dialed 911 with shaking fingers while he reached over to check that Moll was breathing. Moll, this man he valued above all others, lay dying in front of him. So like his friend to sense the situation and leap to protect him. When 911 answered his response came out as a sob. Terry whacked himself on the side of the head to gather his wits.

"Drive-by shooting on, shit, where the hell are we? Third and Main. By the huge elk statue in the road. My friend is shot twice. Barely breathing. Hurry. Hurry."

"Help is on the way. Stay on the line. Repeat. Remain on the line. Are you all right, sir?"

"Yeah, yeah. But Moll may be dying. What should I do?"

"Do not move him. Press something to his wounds to staunch the flow of blood. Repeat -- do not move him."

Terry started crying again and shaking all over in fear for Moll. He knelt down, ripped off his shirt, tore it in half and pressed half to the wound on the back of Moll's head. Twisting slightly, he pressed the other half on his back.

When a patrol car screeched up, a policeman jumped out, ran over, pushed Terry back and checked Moll's pulse. More sirens sounded and another patrol car came down the street followed by an ambulance. Ending the call with 911, Terry dialed Ivy. He needed her and Steve. They would help Moll.

"Moll's been shot," Terry yelled into the phone, choking as the words came out.

"Terry. What? Where?" Ivy asked.

"Near our offices. Drive-by. Moll jumped to cover me. He took two bullets. Still alive, but not conscious. Blood, so much blood."

"Emergency services are on site?"

"Yeah."

"Ride with Moll to the emergency room. Stay on the phone with me. We will meet you at the hospital. Police with you?"

"Several," Terry said, peering around.

"I'm giving the phone to Steve. Give your phone to one of the officers."

The medical guys surrounded Moll where they treated him and prepared to rush him to the hospital. Terry walked to the first policeman on the scene.

"Moll used to serve as an FBI agent. His boss wants to talk to you."

When he spun back to be with Moll, the medics were already loading him onto a stretcher. Terry reached out to him but was thrust away by a medic. His heart aching for his friend, he stood watching, helpless and alone in the face of the tragedy. Moll was lifted up and carried to the waiting ambulance in smooth, fast motions.

As Terry rushed to scramble into the ambulance after Moll, the conversations around him stopped making sense. The medics again pushed him aside. A police officer jogged up, grabbed Terry by the arm and pulled him over to a patrol car, opening the front door and handing him his phone back.

"You hang around with some high-powered friends," the policeman said. "Nielsen is legendary. Worked with him on a couple of cases in the last few years. Surveillance stuff. Com'on with me. I'll follow the ambulance."

Too worried to talk when his phone rang, Terry checked caller id – Ivy. He had to answer. "Taking him up Pill Hill to the Trauma Unit. I'm following in a patrol car with an officer who worked with Steve."

"We're in the car and will be with you in less than half an hour. Want me to call Brian?"

"Yeah and Mathew. Christ, Ivy, I'm scared shitless for Moll. I love him. Now I wish I'd told him."

"Regrets won't help Moll now. Stay optimistic. Pray if you believe. Be there for him. With medical help, we will pull him through. We must."

If sheer determination can heal a person, he, Ivy and Steve offered plenty. Could they help Moll's lifeless form, the wounds to his back and skull, the loss of blood? So much blood on the pavement. If he lived, would he be the same Moll or would his brain and body be forever ruined? No matter what the outcome would be for Moll, Terry vowed to love him still for the memories of him and for saving his life.

Although he wanted to cry again, he forced the tears back and pushed himself up into the seat of the patrol car which turned to head up the hill to the hospital. Now was the time for him to be the strong one for Moll.

"The prognosis is not clear," the surgeon briefing them several hours later said. "The bullet angled in to crack the thoracic number two vertebrae in his back, passing out through his right abdominal muscles which are well-developed for so reedy a man. The shot bypassed his organs. We staunched some internal bleeding, and we will monitor his mobility if he recovers. The spinal cord is severely bruised, but not severed, which means he may or may not be ambulatory."

As his panicked mind tried to make sense of the doctor's words, Terry asked, "His head?"

"More delicate. First we want to stabilize the patient. Once he is stable, we will need to reach a decision. Leave the bullet and monitor him or open up his skull and remove the slug if we can. Either way pressure from swelling and internal bleeding can build up, which may be more dangerous than the bullet itself."

"Any chance he will retain his mental faculties?" Steve asked in a hoarse voice. "Moll is near genius level in creativity."

"The bullet went into his left temporal lobe." The physician placed his hand on the lower left side of his own head. "The area controls some memory functions, such as the ability to recognize people as well as managing certain sensory functions, including processing sounds. The shell may be pressing against the hippocampus which handles the creation of new memories and impacts mood and orientation."

"What do you recommend?" Ivy asked. She reached over to take Terry's hand. The three of them now constituted Moll's family.

"I assume you are his parents?"

"Not quite," Steve said. "His mother became a junkie down in San Francisco. Out of touch and I guess she may be dead. Father never identified. Moll served on my team at the FBI and remains a close friend. My wife and I will stand in place of his parents. This man is his business partner and," Steve paused and shifted his gaze to Terry, "his close friend. Together we will make any decisions regarding Moll. I can start a search for his mother but to my knowledge more than fifteen years passed since he last talked with her."

The surgeon nodded. "For now we must wait to determine the pace of his recovery."

"Which option – the brain surgery or not – gives him the best chance?" Terry asked, his voice breaking as tears ran down his cheeks.

Steve wrapped a long arm around his shoulders.

"I would opt for the surgery as soon as he is stable," the doctor said.

"I want to be with him."

"In a couple of hours. Your friend is in post op now and in a coma. However I believe encouraging voices of friends and family, favorite music, comforting aromas and touch can help a patient. You'll be familiar with what he likes."

"The tapping of fingers on a keyboard. Folk music," Terry muttered.

"Talk to him as you might ordinarily about business, about your life, whatever. Recount events and memories you shared. I am liberal about visitors as long as you give him extended periods of rest."

"Can we be here at any time?"

"We'll take shifts," Steve said. "This might be a long haul. You must keep the business running. Your staff and clients are dependent on you."

"Work doesn't matter now."

"Noble Firs matters to Moll. Doctor, expect either uniformed officers or plainclothes FBI agents here 24/7. They need to stay with Moll when he goes for tests, surgery or any other treatments. Moll and Terry's business helped the FBI nail a number of major criminals by identifying money laundering activities. We suspect this shooting represents a retaliation action and a play to shut down their company."

The physician nodded and turned to go.

"Thank you, doctor. Moll is an exceptional man. We will rely on you to advise us," Steve said and turned to face Terry. "I think we should camp out at Moll's and Brian's house, which is ten minutes or less away."

"I'm not leaving Moll alone."

Steve nodded. "All right, you stay here. If you give us your keys, Ivy and I will collect your Firewire cat, and we'll pack a bag for you. We'll brief Brian and Mathew, shove clothes for ourselves into a suitcase and catch some sleep. I'll be sure to line up protection at the Council Crest house, your offices and here at the hospital. You can anticipate an escort wherever you go. Officer Brandish is still here. Expect him to be relieved at six in the morning. For each transition, you will be introduced to the next person on guard duty. Ivy and I will be back here no later than seven. Call if Moll's condition changes."

Ivy wrapped the car blanket she had grabbed from her SUV around Terry's shoulders and said, "Try to sleep. The staff will wake you."

As he stumbled back to sink into a chair, Terry's sense of isolation increased as if he had been plunked into this hospital scene as an invisible observer. The unreality of tonight's events formed glass walls around him, keeping him from the security of his life before those shots were fired. He needed to see Moll to verify for himself he remained alive. Outside of the antiseptic hospital around him, the world ceased to exist.

Chapter 21
Brian

Brian paced around the gate area at Heathrow, impatient to board a British Airways flight connecting to Portland. His worry for Moll made him edgy. Hanging around with Moll since law school, working with him at the FBI and now partnering with him in business, they shared irreplaceable bonds.

Offbeat, brilliant, compassionate Moll. Would he survive the shooting? The surgery on his back must be over by now. Right when he decided to contact Steve, his cell phone rang with a call from Ivy's phone.

"Steve here. We're leaving the hospital."

"Is he out of surgery for his back?"

"Yeah, but he remains in a coma," Steve said.

Brian listened as Steve related what the doctor had communicated and recapped their plans.

"Makes sense for you to stay at the house. Terry should use Moll's room. You take the master. I'm waiting for a flight now. Should be in Portland mid-afternoon your time."

"Whoa. You were told to stay put."

"Dammit Steve. Moll is my friend. I need to be with him."

"What about your duties at the London office? The Bureau is working with Scotland Yard and the police to organize protection."

"I briefed our manager. We're telling people to work from home, saying the plumbing and water supply in the building are malfunctioning. No one should be at the office this weekend or Monday. I'll come back here to meet with the employees next week, but now I need to be with Moll."

"You should stay in London."

"Did you stay in Mexico when the gang down there peppered Mathew's leg with buckshot? No you didn't. You jumped on a plane back to D.C. with him. Ditto with me in Sofia. And again when Mathew took a bullet in London."

"Not going to convince you, am I? Somehow we must cover both offices. We should not give into these perps by shutting down. Between you, me, Ivy and Mathew, we can keep the operations going."

"We'll talk when I arrive," Brian said in his firmest tone. "Terry can run the Portland office."

"Terry may not be of much help to us. He's too broken up." Steve paused. "Do you think they're involved?"

"Not to my knowledge," Brian answered. "Not important now."

"You're right. Doesn't matter. Moll and Terry are each exceptional guys. Alike yet different."

"Moll and Terry are the best. Like you, Mathew and Ivy." Brian said and paused, only now realizing that his other friends could be in danger. At least at Spook Hills they had retired agent Lenny, a stalwart sharpshooter, who now worked on the vineyard.

As if reading his mind, Steve said, "Send me your flight schedule. Expect Lenny to meet your plane. I'll tell him to bring your gear with him. Put on your bullet-proof vest before you leave the PDX airport."

"Steve, thanks for always supporting us."

Brian ended the call and joined the line for his boarding group, anxious, sad and angry all at the same time. He needed to call Nicola to give her an update before takeoff. When the first call came in about the shooting, she had jumped on her laptop to find a flight to Portland for him. Although they wanted this weekend together to move forward in their relationship, without hesitation Nicola had insisted he should fly out to be with his friends.

She would worry about him, but she would also support him. He needed to tell Steve about their relationship. While this might not be the best time given Moll's condition, Brian wanted to handle the discussion face-to-face.

After spending most of the day at the hospital where Moll remained unconscious, around nine on Saturday evening Brian sat with Steve in the living room at the Portland house he shared with Moll. Terry and Lenny stayed to hover by Moll's bedside at the hospital, while Ivy and Steve expected to relieve at least one of them around four the next morning. At ten the next day the surgeon planned to meet with them to discuss next steps for Moll. After their meeting they would devise their near-term plans for the company.

With the June evening warming up the house, they opened the windows. From where the house sat on one of the high hills at Council Crest, they had expansive views to the south. In the distance the lights of Mountain Park began to twinkle on. When Ivy walked away down the hall to take a shower, Brian decided to talk about Nicola.

"Steve, this may not be the best time to talk about this, but I want to have this discussion with you in person. Do you remember our talk a few weeks back?"

"You ready to tell me the rest of what is bothering you?"

Brian walked over to the window, inhaled the fresh air and leaned against the wall to pull his thoughts together. He turned to face Steve and confessed, "I fell in love."

"Ever been in love before?"

"No. Started in the fall of 2014. This spring I ran into the woman again. After a year and a half, I still couldn't forget her."

Steve tapped his forefinger on the arm of the leather lounge chair, the way he did when thinking, as each tap eliminated one possibility and ushered in a new one for consideration. Surprise came over his face. His lips curved up in a little smile, "Nicola. Realized from the timing. In thinking back I remembered that you regarded her in a certain awe-struck way."

"She and Maxim needed protection. Moll and I committed ourselves to the operation. During downtime in the limo, over meals and on planes, we talked with the cousins. Exquisite Nicola, abused as a child, masqueraded as a man, in all probability a felon. Nothing happened between us during those few days.

"When I made the pitch in Barcelona in June, I saw her again. We met up and went for dinner. We've been dating ever since. She's strong yet fragile too. Her father's abuse left her afraid of men. She's working with a therapist and trying to find ways to put her issues behind her."

Brian shook his head at himself, "Classic, right? The agent falls for the perp?"

"Nothing about any of those Fuentes would be considered textbook. We all liked Nicola and Maxim even though we only spent a few days with them."

"How long before you fell for Ivy?"

"She attracted me from the first. When Ivy stepped out of the elevator, walked into her office space where we waited and reached out to shake my hand -- her smile, her touch, her divine self were unexpected. I acted like a regular prick on the trip because I didn't want her to guess she had walloped me right in the heart."

"You fooled us all until the day you called Ivy and asked her out."

Steve sat with a bemused smile on his face as if he were replaying in his mind those early times with the woman who became his wife three years before.

"Is anyone else aware of your relationship with Nicola?" he asked.

"Mathew, but I asked him not to say anything because I wanted to tell you in person. Steve, why aren't you shocked?"

After cocking his head from one side to the other in the way he did when considering two sides of an argument, Steve said. "Nicola's life started out with such horrid trauma. Difficult to imagine a girl suffering physical and sexual abuse during most of her childhood. She had no real chance at finding her way to a better life.

"You remain afraid of being controlled after the way your mother dominated you. Nicola is a woman who needs you, but she will never try to control you. You are both intelligent, strong, handsome people. I am surprised but not shocked." Steve fell silent and stared out the window before turning back to Brian and saying, "The loves of our lives find us if we are lucky. How a relationship between you two will succeed is a challenge to envision."

"I know that by agreement she cannot return to the United States. I'll stay in Europe if I must, but …"

"One day you may want to live here with Nicola or at least visit the United States with her. What about Maxim?"

"We spent a long weekend hanging out with him – sailing and visiting his glass studio. I like him. Could we concoct a way for Nicola and Maxim to return to the United States?"

"No way," Steve said. "You remember the terms of the deal they made with the FBI. Brian, why is living in the United States so important to you? You like living in London, right?"

Brian sat thinking. "No matter what, I'm an American. Sure I like traveling. I even like living abroad, but this is my home. I want it to become Nicola's home again too. My friends are here. My business is here. While we have a London office, this is our headquarters. Ever since I can remember, I have been proud to be an American."

The two men sat facing each other, one determined to defend the FBI, the other wanting to remove at least this one obstacle from his complicated romance. Torn between his loyalty to Steve and his love of Nicola, Brian searched for a way to gain his friend and mentor's backing.

"What if I guaranteed their good conduct?"

"Take our whole Spook Hills gang to make such a guarantee. Remember their history."

"Don't make me choose, Steve."

The big man rose and in a few big strides reached the doorway to a small balcony where he opened the door and went outside. Brian understood enough about Steve to let him think. Brian rose, walked into the open kitchen and took a bottle of water for each of them from the fridge, pulling out one for Ivy too. After checking the lock on the door to the big deck, he stood in the kitchen uncertain what to do next.

Staying silent as he walked back in, Steve closed the door to the small balcony and turned the lock before speaking again. "Let me ponder how I might present your request to the chief. We will get only one chance at this."

"First thank you for considering a change to the Fuentes' agreement. Even if we decide to live abroad, I would feel better knowing we could come back here at least to visit."

Steve nodded and said, "You're sure you love Nicola?"

"Yes, I love her. Given all the issues we are taking small steps. We slept together for the first time last night. Bit of a minefield with what can bring back bad memories for her. A few weeks ago I heard more about her childhood and her father's brutal and perverted abuse of her. What she suffered tore me apart. She wants to put those atrocious experiences behind her. In spite of her problems Nicola brings a light into my life I never experienced before."

Ivy walked into the kitchen wearing a silken pink robe with her bright fuchsia toenails pecking out underneath. Her dark silver hair tumbled in a mass of wild curls around her shoulders. She shifted her inquisitive gaze from Steve to Brian and asked, "Did I hear Nicola's name?"

Chapter 22
Terry

Early Monday afternoon the group gathered in the Noble Firs conference room to discuss next steps for the company. Brian had held a briefing of the full staff at nine on the shooting, the situation with Moll, and the desire to continue operating Noble Firs. He offered several options to each employee including working from home, shuttles to work with FBI-cleared armed guards and hotel rooms at the company's expense.

Steve, Ivy, and Mathew attended as board members who would serve as interim business managers. Work had slowed at the Spook Hills vineyard, freeing up some of Mathew's time until harvest. Terry participated in the briefing and answered questions, but his mind kept going to the hospital where Moll was in surgery to remove the bullet from his brain. Callie stayed at the hospital and would call when she received an update from the surgeon. Now at two in the afternoon, they expected Brian to leave for the airport by four to return to London.

"To recap today's events," Brian said in his methodical way, "one staff member resigned from fear for her life. Six plan to work from home. Four will commute in our secure shuttle, and two with long drives will spend three days in the office, staying as arranged at the Hilton and working the other days from home. The rest are undecided and will give us their decisions tomorrow after talking with their spouses. They will each send an email to you, Ivy, with their decisions."

"How did your employees react?" Mathew asked.

"Shook up. The incident upset them, both in the meeting and when we talked with them later. News of Moll's injuries affected them. You know Moll, offbeat but likable. He was the employees' favorite, wouldn't you say Terry?"

Terry tried to focus on the meeting when he heard his name, but only after replaying Brian's words in his head did he grasp the question. "When Moll walked into the office space, like after traveling, he made people come alive. Always had something upbeat to say."

"Some people here cried when hearing about Moll," Brian continued. "Others kept up a more stalwart front. We talked with each person one-on-one after giving them an hour to think the situation over and call their families or close friends. One did ask if the news would carry a story."

"The FBI has kept this incident out of the papers so far," Steve said. "However they are scheduling a press release for four this afternoon. A story on the shooting is expected in tonight's local news and in the Oregonian. Time to start our client communications now before any broadcast hits. It may be picked up by the Associated Press or another national news service and may be online.

"As far as the case progress goes, the agents assigned to the case have reviewed the security camera footage in the area but nothing is coming up on the shooting. The cameras are building-specific. Moll and Terry were four blocks away from their building and out on the sidewalk. We have no descriptions of the shooters, so doing a review of any potentially suspicious characters who were captured on film lacks a focus."

Brian nodded and turned to Ivy, "Ivy is our script ready for our client calls?"

"Here are copies. I'll make any edits we decide on and email a revised document to each of you. My advice is to be open but limit your comments. Assure your clients our business continues at Noble Firs."

"I should call our manager in London in case the story makes the morning news," Brian said. "Together we will do staff communications and client calls for the London office as soon as possible tomorrow. Here is the list of clients in priority order, beginning with those who are active now, our clients on contract for periodic analysis, and the ones committed to future work. I've split them up between us. If any clients call in, we need to make those call returns a priority."

Mathew spoke up next, "Starting tomorrow at least one of us will be in the office weekdays from six to six. Expect us to brief each other with each transition and log our activities. We'll send a link to you so you can check on our status here. For the first couple of weeks, we will keep the office closed and secured on weekends and from six at night until six the following morning during the week."

"I arranged for 24/7 office security through the Bureau along with the required escorts and shuttle service," Steve said. "Brian you will be met in London by one of the FBI legal attachés and briefed on a similar procedure."

"Thank you. Ivy, your script for the client calls is what we need," Brian said. "Terry, any comments?"

Terry shook his head. Brian's words floated by his ears while his mind kept drifting to Moll and his surgery.

"Let's start contacting clients now. Any questions?"

Before anyone answered their admin knocked on the door. "Callie is on the line. I am transferring her in."

Every face in the room paled. Terry's heart gave an odd wobble in his chest, and his stomach lurched out of fear of Moll having died in surgery.

The speaker phone rang once. Brian answered. "Callie? We're all here in the conference room. What have you heard about Moll?"

"The surgeon gave me an update." Callie's voice sounded a little shaky from worry. "The surgery went well. All Moll's vital signs are stable. The bullet rested right where the doctor thought."

"Which means he might suffer memory loss," Steve said. "Any chance at least some of those memories will come back to him?"

"We won't know until he wakes up and starts the healing process. The doctor couldn't predict when he might regain consciousness or what his condition will be. Moll may continue to be comatose and unresponsive for some time."

Struck by the impact of those words Terry moaned out loud. Ivy scooted her chair closer to comfort him.

"Callie, when will Moll be back in his room?" Steve asked.

"The surgeon thought as early as five this afternoon." Callie's voice came out of the phone higher pitched than usual. She cleared her throat and advised them in a more normal tone, "We need to be cautious if he does come back to let him regain consciousness at his own pace."

"Brian, you should head straight to the airport when you leave here. We'll call you with any changes or with periodic updates," Steve said. "Callie, we are wrapping up at the office around four today and will be with you right after. We sent everyone home for the day. For now we must each think positive thoughts especially when we are in the room with Moll. He needs to sense our compassion and our hope."

Terry said, "Hard to think happy thoughts now, but I will do my best for Moll. How long before he might be released?"

"Depends on when he comes out of the coma and what shape he's in," Callie said.

"Ivy, Brian, Mathew, Steve and Callie, thank you for all you are doing," Terry said through his sniffles.

"As Moll would say, KTF," Brian said.

"Keep the Faith," Terry echoed back and ended the call with Callie.

Tears shone in each person's eyes around the conference room. Keep the Faith was so Moll. They would do their best for him now.

Chapter 23
Terry

Two days later at the hospital in Portland, Terry worked on his laptop in a side chair but kept an eye on Ivy where she sat next to Moll with her hand covering his. By now the warmth of Moll's hand stayed with him even when not at his bedside. Ivy began talking in a soft voice.

"Remember when I first met you, Moll? Back in your FBI days, you and Brian waited with Steve in the reception area of my offices. Steve acted so harsh when he communicated with me that it made me thankful to have you and Brian as friendlier faces. Having three FBI agents show up demanding data scared the bejesus out of me. That was bad enough without a giant agent doing his best at intimidation.

"Each of us needs you back. You bring a lightness to our lives. We are a gruesome lot without you. Everyone at your company wants you back in the office."

Moll moved his shoulders in a restless motion. He squirmed a little sometimes but did not regain consciousness. This time his eyes drifted open. Although Terry wanted to rush forward, he feared interrupting Moll's return to consciousness.

"Hey sunshine," Ivy said to Moll. "Ready to rejoin the party?"

His eyes drifted closed again and re-opened. "Mom?" he said in a hoarse voice with the single word partially garbled by the tube coming out of his mouth.

"How are you?"

"Love you ... Mom."

When Moll closed his eyes again, Ivy rang for the nurse. Terry walked over to stand on the far side of the bed.

The nurse rushed in and checked Moll's sleeping form. "Something happen?"

"He woke for a moment, and he talked."

"Make any sense?"

"Thought of me as his mother. Brought him comfort."

The nurse checked his vital signs, wrote on the chart, indicated she would alert the doctor and walked towards the door. Before departing she turned and said, "Be happy he came awake so soon. We are lucky that he can talk."

"Terry, our Moll woke up," Ivy said, her voice filled with excitement. "Stay optimistic. It often takes a few short spurts before a coma patient returns to full consciousness. Be encouraged that he can talk."

Terry nodded. "I love him so much. This is the wrong time to tell him, but I will be here to help him in whatever ways I can."

Twice more in the next hour, Moll opened his eyes. Once he tried to speak but the words came out slurred and he drifted away. Around four that afternoon, Moll opened his eyes again and gazed around. When he spotted Terry he raised his arm from the bed in slow motion, curling his fingers together in an effort to make a fist. "Don't ... leave me ... hangin', man."

While worried at his friend's words coming out so slowly, Terry returned the fist bump with a light tap. "Com'on, Moll. Pull yourself together. We need to wander out for a burger and a beer."

Moll smiled, licked his lips and closed his eyes again. His physician stood in the doorway during this exchange. As Moll returned to his comatose state, he walked in and said. "These are hopeful signs. Waking up so close together. Treat him normally, but don't rush him."

The doctor checked Moll's monitors before turning back and opening an eyelid to peer in an eye.

"Bugger off," Moll said, his voice stronger this time as he struggled to swat the doctor's hand away. After tossing out his curse, he raised his knees up.

Terry stared in wonder when he saw Moll moving his legs. A physical therapist had manipulated them, but Moll had failed to move his legs on his own before. As Moll went to push himself up in bed, Terry lurched forward to help him. Between him and the doctor, they raised Moll to a sitting position and pressed the button to bring the bed up to support him.

When Moll pointed to his mouth, the doctor removed the tube from between his lips and wanted to know if his head ached.

"Like man ... who hit me with a ... shovel?" Moll muttered, but he smiled his lop-sided grin. "What's happening?"

Ivy moved to the foot of the bed.

"You're not ... my mother. Musta dreamed ... her. Who ... you?"

"Ivy. Steve's wife."

"Steve's d ... d ... divorced," Moll said searching for words.

Terry found it hard to listen to his normally glib friend having trouble recalling words but he hung on to the hope that since he was having coherent thoughts, his speech would smooth out over time.

"He remarried."

Moll stared at Terry and frowned. "Don't re ... re ... recognize you either. You an agent?"

"I'm Terry. Your business partner and your friend."

"What the fuck? I'm an ... FBI agent," Moll paused and looked at each of them accusingly. "What's ... going on here? Where's Brian? Steve?"

"Brian is in London. Steve and Mathew will be here as soon as I call them," said Ivy trying to soothe Moll's concerns.

"Why am I here?" Moll's eyes darted around and then focused on the doctor.

"You took two bullets in a drive-by shooting. Shot once in the back and once in the head."

Moll reached up and touched his head on the sides, patting the bandage.

"We operated to remove each bullet," the doctor said. "Appears you can move your legs all right."

Moll flopped his knees together, stretched his legs out and wiggled his toes. "What's going on ... down below?" Moll ducked his head under the sheets.

"Tingling?"

"Fucking tubes. Take the fucking tubes out. I'm not some ... Franken-agent."

The doctor glanced over at Ivy and Terry. "Step outside so we can make our colorful friend more comfortable."

"Comfortable?" Moll said crankily. "Tubes sticking into me ... all over. Pull them out. Bring food. I'm like ... starving."

Terry left the room with Ivy, each one smiling at Moll's antics. Tears of relief threatened to stream down his face, but Terry choked them back. "He didn't recall who I am. Didn't recognize you. His mind is stuck in his FBI days."

Ivy nodded. "Memory loss. We must be patient with him. Remember he will be disoriented, like he entered an alternate reality where everything changed. Let him ease into the present. Having Steve and Mathew come here and talking with Brian on the phone should help anchor him and make the changes less traumatic."

She reached over and hugged Terry again. "You're hurt because he forgot you. Be here for him, and he will remember. Put your feelings for Moll second to helping him recover. All smiles now, right?"

She released him from the hug. A wry smile came to her face, and she said, "Like he's still our Moll. Rad as ever. Would you expect him to come back all normal and boring? Com'on Terry, KTF – Keep the Faith."

Terry nodded, clenched his jaw and stuck his chin out in determination before echoing back, "KTF."

"Call Brian. He'll want an update so don't worry if you wake him up over in London," Ivy said as she handed him a couple of tissues. "I'll call Steve and Mathew."

Reaching over she gave him another hug. "Moll is back with us."

Chapter 24
Arielle

Arielle heard about the bungled shooting of the two partners in Portland with mixed emotions. One part of her wanted the Operation Payback completed and behind her. The other part realized the bungle gave her leverage over Carlos for the next time he became too mocking during a call.

Since burying her father she had spent most of her time in Paris, staying in her apartment and conducting clandestine meetings throughout the city with the key leaders in her father's former network. On a weekly basis she met openly with each of the managers of the four legitimate businesses and dropped by each location a couple of times a week. Her other hours were occupied with establishing her control over the rest of her father's operations.

Needing a break she had flown to Barcelona early that morning, sailed for most of the afternoon and now tied up her boat back in the slip. Early tonight she had a call scheduled with Kazimír on increasing the interrupted flow of drugs and underage prostitutes from his operations in Eastern Europe to France and other Western European locations. Glancing around and seeing no one within hearing distance, she nonetheless went into the small cabin, closed the door, opened her laptop, put on her headset and dialed Kazimír.

"Arielle, I am glad we are talking today without Carlos. How are things in Paris?"

"Touchy. My apartment is watched. I have to be careful when I leave the building. My strategy is to conduct meetings in changing venues around the city such as restaurants, hotels, and so on. I openly check on the regular businesses. When things are settled down this winter, we should talk about coming up with a joint legit venture in antiques out of Eastern Europe."

"I will make a note to follow-up with you in December."

Arielle paused for a moment to key a quick reminder into her follow-up list as well.

"What about you, Kazimír? Do you still have people trailing around behind you?"

"They are easy to lose. I had a secure room put in an office that will shield my calls and of course keep changing encryption methods. Most of my work is outside of Prague. Every week I am traveling to one, two, three or more cities. All that hopping around is very tiring and my wife and little girl find it hard to have me away so much."

"I am luckier. Most of the travel I do is only a train ride away."

"When will you be ready for increased product? The trickle you and Carlos are taking will not sustain my operation for long."

"Two of the pleasure houses in Paris will reopen in new locations with new managers in September. The better quality working staff will remain much the same since they were released after facing minor charges. As you know the operation of brothels is illegal in France. However the act of prostitution by a consenting woman over the age of eighteen is legal. I am not rehiring any of the younger ones. For the grand openings, I will need at least a dozen snow whites and six rent boys."

"Excellent. And when will you increase taking the white stuff? I need some blizzard conditions."

Arielle laughed sardonically at Kazimír's humor. "I want to increase the heroin from today's levels by about 20% per month. That should put us back at prior capacity by year-end. I am outsourcing some of the sales which means we will each have narrower margins on about 40% of the product."

"Arielle I cannot do this with these reduced volumes."

"Hear me out. By going this way I expect the volumes to increase next year, maybe not doubling our prior peak sales, but coming very close by next September. Less risk for me and for you if I run fewer street people."

"What about the other brothels?"

"Some will remain shut down. They were marginal on a risk/return basis. The new ones I am opening are luxury emporiums with a broader range of services and beefed up security in more of a club environment. Two in Paris in September and then two in Amsterdam by February."

"What makes these places emporiums?"

"Expanded services. Bondage. Group sex. Wider variety of drugs. Glass rooms with masked participants. I am also considering selling packages of services in coke-fueled auctions. Maybe I will offer bachelor and bachelorette parties. We will include come-down facilities so patrons do not leave incapacitated."

Arielle had come to reconcile herself to dealing in the human sex trade. While the use of underage prostitutes had horrified her when she first learned about that part of her father's business, by now her hardened feelings let her regard them merely as another source of income, one that brought premium prices.

"Interesting. Going after more of the guys with money, eh?"

"And women. About 10% of our business comes from women and that will increase with the emporiums. Another 30% is from gay men. I am thinking of opening an all-gay emporium early next year and a separate one for women the year after that."

Kazimír was quiet for a few moments perhaps mentally calculating what the emporiums might mean to his human trafficking trade. He cleared his throat and asked, "What about that mess-up in Portland?"

"Those fools Carlos sent out bungled the hit. I think you know they left one man alive and one brain-damaged in the hospital. So far the police have not traced the two hitmen back to Carlos. The FBI is in on it too which is not good. We do not need publicity of that type as we work to establish ourselves. We are fortunate to be well away from that mess," Arielle paused before saying, "We must advance our goal of finding new partners in the United States. If Carlos should be identified as behind the attacks, it could be disastrous for us."

"Agreed. I have opened negotiations in Florida, Texas and California. So far no deals, but two of those three show promise. I am shipping sample product this week."

"You must be careful that Carlos doesn't get wind of it."

"I'm using another name in these dealings," Kazimír said. "Even a separate phone. Giving my location as Sofia."

"That is what I like about you Kazimír. You think things through and proceed with caution. Let me know if I can help in any way."

"If I am successful, I will need you to assist in transport, same as with Carlos."

"Usual terms?"

"I may need to undersell the stuff coming out of South America and through Mexico at least at the beginning. Think of a 20% reduction in fees short-term. Within six months we should be able to creep the prices back up."

After some wrap-up conversation, they ended the call. Kazimir must be dumping dope somewhere unless he lost some of his suppliers in Turkey and further east. Where was he selling it if both she and Carlos were taking so much less product? Perhaps he was warehousing the surplus, but that would strain his cash flow.

Finding the cabin too stuffy to work in, she took her laptop up to the deck, pulled out a deck chair and opened her business model in Excel. Each of her operations had a separate spreadsheet, linked to an upper spreadsheet by product line, and then to a top level one to consolidate results. She had set this up for her father and maintained the data for him but with his old-fashioned ways, he always wanted printouts.

Alone on the boat she stopped to remember him. She never allowed herself to fully grieve since she could not afford to let her guard down in this critical time. When she could she did take moments like this to remember him. Rebuilding his businesses and establishing her authority demanded far more time and effort than she expected. Her father made it all look easy, but then everyone in the network were his hires and were loyal to him.

Arielle glanced around. The boat slip where the mysterious woman docked remained empty. She decided to wait until dusk to see if she returned and then dress for a night of clubbing in Barcelona. She wanted a partner for the night. She had not been to bed with anyone in three months and she needed a good romp between the sheets with no ties and no constraints.

She turned back to her spreadsheet and began making a list by region of required actions to demonstrate her leadership. Her next steps would be to waste a few people. Fire others. Threaten families. Those actions would be necessary for her to gain the respect she needed. With more people in place loyal to her and others fearing to be on her wrong side, her now tentative authority would become more solid. She nodded to herself and began to study the spreadsheet for the Amsterdam drug business.

Chapter 25
Nicola

In Barcelona near dusk Nicola angled her small yacht into its slip after returning from a long day on the water. Sick with worry for Brian and for Moll, she had sailed out early in the morning, dropping anchor in a nearby cove where her phone showed availability of cell service. Under an awning, she had worked most of the day on her action series, although her concentration kept drifting away.

Now at the dock Nicola turned off the motor as *Hildalgo* drifted into the slip. After securing the boat to its mooring, she started to pack up for the night.

"Buenos Nachos, senora," said a smooth female voice with a French accent.

From where Nicola tied the awning down, she jerked her head up. As she regarded the woman in front of her through her sunglasses, she grabbed her beach bag where her small pistol rested. On occasion a man would come by to talk, but never before did a woman stop. Whenever a stranger approached her, Nicola turned brusque and spurned any advances.

Although from her days as Julio in Miami she remembered the woman, Nicola gave her no answering response. After running into her at a couple of parties, in her sleek Julio attire she had danced with her at the second one. The woman stood about five-six, shorter than herself, with a curvy build, short dark hair and an air of a stylish French woman. However her allure was marred by a predatory quality visible in the way she held her mouth and in the hard coldness lurking around the edges of her eyes.

"My name is Arielle," the woman said, as she continued to speak in Spanish. "I noticed you here once before when I stopped for the night in Barcelona. Thought I might introduce myself since I don't run into many women who pilot their own crafts like you and I do."

Arielle Moreau. On their last encounter as Julio, she had slid away from her at that party and sidled back to her condo by a circuitous route. The woman was the daughter of a major underworld boss in Paris who had been killed during a police bust coordinated by Interpol when Brian's company contributed evidence to the FBI on money laundering.

Moll shot in Portland. Now this woman shows up here in Barcelona. Coincidence? Might her own cover be blown?

In a fast motion Nicola finished tying up the awning, grabbed her keys, slid her hand into her beach bag and gripped her pistol, ready to fire if needed. She jumped on the dock. "Late for a dinner date," she said in Spanish, making sure to put more inflection than usual in her voice to distinguish the sound from the careful, modulated tones used during her years as Julio.

"Please one moment," Arielle said reaching out for her arm.

Shaking her off Nicola rushed along through the marina and ran up to the street to hail a cab. No shots rang out. For the moment she should be safe, although her heart pounded from the adrenalin pumping through her as she ran. When a cab pulled over, Nicola gave the address of the ABaC Hotel to the driver. The hotel stood near the B-20/B-23 highway, which would take her to the airport in less than twenty minutes. En route she would call Maxim, arrange a flight out and take a different cab away from the hotel to catch her plane.

When Maxim answered she said into the phone, "Maxim? A woman confronted me as I docked *Hildago*. Back when I still masqueraded as Julio, I had met her in Miami. The police killed her father in the bust Brian and his company contributed to."

"Where are you?"

"In a taxi heading to a hotel and catching a different one to get to the airport."

"Try for Geneva or Zurich. I will leave now for Madrid and meet you. Text me your flight info. You should call Brian."

"Too much for him to deal with between Moll and keeping the business going. This may be nothing more than she is a bisexual, attracted to me," Nicola said to conceal her doubts.

"You must tell him. He'll best understand what to do. If you do not call him,

I will."

"I'll give him a ring before I board."

"You carrying an alternate passport and money?"

"Of course – always bring my parachute. In Geneva I stashed away a couple of other identities and more cash."

"Keep in touch. Be careful, my cousin."

"And you." After ending the call Nicola stepped out at the hotel, dialing Swiss Air as she walked into the lobby. Spinning around she made sure the cab drove away with a new fare before walking into the bar where she ordered a Pellegrino while waiting for a Swiss Air rep to answer.

Answering his cell phone on the second ring, Brian said, "Nicola. So sweet of you to call, my love." A boarding announcement blared out. "Sounds like you're at an airport."

"At a gate in Barcelona and about to board. Brian, a woman from my Julio days appeared in Barcelona. I'm going to hide out in Geneva for a few days. Maxim will join me."

A rush of concern and protectiveness flooded through Brian. While aware a day might come when someone from Nicola's past discovered her, he hoped the threat would not materialize so soon and while she was apart from him.

"What happened? Are you all right?"

"Right after I docked my boat tonight, she approached me. Back when I was Julio, I met her at a party three years ago in Miami where she flirted with me as Julio, but I slipped away as I did whenever anyone became too intrusive. Today she acted like she didn't recognize me as I am now, but I am not sure."

"Who is she?" Brian asked.

"Her name is Arielle Moreau."

"Moreau? Is she related to Alex Moreau?"

"I believe he was her father."

"You should leave Barcelona, but come here instead. Come with Maxim. Will you hold on? I should conference Steve in. When I was in Portland, I told him about us," Brian said. "I wanted him to mull it over before I told you."

"Is he comfortable with us?" she asked in a tone edged in doubt.

"He voiced concerns. However given this situation, I want his advice. Hang on."

"Steve," the big man answered in his raspy voice.

"Brian here, Steve. I have Nicola on the line. Something happened in Barcelona."

"Go ahead. Tell me," Steve said.

After repeating what she told Brian, Nicola added, "After she had started talking to me, I left her as fast as possible. I don't think she followed me. I called Maxim. Now I am waiting for my plane. He will meet me in Geneva."

Steve went silent. Nicola listened to a series of taps of a pen on his desk.

"I think each of us must act on the side of caution," Steve said. "I am pretty certain this shooting in Portland is the direct result of the work Noble Firs turned over to the FBI late this spring that brought about the arrests and shootouts in Paris, Prague and Philadelphia, as well as other locations. Nicola, I will arrange protection for you and Maxim. While this woman's approach to you may not be related to Moll's shooting, with your relationship to Brian we must assume that you could be in danger."

He paused to let his words sink in and then continued, "While you are in transit, I will make arrangements. Expect someone to meet you in Geneva. Text me your flight and Maxim's. Stay at the Geneva terminal until Maxim arrives and call me when you are together.

"Brian since we are already organized with British Intelligence, we will find it easier to protect them in London. Can they stay at your place?"

"Too small – one bedroom."

"In that case I'll arrange a safe house. Nicola, why didn't you put this woman and her father on your list of criminals you turned over in 2014?" Steve spoke with an edge in his voice.

"Because I never engaged in any dealings with them. Never met this Arielle's father. Only talked to the daughter at the one party I mentioned. Saw her at another one. Nothing factual to turn over."

"If you are scamming us," Steve said in a cold voice, "we will find out."

When Brian started to protest, Nicola said firmly, "I will never lie to you. That life in the shadows is behind me. If you will be more comfortable, I will send you a list of all my acquaintances and people I would characterize as probable underworld players, despite not being able to supply any tangible evidence."

"Maxim too?"

"When I see him in Geneva, I will speak to him. Right now I need to board. Last call."

"Be careful Nicola," Brian said and added, "I love you."

Nicola hustled to the Jetway for her flight. While still unaccustomed to having people care about her and assist her, she was relieved to have Maxim, Brian and now Steve in a time of need. None of them believed in coincidences.

Chapter 26
Moll

A little over two weeks later, Moll walked upstairs in Steve's house at the Spook Hills Vineyard. Sometimes the disorientation of losing his memories of the last three and a half years of his life overwhelmed him. As he walked across the house, he marveled at the huge living/dining combination. The open windows let a warm breeze flow through bringing in the sweet scents of flowers, grapevines and fresh-cut grass.

Even though he walked with some stiffness, he was recovering quickly. Last week he began twice-weekly visits to a physical therapist and this week added daily swims in Steve's pool. While thankful that he could keep track of current events in his life, the big gap in his past left him bewildered by where he was and how he had arrived in this present he found himself in. He was glad to be living in a sheltered environment as he became overwhelmed with this alternate reality he now found himself in, split between the familiarity of Steve and Mathew and the missing passages of time, events and people.

Where was everyone? Perhaps they worked out in the vineyard. Following the aroma of a pot of chili simmering on the stove, he walked into the kitchen and called out, "Hello?"

Ivy's voice answered from the direction of the master suite she shared with Steve. Imagine Steve landing a fox like her. Sure she might be a silver fox, but he thought her beautiful. Her kindness to him reminded him of his mother back when she still found her way to good days. Right from the start at the hospital, Ivy had insisted he live here to recover. Each day his health improved as he grew stronger. While now steady on his feet, the dissociative memory disorder from the bullet shot into his brain left him perplexed and with limited recall.

Ivy stood by the bed holding up a tailored navy suit. "What do you think? Keep this outfit or send the suit to the career woman's benefit shop?"

"Waz that?"

"Sort of shop specializing in recycled clothes to give women entering or re-entering the job market a professional appearance."

"Cool. Like donate the suit. You're too hip for conservative stuff."

Picking up the cat from a winged chair, he took him to sit on a capacious leather bench by the window in the sun. Funny he remembered the two cats, Druid and Firewire, but not the corgi dogs or the people from the last few years. Must be the sensory element of a cat. Snuggling Druid up by his face, he rubbed his cheek against the soft fur.

Ivy came back out of the closet with two full-length evening dresses. One sported a gold brocaded jacket which she regarded with disgust and tossed on the giveaway pile. Ripples in the fabric of the other gown caught the light in its striking iridescent emerald-green.

"Still stunning. A keeper?" she asked, glancing over at Moll.

White dancing lights began filling his internal vision. Champagne. Food. Green shimmer. Steve grinning. Memories came flooding back.

"Moll?" she said still holding the party dress.

He held up a hand as snippets of his past raced through his head, exiting in a smear of color. They came back in less of a jumble.

"Remembering. The fragrances of Christmas – evergreens, spices like cinnamon and cloves, peppermint. You in the green, shimmery dress. Steve happier than ever before. Lots and lots of little white lights. Small tables with white tablecloths. Long buffets of food. Music. The corgis grubbing crumbs dropped on the floor. Loads of people. Champagne. Me in a tux." Hugging the cat tighter, tears slipped down his face. "I remember, Ivy. Images are coming back. Memories – I never grasped how precious they are, but memories tell us who we are, where we've been and what we shared."

"The doctor said objects, sounds or scents might help your stored recollections to come back. A visual like a dress might conjure up memories too. The senses help us to remember."

"The green –dazzling. Like Holyshmoley. Your wedding?"

"The party after. You set up all those little round tables and helped with the decorations. Moll, your brain is starting to fill in the gaps." With the shimmery dress draped over her arm, she walked over and bent down to give him a hug.

As she moved back to the closet and his mind grew quiet again, he saw darkness followed by a flash of light. New images started flooding his brain.

"Something else." Releasing Druid, he sat still to let him settle in his lap.

Ivy poked her head back out of the closet. After a minute or so he spoke again. "Working in a house with Brian. Where was I?"

"My old house in Portland. You, Brian and Mathew bought the property together late in 2013."

He inhaled. "Right. You brought us a pot of chili like you are making now. And cornbread."

Moll scratched the side of his head with the incision where the hair had been shaved off. A mass of frizz had started growing back, but it itched something fierce. "We worked at testing software for ... for us. I remember now. Noble Firs. We worked on the startup of our company. Us two guys at the dining room table, coding, testing, documenting. Snow fell outside, fat flakes drifting down and covering the deck."

Ivy beamed over at him. His memory must be genuine, not a repeat of what others had told him. No one mentioned the chili, the cornbread or the snow.

"Do we still own the house?"

"Yes. We can go visit this afternoon if you want." She held up an elegant white wool pants suit, smiled and took it back into the closet, coming out with three more suits.

"Totally rad. Fucking A. Remembering all on my own."

"What's the recollection process like?"

"A flash followed by scads of pictures running super-fast forward. The stream stops. A void. All those phantasmagorias shuffle themselves into something I can make sense of. Nothing quiet or tidy. My brain never tended to be neat or organized. Why would the old noggin be any different with those nuggets I squirreled away?"

For a couple of minutes, he sat thinking over those recollections, wondering if something else would pop up. When nothing did he asked, "Can I chug an ale with my chili? And are you making cornbread?"

134

Ivy laughed. He remembered her laughter now and how sometimes this woman in front of him would laugh with brilliant abandon when her amusement became too intense to hold back. Now confident of more of his past returning, life transformed into a much more appealing prospect, and he found himself laughing along with her.

Later in the afternoon with his eyes as wide open as an owl's, Moll prowled around the house in Portland. The layout appeared familiar, yet the details evaded him. The house upstairs consisted of windowed rooms spilling into each other with only partial walls and with private nooks. The funky layout downstairs appealed to him. The lower lounge opened into carefree hidden gardens where shrubs and flowers tumbled together in happy harmony.

"I own this?" Moll asked, gazing at Ivy in wonder.

"With Brian. Mathew used to be a part-owner too, but you two bought him out last year when he built his house at Spook Hills."

"I remember working in the dining room and having coffee on the little deck, but most of the house is as foreign to me as a bear's cave." Plopping down in an oversized chair nestled into a small library with bookshelves on two sides, he stretched out his legs on the commodious ottoman.

Ivy handed him a glass of sweet iced tea with lemon. After taking a sip, Moll leaned his head back, inhaled, frowned and took another sip. When he closed his eyes, another sequence of images zoomed through. He waited to see what they might mean.

"One time I got sick and bundled myself up here in this chair. Brian handed me a hot toddy in a pottery mug. The hot drink smelled of lemon like this tea. I drank two of those babies, slept for hours, woke up, stuffed a couple of sandwiches down and went to bed. All better the next day."

After she had pushed a hassock on wheels out of the living room to sit by him, Ivy picked up her own glass of tea.

"Some clown fired a gun at you here, right?" Moll asked.

Going a little pale she nodded. "I was making Sunday dinner in the kitchen. Gunman shimmied up to the back deck, blasted out the door lock and burst in."

Her knuckles turned white as she gripped her glass.

"Steve rushed in when I screamed, took aim and killed the bastard. A bullet from the gunman grazed Steve's shoulder," Ivy said, and her face relaxed as she chuckled. "Steve said my old Harry corgi rushed to bite the guy's ankle. Right behind Harry, Cleopatra pelted in too. They made the gunman's shot go wide."

"Hard for you to be back here?"

"Not anymore. Now I can focus on the better memories. This house provided a place of refuge and comfort during the last stress-filled years of my career. Steve and I fell in love here. You and Brian are making this your home now."

Needing to pose a critical question to Ivy, Moll hesitated out of worry he might not like the answer.

"In the hospital, I would sometimes drift towards consciousness. Voices sounded far away. Every time, someone held my hand. You, right?"

She gazed at him with a questioning expression, then shifted her eyes away from him and towards the front door like she wanted to avoid answering him.

"Ivy?"

She turned back to face him. "Most of the time Terry stayed at your bedside and only left the hospital a few times when we pushed him out to shower and put on clean clothes."

"Terry?" Moll echoed. "Stayed with me non-stop and I can't remember who the fuck he is? No recollections of him. *Nada. Rein.* Nothing."

"He wants us to meet him and Steve at the office around six. Go for a burger at the nearby VQ before we head back home."

Moll stared out the far windows, remembering him and Brian working together. Ivy said they had bought the house late in 2013. Dates were a jumble to him.

"Why did Terry sit with me and hold my hand?"

"The doctor said human contact would help you. Comforting."

"Why him? Why not Brian or Mathew or Steve? Terry isn't gay or something, is he?"

Ivy's eyes clouded with concern. "Yes."

"Shit. Is he like into me? As far as I remember I dated women and too few of them, I might add."

"This discussion should happen between you and Terry."

With a nod of his half-curly head, Moll closed his eyes. "All this remembering is kicking my butt."

"Moll, be kind to Terry. He's an exceptional man. If you don't desire him the way he wants you, be clear but be gentle."

Did some part of him comprehend Terry's attachment to him? Did he want to forget those insights? Did this explain why he remembered nothing about Terry? Leaning his head back, he closed his eyes. The little flash repeated itself.

He recalled a black car coming up behind him on the street, a window opening. He leaped over someone with long blond hair, tumbling over him to the pavement. A fresh minty smell floated back to him. Terry, the someone was Terry. Moll sank back in the broad, comfy chair. Did he like Terry so much he made the protective move or did his FBI training kick in?

"Let me rest here until near dinnertime. Will you tell Terry I'm not ready to go into the office today? We can meet him and Steve for dinner. We all need to eat, right?"

Ivy nodded and rose to take a plaid throw off a chair in the living room and arrange it over him. Even though the day was warm, the little nook held the cool morning air. He snuggled under the wooly fabric, let his eyes close and drifted off to sleep.

Chapter 27
Terry

The next morning on Saturday, Steve called for a briefing with what he called the Spook Hills Gang. Since he was invited Terry guessed Steve had decided to induct him as an honorary member. They all gathered downstairs in Steve and Ivy's office at Spook Hills while Brian came in on Skype from London. Steve pointed the projector to an empty chair with a high back draped with a white sheet, allowing Brian to appear to be sitting with them. Terry found the arrangement darn clever.

"With Moll on his way to recovering," Steve began, "I want us all updated on the shooting incident."

He hit a button on his cell phone to record the conversation. "Moll do you remember anything from the night of the shooting?"

After sitting back and closing his eyes, Moll said, "Yesterday when the flashbacks started, I remembered the minute or so before the shooting. We were walking to the parking lot – me and Terry. The night was balmy and the moon hung above us shining like it owned the sky. The air breezed past our faces, dry and warm. I remember thinking with summer so glorious I needed to go camping before it was over. Wait."

Moll gripped the chair arms and stared straight ahead. His eyes moved over and down, then widened. He stared into space. Seconds passed. Once more his eyes moved over to the left, and he gazed downward. "Dredged up some things from earlier in the evening. Give me a moment to sort them into a coherent sequence."

Steve turned the recorder off.

Sneaking a peek over at Terry, Moll said, "I'm starting to remember the business. Snippets are popping into my brain."

Terry gave him a thumbs-up sign, relieved to find the man he loved clawing his way into his memories. While Moll moved with some difficulty from the bullet to his back and his memory of the last three and a half years stayed riddled with a plethora of gaps, he was recovering faster than Terry feared he might during those long hours sitting in the hospital with him in a coma.

Moll nodded to Steve to start recording.

"Backing up. Earlier the same evening I remember being in a conference room where Terry spoke to our employees, and he showed charts on the company's financial performance this year. While he talked I stood over by the window listening. Glancing down I spied two men talking on the sidewalk below."

Steve went to speak, but Ivy put a restraining hand on his arm.

"Like a pair of hefty crows, the two men drew my attention in their black shirts and pants. One slicked back his dark hair and wore black mirrored sunglasses, and the other sported gold chains around his neck with his shirt opened almost to the waist. Caucasian. Burly. Not Portlanders. More East Coast mob types. I remembered thinking they looked like a couple of undercover Narcs trying to imitate mobsters. After talking for a few minutes, they stared up at our building and walked away."

Pausing and taking a drink from a bottle of water, Moll swallowed and continued, "Ten or fifteen minutes later, after I nattered on about some topic, Terry went back up to present our new stock program. Cool idea, man." A wide grin spread over his face and he gestured with a touchdown signal to Terry.

"After putting up the needed slide, I loafed over by the window again. The two men appeared like they had taken a slow walk around the block or something. Once more they focused on our building as if they caught me standing by the window. Silly to think they could see me, given the way those windows are mirrored. The two crows walked away by going up Madison. They moved differently than people tend to out here – swaggered the way some bullies or thugs do."

He signaled for Steve to stop recording. Shutting his eyes again he leaned back to let memories flood into him. The group waited, hoping for more.

"Super wine at the party – picked a case up from Rick next door," Moll said. "Hit the old recorder, Steve."

After waiting a moment he continued, "Everyone left the offices. Terry and I gabbed for a while about the stock offer and other office stuff. I remember a glow like everything had clicked at Noble Firs – our business boomed, a solid team worked for us and we had healthy financials. The issues from the past May with that DBA were well behind us.

"Sometime long after nine we left, locking up and flicking the alarm system on. We took the elevator down and walked out the front of the building, saying *Buenas Noches* to old Alberto at the reception desk. Weird I remember his name, but not the names of the people who work for us.

"Like I was saying before, the clear sky, the bright moon, the balmy air ... Behind us, a car started up. When I swiveled around to check, I spied a black town car heading our way, not fast, but running along the curb on Third Avenue. As the vehicle drew closer, the passenger window slid down.

"Shit. Bad vibes, man. I reacted and threw myself over Terry. All my agent training I guess. Shots. At least two. Gun with a silencer. Last I remember Terry let out a yell and started squirming under me."

The room went silent. Moll added more details than Terry had supplied.

"Anything else you can remember about the two men?" Steve asked.

"We're like up on the twelfth floor? Difficult to catch details down at street level. Dark in the car as it pulled up by us. The men were barely shadows inside. No, nothing else."

Reaching out Steve went to end the recording.

"Wait. Oregon License plate. "G-P-J ... All I can remember."

"Tree in the center," Terry said, squinting through his glasses to recall more. "7-4-2. Sorry Steve, didn't realize I noticed the license plate until Moll recited the first three letters. I caught the number as the car sped away."

Turning to his computer Steve searched, opened an email and said, "Bingo. Car lifted from a fleet owned by DeLuxe Limos down in Salem. Parked at the airport at the time. Driver arrived early and went inside to take a leak or whatever. When he came back, no more town car. Found a week later in short-term parking at PDX. Prints had been wiped. I'll instruct an agent to work harder on whether anyone observed anything in the parking lot or wherever. Excellent recall, both of you. If anything else comes back to you, tell me right away."

"The guys arrested in the FBI sting in April included a mob leader in Phili named Carlos Ochoa, Senior," Mathew said. "Steve, I remember you saying the word is his playboy son, Carlos Junior, is suspected of picking up the remnants of the street business and is rebuilding."

From Skype Brian said, "The woman who approached Nicola in Barcelona is the daughter and only child of Alex Moreau, killed resisting arrest in the same sting in France."

"A third leader in the same sting," Steve said, "died two weeks after the attempted arrest in Prague. One Tódor Horak. Eldest son killed in crossfire three years earlier. The younger brother is Kazimír Horak and is now thought to control the business of moving drugs and kidnapped teens out of Turkey and surrounding areas. This Kazimír holds an advanced technical degree from the University of Birmingham. Super bright man. Bit of a loner."

"Any recent chatter on them or on this hit?" Mathew asked.

"Nothing so far. Not on the usual channels and not on Darknet."

"The FBI monitors Darknet?" Terry asked. "I've read about that alternative Internet -- carries porn and trash, right?"

"Steve?" Brian asked and paused to gain his attention. "Nicola mentioned one day she caught a rumor about a new network coming online, but the report is about three years old. Something reputed to be called GodfatherNet or NadirNet. It is being built by the upcoming generation of the criminal world."

"Bureau discounted any such rumor."

"Doesn't mean this NadirNet isn't coming into existence," Brian countered.

"New can of snakes. And no, I don't mean worms but snakes – mean poisonous ones. Brian, schedule a call for us with Nicola and Maxim ASAP today. We should hear firsthand any insights they gathered or what street rumors circulated."

Moll shook his head and tried to remember who Nicola and Maxim were. Nothing came to him so he asked, "Who are Nicola and Maxim?"

Everyone focused on him and then looks were snuck over to Brian. "What's going on? Moll asked. "Why are you all so fidgety and squirrelly?"

"Do you remember Cruze Fuentes?"

"No."

"How about El Zorro Astuto?"

"Yeah man. We chased him for a while before we left the FBI, right?"

Everyone stayed quiet until Moll said, "Look gang you gotta connect the dots for me on this one."

Brian spoke up, "After we left the Bureau, we did consulting back to the FBI. This El Zorro Astuto turned out to be three brothers – Cristo, Cruze and Eduardo Fuentes. Cristo and Eduardo were killed in an FBI bust. We thought Cruze had died earlier in another raid in Mexico. Anyway this brother named Cruze remained alive, but he had left the business. The three Fuentes brothers had a cousin named Annetta. It is a long story but in 2014 when we were again acting as consultants to the FBI, Cruze and Annetta entered the FBI Witness Protection Program in exchange for supplying evidence on many criminal activities. They now live under the names of Nicola and Maxim." •

"So like why are they involved now?"

Brian looked at Steve who returned a bare negative movement of his head and Brian said, "They help us out from time to time and they have become friends."

Moll held his head in his hands, then looked up and said, "One bullet to the old noggin and it is like sleeping through three acts of a five act play. Somehow I feel like you just gave me a couple of scenes from the middle three acts."

As Steve moved on to recount the investigative work done by the FBI and the police on the shooting, Moll slumped deeper in his chair. Terry feared the process of remembering had worn him out.

With Moll acting more reserved towards him, Terry decided to take Firewire and move back to his condo to give Moll some space. Something over three weeks had passed since the shooting. Moll was ambulatory and recovering, although he needed to have people around him as he adjusted to the changes in his lost years. He would have plenty of help and protection here at Spook Hills.

Since Moll needed time to complete his recovery, this was the wrong time to add to his short-circuiting by telling Moll he loved him. Terry would rather remain unloved than risk losing Moll's friendship.

An hour later Steve and Ivy sat in front of Brian on the computer again with Terry, Moll and Lenny nearby. This time Brian called in with Nicola and Maxim on a secure video connection from the safe house in London.

"Thanks for joining a call so quickly, Nicola and Maxim," Steve said. "Brian briefed you on the topic of something beyond Darknet?"

"Is this connection safe?" Nicola asked.

"Blessed by the Bureau. New government setup. Latest in security."

"Back in August of 2013, I attended a gathering on a huge yacht anchored off the coast near Miami. A fluid crowd came to the party using a shuttle running every few minutes back and forth to the mainland. After about an hour some of the bright younger set who skirt along the fringes of crime flew a bit high on cocaine and became somewhat unguarded. They did speak in a kind of code. Versed as I used to be in such communications, I followed the gist of their discussions.

"They chattered at length about colluding on a telecommunications project in their different accents from around the world – Spanish, French, Czech, East Coast American, Australian, Chinese. They wanted to change the way crime works.

"Although I stood with my back to them, I overheard wild speculation about a secret network only they would access as the new leaders in their counter-world. They thought their communications could ride on unused capacity in existing private, public and government grids. While I'm not technology-savvy enough to know if this is possible, the group was convinced poaching bandwidth could be done. An East Coast type called the concept GodfatherNet. Somebody told him not to be old school. After many suggestions and raucous laughter, they settled on NadirNet."

"Nothing more you can tell me – only this speculation by a bunch of kids high on blow?" Steve asked in a dubious tone.

"The group went off to the dance floor. A smaller set consisting of the American, a French woman – this Arielle who appeared in Barcelona -- and a Czech came back. They started talking about a team approach to crime, including drugs, prostitution, and data theft. In this new approach, they planned to divide up the world into spheres of influence. They spoke like the hot-shot MBAs I'd run into over the years, mixing business lingo into their pseudo-language."

Nicola peered sideways at Maxim. "Those young people talked like Eduardo when he speculated about creative ways to succeed through technology."

"Eduardo was never loose-lipped," Maxim said in defense of his younger brother.

"Nor at a party either," Nicola said. "The rest of the gang joined them, and they jumped on the next shuttle to some flashy night club."

Terry listened intently. What Nicola related made sense from a technical perspective. Criminals used technology to steal data and money. Why wouldn't the underworld establish its own network? He shifted his eyes to Moll who lounged in a side chair. Terry could see that as casual as he appeared, every fiber of Moll's brain or at least those not severed by the bullet, focused on this technical possibility.

Tapping his pen several times on the desk, Steve sat back thinking. When he spoke his voice sounded removed as if his thoughts snuck out unfiltered. "Inevitable I suppose. The Millennials, as they are called, operating in the underworld will be a lot like their counterparts elsewhere. They are computer-adept. They socialize and consume together. They collaborate and cooperate, seek out adventure, are passionate about values – in this case their warped values. We need to find out if they built or might build an undetected web of their own."

Nicola hesitated and asked, "Ever meet or hear of a telecommunications consultant out of Iceland?"

"Tell me about him or her."

"Back when I played on the other side, I needed help on how to use technology to communicate, to unearth useful information and to protect myself. After searching and checking out various resources, I found a guy with the handle of 'BentLight'.

"In our discussions I kept him ignorant of my work in the underworld by making him think I handled sensitive information for a startup company and I needed to keep my communications confidential. The guy is legitimate. If he had figured out what I did for a living, he would have terminated all discourse with me and called the cops."

"You think this Bentlight can tell us more about NadirNet?" Ivy asked.

"Not necessarily, but he can figure out the telecommunication underpinnings."

"You still in touch with him?"

"In May he helped me find a couple of people to consult on this animation project I'm experimenting with."

"What's his real name?" Steve asked.

"Mikael Sigurdsson. Operates out of Akureyri."

"Way up north in Iceland. Bet he took the name Bentlight from the polarizing effect of Icelandic calcite or spar. How do I make contact with him?"

"I'll send you his info."

A troubled expression came to Nicola's face. "You should be aware of his background. He lost his feet and part of his lower legs as a teen in a skating accident due to severe frostbite. Now he uses a wheelchair. Mikael is brilliant and likable and wants no pity. You'll take to him, I think."

Steve's hard agent's eyes softened when he learned of Mikael's disability.

"Expect him to be cautious with you," Nicola continued. "A few weeks ago I hinted at my less than honest past and turning state's evidence for the FBI, putting myself under non-disclosure."

Ivy searched the Internet. She brought up a website and pushed her laptop in front of Steve. Terry leaned forward to examine a photo of an appealing, chestnut-haired, youthful man named Mikael Sigurdsson and to read about his experience and expertise.

After skimming the text Steve said, "Impressive creds. I'll contact Bent. Okay to refer to you to confirm I am who I say?"

"Of course."

Maxim spoke up. "From the last time we discussed using technology, I remember Eduardo talking about this new system that he came across while researching security back in 2012. Didn't pay much attention because I'm not at all technical. However I remember him saying legitimate front companies planned to build a private telecom net to sell bandwidth but would retain a portion for what they called private communications -- in other words, for their illegal operations."

"Quite plausible Maxim. Two channels to follow – one about stealing spare capacity and the other about services posing as legit but with devious undertones. Ivy, I may need to travel next week. You up for a trip?"

"What about Moll?" Ivy asked with a glance across at Terry and Moll.

"I'll check with Mathew to find out if he will let Moll and Terry move over to his place. We might leave as early as tomorrow. Maxim and Nicola, if I sent you lists of the contacts on the cell phones of Cristo and Eduardo, would you help us decipher them? Many only went by code names and the lines turned out to be disconnected when we tried them."

Maxim nodded. Nicola agreed.

"Enjoyed speaking with you both," Steve said. "Good info. Thank you for collaborating with us."

Chapter 28
Moll

Two hours later Moll jogged down the stairs to Steve's office at Spook Hills for a call with Nicola and to be updated on Steve's recent conversations. After their meeting in the morning, Terry indicated he wanted to move back to his condo and left after lunch. Working with Steve to participate on what resembled an FBI case made Moll comfortable. The investigative topics under discussion wrapped around him like a security blanket. Most of the time in the present, he masqueraded in someone else's life.

"Nicola? Steve Nielsen here with Moll O'Leary. Can you talk now?"

Nicola inhaled from the surprise of Steve calling her directly

"Is this about BentLight?"

"Related. I did talk to Bent. Reminds me of Moll and Terry. Each of the three men is loaded with more brains than he can keep in his head," Steve said with a nod at Moll. "We're linking up on Tuesday at the FBI offices in D.C. to meet with a gang of their experts. Ivy and Moll will join us.

"Since telecommunications is not my area of expertise, Bent will be an asset. He will give me support as a technical authority who believes this NadirNet likely does exist despite with what the FBI's own experts say. During a discussion with Director Comey mid-day, he asked me to head up a research project to explore the possibility.

"I'm sure Brian told you he talked to me about the two of you. While he surprised me, the way he regarded you when you first met told me he found you intriguing. To reassure you let me say I will support your relationship with him. However I am not fond of extended periods of subterfuge among friends, nor is Mathew. I have not shared this with Ivy yet, nor has Mathew with Callie. With your

Later in the afternoon while Steve spoke on the phone, Moll went in search of Ivy. One advantage of this period of recovery was the freedom it gave him, leaving him unfettered by work responsibilities. Ivy bent over a long clay planter in the conservatory, fussing with the herbs she grew year round. The glass room, located between the garage and the kitchen, attracted light whether the sky was sunny or cloudy.

"Hey Ivy. Waz up with those herbs?"

"Trimming them," she said, bending to pick up a few stems. "They grow faster than they can be used and I want to keep them pot-sized and healthy. Take some tea. Should be brewed by now."

While not much of a tea drinker, Ivy kept trying to convert him. He liked the orange spice one she picked this time, so he poured out a mug, added a little honey and sat in one of the cushy chairs by a glass table.

Ivy came over, brushing herself off and tossing the pungent rosemary trimmings into a wicker basket for composting. She nodded when he pointed to the teapot, and he poured tea into a red stripe mug for her.

"Honey too please," she said and picked up a swirled cookie. "Love these thyme-cardamom cookies – sweet yet savory too."

"Ivy, what should I do about Terry? I remember him now, and I like him. Used to think of him as my brain-twinner."

"But you aren't attracted to him?"

"That's the scary part. I am attracted to Terry." Moll paused to think about how much he should disclose to Ivy. "Guess I always recognized this tendency in myself. No matter how hard I try to bury my attraction to men, sometimes a certain magnetism surfaces. All I want is to be one of the guys, you know? Someday soon I want a home and a family. I like hanging out with Brian, Mathew and Steve. No way can I taint our friendships by letting myself get into a relationship with a guy."

"Does this explain why you keep dating women but never advance your relationships?" Ivy asked.

"I'm such a screwball. The proverbial geek of a guy who never quite fits."

"Like Steve."

"Steve is a powerhouse. A leader. He always fits."

"Not in his mind. He sees himself as lacking in social skills. I developed a fragile veneer of grace to cover my own awkwardness, but underneath I remain the too-intelligent, too-tall woman who was always different."

"None of us ever thinks of you as anything but charming, if a little feisty."

"We each carry different images of ourselves than the world does."

"This gay thing. Coming out is such a huge step, making me afraid everything will change. I don't want to find myself sucked into going to gay bars, becoming effeminate, whatever."

"No reason to assume the role of a gay cliché or alter who you are. Men who act like regular guys can prefer the love of another man."

"Steve won't understand."

"He can't identify with homosexuality. Doesn't mean he won't accept you. Steve buddied up to Terry, right?"

"Yeah, but Terry's not one of us. He's not ..."

"FBI?"

"Yeah, I guess."

"Moll, considering this variation of lifestyles is monumental to you, representing a decision you must be comfortable with inside yourself. Those close to you accept you for who you are. You are the authentic, intelligent, quirky Moll who brings a bright light to our lives. That will continue whether you are gay or straight. You challenge us to envision other possibilities. Who you love will not change how we relate to you, as long as you choose someone worthy of who you are."

Moll curled over himself in his chair, afraid to face a decision he had never wanted to make. What Ivy communicated made the choice his alone. He remembered the first time he realized he might be different. At the time he had been about twelve and had gone out to play Frisbee golf on the beach with a guy his mother brought over sometimes. After making a tricky shot, the fellow ran over and hugged him. His pre-pubescent reaction was so intense, it had scared the bejesus out of him. He had run away from the guy, left the beach and hid in the library. He became determined not to grow up to be, what they called in those days, a pansy or worse a pussy.

"Always worries me when I want to learn about things from you, like cooking or how to decorate a house. Concerned my interests are not masculine."

"Those artificial definitions changed. Women's roles changed. Men's roles are changing too. Do you think any less of Steve for making scones? Or doing dishes? We're human, and we each possess varying degrees of what might have been considered masculine or feminine. Am I any less of a woman because I like to work with Steve on FBI cases or the important training development project we did for the Bureau?"

"You're feminine, but not a giggly girlie-girl. Ivy, didn't you ever want children? Do you regret having a career instead?"

Ivy's face became thoughtful and sad too, making Moll regret his questions.

"The truth is, Moll, I can't have children. My own fault – back in college I diddled around with a guy, became pregnant and realized I had made a terrible mistake. An abortion went bad. If children were possible for me, would working still come first? Deep inside, I craved, and still yearn for the intellectual challenge, the sense of worth and the independence. Never a stay-at-home sort of mom."

"I want children," Moll said.

"You can adopt."

"But like what would they call us, Dad and Daddy? Too weird for kids."

"Kids are more accepting than adults, don't you think? Left to themselves, would they ever act prejudiced?"

Moll faced a decision only he could make. Terry's move back to his place in Portland would give him room to think. No matter what Moll wanted to keep Terry as a friend and as his business partner.

Chapter 29

Brian

The next morning Nicola and Brian sat across from Maxim at breakfast in a hotel not far from the Noble Firs London office. As the two men dug into omelets, Nicola nibbled a healthy concoction of coconut yogurt laced with fruits and toasted grains.

"Steve called late yesterday asking Maxim and me to help him decode messages on NadirNet," Nicola said, choosing her words with care.

"If such a criminal network exists," Brian said.

"If Eduardo recognized the power of such a private network, our former competitors picked up on the idea too," Maxim said.

"You will do office work only," Brian said in a firm voice. "Deep background."

"Yes," Nicola agreed. "Steve nicknamed our research 'Project Anti-Camorra'. A camorra is a secret group united for devious or unscrupulous purposes."

"Meaning we are aiming to do the opposite –identify the Camorra. Not sure what I can do," Maxim said. "I'll try but I'm not a techie."

"Your mind is excellent," Nicola said. "I will show you how to decode messages. You need to perceive patterns. Think of words as objects forming arrangements."

"Patterns appear to me in nature, in glass, in architecture. Back in school I enjoyed art of course. Mathematics, yes. English not so much, but I still enjoy reading."

"Pattern recognition requires keen observation, the ability to collect data and let your mind process the information represented," Brian said. "When we hire people at Noble Firs to analyze data, we try to attract keen observers. One guy came to us after a stint as a star quarterback in college. While his arm was decent, his real strength lay in recognizing team formations and adjusting plays as he thought best. An injury to his shoulder ended his football career.

"His coach called us because the guy lost his ambition after the abrupt termination of his future in sports. We took a gamble, interviewed him and taught him to apply his skill to data analysis during a summer intern program. After graduation he joined us full time and has become one of our best analysts. When training him, we discovered a neat approach called Visual Thinking. I'll send you a link to a short article."

"Nicola and Eduardo have the brains, although I used to be a fair student. While I can't promise to make a contribution, I will try."

"No one with eyes as keen as yours is limited by intelligence. Nothing escapes your notice. You'll make a solid impact on the results," Brian said. "Besides people respect you because you speak only when you have solid insights."

Nicola said, "If we do this – make this contribution to the FBI – Steve agreed he would work to allow us back into the United States, lifting the term of our agreement."

"He agreed?" Brian asked. "As Moll would say, Zoinks."

"Our work on Project Anti-Camorra would give him leverage to open the negotiation. Steve also thinks we should tell Callie about us and he wants to advise Ivy too."

Brian reached over to take her hand, cradling her slender fingers. "Are we ready?"

Maxim put his glass-nicked fingers on top of their intertwined hands. "Your best friends will share in your joy, as I do."

"Will you call Callie?"

Nicola nodded her confirmation.

"Then I will give Mathew a heads-up on it too," Brian said. "Maxim let me know if I can help in any way to get you started on Project Anti-Camorra."

"Understand this, both of you," Maxim said with a stern expression. "If I cannot make a valid contribution to the decoding work on this Project Anti-Camorra, I can't ask Steve to negotiate on my behalf. I must achieve my own freedom."

At two that afternoon Brian closed the door to his office and called Mathew.

"Hey Brian. Let me walk to my den," Mathew said. "Heading there with a freshly made Caramel Macchiato. I've become a pretty talented barista. Glad you called early. Full day on the vineyard ahead of me."

He waited as Mathew clomped across the wooden floor in his house and settled into a chair before saying, "Mathew, I continue to see Nicola and with her now living in London, I will see her more. I wanted you to know that I love her. She's still troubled by what her father did. The extended abuse she suffered scarred her and now she's working on her mental and emotional issues. I will help in whatever way I can. While hard for her to trust and to love, I think she is letting herself love me. Steve is telling Ivy about us this morning. Nicola will call Callie and let her know about our relationship. Steve thinks both women have already guessed."

"Callie whoop with joy. You the playboy committing to a woman? Almost harder to absorb than you dating Nicola."

"I've started going to a counselor to help me understand her."

"If anything proves you love her, going for professional help does. Weren't you the guy who wanted action in no more than three dates and dropped head cases like the proverbial hot potato?"

"What a cad I was."

"Not a cad. A guy scared of commitment. Why aren't you troubled by committing to Nicola?"

"Steve summed up my trust of her best. She is so independent she will never try to control me. She needs me. I find I like being needed as well as wanted. I want to marry her, Mathew."

"Well I'll be damned. You have changed."

"Yes, I have." Brian said, becoming so lost in thought that when Mathew spoke again, it surprised him.

"I know this is off topic but I want to ask you something important to Callie and me. Callie and I are going for fertility tests next week. If I'm the problem, would you be a sperm donor? All test tube stuff of course."

"Think you're a little ahead of yourself. Find out the problem first. You may not be at fault. Why not Steve?"

"Complex situation. When I asked him he thought himself too old."

The dismissive tone of Mathew's voice and the way he rushed the words out made Brian ask, "More to his refusal than what you are saying?"

"You can't talk about this, but Steve discovered his son isn't his son. His wife fooled around with the man who became her second husband far longer than she let on. The son asked Steve to do a paternity test, and the story tumbled out."

"How's he handling the revelation?"

"Unshakable as ever. Never told me anything until we talked about the sperm donating thing."

"Why wouldn't he want to donate now?"

"Doesn't want to upset Ivy. A part of her wanted kids, but she couldn't become pregnant. He thought a little Stevie running around might distress her."

Brian took a moment to think about Ivy who had never let on about wanting children. "I thought of Ivy as a total career woman. Anyway in answer to your question, I would consider being a sperm donor if Nicola and Callie agree."

"Either way, I'd want you to be the godfather."

"Thanks. You indicated you wanted to talk about two problems. What's the second?"

"Torn down the middle. Brian, I want to help you, Moll and Steve like I used to, but my family is my priority now. Callie is afraid having Moll here at Spook Hills could endanger Susannah if the thugs decided to finish him off here. That's why Moll is traveling with Ivy and Steve next week. Terry moved back to his own place yesterday."

"Your family comes first. We'll always help each other, but one-by-one we will move into our own lives like Steve did. This is why we stopped being FBI agents and started new careers."

"The following week we're taking Susannah down to California to visit her father," Mathew said. "Thanks to your help in coming up with terms John Henry would accept, we are close to adopting her. One of the terms of the adoption agreement is visits with her birth father, John Henry, if she wants to see him. We want to do this now as a gesture of goodwill. We expect the adoption to be finalized in September."

"Susannah wants to see her father?" Brian asked.

"She is willing to go as long as we are with her. She'll stay in a hotel with us and spend a couple of half days with John Henry. Susannah hasn't been back to California since the kidnapping two years ago. We think she needs to go to silence any ghosts of that horrid event."

"Sure hope she can face down those memories without too much emotional trauma. Is her birth father staying sober?"

"As far as we can tell from a distance. He tested satisfactorily every week for the last month."

"Give me a call to tell me about your trip."

Brian ended the call and took a few minutes to think about Nicola. They spent time together most days, if only for a quick breakfast or lunch when he became too busy at the office. The routine of seeing her with such frequency charmed him. Several evenings a week now she would either stay at his apartment, or he would stay over at the safe house. With more time together, their relationship deepened and Nicola appeared to move further away from the memories of her past.

He wanted her as he never wanted any other woman. Not for the night, not for the short-term, but for the rest of his life. If things moved forward on Project Anti-Camorra, he would spend less time with her. On the positive side she and Maxim were grappling with the possibility of clearing a path to a better future, essential for each of them and for him. He was glad they had this opportunity to prove they changed their lives.

How strange love is – makes a man happy, exhilarated, edgy and patient all at the same time. Always an optimist Brian focused on his future. Despite the danger popping up in the Noble Firs business, his horizons glimmered with potential more than ever.

Chapter 30
Arielle

Early the first Monday evening in September, Arielle spied on Brian Tovey in London as he left his office building accompanied by a burly man suspiciously like a bodyguard. She stepped out of the café where she sipped coffee to follow the two men at a distance, using the camera hanging from her neck and her casual clothes to appear as a tourist. First they walked in the direction of Tovey's apartment, but then they detoured and dropped down into Bank Station. After delaying a minute she followed the two men down the stairs.

Spotting them where they stood in front of her on the platform for the Central Line heading west, she hung back and then boarded the next to last car when the train came in. The two men exited at the Hyde Park station. When she went to step on the platform, Tovey's eyes focused on her. He muttered something to the muscular man, and they hastened to an exit.

Had the woman she approached in Barcelona alerted him, and he recognized her? Should she follow them now or send one of her men to tail them? For a couple of minutes, she walked along behind them at a distance. With a call scheduled in half an hour, she turned in another direction and hailed a cab back to her hotel. The chase would wait for another day.

She needed to find out more information about the woman in Barcelona. The registration of her boat had showed a Maria Velez who kept an apartment in Madrid. When she went to the address, Arielle had found a small apartment in a middle-class neighborhood with the name of M. Flores. With no one answering the buzzer, she had weaseled her way into the building, gone up to the second floor and banged on the door. When only silence answered her knock, she had jimmied the locks and peered inside to see only a little furniture and a layer of dust. The flat had indicated no signs of recent habitation. Either the woman in Barcelona seldom came to Madrid, or she did not want to be found.

Stepping out of the cab at the Mandarin Oriental hotel, Arielle hurried to the elevator, not wanting to be late for her call with Carlos and Kazimír. She sat down at the desk to pull up the access to their private network. While her computer woke from its slumber, she opened her iPad to her notes for the meeting.

The items on her hotel desk sat a little differently from the way she had left them. The laptop was pushed back from where she left it earlier. The maids had freshened up the room while she went out to spy on Tovey. Perhaps they had tidied the desk.

When her computer beeped she logged into their video conference. Carlos and Kazimír appeared on the screen.

"Kind of you to join us," Carlos said in a sarcastic tone.

His tired face exhibited a two-day beard. Did his playboy's lifestyle take its toll or did his business responsibilities weigh on him?

"Following Tovey here in London," Arielle said.

"Why not let my guys finish off the other geek out in Portland?"

"Better to torture them a bit more. My men will hit Tovey this time. One brain-injured and the next one dead should make them close up the business. Tovey walks around with a bodyguard." She would continue to keep the information about the woman in Barcelona to herself.

"Well if you can't handle a couple of pansies in London, I'll fly some guys over," Carlos said.

"Let's move on," Arielle said. "Kazimír, did you develop a new language protocol for us?"

"About half of the words will be changed. Some of the old words carry new meanings. Others are added. We'll also put text messages into native Welsh. Use the Google translator. My instructions and the synonym dictionary will be dropped in your inboxes on the new server as soon as I verify security."

"This is on NadirNet?" Carlos asked.

"Yes. Keep in mind that we control the access, the encryption algorithm and the pseudo-language for our sphere," Kazimír said.

"Where did this new encryption come from?" Arielle asked.

"I took a formula from a PhD thesis out of MIT and made a few changes. As far as I can tell, no one is using the student's approach, but the logic is cracking fine. The United States National Security Agency hired the kid who wrote the encryption method. Now he is on loan to the FBI. We'll change the technology up every year or so. This particular formula regenerates the protocol every day."

"The new servers are where?"

"Norway. Excellent security and low power consumption."

"When will we be up and running?" Carlos asked.

"Targeting Tuesday."

They moved on to discuss pricing on drugs moved, some issues with the quality of the teens for prostitution coming out of the Ukraine and improvements to the logistics for running them through Slovenia and Greece.

"Carlos, your operation is taking 60% less product than before. I thought you aimed to rebuild the network," Arielle said.

"Takes time. You should appreciate this is hard with the Feds still sniffing around. Shit, you didn't reopen all your ops. The upper levels of my outfit are rebuilt. Now my guys are recruiting for the middle layer. The street people are always easy to find."

"When will you be operating at previous levels? Kazimír and I are stuck with warehousing product which is negatively impacting our cash flows."

"Two more months and we should be back at prior capacity. The plan is to be running 20% more product by year-end than we did on a monthly basis at the beginning of this year so don't go selling off what you stockpiled."

Arielle raised an eyebrow at Kazimír. He gave a slight nod of acceptance.

"When will you hit this Tovey?" Carlos asked as they prepared to end the call.

"Not until we can take a clean shot," she said. "We will keep Tovey under surveillance for the next week or so and put our plans in place."

"Any chance we can turn him to work for us?" Kazimír asked.

"That would be sweet revenge," said Carlos.

"From what I understand of his history, he and his friends are not corruptible," Arielle said.

"Fear for loved ones can make a man change his values. What's the matter, Arielle, can't you grow the *cojones* for the rough life? Who's he got besides his partners?"

"Mother in Boston. A girlfriend." She smiled to herself over her reasons to find out more about Tovey's woman.

"You run down the babe," Carlos said. "I'll send a guy to scout out this mother in Boston."

"Wait, are we agreed this is what we want to do? Kazimír?" Arielle asked.

"I say we check the dear ones out and reconvene next week to make a decision. Forcing Tovey to work for us would give us clear sailing with some strategic banks."

"Rad thinking, Kazimír. I like this possibility," Carlos said.

Ending her session Arielle sat back to think. Since she needed to return to Paris, she would send a man over to tail Tovey while she shifted into the background. Once her man marked him with his girlfriend, they should be able to find out more about the woman. Could she be an undercover operative of some sort? Why did she seem familiar? Where had she run into her before?

Chapter 31
Moll

On the first Tuesday morning in September Moll marveled at being back in the FBI offices. Instead of feeling welcoming, the building generated a colder atmosphere like it understood he no longer belonged there. As he often did since the shooting, he experienced a sense of dislocation as if they might be travelers returning home to find strangers living in their house.

Usually as solid as granite, Steve appeared keyed up when he went through security for a quick pre-meeting with the head of the FBI. While they waited Ivy ran out to pick up lattes from a Starbucks a few blocks away.

A man sporting heavy auburn hair and a friendly smile rolled in through the front doors, hand-powering his wheelchair with determination. The intensity in his eyes sparked his face into a beacon making Moll like him on sight. Draped over his knees, a beige and brown plaid throw made from rough wool lay in a neat wrap. The toes of hiking boots sticking out of the bottom made Moll curious since he understood this fellow, Mikael, had lost his feet and part of his lower legs to severe frostbite. Perhaps he wore prosthetics.

Mikael followed his gaze, "Fakes. People become uneasy when they don't spot shoes or boots. Gives me a place to put my stumps – always chilled from bad circulation."

Moll grinned at the guy with the sense of finding a new friend who appeared to be forthright and who wanted dispel uneasiness, not garner pity. He held out a hand in greeting. "Moll O'Leary."

"Mikael Sigurdsson. Neat hair you've got there," Mikael said as he reached up for the handshake. "Fine pair to be here, aren't we?"

Moll touched his half-shorn head where the hair grew about half an inch long on the shaved side. "The best and the brightest. Brain still works, but the old memory is a bit quirky. Took a couple of bullets a few weeks ago. One knocked out some of the indices to my storage unit. Rebuilding, but lots of gaps."

"Having impaired brainpower would be the worst."

"Guess you could call me lucky."

"Me too."

Ivy walked in and handed each of them a latte. "Hi. I'm Ivy – Steve's wife." She put down the carrying tray and shook Mikael's hand.

Talking on his cell phone, Steve appeared on the far side of FBI security and motioned them in. They picked up their clearance badges, laid their briefcases on the scanner and started to move forward. Moll glanced over at Mikael.

"Go ahead, man. They'll pat me down and wand me. I'll let out a yell if the guy is too chummy."

Up in the conference room, a couple of people waited. Steve moved a chair aside for Mikael. "Here, Bent. Take the power seat."

Mikael wheeled up and pushed the chair back next to him. "Hey TimeLapse. Sit next to me. Us disabled folks need to stick together."

Steve brought over a signed contract for Mikael's consulting work as well as a copy of the required FBI confidentiality agreement. Moll watched the man glance at the signatures before tucking them into the slim briefcase slid between him and the arm of the wheelchair.

"You're one of us now," Moll said. "No going back."

"Steve already gave me the old 'loose lips sink ships" lecture. No matter who I work for, each situation demands my absolute silence on the details of the work. Is Steve as tough as he comes across?"

"For FBI work he's even tougher. As a friend and a mentor, he's thoughtful and helpful. As a husband I think he is the ultimate old softie."

Within five minutes all twenty seats in the long conference room filled up. Moll remembered a couple of the encryption experts from a case he worked on. Steve shook hands with two of the managers and a few of the technical staff. A tense vibe permeated the room. Several people appeared to be outright resentful about having their work called into question by Steve's inquiries on NadirNet.

Right when Steve moved to the front of the room to kick off the meeting, the head of the FBI walked in. The surprise of having Director Comey join them stopped the meeting participants in mid-sentence. Several of the agents sat at attention and four jumped out of their chairs to stand respectfully.

The Chief, as Steve called him, raised a hand in greeting. "Good morning. I designated former Senior Executive Agent, Steve Nielsen, to re-open the topic of an underworld network coming into existence and dubbed … What did you say the name is, Steve?"

"NadirNet, sir."

The Chief gave a brisk nod. "NadirNet. If this network exists and we are not monitoring the traffic, we will be missing opportunities to stop crime and to head off terrorist attacks. This is the tool of the new generation of criminals – a rich, hip international set who are tech-savvy and willing to work in cooperation against the society we are sworn to protect. You were hand-picked to attend this morning. You may not discuss what is said here with anyone not in this room. At the end of today's session, we will be requesting a few volunteers to work on the study. Expect me back at eleven-fifteen to go over your conclusions."

When the director left the room, Steve elaborated on his kickoff comments and introduced Mikael. "Mikael is an international telecommunications expert based out of Iceland. His credentials are impeccable. Behind his boyish face is one of the best minds in communications security and networking."

Mikael turned red at the compliment. "Thanks, Steve. While I do possess expertise, I am sure every person in this room can match me."

He looked at the various people in the room as if trying to assess who his allies might be and then Mikael said, "So far we devised several possible ways this NadirNet might exist and evade detection. First this underworld network may be stealing spare capacity on existing networks, riding along behind legitimate voice and data communications. This would require an artificial intelligence system and super-skilled hackers to penetrate the security of various private, public and government networks."

"Not possible," one of the resentful FBI technical staff said. "Several Cray computers would be required to monitor, model and steal the capacity."

Undeterred by the agent's belligerent tone, Mikael nodded and smiled, "The Chinese equivalent – I am guessing one or more of the Sunway TaihuLight which can run a theoretical 125.4 petaflops."

"What's a petaflop?" Ivy asked.

"A unit of computing speed equal to one thousand trillion floating-point operations per second."

"Super-fast. Way faster than a Cray," Ivy said.

"Let's remember," Steve said, "money is not a hurdle for these criminals. Most of them inherited their illicit operations along with the fortunes made by their parents and even grandparents. These are not raw, spunky delinquents clawing their ways out of the ghetto. They are college-educated at the best schools. Most hold advanced degrees."

When Steve talked he let his eyes rove from person to person, fixing each one with a penetrating gaze. Remembering this tactic of Steve's, Moll understood it was his way of saying, 'Get on board with me or get left at the station.' Only the stupid did not jump on Steve's train.

Steve made a circular motion with his hand to Mikael, indicating he should resume.

"Second, one or more networks run by so-called legitimate front companies may exist. They sell bandwidth to the legitimate computing world but reserve a significant portion for the use of their not-so-savory businesses."

"You think we're a bunch of dummies?" the same FBI agent retorted. "If such a network exists, the sucker would be identified."

"Are you sure? Do you monitor all networks in every telecommunications space?" Mikael uttered the words without malice.

By not budging from his suppositions, Mikael staked his claim as an open-minded telecommunications guru as opposed to certain of the technical FBI staff.

The FBI agent glared at Mikael, his disgruntlement escalating from Mikael's questions.

"Third, and this may sound sci-fi-ish, the messages may be running on the open Internet using a technique called Oblivious Ram to hijack existing server memory and alter transmissions for their own purposes. In my opinion this is the least probable and should be explored last.

"This underground communications system might be a combination of the first three. Other possibilities may exist. Our job will be to detect any such networks and out-think the engineers behind them. Your help is needed on detection and on decryption. For messages communicated in a short-hand pseudo-language inside the encrypted packets, we are contracting with a resource familiar with such jargon."

"Bent," Steve said, "would you elaborate on the third type of network NadirNet might ride on?"

One of the younger techies jerked his head up and stared at Mikael. "Are you Bentlight?"

"Bentlight is my personal handle for certain pro bono work and paid consulting I do."

The young technical agent jumped up and directed a penetrating gaze around the room. "Listen to this guy. He's brilliant. Two years ago when doing my PhD work, I came up against the proverbial brick wall. My mentor insisted the proof of my encryption theory contained flaws. Of course I panicked. After an agonizing week of reviewing my theory, I found the issue but not how to remedy it. My thesis was due, and I foresaw failure.

"In desperation I put a post out on a techie site. Within two hours this guy with the handle of BentLight responded. He offered to review my work, and within four hours he solved my dilemma by pointing out a mistake in one of my premises. Once I corrected the logic, the flaw disappeared. This man is a telecom god. I'll volunteer for this project to work with him."

"You're 'QuickNick'? Mikael asked. "Your thesis -- totally brill. Real breakthrough in encryption technique."

The younger man nodded and turned beet red. "That encryption theory got me a job at the National Security Agency who loaned me to the FBI."

A seasoned agent pushing towards retirement shoved back his chair. "Two gods in one room," he said without a hint of sarcasm. "I'd be a damn fool to pass up working on this project. I would sign up to work with you, Nielsen. You're still a legend here at the Bureau. And BentLight. I've heard about you. You did some work for the United Nations, right?"

"In 2013. Most of the clients I consult with are international companies, but to work with the U.N. came as an honor. Now let's talk more about Oblivious RAM."

Listening with care to the discussions, Moll began typing notes on his laptop. Telecommunications formed an important part of what he could recall about their Noble Firs business. If banking transactions became hijacked and altered midway through transmission, their bank audits would be invalidated. Provided Steve would permit it, he would send the information on to Terry and Brian.

The Chief walked back in the room to listen to the summary comments. Steve added two encryption experts to his team, in addition to the agents who had volunteered. One, a dumpy pale-haired woman in a worn suit, sat hugging her laptop to her flat chest. The other, a tall blonde with the shoulders of a linebacker, narrow waist and curves she made no attempt to hide, made Moll wonder if she might be transgender. Three agents skilled in telecommunications also volunteered, including the agent who had been angry and resistant. Once the Chief left, Steve dismissed everyone not on the list of volunteers.

"We're going to be working at a safe location a hundred miles or so from London," Steve said. "For the next weeks or months, expect to be sequestered until we find this NadirNet. Services will include super-fast connectivity, mega server power, a couple of Crays, a chef and a gym. Expect long days, seven days a week. All findings and conclusions will be verified by at least one other team member. Nothing is to be written down. All discoveries including dead-ends are to be documented in a database we will set up.

"The four of us depart this afternoon. The rest of you will join us in two days. Former Agent O'Leary is assisting with the logistics of the setup. If you require anything out of the ordinary, contact him. Be prepared to work in a tight team environment."

The FBI team members nodded and left the room. Steve remained somber. Sometimes he play-acted as a harsh man, but this morning Moll sensed that his dark mood sprang from genuine concern.

Steve waited until the door closed before he spoke. "Bent, as I said before, you are going to hear and learn about topics that are highly confidential. I need your word that you are 100% with us on this. The lives of innocent people may depend on it, just as the identification and capture of many crooks will."

"You have my word. I will not disclose any information outside of this immediate group. Steve, the nature of the work that I do on the security of major telecommunications systems mandates that I must be not only discrete but absolutely tight-lipped."

"Right. Brian called this morning, right before our meeting. Last night the same woman who confronted Nicola in Barcelona followed him and the British guy guarding him. As a precaution we've moved Nicola and Maxim to a different location. No sign anyone traced them to the safe house in London, but we can't assume they would continue to be unknown there. They will be flown to our new secure location by helicopter to arrive a little before we do."

"Who are Nicola and Maxim behind the front story?" Mikael asked. "No names. Like to understand them better."

"Long story," Steve said. "FBI-confidential. Let's say at one point they made a deal with the FBI leading to the incarceration of almost a hundred bad guys, with three on the most wanted list. In return the U.S. Government allowed Nicola and Maxim to start over in their Witness Protection Program. They volunteered to work with us on this study. Recent events show Nicola's life, as well as the lives of Moll and his two business partners, are in danger. We suspect the daughter of a deceased French gangster is acting in collusion with at least one other criminal responsible for the shooting of Moll.

"A new twist popped up for our consideration, which may affect Moll and which will impact Terry too. Your shooting may be a demonstration of what these people can and will do. Brian is afraid, not for himself, but for those close to him. Nicola, we are covering. Brian's mother will be moved to a secure location until we can sort this out. Since she is mega-controlling, this change will be difficult for her and for those who protect her."

"And Terry?" Moll asked. "His parents are retired and living down on the Oregon coast."

"We are offering them a safe house. If they don't want to move, we will send agents down to patrol 24/7. Terry is talking with his mom and dad this morning. He will continue to be given protection at the office, around his condo and while he is out and about. Lenny will serve as his personal bodyguard."

"None of us would ever cooperate with criminals," Moll said.

"If someone you love is in danger, your perspective can change. During Ivy's abduction two years ago, my thoughts honed in only on her safety. As the kidnapping worked out, I did not face a test of what I would do for her well-being.

"One of the reasons we are bringing you along on this trip, Moll, is because

Mathew and Callie voiced concerns for Susannah's welfare. Callie became afraid that having you at Spook Hills would attract these thugs. She's right -- your presence might prove dangerous. In addition Mathew wants us to remove his name from the Noble Firs website."

"He's deserting us?" The action hit him in the gut, leaving him shocked and sorrowful.

"Only from a public perspective and until these folks after you are in custody. He came over to share his concerns with me Saturday night, and we devised this course of action. Mathew needs to put his family first now."

Ivy glanced up from her phone. "Our car is downstairs waiting for us. Are you with us, Mikael?"

A slow smile spread across his new buddy's face. "Think my super-hero cape will float along behind me as I putt-putt down the sidewalk? How about a bright red one? You bet I'm in. By the way I need some things from my place in Iceland. Didn't realize this would turn into a sojourn in the English countryside."

"Make a list as we go to the airport and tell me how to access your place," Steve said. "I'll arrange for an FBI legal attaché out of Copenhagen to fly to Akureyri to pick things up and get them to you. Post Wiki-Leaks that overseas FBI office covers Iceland."

Pushing his chair over to give Mikael room to maneuver, Moll stood. He wouldn't mind having a red cape draped across his shoulders too.

Chapter 32
Brian

Over near a tiny village, Brian walked with Nicola around rolling fields in a huge country estate, something over a hundred miles from London. The lord who had inherited the mammoth house and acreage had loaned it to the UK government. As a part of its makeover, the facility included a basement operation with a robust server farm and secure telecommunications, allowing it to function as a supplemental site for the various British Intelligence agencies referred to as BI. In addition to the well-equipped and luxurious location, BI supplied both the computing power and several skilled technical officers for the NadirNet study.

Brian stayed with Nicola and Maxim to help them settle into their country work site. For Nicola cities signified her places of comfort, and he wanted to help her adjust to her new surroundings. Near the beginning of their walk, Maxim split off on his own to scout out the other side of the extensive property where a herd of horned cattle grazed.

"Check out the gully," Brian said to Nicola and pointed to a long dip between the fields. "If a person needed to, he or she could flatten themselves out in the bottom and follow the dry stream bed to a road to run for help or crawl into a drain pipe to hide. Disappearing in the copse of oak over there is another option. Those hedgerows, which may be blackthorn or hawthorn, can give cover too. You would need to take care as they often sport nasty briars."

Stopping to stand opposite her, Brian placed his hands on her arms and searched her striking face, finding warmth, curiosity and a tinge of fear. "Is this helpful or are you more uneasy out here?"

She studied the landscape. "Helping. For sure your tour and pointers are useful. I can begin to fathom how to slide away now. Thank you."

Dusk approached, and the sky lit up at the horizon. The drone of a helicopter sounded overhead.

"Incoming." Brian said. "Likely Steve, Ivy, Moll and your friend, Mikael. We should walk back. I think they said cocktails at six and dinner at seven – Steve's an early to bed sort of guy, but he is up and either working or exercising at four-thirty every morning."

"Now when he is retired? Every day he jumps out of bed that early?"

"Unless Ivy tempts him to stay and snuggle."

Huffing a little from the climb, they crested a hill overlooking the house lying in a protected small valley east of the nearby village. The upright structure with its two wings stood tucked behind a copse of trees and reachable down a long, twisty driveway. Built with local sandstone, the buildings glowed a golden honey color in the slanted rays of the late afternoon sun.

Cuddling up next to him, Nicola said, "How lovely to be here in this seemingly unchanging scenery."

Brian inhaled the fresh air. When he did his year at the London School of Economics, England's rural counties fed his soul. He judged this area to be somewhat north of where he stayed two Christmases ago. The terrain, natural beauty and harmonious blend of buildings and landscape reminded him of the Cotswolds.

The helicopter sat in the middle of a small helipad, tucked out of sight behind the former stables. Three people scrambled out. Ivy ran bent over away from the slowing whir of the propellers, while Steve pulled out a wheelchair and assisted the man who must be Mikael out of the helicopter. The pilot pulled out a ragtag collection of luggage, which the groundskeeper tossed into an old Land Rover. Brian waved an arm overhead as Steve surveyed the countryside. He returned the wave before turning to follow the others to the house.

Taking Nicola's hand Brian tugged her into a run down the hill. Laughing like school children at recess, they reached the bottom. She seldom laughed, but when she did, his heart beat a little faster at the fresh tingling sound, as if the joy came from some happy hours of her childhood, perhaps those she spent with her cousins.

Brian planned to stay for the kickoff meeting before returning to London. With Nicola, Maxim, Moll and his mother protected in secure locations, he could tend to Noble Firs business and stay vigilant in case anyone turned up to follow him again.

While this estate appeared open and casual, a plethora of cameras and sensors patrolled the house and grounds. Every staff member from the groundskeeper to the chef contributed to the protection of the site and its residents. Nicola would be safe here, and Steve would ensure her well-being.

Terry worried him since he was working on his own in Portland. Surveillance continued at the Noble Firs offices, and Lenny accompanied Terry whenever he left the building or went home. What concerned him was that without Moll, the sensitive Terry would feel isolated. Brian resolved to find reasons to call Terry a couple of times a day, including weekends.

Chapter 33
Arielle

Back in her apartment in Paris, Arielle stared at the text message in front of her from Carlos sent early that evening.

"RABBIT to/fro office with old geezer. MYBE BDY GRD. Wz up wth CHINCHILLA?"

Not surprising for the Rabbit, as they called the guy named Terry Fenwick, to have a body guard. The Chinchilla, their name for Brian Tovey in London, had gone out of town, perhaps with the girlfriend who seemed to have left Barcelona immediately after Arielle approached her on her boat. Some linkage existed between that woman who looked familiar, the Chinchilla and the FBI, something more than his formerly working as an agent, but she had not yet figured it out. She sensed more was up than she knew.

Keying quickly, she texted back, *"CHNCHLLA off grid. WILD HARE appear?"*

Her phone rang. "Hi Carlos."

"Hey look, these guys have some tie to a vineyard in this podunk town called Dundee less than an hour from Portland. We tailed the Rabbit down there. You know anything about that?"

"Who owns it?" Arielle asked.

"State records show the business name is registered to a guy named Mathew Heylen and a partner of Steve Nielsen. Who are they?"

"Give me a moment," Arielle said, flipping open a document to confirm what she remembered. "Former FBI. Worked with the Chinchilla and the Wild Hare. Nielsen was some sort of bigwig executive with the Bureau."

"That fits. Street rumor associated his name with the hit on my old man."

"You have someone watching the vineyard?"

Carlos gave a disgusted groan, "Damn hard. Wide open spaces there. Too easy to be copped. They did see three people leave in a town car the beginning of last week and tailed them to the airport. All three boarded a flight to D.C."

"Who were they?"

"The Wild Hare, some big tall guy around sixty and a woman with this wild silver hair about the big guy's age. I'll send you the cell photos I got."

She waited and clicked open an email with three photos attached. She looked over at the document she opened earlier.

"Pretty sure that big guy is Nielsen. If they are off to D.C., they could be going to the FBI."

"Not good."

"Let's stay with just observation until our next call. You have your guys stick with the Rabbit. I'll let you know the next time the Chinchilla surfaces."

"Hate these guys. We need to get them out of the way."

"Yes but without bringing the FBI, Scotland Yard, Interpol and the police down us."

"Yeah. Gotta go, Arielle. This fucking business has me running from city to city."

Arielle ended the call. Right as she turned her thoughts to those FBI consultants and the girlfriend, her phone rang with a call from her middleman in Marseilles. He was a good man who only called when he had an issue or an increased need for product. She hoped it was the latter.

Chapter 34

Brian

True to their word the British supplied a talented young chef, making the dinners remarkable and the buffet breakfasts hearty enough to fuel them through the mornings. Two evenings later the full team of more than a dozen gathered in the spacious library of the west wing of the house. Steve reorganized the space to allow room for everyone to gather on chairs and sofas in the center, placing long tables on each end by the floor-to-ceiling polished walnut bookshelves.

As he did with newly assembled FBI squads, Steve asked each person to give a brief summary of their credentials. At the end of the individual's spiel, he added something about the agent or person as his way of complimenting each individual and revealing his familiarity with his or her background.

"To continue on logistics," Steve was saying. "Our six encryption specialists," he paused to point to four of the FBI folks and two BI men, "will work in the west drawing room."

"As a first step I want you to create a comprehensive inventory of the doctoral theses on encryption in the last four years. Start with the major high-tech universities and work your way down. Try to find out if each one is in use. Log your findings into a folder on your website and put them in either a database or an Excel spreadsheet."

The team members started to gather up their things.

"Wait. Let me plow through the rest of this," Steve said. "You five." Steve pointed to Mikael, two FBI telecom agents and two of the British experts. "As our telecommunications squad, your job is to find the physical net and determine its platforms. Once you make any discoveries, our excellent hackers will break the encryption for us while you continue to search for similar setups and backup sites."

Steve pointed to a map of the house on a white board. "The room you will work in is a modernized version of the old servants' hall. The elevator is nearby.

"The decoders and logistics folks will be in here, one group at each end of the room. Nicola and Maxim, take the far table with Moll. Ivy and I will be at the other table. For each team, expect me to visit you each day wherever you are working.

"Before we disperse, I asked Maxim and Nicola to brief us on how major drug lords and other underworld gurus think. Even if you've heard information like this before, listen to their recap. You might gain some insights. Ask questions, but not about where their info came from."

Maxim moved to the front of the room. When Brian perceived his nervousness about speaking to the assembly, he walked up to join his friend and pulled three chairs close together. A fire burned lazily behind them in an enormous open fireplace. The estate cat, Ginger-Pinger, slipped into the room and sat at attention by the fender, as if assessing the new group.

"Let's treat this," Brian suggested, "like a fireside chat. Nicola, switch seats and join us. Maxim, tell us about this younger fellow."

The evening before Steve and Brian had talked with Nicola and Maxim about presenting this material, using Cristo and Eduardo as models.

Maxim sat back to organize his thoughts before leaning forward to speak in a soft, captivating voice. "He was damaged, this fellow I ran into, by an incident with some druggies in his youth. Even though his body healed, the experience had left him so fearful, he became paranoid which drove him to become so reclusive he seldom went outside."

Maxim let his eyes move from person to person. Each of them shifted in their seats to catch his every word. Brian had never observed a band of agents so quickly enthralled. He glanced over at Steve and saw a little smile curling his lips. Even now as a successful businessman, Brian realized he could still learn from the big man, in this instance noting his quick understanding of how to increase the commitment of the team members to the goals of the project.

"Co-existing with those fears, he aimed to found an empire of power and wealth. He became the brains of the operations. This man was self-taught. Dropped out of school in his early teens. Home-schooled himself, read for hours each day – from novels to the densest works of physics. He enrolled in or audited many courses on the Internet, talking his way into online programs at the best universities in the nation. He became an expert on everything from gourmet cooking to setting up complex computer configurations to programming them and developing complex investment modeling software. The Internet functioned as his lifeline. You would view him as the extreme of an introverted nerd or what my friend Moll here calls a technogeek.

"This man set up an elaborate organization of real and shell companies with officers who assumed various identities and disguises as needed. The money came from moving drugs. Massive quantities of drugs. He handled huge amounts of money – the total investments and cash generated by his enterprises are estimated at one and a half billion U.S. Dollars. This is profit, not revenue."

Maxim paused and drank from a glass of water.

"His ingenious schemes ran money through the international banking systems, initiating, moving, investing, moving, reinvesting. In the end the FBI discovered and killed him. I understand about a third of the money remains hidden. For many years this adroit and intelligent man figured out how to work the system, how to cover his tracks and how to outsmart the best minds in U.S. and foreign government organizations."

Maxim stopped speaking with a glance towards Nicola. The cat left his spot by the fire and marched in commanding confidence over to Mikael where he sat in his wheelchair with his hands resting in his lap. Very politely, Ginger-Pinger reached up and tapped the stump of his right lower leg twice. When Mikael moved his hands out of his lap, the cat neatly leaped up, turned around twice and settled down, curving his body into a tidy circle.

"More people like this man will surface," Nicola said. "I was acquainted with him and certain others. Their histories will vary. Most will be well-educated. Each will either operate alone or with a tight clique where they act in collusion to achieve a goal. Every generation of gangster evolves and becomes different. The stereotype *Mafioso* are becoming anachronisms, and the Colombian *banditos* are disappearing.

"The underworlders of today often operate as a part of our society. Some are introverted, but many are playboys and playgirls. Think of sleek boats, showy condos or houses, fanciest of nightclubs. They slide between worlds, lunching with legitimate business people at the golf club at noon and negotiating major drug deals by phone on a yacht the same afternoon.

"These crimesters, as my friend Moll calls them, will organize into small consortiums. Each will operate from a core faction. Their goal will be to make their businesses run as smoothly as legal ventures. They plan to carve up the world into spheres of influence. While they will maintain the old cash cows like gambling, prostitution and drugs, they are today into cybercrimes including electronic theft of money and other assets, identity theft and manipulation, hacking into government systems to find information to sell. They make arms deals with terrorists not just for the money but because chaos benefits them for short periods. Long term, such disruption is bad for business."

Maxim leaned forward, clasping his hands together and studying each of the people in the room where they sat spellbound by his and Nicola's delivery. "Do not be foolish and underestimate these people. They can and will outsmart us. What we are undertaking is admirable, but assume we will encounter many turns and twists along the way. Expect detection barriers like you never encountered before when you try to hack into one of their networks."

Sitting up straight Nicola spoke with reserved authority as she said, "These men and women will devise contingency plans multiple layers deep. They do risk analysis in brainstorming sessions, the same way you do. Every technique developed for managing legitimate operations is at their disposal. You should expect them to take those tools and use them for what they consider their alternative enterprises. Not only will they be one step ahead, but they will aim to be several steps."

Holding up a hand to stop Maxim and Nicola, Steve said, "For sure several steps. We chased one of these guys on and off for years. When we cornered him, we found out three of him existed and, as if they used a replicator, two of those three men trained actors to imitate them. These guys liked to appear to pop up anywhere at any time. Made for one hell of a hunt."

"Like all people, these young criminals are flawed," Maxim said. "Success can lead to arrogance, which in turn may lead to carelessness or blind spots."

"And like any humans, the most creative will think and act in patterns," Nicola said. "While they will use their brains to morph those arrays, the patterns will exist and we must find them."

Steve stood, towering over the seated assemblage. He smoothed down his blue shirt and let his gaze rove around the room at each person.

"Let me be clear about two things," Steve said. "First, we are here to find the networks, break them and decode communications. When we are successful, the FBI, BI, and Interpol will take over. We will not be undertaking field work.

"Second, if anyone leaks what we are doing or what we find, they will be considered traitors. This work you will be doing is vital. You may be thinking we need hundreds of people working on this. However I believe a small collection of motivated, exceptional people can be more creative, more agile and more successful. Be proud you are here to work on this project. If we succeed, you will be part of a victory you can tell your grandkids about."

As so often happened with Steve's kickoff meetings, the group rushed from the room to their new locations in a flurry of motivation, excitement and fear of failure. Although he had been a part of many of Steve's projects, even today the thrill of the upcoming chase piqued Brian's interest.

He needed to thank Steve. Nicola and Maxim were both apprehensive about working with this group of high-powered technicians. By inviting them to speak to the group at the kickoff meeting, Steve established their authority and knowledge in their domain of decoding. They spoke like seasoned field operators, and they would now enjoy standing within the group.

Chapter 35
Arielle

At her family's Loire Chateau, Arielle sat uneasily in her father's old office. That afternoon she had cleared the desk and devised a plan to go through his old papers which appeared to only deal with the affairs of the estate and vineyard. His broad leather desk chair reminded her of times as a child when she had sat on his lap, often coloring or drawing, while he talked on the phone or met with his vineyard manager. The office smelled like him as if the brandy he drank in the evenings and the rich pipe tobacco he sometimes smoked seeped into the leather and the books lining the shelves to the right of his desk.

She had moved the photo he kept of her over to the credenza and replaced it with her favorite one of him cutting ripe grapes from the vines. For a man as accustomed to Parisian life as he had become, he always loved getting close to the land and never missed working on the vineyard at harvest and crush. He lived on in her heart as frozen in time as the snapshot of him, the one person she ever felt close to.

Her cell phone buzzed with a text message.

"Must talk. Secure line. NOW. Carlos."

Puzzled by the immediacy of the communication, Arielle was about to dial Kazimír when a new message came in from him with a secure call in number. She dialed rapidly and entered the call right before Carlos.

"Carlos, what's up?" Arielle asked.

"Feds linked those two goons who did the hit in Portland to me. They brought me in for questioning but didn't charge me, not yet anyway. They have the two hitmen in jail. I think they don't have enough evidence yet that I was involved. If either of the goons talks, I'm in deep shit."

"What incentives have you offered the men in jail?" Kazimír asked.

"The usual. Surreptitiously I will pay for their attorney. Ditto with family support. Bonus for them when they get out."

"We each must be very careful," Arielle said, squirming in her chair. "I suggest we temporarily halt Operation Payback. Resume when things cool down and then only use anonymous third parties for any hits."

"My old man won't understand if I don't get these guys wiped out."

"Your father is in prison awaiting trial. Deal with it, Carlos. You're the man in charge now," Kazimír said. "Go buy a new cell phone. Change it frequently – different brands, different phone numbers, new services. Post each new number on our secure server. Communicate with us as little as possible. We'll ship product at the same rates as you have been taking it."

"Carlos, is your father still trying to run the business?" Arielle asked.

"Yeah. Hampers my every move. I made changes without letting him know. He is furious with me and he is threatening to take me off his accounts. This so sucks."

While they continued talking, Arielle made notes for a follow-up call with Kazimír. They had to strategize on how to survive a possible shutdown of Carlos's operations by the feds and the potential loss of his father's money to support his cash flow. If they were not cautious, Kazimír would be out the money for the goods he supplied to Carlos and she would lose compensation for handling the logistics of the product movement. Even worse they would be left without the sizeable drug and prostitute market that Carlos represented. She would stay solvent with her own operations, but if Kazimír carried too much debt, his business might not survive to continue as her supplier.

If Carlos's father was going to run the business from prison, that would create another bad set of dynamics potentially putting them all in precarious positions. She wondered if they would be better off if his father were somehow neutralized. It would be a dirty play but this was business after all.

"Carlos, any chance the feds might link those hit men to your father?"

"Why? What are you driving at?"

"If he were linked to them instead of you, the feds might put him in solitary confinement, take away visiting privileges and ban his cell phone."

181

"Arielle, you are a real bitch, you know that? This is my father we're talking about."

"He's not playing fair with you, is he? He is limiting what you can do. If he takes away your financial reserves, you will be in trouble."

Kazimír said quietly. "Arielle may be on to something. Look we are not suggesting you bump your father off or anything. Don't you want the freedom to operate the business the way you see fit? You can't do that if he is interfering or putting you in an untenable financial position."

"You two are just worried about the impact on yourselves. I've got to live with my family, you know."

"Think about it Carlos. Just think about it." Arielle said. Carlos would always put himself first. Once he stepped back and saw the benefits of limiting his father's influence, he would act in his own self-interest. All he had to do was incent the two hitmen into revealing that they undertook the attack in Portland under direction from Carlos's father.

She smiled to herself at her own cunning and yet she wondered if their positions were reversed and her father were incarcerated instead of dead, could she do what she was suggesting to Carlos? On the other hand her father would have already instigated the scenario to take the focus away from her.

Chapter 36
Moll

Moll's teammates assembled the next morning in the drawing room in silence. The easy laughter from last night's introductory dinner no longer filled the air since now each person focused on their assigned work. Glad to be working with Nicola and Maxim, he sat down with them, thinking about what his role should be. While knowing this was Nicola's effort, his familiarity with Steve's expectations made him realize he needed to act as a mentor.

By way of beginning Moll said, "We will be the last team to be activated in terms of real transmissions to decode. I suggest we spend this time organizing so we can act fast when needed. We should define a database to record our research and findings. Steve wanted me to bring along a copy of the Noble Firs software, and I installed the programs and database on the servers downstairs. Last night I set you up with access rights. We could begin with a demo of its capabilities.

"Afterward Nicola you can explain how you go about decoding, what the elements are and how you detect patterns. While we will change the contents as we go, the software will help us analyze hefty quantities of message data."

"Moll, could we reverse those two tasks to give me a better context?" Maxim asked. "For my benefit, Nicola would you explain what a coding scheme might be like? While I understand the concept, walking through an example would help me to visualize what we are trying to tackle."

Before speaking Nicola thought for a moment. "Let me take an illustration from information I needed to acquire in 2009. While this job offered certain challenges, from an encoding viewpoint, the task was fairly straightforward once I found the patterns. You remember Alligator Alfonso? Arrested early in 2015? One of the criminals we turned over?"

Maxim nodded and Moll asked, "Why was he called Alligator Al?"

After exchanging a glance with Nicola, Maxim said, "Alfonso was as tough

183

as they come. He hated alligators. If one so much as crossed his path, he would have it killed. His brother was attacked by one when he was a kid. It tore off his leg, and he died from infection. Al saw the attack when he was about five. The horror of it stayed with him."

Nicola nodded. "Alfonso wanted to disrupt a building materials scam run by the *Rossiyskaya Mafiya* -- the Russian Mafia -- and take the operation over. Their swindle stole building supplies from major construction sites while they masqueraded as a legitimate supplier. Often these materials took time to order. This scam supplier would be the sole vendor with the specific inventory in their warehouse because they now stored the supplies stolen the night before. They targeted the foremost projects – high-rise buildings, hotels, shopping malls, condo developments and so on."

"Alligator Al wanted to learn what site would be hit when," Maxim said.

"Right. As an interloper Alfonso planned to move in before the *Mafiya* and take the goods. He also planned to put out misinformation on what goods would be at which construction site."

Moll frowned, "How much profit materialized?"

"Enough to pay me about a million and a half to provide the information to start their business. They planned a national operation. The way the *Mafiya* setup worked, they ransacked one, two, three jobs around a city and moved on to another city. Their local supplier continued to operate as a regular business. They made the thefts random to avoid leaving a trail. A couple of years later, they returned to the same city and raided a few building sites again. By making the hits appear haphazard, the insurance companies and the police failed to catch on."

"What about the contractors? Didn't they think something was up?"

"The *Rossiyskaya Mafiya* is merciless," Maxim said. "The contractors kept their heads down, filed claims with the insurance company and bought the goods back. The big construction crews knew about the scam, but no one would risk squealing. Each one understood they and their families would be butchered if they did. Julio was playing a very dangerous game with this job."

The three of them sat silently absorbing what Maxim said. Nicola cleared her throat and continued. "Back to the decoding. Here's the tricky part. The communications went mostly by cell phone conversations, although a few texts and emails popped up sometimes. We needed their cell traffic. I hired people to follow the fellows around to grab their cell conversations with a transponder. Experts decrypted the transmissions, and I tackled decoding the messages. Most communications took place in Russian. The snoops with the transponder and the decryption were outsourced. The setup worked. I translated the Russian with reasonable accuracy."

Nicola so impressed him with this work from her past, Moll's mouth dropped open. Even though he understood she traded in information, he had never received the details of her transactions. Until she and Maxim, as Annetta and Cruze Fuentes, turned their compendium of criminals over to the FBI, she never surfaced on a suspected criminal list, not as Julio and not as Annetta. Before today he had thought of Julio as a sort of underworld snitch, but clearly he had honed sophisticated talents which Nicola still possessed.

With a wry chuckle Maxim said, "Nicola is a linguist. The Romance languages, Germanic ones, Greek and Cyrillic. Arabic and Asian languages to a lesser extent. Nicola is as smart as Eduardo and self-educated."

Nicola regarded him with those disturbing turquoise eyes of hers as Moll rose, stretched, walked over to the window and stretched again. Ever since taking the bullet along his spine, sitting made his back tighten up.

"Does Brian appreciate how talented you are?" Moll asked as he turned back to the table. Although he was fond of Nicola, he still found her relationship with Brian to be a shocker. Brian, who never wanted to commit himself to a relationship, had fallen in love with this un-convicted felon.

"We do not talk about my criminal past except in general terms. Brian is kind. He accepts me for what I am today."

"Will you ever tell him?"

"I will tell him whatever he requires about my past. My past made me unworthy of love from a man like Brian. All I can do is transform my present and my future to earn his regard."

Moll stretched a third time and returned to his seat. Steve likely understood as much as anyone about the crimes Nicola and Maxim had committed. If Steve accepted them, he should be able to. After all he had helped the cousins escape to their new lives.

"I'm all right with you and Brian, Nicola," he said giving her his lop-sided grin. "The difference between general knowledge of your past and finding out specifics is what struck me. You and Maxim should write a book."

"One day under pseudonyms we might. In the meantime ..."

"Tell us about how you deciphered those communications."

"They assigned a pseudo tag to each place they targeted. The days and dates threw me. Turned out the Russians referenced the old style Julian calendar historically used in Russia, which is twelve days off our Gregorian calendar and the new year falls on September first. Once I derived this insight by analyzing past operations, I was positioned to calculate the upcoming date of any particular planned theft.

"Time became another issue. After studying the data for a bit, I realized the parties cited Moscow time which is three hours later than GMT, allowing for any variations in Daylight Savings. Since the people communicating worked in various cities in the U.S., I also adjusted for the local time zone.

"Makes sense. Russian operation."

"Some came from Russia. Others lived as second and even third generation Americans of Russian descent. I also addressed the place nicknames which were in Russian. They came up with a rather inelegant solution. First I made a compendium of American cities in descending population sequence and second compiled a similar list of cities in Russia, throwing in countries of the former USSR."

"And matched them up," Moll said. "Reminds me of how Eduardo named the companies and officers in the many Fuentes Enterprise companies."

Maxim smiled with a certain sadness in his expression. "*Si,* I mean yes. Although born in America, my brothers and I often communicated in Spanish, as these folks Nicola discusses communicated in Russian. Eduardo did name our companies in an alphabetic way. You figured that out, did you? Another instance of patterns."

"So you identified the city, what about the names of the individual projects?

"Finding the locations proved tedious because I had to research detailed maps of each Russian city to locate sizeable buildings of the same type. A hotel in New York might be nicknamed after a hotel in Moscow. In general practice names of office buildings are often linked to streets. Similarly condo and apartment developments often carry names derived from streets or local areas. Shopping malls might be dubbed with monikers after department stores or shopping districts. I pulled together an index of significant building projects in each city that Al wanted insights on and mapped them to the snatched calls."

"You became successful?"

"Of course. Once the Russians showed up to several job sites to find the building materials already gone, they began nosing around. The conflict escalated into a nasty bloodbath. After some weeks the warring parties called a truce and divided the nation between them. They continued to operate until late in 2014 when we turned our collection of known criminals over to the FBI.

"This represents a somewhat simple example to explain decoding. Do you see what I mean by patterns better now, Maxim?"

"The trick is to think as they might."

"What happens if they use arbitrary choices for the crypto-words?" Moll asked.

"We are screwed," Maxim said.

"Random would be too hard to remember," Nicola said. "These coding schemes exist to be catchier. We need an inventory of all detected coding schemes. To give us a starting place, I dug a file out of my archives. The file contains summaries of the coding schemes I knew about when I worked on the other side."

Nicola searched on her laptop. "Here's my catalog in a Word document. On its way to you, Moll, to upload into this database of yours. My list is limited by what I found on my own, and I haven't applied any updates since mid-2014. Refreshing the contents should be one of our startup tasks."

Maxim asked, "Where did you find such information?"

"Sometimes I learned about schemes through my network of contacts, and I hired hackers to break into various systems. News stories, books and so on also proved to be reliable sources."

"Let me take online research for relevant news stories," Maxim said. "Despite my limited technical skills, I can run down info with search tools."

"I'll arrange access to the FBI and other crime databases," Moll said. "Steve will tell me about any additional sources he knows. I'll check with the encryption guys here to find out what they can share, and I'll call our partner, Terry. He might bring a fresh perspective of places to search."

"I'll talk to Mikael," Nicola said. "He may be able to help, or he can point us to other sources through his network of experts."

Moll went through the information in Nicola's document, finding it neatly organized into key parameters in an extended Word table. She included such elements as language, date and time logic, place names, nicknames for goods, and so on.

Steve walked up with Brian and asked, "Are you pulling a plan together?"

"Sure," Moll said. "Nicola, why don't you giver Steve?"

In her poised way Nicola filled in Steve and Brian.

Steve asked a few questions and then gave a nod of approval. "Good starting place. Be interesting to see your expansion of Nicola's inventory of coding schemes."

From outside the sounds of a chopper landing came through the open window.

"That's my ride," Brian said. "Walk out with me, Nicola?"

As they left the room, the way their shoulders touched showed they shared the familiarity of a couple. What a striking pair they made too, both tall and slender with dark hair, polished physiques and moving like they had stepped off a page of *Gentlemen's Quarterly, Horse and Hound* or some other classy magazine. Thoughts of couples brought Moll to himself and Terry. For now he must push his conflict away and worry about Terry after returning to Portland.

While working on this project, he enjoyed the respite from the pressure of remembering. Gaps still existed in his memory for the last three and a half years. When he had sat down to load the Noble Firs software the previous evening, apprehension had settled on his shoulders. Would he remember how to use the programs he had created? Working with the technology had stayed with him. Everything he had tried t made sense. In addition he had recalled the data for a number of clients.

The memories of people and situations with people tended to be what remained lost or evasive. Most of the employees at Noble Firs and their clients stayed either faces without names or names lacking associated faces. Situations with them and meetings eluded him. As the weeks of his recovery pushed towards a month, he feared he would need to learn to live with the gaps.

Chapter 37
Brian

Three weeks later on the last Friday of September, Brian flew to Portland to meet with Terry over the weekend and travel with him to pitch a prospective client the next week. Mathew invited them down for dinner Saturday evening.

Lenny served as Terry's bodyguard, sleeping on his sofa, driving him to and from work and doing surveillance at the office. Though he had driven Brian's rental car down to Spook Hills, he passed on the dinner invitation, wanting some well-merited time alone in his half of the duplex called Caspar's Cottage at Spook Hills. The three of them planned to stay at the vineyard for the night. Brian and Terry would fly out to Atlanta on Sunday morning with Lenny acting as their protector.

When Susannah ran out to greet them with sweet hugs, she smiled with less happiness than usual. As she skipped into the house with her hand slipped into Terry's, Brian took the opportunity to ask Mathew about their trip to San Francisco for Susannah to visit her birth father.

"Our visit turned into a bad time for Susannah. For the first afternoon she went with John Henry to the zoo, rode the trolley car and did other fun activities," Mathew said and stopped before entering the house through the sun room that linked the house to the garage.

"The next morning we took her over to his townhouse around ten, but he didn't answer the door. After doing some reconnaissance, I found his car in the carport, his place locked up and the drapes closed. I sought out the manager of the complex and discussed my concerns. He agreed to open John Henry's door for me.

"Worried about what we might find, I told Callie and Susannah to wait in the car. Glad I did. Judging by the empty wine bottles and the drained vodka bottle, John Henry had tried to drink himself to death. He was sprawled unconscious on the bed, covered in vomit. After calling 911, I sent Callie back home with Susannah."

"Is John Henry in rehab?"

"He is. I can only hope he will follow the program all the way through. Perhaps he somehow faked the sobriety tests or seeing Susannah and Callie with me upset him. While his department head at Berkeley will support him through the sobriety program, this event marks the end of his patience with John Henry. Luckily Callie kept phone numbers for his family. She conferred with his brother back in Boston and convinced him to fly out."

Mathew shook his head, shoved his hands in his pockets and turned to stare out at the vineyard. "We're staying in touch with the rehab center and with his brother. Although I dislike John Henry, I never wished this addiction on him."

"Susannah didn't need this upset either," Brian said.

"Neither did Callie. I'm glad they didn't witness the mess. A service I hired went in to clean up the townhouse. Brian, you relate to Susannah. Try to distract her while you are here. Lenny agreed to come over in the morning for breakfast and play some backgammon with her."

"You're a brick, Mathew. Does Callie understand how lucky she is with you?"

Mathew smiled. "After what she went through with John Henry, she does appreciate me. One bit of decent news – nothing wrong with us in the baby department. Although my sperm count tested a little under optimal, the doctor thought nothing should prevent a pregnancy. We are again hopeful."

"Can't let those splendid genes go to waste, can we?"

They walked into the house where Callie greeted them. "Brian, how's Nicola? How happy I am for both of you."

Brian found himself grinning until he realized Terry scowled at him. With everything going on, he had failed to fill his partner in. Terry listened to the news with a frown on his face.

"Let me make sure I understand you," Terry said. "This is the same woman you and Moll helped to escape out of the country a couple of years ago, right?"

"Yes. Nicola and her cousin are now collaborating with Steve."

"Will those two ever be able to return to the States?"

"Part of the deal for them to work on Project Anti-Camorra is to be allowed back here as long as they live crime-free."

"You'll like them, Terry," Mathew said. "Nicola is intelligent and curious about technology."

"She's beautiful, sweet and a little naive too," Callie said from the kitchen. "We are becoming close friends."

"And this Maxim guy?" Terry asked as he accepted a glass of pinot noir from Mathew.

"In a word I would describe him as sharp. He's also somewhat introverted, but I find him loyal and likable. He has the soul of an artist, and he works with glass in his personal studio in Spain."

A wry smile played across Terry's face. "Heard some of their background from Steve, but I feared he would cut my tongue out if I didn't stay quiet. Guess I can talk now since you are discussing the cousins. Is Maxim married or anything?"

"Kind of an island, but judging by the way his eyes move in mixed company I am certain he likes women. Life is hard for Nicola and Maxim. They each find developing relationships difficult because of their pasts," Brian said and paused to drink a little wine. "When I met Nicola, a thrill reverberated through me like a hit from a stun gun. Instant attraction. For the first eighteen months, her past and my commitments to the FBI stood in our way. Now that we are together, my knowledge of how she lived and what she suffered helps me to understand her. When this Project Anti-Camorra is over, I want to ask her to marry me."

Callie hugged him again.

Terry said in a quiet tone, "If you want to live in Portland, I will take over the London office."

Brian slung an arm over Terry's shoulder. "Hard to say what twists lie ahead of us. Let's talk again after Moll is back working at Noble Firs."

With his face hard and unyielding, Terry turned to stare at him. "Ivy told you?"

"Ivy never said a word. When you wouldn't leave Moll's side at the hospital, I guessed your feelings. Steve figured out that you're in love with Moll too."

"Damn. What did he say?"

"If Moll wants a relationship with you, Steve will support you and him because he wants each of you to be happy. Difficult to predict Steve. After thinking

191

he would go bonkers over me dating Nicola, he surprised me by acquiescing to our relationship. After all he accepts you."

"Moll doesn't, though."

"Did you talk with him?"

Terry shook his head and took a long sip of wine. "The time is never right. Before they all flew out, I could tell he'd figured out that I love him. He appeared a little sad and wary of me like he was sorry he finally remembered me."

"Not sure with a brain injury, a person can control what memories appear when," Brian said. Turning to Susannah where she helped her mother set up hors d'oevres in the kitchen, he said, "Hey Susannah, how about beating your uncles at a game of Scrabble or something while we eat munchies?"

"You're on," Susannah beamed at him with one of her enchanting, merry smiles and ran into the family room to pull out a game. Brian followed her wondering how he would get her to talk about her birth father.

"How about Tri-Ominos?" she asked. "I can teach you. Com'on Uncle Terry, you play too."

As they played the game, Susannah asked, "Did you hear about my other daddy?"

Brian nodded. "Your mom and Mathew will make sure he receives help."

"Why does he drink so much?"

"Alcohol can become an addiction. A disease. Some people experience more emotional pain than they can deal with and want to escape."

"Did I hurt him?" Susannah posed the question with tears in her eyes.

"Your father hurt himself. He lost you and your mom through his drinking and nastiness. My guess is his own actions upset him. Only he can find a way to live sober and become reconciled to his past mistakes. The people at the rehab center will try to help him recover."

"My daddy used to be nicer, at least to me. We enjoyed our first afternoon. Why can't he always be nice?"

"Inside of us desolate spots appear from our own weaknesses or painful memories or acts we regret. Hard to find ways to heal them."

"You too?"

He leaned forward and whispered conspiratorially, "My mother was a controlling witch who wanted to be my constant guard. My safety became her obsession. She wanted to protect me, but like any kid, I needed to grow up in my own way."

"What happened to her?"

"Usually she lives in the apartment in Boston where I grew up. Sometimes I call her. When I visit her, I find talking with her hard because she still wants to control me. The neighbors tell me she is proud of my accomplishments. Always bragging about 'her Brian, the FBI agent' or 'her Brian, the entrepreneur'. If she backed off when she is with me, I would spend more time with her."

"Adults sure are complicated," Susannah said.

"Remember those words. Stay sweet, smiling and charming."

"Attractive too? Like my mom?"

"You will always be attractive but remember real prettiness comes from the inside," he said thinking of Nicola.

Susannah played her next tile to gain a high score. "You better hustle to keep up with me," she announced with a grin.

Susannah was so darned cute that he wondered if he and Nicola should consider having children. She neared menopause. While he never envisioned a family, spending time with Susannah always led him to think of one. He would be happy with Nicola, but a child or two might be appealing. As he told Mathew, it would be a shame not to bequeath their strengths to a future generation. In his mind he pictured a couple of children with brilliant turquoise eyes.

Chapter 38
Arielle

Frustrated by learning her revenge target had flown to the United States and his girlfriend had vanished, Arielle sat down for her update call with Kazimír and Carlos in a foul mood. She did not want to give Carlos this opportunity to hijack the chase. On the other hand, they needed to be sure that Carlos was free of his father's influence and would stay in business.

"Carlos, what is the story with the Feds?"

"I handled the deal with the hitmen so well the feds fell for it completely. Sure I feel bad that my old man is in solitary, but I gotta run the business right?"

"So my idea worked?" Arielle asked wanting this edge over Carlos.

"Your idea? I already had decided on that course of action. Just wasn't going to discuss it until it was successful."

Arielle put the phone on mute and pounded her desk a couple of times in annoyance. Damn Carlos always had to twist circumstances to make himself look good. Switching her phone back on, she said, "Our first update is on Operation Payback. I know we agreed to put it on hold, but then Carlos you were still going to do some sleuthing. What did you find out about Tovey's mother?"

"According to her neighbors the old bat left for a vacation in Florida that her son sent her on – had her picked up in a town car. Haven't been able to find her."

"How long ago?"

"The day after our last call."

"Did one of your men tip him off?"

"Hell no."

"Kazimír, is someone eavesdropping on these calls? Too much of a coincidence for both Tovey's mother and his girlfriend to disappear about the same time."

"The calls are all encrypted. A bug in your hotel room?"

"Did a sweep before the call. What about your locations?"

"Standard Operating Procedure, SOP," Carlos said, meaning he swept his calling location too.

"Ditto," Kazimír said. "Let's end this call and hop on to another service. Check your secure email for the next call-in number. And use your iPhones, not a landline."

Arielle went from irritated to worried. If their phone call had been compromised and their ideas for Operation Payback revealed, why didn't Tovey go underground? Why did his other partner still go into the Portland office? Despite the protection of a bodyguard for each one, skilled gunmen could execute a hit. What were these yuppies playing at?

She checked her secure email for the new call-in number, dialed and waited with Kazimír for Carlos to join them on the line.

"We should attack the bastards the next time they are sighted," Carlos said. "We can pick off the guy in Portland any day when he comes and goes from the office. His defense is some grizzled old geezer who probably shakes too much to fire back. We'll scoop up Tovey as soon as we locate him here in the States or you can grab him when he pops up again in London."

Arielle said, "What is troubling me is how they learned about our plans. What if someone is able to tap into our communications? This time they sold the info to the fucking FBI. Next time they might sell to our competitors. In case we do have a leak, Kazimír, you need to find out if a weakness might exist and come up with a fix."

"My total focus will be on it," Kazimír said.

"Arielle, what do you know about Tovey's girlfriend?" asked Carlos.

"Didn't I talk about her on our last call? I thought I did back when we made a decision to convert one of these so-called Noble Firs guys to use him for our own purposes."

"I kept a transcript of the call. You never gave us any detail. Not by name, not by implication."

"You made a transcript? You documented our call? Did someone type the recording up? Now we can identify where our vulnerability is," Kazimír said.

"No fucking leak in my outfit," Carlos said. Stop trying to squirm away from the technology issue. Find out where the exposure is."

"Wait," Arielle said. "This is how the feuding starts. This is why our fathers never learned to work together. They pointed fingers, argued, fell out with each other and never expanded their businesses together. We swore we would not be like them. Here we are at the first hurdle and we are bickering like they did. We must stop arguing now. Do we trust each other or not?"

"What do you suggest, we ignore the issue?"

"Carlos, you need to check if anyone accessed and sold or passed on the information from our last call. Kazimír, you must assess the technology."

"What about you, princess?" Carlos threw the words at her in a menacing tone. "Your goons reveal our tactics?"

"No one in my organization is aware of our goal to avenge our fathers. Nor do they know about the twist to recruit one of those so-called Noble Firs guys. Over in London one of my men is following Tovey, but he has not been told why. Remote possibility someone hacked into my link from the hotel in London, unless ..."

"What?"

"The FBI made a lucky guess on our next steps and expanded their protective net as a precautionary measure."

"Two out of three of them worked for the FBI. Their board is also FBI," Carlos said. "Conceivable they guessed our next move. We should now bump the three of them off, right? Each one as soon as we can."

"As long as we use people for the hits who can't be traced to us," Arielle said. "Kazimír?"

"Going back to our last approach, I still think we should try to turn one of them to work for us. You two decide. I'll be fully occupied delving into our technical platform and security."

"Let's discuss other specific items in our current business and talk more about these troublemakers on our next call," Carlos said.

"Agreed, "Arielle said and turned to her list of agenda topics.

Chapter 39
Brian

Down on Sanibel Island, Brian rode in an FBI car with an agent from the airport to the condo complex where his mother stayed as if on vacation in a safe house with agents guarding her. Criminals and gunfire he faced, but this discussion with his mother would test his resolve. While Terry flew back to Portland with Lenny, Brian spent the previous day with the new client in Atlanta. Working into the night, their extracts ran right before midnight, and their data now resided on a secure server in Portland waiting for analysis.

A few minutes later with the FBI agent who acted as his driver, Brian walked up to the door of a four-story building which he guessed housed about eight luxury living units. His mother stayed up one of the two penthouses. After her little apartment in Boston, this spacious condo must ensconce her as well as a palace. The FBI supplied the agents who guarded her, but he insisted on paying her expenses. While she was over-controlling and often negative, his mother asked for little in the way of material luxuries, making him glad to mix a vacation atmosphere into this protective sojourn.

Bracing himself for her effusive greeting, Brian rang the bell. An attractive female agent in a beach dress greeted him at the door with her gun drawn. After lowering her weapon she nodded at his driver. His mother hurried past the agent to give him a hug and an enthusiastic greeting which included saying "my Brian" at least three times.

"Brian? This is Sheila, my day companion. We're setting up brunch for you."

Inwardly Brian groaned because his mother used food to prolong his visits. Although she cooked scrumptious meals, her dishes featured carbs and butter. He gave her the obligatory kiss and hug, wishing he loved her more, but too many years of asphyxiation stood between them.

"Sheila, show him my beautiful condominium. This home is enough to make me want to move to Florida. The weather and the beach are like a scene from paradise and no horrid cold winter like in Boston."

Brian submitted to the tour which ended on a rooftop patio with a table set for brunch. His mother bustled up with a laden platter of vegetable strata, blueberry muffins and bacon. After Brian had taken the food from her, his mother poured fresh-squeezed orange juice and coffee. A collection of shells drifted down the center of the brunch table in a whimsical swirl. Below them the beach stretched in both directions with its resplendent white sand sparkling in the sun.

The agent joined them for their meal. Before she left for a walk on the beach, she handed Brian a card with her number. He poured another cup of coffee and walked over to stare at the Gulf. The delicious blue pulled his thoughts to the time he had spent with Nicola and Maxim sailing on the Mediterranean.

"You are so sweet to me, my Brian. Staying here is the best of vacations."

"Mom, we need to talk. If you want to move to Florida, say so. I will buy a condo for you. Perhaps you and Aunt Berthe ..."

"Not Berthe. The old biddy wants to control everything. Perhaps my friend Marnie. But you, as usual you are too thin. What danger are you in?"

"My company is collaborating with the FBI to catch certain criminals, here and abroad."

"Why not quit and come home to live? Come here to Florida."

"Mom, I want you to be quiet and listen," Brian searched for his agent's voice. He always struggled around his mother not to revert to the sheltered, intimidated boy of his youth.

"My work is important to me and to preventing and solving crimes. Although I will always be your son, I am a man now – a mature man in my forties. You must stop trying to control me, shelter me, or smother me. If you continue, you will drive me further away."

"How can you use such a nasty tone with your mother who only loves you? Now you sound like your father after that hussy seduced him."

"Mom, you drove Dad away by over-controlling his life."

"The hussy stole him away."

"I overheard the fights. Let's not dwell on the past, not while I am moving into my future. If you want to be part of my life, you must accept I will offer you what I can, but I will not give in to you. I will not be controlled."

"I am not ..."

Brian held up his hand. "I met a wonderful woman. I am going to become engaged, if she will agree."

"Did she put you up to talking to your mother in this manner?" his mother said in a jealous way, reminding him of when they argued over his teenage friends.

"No, she talked to me about the importance of family. While I want you to meet her, you must treat her with respect. Any of your scornful remarks and I am done with you. Nicola is precious to me."

His mother sat still for some time. He expected tears or anger, but not this stillness.

"Do you carry a picture of her?"

Pulling out his cell phone, he brought up a photo of Nicola taken in Hyde Park in July.

"She is beautiful, but beauty ..."

"No buts Mom. Nicola is beautiful on the inside too. You will not hurt her, and you will not interfere in our relationship."

Again his mother was silent and he decided to wait her out. After a couple of minutes, she asked, "Do you want children? Is she your age?"

"Yes, if we can."

"I want to play with my grandchildren." Walking to the railing, she turned her back to him and stared out at the Gulf of Mexico. After several minutes she turned around and said, "Brian my sweet boy, I don't want to be the way I am. I want to change. Help me to be the person you want as a mother."

Of all the reactions Brian expected, her asking for help had not made the list. Did she conjure up this new trick to lure him into staying with her?

"Would you try working with a counselor? Someone to help you make the changes you want."

"How am I to pay for such expenses?"

"If I pay the fees, will you start while you're here?"

"To spend time with any future grandbabies, I would swim to Cuba and back again. Will someone come here?"

"An agent like Sheila will take you to appointments."

"Brian, are you able to afford this condo for me?"

Was his mother's willingness to cooperate because she wanted to live in Florida? Whatever the reason if she offered to try, he would support her.

"Let me talk to the owners to see if they will sell this place. If not, we will find a similar one."

"This one because I adore the hominess here -- the space, these furnishings and the views. Every day I go out with my bucket and find gorgeous shells. My plan is to learn to make wreaths and mirrors with them and to sell them as one of those cottage industries," she said with a wistful giggle.

Standing in front of him on the sunny rooftop deck, his mother appeared healthier -- thinner, tanned and younger. Silver streaks ran through her dark hair, now worn a little longer and tossed around in loose waves instead of the dyed, crimped style she used to wear. If his mother found ways to change and meet him part way, he should give on his side too.

"When will I meet her, my soon-to-be daughter-in-law?"

"For now she is obligated to stay in Europe. We will come to visit you in a few months."

"We don't need to wait. Why can't I go to Europe?"

"You always believed flying would terrify you."

"Not anymore. Sheila had me drink a mai tai at the airport before boarding the flight down. My fear of flying was silly apprehension. The flight was so enjoyable. Nothing to do but sit and read my magazines. Every night now before dinner, I make a mai tai."

"How about we rent this place for a year?" Brian asked. "I will pay for the condo and for the counseling. After the year if you still want to move here, I will try to work out a deal with the owners."

"Will you visit me more often? And call more?"

"Yes as long as ..."

"Menopause did something to me, Brian. Now I see the negative, controlling side of me. After I reaching my sixties, a lot of the noise in my head went away. Until my teenage years my disposition was happy and contented. Here I sense I might become more like my childhood self."

Brian glanced at his wristwatch, seeing he needed to leave for the airport. For the first time he remembered, he would leave his mother too soon.

Chapter 40
Nicola

Over at Great Snoop Hall as they called the estate where they worked, Nicola sat opposite Maxim at lunch. Ivy dined next to him and Nicola found herself comparing the difference in her own eating habits with the other woman's. Ivy ate with the gusto characteristic of her enjoyment of life. She polished off about two-thirds of her full plate from the buffet before pushing the remainder towards Steve. Nicola dilly-dallied over clear consommé soup, some crackers and a small salad. Lately she felt as if no matter how little she ate, her tummy seemed unhappy with it.

The estate featured a well-equipped workout room in the former stables and a lap pool to the side of the conservatory. Although she swam laps at the pool early most mornings, perhaps if she took more exercise, her tummy would settle down. So much was riding on her and Maxim having success here through their decoding efforts that it must be affecting her nerves.

"Maxim, I'm going to take a long walk around the estate after lunch. You want to come with me?" she asked.

"Let's grab some boots and stuff. I want to head to the far corner of the property to explore and an old stone barn I spotted."

The two of them walked to the cloak room where they struggled into wellies and anoraks to protect themselves against a damp autumn wind. Once dressed and outside, they started off at a brisk pace. Since the long walk took them up and down hills, they huffed along as they made the last climb to the barn where it nestled near a high stone wall.

After poking around the outside of the barn and inspecting a few pieces of well-tended farm equipment in an attached shed, Maxim propped the broad door open. The inside housed a neat block of hay stacked near the back.

"An old tithe barn," he said, admiring the arched wooden beams coming out of the walls overhead. Maxim took out a little notebook he carried and started a sketch of the arched beams.

Nicola walked in a couple of paces and stopped, awed by the height and breadth of the building. As she stared upward she found herself wobbling in place. Although she struggled to stay upright, suddenly she was sinking to the ground as the light around her faded.

"Nicola, Nicola," she heard Maxim calling. She opened her eyes and saw him kneeling over her, rubbing her hand.

Maxim checked her pulse. "Not strong and a little fast. Perhaps the walk overtaxed you."

He raised her up and cradled her in his arms. "I'll call to get us picked up. You'll get chilled here."

Her eyes fluttered shut and then opened as she took in the concerned face above her. "What happened?"

"You fainted," Maxim said in a gentle way, "and no wonder. You work, you exercise, but you are not taking in enough food."

"You know I never eat much," Nicola said, pushing herself into a sitting position.

"Is this the first time you've fainted?"

"Yes but on occasion recently a little dizziness comes over me."

"I think you should see a doctor." Maxim used a firm voice to put off any argument. "I'll get the housekeeper to arrange an appointment for this afternoon."

"Maybe you should. My tummy has been rocky on and off lately."

Maxim regarded her for a long moment and then asked, "Nicola? When did your last monthly cycle come?"

"About two months ago? It has tended to be irregular the last couple of years."

"Could you be pregnant?"

She stayed still in stunned silence. Her hand slid to her tummy. "Brian's baby," she whispered. "Possible, yes. A couple of spontaneous moments."

"Let me help you up off this cold cobblestone floor. The doctor will confirm if you are carrying a baby or not," Maxim said.

"If I am pregnant, I don't want Brian to be told," Nicola said in a stronger voice. "He doesn't need more to think about than his Noble Firs business and these people who are after him."

"Let's see what the doctor says first. You must eat well and be careful with yourself."

"Not a word to Brian. You must promise me." She stared at Maxim until he nodded a reluctant agreement. As she walked outside Nicola could feel herself smiling just a little in love, pride and wonder.

If she carried a baby, they would all mollycoddle her. Her baby would be born with at least four self-designated godparents hovering around and worrying. Tears prickled at the corners of her eyes. Her dear cousin might become an uncle and she might be a mother, something she had never expected to happen. And her dear Brian, whatever would he say when she did break the news to him? No matter what she would not trap him into making a commitment for which he was not yet ready.

Chapter 41
Moll

At three the same day, Moll glanced up when Mikael wheeled himself into the library and over to Steve. His teammates hovered in the doorway behind him. Since Moll worked alone that afternoon, he sauntered over to join Steve and Ivy.

"The rest of you, come in," Steve said and waved an arm over his head. "Do you have some news?"

"After much digging and searching, we found a network registered under the name of 'Telecommunications Emporium Network Enterprises' or 'TENE'," Mikael said. "From what we ascertained, the configuration is a multi-pointed star pattern with servers in Hong Kong, Istanbul, Oslo, Miami, Mexico City and Rio."

"Not Bogota?"

"Satellite site. Many satellites are attached to the star system. Each one seems to define a sphere of communication."

Letting out a whoop of joy, Steve grinned in his boyish way. "Let's bring the full gang in here now."

For the next hour Mikael and his co-workers explained their findings. "This network runs in an area called DeepWeb or DeepNet, which is not accessible to most browsers."

"Isn't DeepNet the same as Darknet?" Ivy asked.

Mikael brought up a slide to project on the wall screen. "Check out this diagram. The shape in the center is not unlike a glacier. The top – the part above the water line -- is what we think of as the Internet which are the websites accessible to common browsers. Underneath is an extensive layer referred to as DeepNet or

DeepWeb. Much of DeepNet is legitimate, such as banking data, private communications and so on. As shown in this diagram, Darknet sits at the bottom. Its purposes are devious."

The door to the library opened. Nicola and Maxim slid quietly into the room followed by the cat, Ginger-Pinger. They tiptoed around the side and found the seats near Moll when he motioned them over. He leaned over to give them a hushed, quick recap.

"From what I can tell," Mikael continued, "TENE runs as an authentic offering and sells bandwidth to legal entities running regular businesses in the legitimate DeepNet space. However in examining the financial records for TENE, they sold only about 30% of their capacity, and yet their telecom traffic loads run seventy percent on average. This is not peak loading I'm talking about. This is a steady stream which indicates the bandwidth is otherwise allocated. Both the sold capacity and this unknown stream share the remaining 30% during peak load times. NadirNet might live in the unsold 40% of the setup."

"You say might. What makes you think this is a candidate for NadirNet?" Steve asked.

"The encryption in the TENE free space appears to vary on a point-to-point basis, which indicates subgroups may be generating the traffic. Families of encoding surfaced in six spheres, one on each point of the star network. One sphere of particular interest bounces through Norway and into Paris, Prague and Philadelphia."

"Bingo. The three Ps are where our three suspects operate."

"From those hubs communications go elsewhere. The encryption scheme must be broken to discover more," Mikael said.

"Is it possible for this company to have clones?" Nicola asked.

"Yes. Ryan here," Mikael pointed to the BI member of his team, "is searching for copycat operations. Thinks he found two more with similar patterns but they are older. More of the capacity is allocated to valid sales – about 60%. TENE may be the third generation of this model. As you told us on the first day, Nicola, expect multiple layers of contingencies."

"When did you find the first one?" Steve asked.

"Two days ago. The company appeared so obvious we thought we must be missing something. After spending time poking at the traffic and doing more searches, we found the copy-cat networks. Since we already logged a dozen false-positives, we didn't want to raise everyone's hopes until we were certain this network could be a candidate. When we break the encryption schemes, we should be in business to assess the actual traffic."

"Can you isolate the packets or whatever you call them involving the Norway center and the three Ps? Why Oslo do you think?" Steve asked.

"We already lifted communication streams from the Philadelphia-Paris-Prague pyramid linking through Oslo. Norway is becoming the center of choice in Europe for locating data centers, hosting server farms and handling telecommunications. About 40% are concentrated in Oslo. The remaining 60% is spread out in other cities such as Bergen, Stavanger, and so on. I'm proud to say Iceland is up and coming as a host country too."

"Aren't the temperatures too cold in both countries to run large computing centers with any efficiency?" Moll asked.

Mikael stroked the cat who had settled in his lap. "Like our warm Ginger-Pinger here, servers generate heat. A cold climate saves data centers money. In addition Norway and Iceland developed plentiful natural sources of electrical power. Norway uses hydroelectric power and Iceland utilizes geothermal energy sources."

"Cool, in both senses of the word," Moll said.

Steve nodded and said, "What a discovery! Congratulations to the whole networking team. Once we prove this theory after decryption and decoding – and those are two colossal efforts – we'll turn this information over to the FBI, British Intelligence and Interpol to pursue the rest."

For the next hour Mikael and his teammates filled everyone in on the more technical aspects of their discovery, including how they had determined the usage patterns.

When they finished answering questions, Steve said, "Excellent work. Keep digging in case more of these companies and services exist. Turn what you snatched over to the encryption group. Also I would like the decoding folks, plus Ivy, to examine the related company names and stock ownership to explore links to other businesses which may serve as fronts for illicit activities."

A satisfied grin spread across Steve's face, "Project Anti-Camorra is in business. Champagne toast at dinner."

Applause burst out. Each of them had harbored doubts about their small group's ability to snoop out a clandestine criminal network. The discoveries of Mikael and his team might prove to be a major victory. While they could still endure a long wait until the encryption gang broke the code, at least a possible platform had been identified.

Once the room emptied out, Maxim leaned over to Moll and murmured, "Nicola has an appointment with a specialist -- woman troubles. We will have agents escorting us in both directions and around London. I had the groundskeeper set it up. I just need to let Steve know."

"Sounds serious. Is it?" Moll asked.

"The local doctor thought not, but he wanted her to be checked by a first-rate gynecologist to be sure."

Chapter 42
Nicola

Right after arriving back at Great Snoop Hall from London, Nicola pulled Maxim into the now quiet dining room. They had agreed to remain silent about her pregnancy until she had seen the London doctor. To their surprise Brian had been waiting on the helicopter when they reached the helipad so they had no time to talk on the flight back.

Maxim said, "Now that you are confirmed as pregnant, you can tell Brian."

"Not yet."

"Why the heck not?"

Nicola was uncomfortable explaining her feelings. She walked over to the windows that ran along the whole side of the dining room, giving views of the side garden. Taking a deep breath, she turned back and said. "Brian has so much on his mind right now that I don't want to add to his troubles and I don't want him to feel compelled to marry me."

"You don't love him?" Maxim asked.

"Of course I love him, but I am afraid of making him feel trapped. He has been so fearful of commitment and of being controlled after the way his mother stifled him. If he were ever to ask me to marry him, it must be because he wants to, not because he sees it as the noble thing to do."

Maxim regarded her with those sharp blue eyes of his that missed nothing, but he nodded his head. "What else?"

"As well as we can calculate, I am probably only six weeks pregnant. The doctor wants to do an ultrasound at eight weeks to confirm that all is well. I don't want to cause Brian worry in case I have a miscarriage.

"He has a right to know," Maxim said firmly.

"I want to wait until after the ultrasound."

"You are putting me in a very awkward position. Brian has become my friend. If something happens to you during those two weeks, he would feel betrayed by me and rightly so. Moll mentioned to me that Steve brought Brian down here today to take on a special duty on this case, although Moll didn't know what it was. British Intelligence is to keep him under their protection during this time."

Nicola's face showed her fear for Brian's safety, but she said, "Please agree that I can wait two weeks before telling Brian about the baby. I'm supposed to have tea with him right now in the music room."

"Agreed," Maxim said, "as long as you will eat more and let me know immediately if you have dizziness, pain or other issues."

"I'm not used to being fussed over," Nicola said.

"You must think for two now, three if you count Brian."

Nicola nodded, rose and moved to the door. She would make a start by eating something at afternoon tea rather than taking only her usual cup of black Darjeeling.

Chapter 43
Brian

Decorated in a comfortable style, the small music room sat cozily around Brian and Nicola. A small pianoforte stood in one corner and a harp in another. A tray with a formal tea was set on the polished cherry table invited them to sit down on an overstuffed loveseat.

Since Brian had decided to ask Nicola to marry him as soon as he found time to be alone with her, the prospect made him both excited and nervous. Despite his eagerness to talk with her, he had managed to sleep on the flight across the Atlantic allowing him to arrive at Heathrow refreshed.

He tapped the pocket of his suit jacket to confirm the presence of the ring he had selected and ordered a few weeks ago from Cartier's in London. The keepsake featured a magnificent oval diamond set with pavé side diamonds in platinum. Now with the moment confronting him, doubts crowded into Brian's head. He had no reservations about his intentions and desires, but he worried about whether Nicola thought of him as the man to share her life. Would he be rushing her? Should he wait? Once more he pressed the little box in his pocket.

Nicola poured for each of them and selected two of the small, round sandwiches. Too nervous to eat, he did take a sip of tea. She appeared to have her guard up more than usual, and yet she glowed like she gloried with an inner joy. He hoped she was coming to love him so much that seeing him again made her too happy to suppress how she felt.

"Nicola," he said, taking her hand and trying to keep his voice from shaking. "I want to ask you something."

Should he kneel? Would such a romantic gesture alarm her or would she find his action endearing? Sliding off the loveseat, he balanced himself on one knee. Nicola stared at him, her eyes widening with surprise.

"My sweet Nicola, I love you. You captured my heart in a way I never thought possible. Would you do me the honor of marrying me?"

Her hands flew up to her face in surprise. Tears welled in her eyes.

After pulling out the little red box, he fussed the catch open and took out the diamond he hoped she would like.

"Brian, this is all wrong," she stammered out. Her tears spilled over and trickled down her face. "Did Maxim tell you? Did he break his promise to me? I can't do this. I must go."

When he took her hand, she pulled back, tossed down her napkin and ran out of the room. Stunned by her hasty exit, Brian remained on the floor. What could Maxim have told him? What was the promise he made to Nicola? Had Nicola decided to break up with him during the days he had traveled to the States?

He crawled back up on the loveseat, too hurt by her fast exit to think straight. The ill-fated ring lay on the floor by his feet. The world in his head so full of happy potential now lay in tatters around him.

Sometime later Steve walked into the room. "Here you are. We have to discuss an intriguing negotiation I need you to take on."

As Steve approached him, Brian struggled to pull himself back together. He reached down, feeling far older than a few hours before, and scooped up the ring and the box.

"What's this?" Steve asked. "What happened here?"

"What's going on with Nicola?" Brian asked, hurt and angry. "Do you know about this secret I'm not privy to?"

"No idea."

"When I asked her to marry me, she erupted into tears, thinking I was aware of something she wanted concealed from me. Before she let me understand what had caused her upset, she ran away. I can't stay here." He jumped up, put the box in his pocket and went to leave the room.

Steve grasped him by both shoulders. "Whatever you are thinking, Nicola loves you. Look she might have sort of woman troubles. She went to a specialist up in London. Maxim said she is okay but maybe she needs to heal up or something. Women get a little secretive about these things. Give it a few days and talk to her again.

"Right now we need to discuss this work I need you to do and then you must get back up to London tonight. This assignment will help take your mind off of Nicola. And don't worry. We will all look after her."

Brian was uncertain what he should do. Should he stay here and try to talk with Nicola again. What was wrong with her? Was it something more serious than she was letting on? Yet she looked so healthy. Why did she act so differently with him? A week ago their love was blossoming in sweetness.

Part III: Asunder
October -- November, 2016

Chapter 44
Terry

The second Monday of October, right before seven in the morning, Terry walked with Lenny from the parking garage to the Noble Firs office building six blocks away. He had grown to appreciate the taciturn, grizzled Lenny at his side. While he might talk but little, Lenny spoke meaningfully when he did speak. With the fog rising off the river, the predawn morning carried an air of mystery. Up above the city where his townhouse stood, the sun would soon be shining, but down here they strode along in a white mist made eerie by streetlights.

As they walked Terry began planning his day in his head. He needed to make two client calls, meet with one employee, conduct a project review and check-in on three projects for a status update. He also wanted to start a quality control review of one project's findings.

Lenny automatically turned into the coffee shop they frequented. Unlike his Starbucks-fueled partners, Terry preferred a smaller local barista for his morning cappuccino. Lenny ordered his usual grande coffee, loading it with sugar and cream. After waiting for their toasted multi-grain bagels slathered with cream cheese, they walked back out to the street. As usual he carried the drinks and bagels, leaving Lenny with his hands free to grab his weapon should it be needed.

They moved along as he remembered walking with Moll with him on the building side and Lenny nearer the curb. He supposed that was their FBI training as a way to shield the one they were protecting. It seemed peculiar now that he thought about it. Why had Moll wanted to protect him?

Halfway to the office, running feet slammed up the sidewalk behind them. Terry turned to look and caught a brief image of two men in dark clothes pelting towards them, jackets open and flapping. They pulled guns out. Terry glanced around wildly for cover and saw an inset building entrance just ahead. The men were within thirty yards.

In a fluid motion Lenny shoved him into the doorway, jumped in front of him, spun to the right and opened fire. Four shots, fired one after the other as Lenny slightly changed the position of his gun. All went quiet. Holding his weapon in front of him, Lenny eased away. Terry's heart pounded in his ears and he found himself gasping for air when he went to get up.

"Stay put," Lenny yelled as he moved slowly away.

Terry peeked out to spot the two thugs curled up on the ground. One groaned and held his hand while blood streamed from his left leg. The other fell backward with a bullet to his right shoulder and a hit in the leg. Keeping his heavy Glock trained on the two men, Lenny scooped up one weapon from the ground and wrestled a second piece away from the guy with the bleeding shoulder.

In his gruff voice he said, "Give me one reason to finish you two off. I only need one."

Each man went still.

The action in the street surprised Terry. Two men ran up with guns drawn, one in the garb of a homeless man and the other dressed as a businessman. A woman in heels sprinted over from across the street, stopped in a commanding stance and pointed her gun at the men on the ground.

"FBI, don't move," the woman yelled out.

Lenny returned to check on him. "Didn't think I'm the only one guarding you, did you kid? This is the FBI, not some slapdash rent-a-guard outfit."

Shaking with fear and relief, Terry leaned against the building. Although chilled with fright, anger coursed through him. No one possessed the right to kill them or to shut their business down – first Moll and now him. Given the danger how could they keep going?

He needed to hustle to the office to call the employees who still came in to tell them to work from home. None of them signed up for this threat. They had lost five people after the first shooting. They would lose more once their people heard about this attack. As soon as possible he must talk with Brian and Moll. This second shooting put their Noble Firs business in further jeopardy. How could they take on any more clients without sufficient staff to work on their projects?

Lowering his weapon to his side, Lenny walked over to him. "Right about now you think this will be the end of your business. Remember as you go through the next few hours, days and weeks, this shooting might be the beginning of something else."

Lenny pulled a flask out of his jacket. "Take a swig for shock. You'll pull through this, Terry. Let's go call Steve."

Snatching the shiny metal container, Terry unscrewed the top and gulped a mouthful down. The bourbon stung his throat. He took a second gulp and handed the flask back, letting the warmth thaw him out enough to move out of the doorway. Twice in the last month, a man had acted to save his life, actions he could never pay back.

At least Moll stayed clear of danger on the protected estate in England. He worried about Brian and hoped he would not continue to offer himself up as bait in London. Whenever they poked their heads outside, they became targets for gunmen. This marked the second time he had found himself in real danger. How had Moll and Brian handled this terrible fear and shock of gunfire in their FBI careers? If it weren't for Lenny, he would be lying dead back there on the sidewalk, just as he could have been last June when Moll saved him.

An hour later after calling their employees, Terry signed on to a teleconference on the Noble Firs business. His partners phoned in from London and the undisclosed place they referred to as Great Snoop Hall.

"What I don't understand is why the FBI can't arrest these gang leaders when they are aware they are behind the attacks," he said as the call started.

While Brian countered with a discussion of needing proof to stand-up in court, Terry worried about their business. He needed to hang on to Noble Firs. He suspected each of them did.

Moll said, "Lenny wounded those two gunmen instead of killing them so they can be interrogated. Steve's orders. We must find definitive proof before going for an arrest. So far we only have suspicions, not the evidence we need."

"Why are they taking so damn long to break into the criminals' telecommunications networks?" His fears for their employees, himself and their company made him irritable and impatient.

"Progress is being made. At least one possible network is identified. Encryption experts – the best in the world – have begun to crack the algorithms."

"I thought the feds can hack into anything or do they go for the easier pickings of communications between honest citizens and among businesses?"

Brian jumped on the line. "Terry, I appreciate how much you are stressed from the shooting this morning, but sarcasm isn't going to help us. The team is working long days, every day, seven days a week. Finding this network at all is an incredible achievement. Our focus for this call should be on what we need to do under the circumstances. Should we shut down?"

His question hit Terry deep inside, sending a chill through his body. Did his partner want to quit?

"No way are we letting them win," Terry said. "We must find a way to keep going."

"Thank goodness," Moll said. "While I dropped out of things, I still hold Noble Firs close to my heart. To shut down the business would turn our dream into a nightmare."

"Are you ready to return to work?" Terry asked, annoyed with himself over the edge in his voice.

"Moll is needed on Project Anti-Camorra," Brian said. "Besides he's not ready to be wandering around on his own."

"All right, you and I will decide what to do next."

"No," Moll shouted. "Never just the two of you. Been down but not out. Let me talk to Steve. I'll split my time between Project Anti-Camorra and Noble Firs. A guy can only stand so much coddling and extra sleep."

"You must first go to a doctor to confirm you are able to work more hours," Terry said. "No matter what, your recovery is our priority. While I may be a determined asshole at times, the world will not end if we are late with a client project. Do we agree on this?"

"For sure I do," Brian said.

"Yeah, especially on your being a determined asshole," Moll said with a chuckle. "No matter what, I don't want to lose either of you, not as friends and not as business partners."

"Everyone who stays with us will work from home," Brian said, "but I have two in the London office who don't live in situations where they can work in a productive manner."

"Same here," Terry said. "Lousy telecoms for one guy and a single mom's three kids are too rambunctious."

"Let's find office space near their homes until this is over. Either an executive suite type arrangement or a hotel room set up as an office."

"I'll arrange a doctor's appointment," Moll said. "My records are with a specialist in London – already seen him once. Noble Firs remains in business. All for one and one for all, right guys?"

"Always," Brian said.

"Hell yes," Terry echoed.

Each man was silent for a minute feeling glad for the commitments from each other. Having Moll back at work, even on a part-time basis would make the going easier and he would lift their spirits.

"Terry, I think you should fly over and work here at Great Snoop Hall," Moll said, breaking into his thoughts. "Brian needs to remain in the city, and I will be more re-assured if Lenny guards him. You'll be safe out here on the estate. The helpful gray-haired housekeeper is a trained sniper. The cook keeps assault rifles in the pantry. No telling what the maids and gardeners are packing."

"Are you sure? Don't want to be underfoot."

"Of course I'm sure. We're best buddies, aren't we? This is a big place. Steve will find room for you."

"Thanks for the offer. I'll organize things here this morning, and we'll catch a flight this afternoon. Lenny earns the title 'awesome' in the best sense of the word. If anyone can protect a man, he can. But Brian why should you stay in London?"

"I have a screening pitch to make in a couple of days in Amsterdam. I'll meet you at Heathrow and arrange a chopper to take you to Great Snoop Hall. Book yourself and Lenny in Business Class. Text me your flights."

"Can I bring Firewire?"

"Lots of regulations around shots and things," Moll said. "We're hoping this is not for too long. Leave her at Spook Hills where she can be taken care of along with Druid and the corgis."

"I'll call Mathew about Firewire. Moll, will you bring Steve and Ivy up-to-date? With those communications complete, we should start calling employees."

"I talked to each person who still comes into the office, so they are aware of

218

what happened this morning."

"Let's do a Skype to announce our intentions to our staff," Moll said. "After the general announcement is made, we'll touch base with each employee. Terry, send me a list of people, and I'll do my share of the calls."

"I'll arrange the session. Today?" Terry asked.

"Ten your time," Brian said. "Let's begin with the positive news of Moll being back with us and second describe the rest as safety precautions. More people will leave and I don't blame them, but the rest of us will fight on."

Terry ended the call and breathed a long sigh of relief. Each of them had worked too hard on building the Noble Firs business to cease operating altogether. Moreover if they allowed the criminals to win by closing down their company, they would lose respect for themselves. They were all fighters, and while he never considered himself courageous, he planned to preserve their business.

That evening while waiting for their connecting flight out of Chicago, Terry found himself trembling with a fit of nerves. All morning Lenny had stuffed bagels and ginger ale into him to keep him steady. Taking a look at him now, Lenny grabbed him by the elbow and guided him into a nearby restaurant, ordered a burger for him and then slammed an ale on the table, with a strict order to eat and then drink. While he only got about half of the burger down, Terry boarded his flight feeling a whole lot less rocky.

Right after dinner on the plane, Terry slid down in the business class seat, put on his headphones and hoped to sleep. The weeks of tension had left him more stressed and tired than ever before. Today challenged his already stretched nerves. Another beer and a shot of bourbon with dinner on the plane settled him down enough to make it through the flight. Usually he had trouble sleeping on airplanes, but he wanted to catch an hour or two on this flight.

With no awareness of the short night passing, the next thing Terry noticed were the interior lights in the business class cabin winking on. He struggled with the controls to sit back up and grab the mug of coffee the stewardess handed him. Grateful for having slept through to morning, he bent over to check on Lenny. As grizzly as usual, Lenny yawned over his breakfast on the opposite side of the plane.

After making himself somewhat presentable with the airplane amenities kit, once the plane landed Terry filed off and waited for Lenny. Walking away from the gate at Heathrow Terry felt more refreshed than he anticipated. After clearing immigration they exited the crowded area outside of Customs. Scanning the myriad of faces lining the long exit walkway, he spotted Brian with what must be his British Intelligence bodyguard.

"You're bright-eyed after your long trip," Brian said as he slapped him on the back.

"First time I slept well in weeks. After worrying about snipers and drive-by shootings, I think my brain gave up fretting on the transatlantic flight. Great to be in London again. Been a long time. While I'm in town, will you take me to visit our office space here?"

"Not now. We want you on the chopper out of here without anyone aware you are in London. Before you go back home, we'll visit our office space for sure," Brian said and turned to Lenny. "How are you holding up?"

"Just like Terry I zonked out as soon as I got dinner down. A glass of red wine plus a hit of brandy and bam. Those long days caught up with me."

"I'm glad you both got a flight over so quickly. Terry, I know you're not ready for more work but you should know I made a pitch in Birmingham yesterday afternoon and landed a new client. Even though we are backlogged, I thought we should sign new clients whenever we can given the course of events this year."

"We've lost another three people," Terry said in protest. "How are we going to do the work?"

"Steve lined up four recruits from British Intelligence who will be on your helicopter. If you can believe this, he's set up the ballroom for you to work in. It is wired and equipped. Moll will shift over to work with you in the evenings too, so you can cover the British agents and our employees in Portland. When the first four are trained, BI will supply four more if we need them. Steve convinced them it was a terrific way for those rookies to become versed in identifying money laundering."

"Steve remains quite influential, doesn't he?" Terry asked. While aware of Steve's past role as an FBI bigwig, he found Steve's continuing sway with the Bureau impressive.

"Brash and demanding as he is, Steve earned friends in high places, although I am not sure how long his sway will last after the Administration in Washington changes. If Director Comey is replaced, Steve loses his high-level supporter."

"You look older, man," Terry said to Brian as they settled into the back of the waiting town car. Lenny slid into the front seat by the British agent.

"Been a hard few weeks. I only slept well at Great Snoop Hall."

"You coming out with us?"

He shook his head. "Lenny and I will stay here."

Puzzled by Brian's stance, Terry said, "Thought you would want to spend time with the lovely Nicola."

Brian inhaled and exhaled with a little shudder. "We seem to be taking a break from each other – her decision, not mine."

"Unlucky at love, aren't we? The three of us. No wonder we prefer working and dodging bullets."

Brian nodded but didn't meet his eye. "Noble Firs may be our sole legacy."

"At least you can point to your company," Lenny said.

Leaning forward Terry clapped him on the shoulder. "You are leaving the best of legacies, Lenny. People like me remain alive and safe because of you. What can be finer than saving peoples' lives?"

Under his hand Lenny squared his shoulders. The loneliness flashing over his face disappeared, and he once again became the stalwart man they all admired.

"How is Moll doing?" asked Terry.

"Health-wise, about 90% excluding the memory loss, but he is different. Quieter, less goofy, more thoughtful. While he keeps trying to bring back more recollections, something else may be on his mind. Be good to hear what you think. The doctor in London is allowing him to work more hours with a strict limit of twelve a day, although he has to go back for a checkup in a week after working the extended hours. When we talked on the conference call yesterday, I almost cheered to hear him sound so emotional about Noble Firs."

"Sure surprised me when he wanted me to stay at his location."

"Moll does care about you in his way."

"As a friend and as his business partner. After his shooting I told myself I would learn to live with however he turned out, as long as he remained with us. Looks like I will need to muster my determination to deliver on my commitment."

As they arrived at the helipad, Terry found himself nervous about the prospect of seeing Moll again. He still loved Moll. Now he would see him every day again. Could they fall back into a comfortable working relationship?

Chapter 45

Moll

With mixed feelings Moll watched what he called the whirligig land with Terry, two agents from British Intelligence and the four new BI recruits to be trained on Noble Firs analysis work. While he wanted his partner to be safe here at Great Snoop Hall, he worried that at some point they might come to a showdown on Terry's feelings for him. Terry remained his best buddy, but Moll could not see his way clear to a relationship between them.

The rotors slowed and the groundskeeper walked over to help Terry jump down from the cabin, then he grabbed Terry's bags before unloading the ones for the agents.

As soon as Terry was clear of the helicopter, Moll walked over and surprised himself by pulling him into a manly hug. "Good to see you in one piece, man."

Terry nodded and Moll could see a question forming in his eyes but each of them understood this was not the time for any sort of discussion about personal feelings. The agents had to be settled in, orientation given that afternoon and a plan laid out for their training. Moll grabbed Terry's rolling bag and duffle, leaving him to bring his light backpack and briefcase.

"Wait till you see your work digs," Moll said. "The ballroom is freaking awesome. The murals are a bit faded, but zowie it is one beautiful room. The ceiling trim is even gilded. To start with I had them set up tables as a square in the middle for training purposes, but then you can get it organized however you want.

"Let's have the new recruits dump their luggage into their rooms and meet them at the top of the stairs in the East Wing. We'll take them to the dining room for lunch. You and I will eat fast so I can give you a quick spin through the facility and then we'll do a slower tour for the agents. Tell me when you start to fade and I'll handle the rest of the afternoon. Sound okay?"

Terry nodded. "Thanks for having me here, Moll. This place must agree with you. You're acting more like your old self."

"Still have gaps. When this is over, I am going to put together a chronology of the missing years and get everyone to help me fill in what I can't remember. Isolated here, away from places and people that should be familiar to me, the recall of the missing memories stopped."

When Moll grinned in his lop-sided way at Terry, he realized they would be okay working together at Great Snoop Hall as friends and as partners. Any other discussions would have to wait until after this work was over and they could safely return home. He hoped that their friendship would not be irreparably damaged by their personal feelings. The truth was he was unsure what he felt for Terry.

When he heard about the shooting in Portland, he found himself in a quandary of fear for his partner and a strong desire to keep him safe. Today meeting the helicopter, a jumble of emotions swirled around inside. When his friend stepped down from the helicopter, he felt a surge of what he could only describe as joy at seeing him. Even so he remained reluctant to change his lifestyle.

Late the next afternoon shortly before pre-dinner drinks, Moll wandered over to talk with Steve as he wrapped up a meeting with Mikael. Right then the youngest member of their team, QuickNick, came in. A quiet, intense young man, they referred to him using his online handle. He approached the table hesitantly, like half of him wanted to be running in the other direction.

"I need to leave the project," Nick said in a high-pitched whisper.

Surprise flitted across Steve's face followed by annoyance, but when the young man's trembling came to his attention, he pulled out a chair for him. "Sit down and tell us why, unless you want Bent and Moll to leave."

"Doesn't matter. Everyone will soon comprehend what a disgrace I am."

The drinks cart rumbled by on its way to the drawing room.

"Give me a minute," Steve said, rising and heading for the door.

He returned with a glass of brandy and handed the snifter to Nick. "Drink about half of this, take a deep breath and tell us."

While not much of a drinker, Nick clutched the snifter and chugged half the contents down. Even with the fortification his voice quavered when he began. "Remember when we did the kickoff meeting in D.C.? I mentioned how Mikael rescued my thesis."

"Yeah. You helped establish his credibility with the FBI."

"While working on the encryption for the Norway sphere, I spotted a familiarity in the patterns. I applied a decryption technique I wrote back in my doctoral program." Nick stopped to take a couple of deep breaths.

Waiting the way he did when he thought he might learn something of interest, Steve sat back in his chair, never taking his eyes off Nick.

"My decryptor worked partially. Enough for me to tweak the code and keep trying."

"So what's the issue?"

"Those fuckers are using my encryption algorithm," Nick said with the words hissing out between his teeth. "They stole the code out of my doctoral thesis and are applying it in the Norway sphere. This is my fault. Their communications are hidden because of me."

"Finish the brandy." Steve struggled not to smile as Nick downed the last of his drink. The glass might be more alcohol than the young man ever drank at one time.

"The bastards tweaked my code, but they are using my algorithm."

"Didn't you file the work encrypted?" Mikael asked.

"Yes. They must have hacked the database. The encryption technique is all mine. No business has picked up the approach yet."

Leaning over, Steve clasped his hands between his knees and spoke to Nick in an encouraging tone. "As for your needing to leave us, nothing is further from the truth. This problem is not yours, Nick. Finding this out and disclosing the discovery right away says everything for your character and integrity. Your intimate knowledge of the encryption algorithm will make all the difference to our progress."

Nick sat staring at Steve in shock. He flushed a bright red, although whether from embarrassment or the unaccustomed hit of brandy Moll found hard to ascertain.

Moll clapped Nick on the back, "Super finding, man."

Mikael grinned at him, pounded the table in applause and said. "What a great break for us!"

Stretching over Steve shook his hand. "You made my day, QuickNick. Now we can make some real progress." His suppressed smile spread across his face in a toothy grin as he called across the room, "Ivy, Nicola, Maxim. Decrypted text will soon be available to decode. Come over here. Another champagne toast night is ahead of us."

As Moll sat back to think over the conversation, the realization of kindness taking many forms stood out. Without offering any condolences to QuickNick over the theft of his intellectual property, Steve had treated him with respect and given him a hero's welcome for his discovery. He would add the technique to his own arsenal. Adults sometimes needed respect more than empathy. Nick just conquered a rite of passage in his life. He encountered an issue and demonstrated his personal integrity by facing the potential consequences.

Chapter 46
Moll

Late the next day Moll stared at the encoded texts that Nicola projected on a small screen in front of them.

1. *"Gêm fwrdd a osodwyd antur nesaf @kili"*
2. *"Eich chwarae. Pob lwc, Kili @taureil"*
3. *"Gringotts Transfer. Ten prime models. Grecian runway? Need budget. @taureil"*
4. *"Park Place. Five million Es @nori"*
5. *"Trychineb Cwningod. Dau Lawr. Trolls on Scene @kili"*
6. *"Yodel 1800 Sandwich @taureil"*

Such read a small sampling of text messages in front of the decoding group where they gathered around their table – Ivy, Nicola, Maxim and himself. All of the texts dated to the day of the last shooting in Portland. Ivy started running searches on her laptop.

Nicola began to play the referenced recorded conference call. Damn fools must have been so confident in their security measures, they spoke in English on their phone call. Perhaps they would switch to code as the topics grew more sensitive. The callers came in from Atlanta, Marseilles and Sofia on a teleconference which began at 18:00 GMT. All three of their persons of interest must be traveling.

Now they confirmed "Yodel" meant conference call and they figured out the time zone used. The Triad did not appear to be too ingenious. Nicola paused the recording of the call when Ivy showed a display on the wall screen using the wireless projector.

Welsh used in texts:

227

1. *Gêm fwrdd a osodwyd antur nesaf* = Game board set. *@kili*
2. *Eich chwarae. Pob lwc, Kili* = Your play, *kili*. *@taureil*
3. *"Gringotts transfer. Ten prime models. Grecian runway? Need budget. @taureil"*
4. *"Park Place. Five million Es @nori"*
5. *Trychineb Cwningod. Dau Lawr. Trolls on Scene* = Rabbit disaster. Two Down. *Trolls on Scene. @kili*
6. *"Yodel 1800 Sandwich @taureil"*

"Let's take this a little further, Ivy," Nicola said, "and add our best guesses at the rest of the text using our conventions as you did so we can start to create our dictionary."

Ivy pushed her laptop over to Nicola where she began adding to the text until she had a more intelligible version:

Text Translations

1. *Gêm fwrdd a osodwyd antur nesaf* = Game board set = <u>Carlos is ready for the hit in Portland.</u>
2. *Eich chwarae. Pob lwc, Kili* = Your play, kili. @taureil – <u>Arielle tells Carlos to go ahead.</u>
3. *"Gringotts transfer. Ten prime models. Grecian runway? Need budget. @taureil"* = <u>Arielle wants to use her bank transfer method and the ten top quality humans should be moved out through Greece</u> (likely to France).
4. *"Park Place. Five million Es @nori"* = <u>Kazimír says the human goods are top quality and wants five million euros.</u>
5. *Trychineb Cwningod. Dau Lawr. Trolls on Scene* = Rabbit disaster. Two Down. Trolls on Scene. @Kili = <u>Carlos says they didn't kill Terry. The two hitmen were shot. FBI Agents on Scene.</u>
6. *"Yodel 1800 Sandwich @taureil"* = <u>Arielle calls for a conference call at 18:00 GMT.</u>

Ivy followed along as Nicola typed, "Good. Gives us a full audit trail from start to finish, so if we later need to make corrections, we can."

Maxim smiled a little, "Not as hard as I thought pattern deciphering would be. With this context, let's listen to the call and figure out how much we can understand. This is good. I can do this."

They found the call easy to follow, since they possessed the background and the call proceeded in English. The American, who they thought to be Carlos, had hired two assassins through a third party out of Detroit.

"Do they have your name?" the woman with the French accent, who they believed to be Arielle, asked on the call.

"The beauty of this service is no names are required. You fill out a form on their website. The website gives you back a price, a bank routing number and an account number. As soon as the money arrives, the strike moves forward. No questions. The operatives record a 95% success rate."

"We fell into the 5%. What happened, Carlos?"

Nicola hit the pause button but hovered her fingers over the play button. "Carlos confirmed."

"Now us bloodhounds can start baying," Moll said.

She again hit the play button.

"Word is the old geezer guarding the Rabbit moved like lightning. Sharpshooter. Formerly a troll. Three more trolls popped up at the scene – dressed to resemble regular dudes. The geezer wounded the two gunmen, and the trolls took them away. The hitmen can't reveal who hired them because they have no freaking idea. The service asked for facts on the necessary action and moved ahead when the total fee reached their bank account."

Nicola stopped the recording of the call and nodded over at Maxim.

"I think you are aware," Maxim said, peering over at Ivy and Moll, "My brother, Eduardo, had devised a similar enterprise to handle any necessary shootings back when Fuentes Enterprises still operated. Like the other operations, the FBI shut down the company and arrested its hired guns."

"I remember. Steve nicknamed the company 'Kruiser Killers' because the killers drove Toyota FJ Cruisers," Moll said.

"Nothing new on the circuit with this approach. Someone resurrected the idea and is operating out of Detroit. This is a bit cleverer since no one, including the owner of the service, receives any info on who is requesting the hit."

He pushed his chair back, stood and walked to the window, staring out at the rain pelting against the old wavy glass. When he turned back to the group at the table, he said, "Now as I work here on this side, I better recognize the awful magnitude of what me and my brothers did. At the time I understood the wrongness of our dealings, but I passed our actions off as business. How I hate the man I lived as in those days."

Maxim sat back down and slumped in his chair. Seeing his distress, Nicola reached over and pressed his hand.

"We can only move forward, Maxim."

Moll and Ivy each nodded. A few moments passed before Ivy posed a question to Moll, "Can we trace the payment transaction?"

"Without the bank number, account or an amount, too difficult. Likely the bank is not in Detroit. Might be anywhere. Only a rough idea of the date. No amount."

Hitting the resume button, Nicola restarted the call.

Arielle asked, *"How much are you out?"*

"Five hundred grand. They weren't aware trolls would be present. Price would have been much higher."

Nicola stopped the call again.

Moll began keying on his cell phone. "Asking Steve to finagle time from the FBI in Washington to search ACH transactions or whatever. With such an even amount, we may find lots of records. We'll start a week before the attempted action on Terry. Identifying the right transaction will be difficult. The website could be operating out of Detroit, Chicago or Algiers -- anywhere in the world."

He nodded over at Nicola, and she restarted the call.

"Where did the Chinchilla go?" Arielle asked.

"We traced him to Atlanta. After landing at the airport, he went off the grid."

"I'll have him tailed when he returns to London."

Nicola gripped her hands together until her knuckles turned white. After inhaling deeply, she unfolded her hands and pressed the stop button. "The Chinchilla must be Brian."

"Wonder what they call me?" Moll asked.

Right when Nicola turned the recording back on, Arielle asked, *"Any word on the Wild Hare?"*

Moll started laughing. The nickname suited him so well. Nicola halted the recording again.

"What are you laughing at?" Steve said to Moll when he walked up.

Turning to face him, Moll formed his mouth so his front teeth stuck out. "Only one way to stop a MAD WATCH."

Steve shook his head, bewildered.

"The Triad call me the Wild Hare – can ya dig it? Wild Hare, March Hare?"

"Alice in Wonderland." Steve raised both eyebrows at Moll's antics before saying, "You received some decrypted stuff to work on? Tell me what you found. If you are the Wild Hare what do they call Terry and Brian?"

When Steve mentioned Brian's name, he stared at Nicola with those eyes of his frosting over like chips of blue ice. Moll sensed he wanted to ask the same question they all thought. Why can't she accept Brian's proposal?

"The Rabbit for Terry and the Chinchilla for Brian. Arielle is waiting for Brian to resurface in London," Nicola said in a strained voice.

From the way Steve regarded Nicola, Moll appreciated the level of his frustration over her relationship with Brian. In his direct way Steve would confront Nicola and given his impatient disposition, not much more time would pass. She needed to be fair to Brian.

Chapter 47
Nicola

On Friday morning of that week with Maxim trailing along behind her, Nicola went out for a walk on the estate to clear her head. Already it was mid-October. They had been at Great Snoop Hall for over five weeks. She supposed Maxim perceived protecting her as his duty, especially now with a baby on the way. The crisp late morning air hit her cheeks as the day began to turn bright and sunny while she walked up the crest of a hill to gaze north.

Down below her a sizeable man sat on a stone wall with his back to her. Unsure who he might be, Nicola froze mid-step. Dressed in a bright red jacket, the man was making no attempt to hide. When he turned his head and waved to motion her down to him, she recognized Steve.

"You shouldn't be out alone," Steve said as she walked up.

"Maxim is trailing along behind me."

"We all want you to be safe."

"Not accustomed to people caring about me. Maxim and his family offered me the only refuge I found."

"Consider yourself part of a more extended family now. What's going on with you and Brian? You devastated him when you refused to marry him."

"This is between Brian and me."

"Brian is like a favorite nephew to me. Moreover everything that happens on this project is of concern to me. Whether you want us or not, you are part of our lives now."

Nicola sat down on the stone wall a bit distant from Steve and studied the grass by her feet. The caw of a rook sounded above the chatter of the smaller twittery birds that hopped around in the hedgerows. England sounded and smelled different from anywhere else she lived, but then her entire life had been spent in cities.

"I don't want him to feel trapped. His fear runs deep of someone trying to control him like his mother did."

"His pattern is to date a little while and quickly break off with each woman. Until you."

"Are you saying what you hope will push me back with Brian?"

"Why can't you accept the truth? From my own experience as a loner most of my life, when you find the right person, every fiber of your body and heart thrills with joy. All the other stuff standing in your way fades and disappears. Is Brian not the man you want?"

"When a woman goes through what I did, trust becomes hard," Nicola said.

"Do you value Brian so little? Do you think of him as shallow?"

"He is a much better person than I am. How can I deserve him?"

"Stop concentrating on the negatives in your life. Think of the positives," Steve said.

"Never been many."

"You had Maxim and his family. Anyone would consider you striking. You stashed away a sizeable amount of wealth. By sacrificing your personal safety to give the FBI evidence to incarcerate dozens of criminals, you paid your debt to society. Now you have friends who are loyal to you -- me, Ivy, Moll, Mathew, Callie, and Maxim. Not only are you intelligent, but you can focus your mental powers. You attracted a terrific man who loves you. For chrissakes Nicola, quit wallowing in your past. Your present and future gleam with potential."

His words stung. Was she so lost in her past she prevented herself from grasping the sweet realities of the life in front of her?

"You don't understand my issues," Nicola said and jumped up to face Steve.

"While I may not be able to identify with your suffering, I do apprehend you are putting a happy life with Brian at risk. Of my agents, he is the cautious one. The best planner. The most meticulous analyst and businessman. In ways I used to underestimate, he is brave. He opened his heart to you, and you ran away. Aren't you being selfish? Are you afraid he will one day hurt you? If you are, you are wrong. Completely wrong."

The big man stood and turned to her. "Back in my career with the FBI, I devoted all my energies to my cases. Now with my scope expanded, concerns for my friends distract me. Today I came out on this walk to gain focus on the two intertwined efforts we are tackling – to gather enough evidence to arrest those folks after Brian, Moll and Terry and to assemble sufficient information to point the FBI, BI and Interpol in a direction to unravel this New Age criminal grid.

"You need to resolve this situation with Brian if for no other reason than for your dispute to quit bothering me so I can concentrate on this project."

The intensity of Steve's words made Nicola step away from him, tripping over a stone fallen from the wall. In a fast motion, he reached out to steady her on her feet.

"This is what you sometimes do, isn't it?" she said. "Help people find their footing. This much I can promise -- I will think about your words. Callie told me you share nuggets of wisdom. Sometimes all the pieces are in front of us, but we can't sort them out."

"Emotions are the best of us and the worst. For now we need your brain on our decoding effort. Despite this requirement, find a time each day when you think only of Brian and your future. The rest of the time, focus on decoding."

Steve's eyes roved the hills until he spotted Maxim where he leaned against a tree on a nearby knoll. After motioning him over Steve turned to walk back to the estate house, striding off in his purposeful way.

Might Steve be speaking the truth? Did Brian want to marry her only because he loved her? The thought appeared too wondrous a discovery to absorb all at one time. She would take Steve's advice and set aside a time each day to think about her future.

Maxim jogged up. "Are you all right? From the distance I thought Steve upset you."

"He did but with a positive twist. He wants me to examine my love and trust of Brian."

"Let's walk back, Nicola. The lunch gong will soon sound, and you must eat for two."

"Not hungry."

"But the baby is," Maxim said and pulled her down the hill. "No way am I letting my niece or nephew arrive all scrawny. Eat lunch and think about yourself and Brian."

The next day after working most of the night on decoding messages, emails and phone conversations, the decoding team reviewed their findings over breakfast. As soon as they finished, the group met to brief Steve. Mikael and Nick joined them to gain an appreciation of what their efforts in networking and encryption had provided.

"We went back over the texts, emails and phone calls for the last two weeks," Ivy said. "Next Nicola is having us go back through the two weeks prior before we catch up on anything from today."

"Once we are up-to-date, we can handle the monitoring concurrently," Nicola said. "From what we accomplished yesterday and last night, we are starting to have a reliable dictionary of the code words encountered. Since some still puzzle us, we are going back until the use of the network began about a month ago. This sphere of traffic out of Norway did not appear to be used earlier except in testing."

"Any files transferred?"

"Yes," Moll answered. "Three. Small, but enough to say they are beginning to steal and sell personal information. This may be a pilot for one of their planned initiatives."

"We are following the flow of drugs and young teens either through Bulgaria or other Balkan countries as well as through Greece," Nicola said

Steve almost shouted, "Bulgaria again. We shut down a human trafficking operation there in 2012."

"Bulgaria continues as a primary conduit for contraband coming out of the Middle East through Turkey. Kind of a modern-day Silk Road but for heroin."

"The Bureau put a squad in Bulgaria to work with their government on improved controls to slow down or stop the movement of drugs. It is part of a mandatory requirement for Bulgaria by the European Union."

"Here is an article on why this is such a difficult situation," Ivy said. "Hundreds of trucks are lined up every hour of every day at border points from Turkey into Bulgaria. Most are carrying produce and legitimate goods from Turkey. The prohibited products are hidden in certain trucks, either under the goods transported or in secret compartments."

Flipping up a colorful slide, Moll leaned over to catch Steve's eye. "Check out this map. We're at the beginning, but we are piecing the flow of drugs together. This guy in the Triad, Kazimír, inherited control over this movement of drugs into and out of Bulgaria when his father died in prison, following the multi-country action last spring. As you know the Horak family is based in Prague."

Steve reviewed the map Moll showed him with the possible routes used from what they had gleaned so far in their analysis. "Moll, keep building the map. We'll need to document as many drug routes as we can. Maxim, what are your impressions of these three criminals from the communications?"

As usual Maxim collected his thoughts before he spoke. Steve directed his question at him to probe for an insider's view as well as to gain a thoughtful appraisal.

"The way I read it, this Carlos in Philadelphia is the hothead. Not as smart as the others, although he is street-smart. Reminds me of Cristo. Of the three he likely will blunder first because he is impatient for results.

"Kazimír is the most deliberate of the three. Kind of a mix of Eduardo and me. He answers all the questions on technology, and he sets up their sphere's technical solutions, but as we suspected, a more sizeable, tech-savvy force is behind the infrastructure.

"Let's call this larger force the Nucleus for lack of a better name," Steve said.

"Our Triad – Arielle, Carlos and Kazimír -- do not want their transactions, directions and decisions disclosed to what you are calling the Nucleus. They do separate calls, use a different encryption system and likely will use a dissimilar anti-language with the Nucleus than the one they use with each other in the Norway sphere. We did not yet penetrate the larger communications net. We need help from your groups, Mikael and Nick."

"Continue," Steve said, "and we'll come back to your point."

"This Arielle is the schemer," Maxim said. "Although she is restrained about her approach, I can tell she's manipulating the other two to achieve her personal goals. In my opinion she wants to become the leader over time. Arielle is the kind of woman I would not want to meet when alone. She is a cold one.

"Her hiding the information about knowing Brian's girlfriend is interesting, but she misspoke, and she let it slip out on one call. Carlos jumped all over her blunder. I am puzzled by why Arielle is keeping the info secret about Brian's

236

girlfriend. Is she attracted to Nicola? Do you think she knows who Nicola was?"

Nicola said. "She gave me the impression of a bisexual when I paraded around as Julio. She looked at eye-catching women the same way she looked at me in my Julio role. When she approached me on the *Hildago* in Barcelona, she seemed attracted to me. However I couldn't tell if she recognized me from my Julio days. I just don't know."

"The three criminals appear to share a history," Maxim said. "Perhaps they hung out growing up when their fathers brought them along to so-called business meetings. The drugs and prostitution activities date to their fathers' times."

Maxim paused to consider something, and then asked, "Steve, would you do a favor for me? Would you ask the FBI to de-age the photos of these three – Arielle, Carlos and Kazimír – by going back in five-year increments? Would you also request copies of any pictures from their files? I think the images may jog a memory or two. This Arielle is familiar in a vague way. The name Carlos is common, but if I studied a photo of him a few years younger, I might recall some circumstances."

"Like you did with the double agent PercyNarc back in 2014?"

"*Si.*"

"The question I am struggling with is when we turn this info over." Steve tapped his pen in the slow, methodical way he did when going through points in his head. "I'm worried the bigger joint operation will take over, make arrests in other areas but spook the three we are after, driving them into hiding."

"Leaving Moll, Brian and Terry and the rest of us still exposed," Ivy said.

Steve lifted an eyebrow at her and nodded.

"We should wait," Maxim said, holding Steve's eye until he again nodded his head in agreement.

"We should try to develop a relationship with one of the three perps identified," Nicola said. "Since Arielle is attracted to me, I could ..."

"No way," Steve said, slamming his hand on the polished mahogany tabletop. "None of us will be involved in any live actions. The FBI, Interpol, BI and the in-country police are responsible for taking this forward."

"But you have left Brian in London as if he is bait." Nicola's voice sounded distressed, and her eyes began to tear up.

"If you will train an agent to cuddle up to this Arielle, I will call Brian back in here."

"Will he come back?" Nicola asked

"If he won't, I will pick him up and manhandle him onto a chopper," Steve said. "When we're finished here, I'll make the request for a convincing undercover agent. Nicola, you will need to help me select the right talent and bring her up to speed."

"The FBI maintains an international suspect list for the key people in the other spheres, right?" Nicola asked.

"Yes, so does British Intelligence, Interpol and so on."

"Coming back to Maxim's request. Would you expand the scope to include other possible leaders around the world, so we can review current and reverse-aged photographs of them? Possible one of us ran into them in Miami or somewhere, such as the party on the yacht I mentioned. Between Maxim and me, we might come up with something."

"Good ideas. Too bad I didn't think of the photo reviews earlier," Steve said.

Steve turned to Nick. "QuickNick, go tell your gang to join a meeting in 30 minutes in your area. Most of your team should shift their work to the decryption of traffic within, into, and out of the Nucleus. We became lucky with the Europe gang using your encryption method. The rest may prove more challenging."

"And me, Captain, my Captain?" Mikael asked. "I assume you didn't ask me here to admire my handsome face."

Mikael grinned at Steve in a way construable as impudence and yet Nicola knew it was only good-natured teasing. Right before Nicola's early morning swims, when Steve and Mikael swam laps in the pool, Mikael referred to the big man as his lifeguard. A couple of times Nicola had arrived early and witnessed Steve helping Mikael out of the pool and assisting him out of his swimming prosthesis and into his ones for walking. Since the walking devices hurt his legs, he limited his time in them. Those actions by Steve gave her a further insight into the caring underpinnings of his nature. She could see that Mikael respected Steve, but he wanted to draw out his lighter side.

"Bent, I want you and your folks focused on cracking this worldwide network. First try to grab the traffic within the controlling hub – the Nucleus. Capture and record as much as you can. Plus calculate volumes on the major traffic patterns between the spheres and within each sphere."

"Aye, aye, Captain." Mikael gave a little salute and grinned over at Moll. "Later, TimeLapse."

"Briefing for everyone at 18:00 today."

"Not more bloody champagne," Moll said with a pretend groan. "Oh well, I'll force a glass or two down somehow. When do we celebrate with the spendy stuff?"

"Saving the Dom Perignon for when the first arrests are made, and we can all go home."

Although champagne was her favorite alcoholic drink, Nicola was avoiding drinking any alcohol because of the baby, but perhaps she could risk a tiny sip of what Moll called the spendy stuff.

Chapter 48
Nicola

As she was getting dressed the next morning, Nicola took the time to think about her relationship with Brian. She wanted to prove her worth to gain the freedom to live in the United States again, for Brian's sake as well as her own. While it could prove risky for her to return to her homeland, she preferred that the baby grew up as an American. Fearful if she did not produce concrete results, Steve would not be obligated to pursue their deal with the FBI. Moreover as she worked more with her team on decoding and with the others on Project Anti-Camorra, she became drawn into their commitment to outsmart the international criminal threats.

Even though she had pushed Brian away, she hoped in secret one day he might come to her out of love and not feel obligated to marry her. While Maxim assured her Brian remained ignorant she carried his baby, she loved him too much to trap him into marriage. Nevertheless Steve's comments were making her reconsider why she avoided Brian. Did her reservations about herself and her hesitation to rely on Brian stand in her way? She loved him. Accepting him in marriage meant she must believe in him too. She continued to worry that he would act out of a sense of duty by marrying her when he learned about the baby, but ultimately he would feel he had been trapped into marriage.

Even with the modern heating system, chilly air came sneaking around corners in the old manor house as the autumn days cooled. After pulling on a pair of warm leggings, Nicola tugged on a loose sweater. She needed to make a second visit to the doctor in London for additional prenatal tests. All this baby stuff was new to her and given her age, she found it more than a little scary. The additional food she was consuming took away the dizziness she had experienced earlier. Soon she had to talk with Brian. Was she ready?

Nicola arrived first in the library following an early breakfast of granola, fruit, yogurt and brown toast. While eating more she concentrated on the healthier selections. Opening her laptop she began reviewing the notes left each day by any of the team who worked later than she did.

The texts indicated that the three persons of interest, as Steve called them in a sarcastic tone, planned to yodel at eleven this morning, assuming they stuck with the GMT they used for the last call. Picking up her phone, she dialed Mikael.

"Bent here," Mikael answered.

"Steve's nickname rubbed off on you," Nicola said.

"Better than Stubbs or something."

"A question -- can you grab a conference call live on NadirNet in the Norway sphere?"

"Must be careful. Not only can we not leave footprints, but we also can't give any indicators of time delays or noise on the line or anything. What's the call about?"

"All I know is that in their lingo the Norway sphere is yodeling at 11 GMT, if they follow their time zone pattern."

"What if we delay the call by a couple of minutes and pick up the stream in a delayed mode? Safer."

"Perfect. They are tracking Brian, aka the Chinchilla, with Lenny who they nicknamed the Cougar."

"Better pull Steve into the eavesdropping too. I'll alert Nick so he can monitor his decryptor."

"Thanks Mikael. I'll advise Steve next."

"All right if I wheel over for the call?"

"You are always welcome," Nicola replied. As she ended the call, she realized someone loomed over her. After having her father sneak up on her, even now the silent approach of a person behind her made her fearful. She swiveled in her chair, looked up, saw Steve and forced herself to relax.

"Mikael is going to conference us in on a so-called Yodel this morning at 11," she said. "He will put us on a two-minute delay to avoid detection."

"I'll sit in." He laid a plain folder in front of her. "Draft Addendum reading to the effect of in recognition of critical services rendered to the FBI during international investigations, Cruze Fuentes and Annetta Fuentes will now be allowed to return to the United States under new identities without travel restrictions."

Nicola regarded him in surprise.

"You and Maxim are fulfilling your side of our bargain, and I guess you will continue your work with or without this document."

"We will."

"As you read the terms, note this part." Steve flipped over to the second page and pointed to a sentence. "All your rights as U.S. citizens will be restored. However if either of you are found to be part of any wrongdoings, you can and will be prosecuted for current and past crimes."

"We won't be anything except decent people."

"I'm required to act as a sort of parole officer. You don't want me coming after you."

"Maxim and I now pursue the lives we want and always wanted. Growing up we lacked any real idea of how to achieve them or perhaps we each took the easier way out."

"If you come up with any changes to this document, we'll discuss them. Then I will present the addendum to the Chief. Give Maxim a copy to peruse. When you go through the text, you will note some adjustment for alternate identities allowing you to live under new names as we do with anyone in the witness protection program."

Nicola held the document tight in her hands. When she and Brian dated, she dreamed of one day returning to the United States. At heart she remained an American and she wanted the baby to be born a U.S. citizen. She continued to feel torn in her love for Brian between wanting him always and frightened of marriage proving too confining for him.

For him or for me? She needed to figure out the answer. Putting the folder aside with a reverent pat, she went back to reviewing the text traffic on the line.

At eleven the decoding team, joined by Steve, Mikael and Nick, sat around a speaker phone. Out of caution or technological superstition, they placed the phone on mute.

They listened to the preliminaries and Moll began taking notes as the criminals discussed payments for services.

"Carlos, you are in arrears to Kazimír and to me for nine and a half million euros," Arielle said.

"Can't be."

"Two days ago I sent you the reconciliation in a secure email. Didn't you receive the Excel spreadsheet?"

"Our fathers reconciled once a month."

"We are not our fathers. We agreed no balances between us would exceed two million euros. Open the email."

"Got the damn thing. I'll need a day to go through your analysis."

"We either collect the amount owed by wire transfer tomorrow or no more goods will be shipped."

"What about your shares of the job in Portland?"

"Aren't you going to recover your money since they botched the hit?"

"Shit, Arielle. They're claiming I set them up by not telling them about the trolls. How could I expect trolls to be hanging around?"

Kazimír spoke up. *"Quit playing dumb. These are former FBI agents. Of course they would protect their own people after they left the organization. If you can't recover the money, this becomes a lesson learned for you, but don't short us on the disbursement. The bungled op should be addressed separately from this payment."*

The conversation went back and forth for some time, ending with an agreement to discuss the fee for the hit in Portland again in a week. Provided Arielle's summary proved to be in order, she and Kazimír pressured Carlos into a commitment to wire the nine and a half million euros the next day. Until the money arrived, no additional product would be shipped.

"How's the sale of the personal data going?" asked Carlos.

"No one wants the small lots we picked up so far," Arielle said. *"My recommendation is to put them up for auction as one lot next week."*

"How does the sale work?"

"eBay knockoff. Think they stole the code," Kazimír said. *"Put what you want to sell on this website called eWharf.onion on Darknet with an opening price. Give the auction so*

many hours or days and the high bidder wins. Usual payment method is through bank transfer."

"Cool. So like if I bought too much blow, I can put one or more lots up for bid?"

"Yes."

"Sounds like this eWharf would beat dealing with local gangs and street pushers. How do you make delivery?"

"FTP drop for electronic data. FEDEX or whatever for the product, unless a courier makes sense."

"Could we use this facility as a way to move into new territories by underselling the current suppliers and blindsiding them?"

"Since none of us used this service before, let's gain some experience with the personal data." Arielle said. "If all goes well, we should each try a local experiment and discuss results."

Steve pointed to Mikael who mouthed, "On it."

The call moved on to a quality issue with three of the teens supplied in what Carlos called the last shipment.

"The rent boy refused to cooperate. He hung himself with his sheets after his first encounter. The blonde minx brought a high price for her first night. Turned out she was not a virgin. The customer threw a shit-fit. The madam placated him with a free ride. Are you trying out these babes first, Kazimír?"

Steve gave a groan of disgust.

"Maybe you fucked her in your wet dreams," Kazimír said. "She left here as a snow white. You better check out your handlers. And the other one?"

"Arrived with the clap. Shoved pills down her. No effect. She's riddled with some new fucking drug-resistant strain. Trying something else, but I'll dump her if she can't perform. You need to cut me a deal."

"Take this off-line," Arielle said. "Text me if you work your differences out with replacements or if I must account for a credit. Moving on, any signs of the Rabbit or anyone in Portland?"

"Nothing. The office is shut. No one comes or goes. Thought you kept a tail on the Chinchilla in London, Arielle."

"He walks around with a new handler. Sending a photo. Check if this is the

bodyguard troll from Portland."

The group went quiet until Carlos said, "Shit-head Cougar. What are you going to do about them?"

"The Cougar is also an errand boy. He goes out for coffees and lunches. The Chinchilla is addicted to Starbucks lattes. We are going to intercept the Cougar and bring him in for questioning."

"After you pump him for info, what will you do?"

"Waste him and seize the Chinchilla."

Steve's face paled to gray before he flushed red. He pulled out his phone but held off dialing until the call ended.

"Wait," Maxim said when Steve went to dial. "Put Lenny on sniper duty. I'll be Brian's bodyguard. If they take me in, I'm strong and can hold up for some time. Just don't abandon me for too long."

"Maxim, no," Nicola said.

Steve held up a hand. "Mikael and Nick, start searching for this Darknet auction website. We might find solid proof of all sorts of illicit activities."

After the two men left the room, Steve turned to Maxim, "Why would you offer to guard Brian? You are meeting the requirements of our deal."

"Brian is my friend. I must do this for him and for Lenny too. Lenny helped us out of the blood bath in Albuquerque and made sure we escaped safely on a plane."

"I'll guard Brian," Moll said.

"No way Moll, not after you've been hit once already," Steve said. "Not putting you in the line of fire again. Lenny is a trained federal agent and the best sharpshooter I know. Just like with Terry in Portland, Lenny is not the only one guarding Brian. BI has agents dressed as regular city people guarding him too. At least one patrols around the outside of his safe apartment at night and Lenny sleeps in second bedroom, gun at the ready."

"That certainly lowers the danger for Brian. I just feel I should be doing something."

"I'll make some calls about logistics. Let's talk again right after lunch."

"I'm going to brief Terry," Moll said.

Steve spun around and strode out of the room with Moll hustling along behind him. After the long weeks here at Snoop Hall, Nicola found the action now proceeded all too fast. If Steve brought Brian down to Great Snoop Hall, how would she handle seeing him again? Should she tell him right away or hold out until she had the pregnancy confirmed with the ultrasound? The time apart let her know that she loved him, perhaps more deeply than she previously appreciated.

He had already asked her to marry him. If he really was unaware that she was carrying a baby, then his love for her must be strong enough to have overcome his fear of becoming controlled by another person. She would have to ask him that question outright and decide what to do depending on his answer.

Only Ivy remained at the table working on her laptop. Ivy worked independently, always willing to help yet following ideas as they came to her. Nicola decided not to ask, turned and walked from the room needing a few minutes alone to think about Brian.

Chapter 49
Moll

The group waited anxiously for Steve in the dining room. When the staff appeared to clear up, Ivy rushed to make sandwiches for Steve. Right after she finished wrapping up his lunch, Steve strode into the room.

"It's over," Steve said without preamble.

"What is?" Ivy asked.

"This research project. After advising the Chief of our findings, he said for goddam political reasons we must transition everything to a takeover team. Agents from the FBI, BI and Interpol will be here by dinner time."

"What about Brian?" Nicola asked, struggling to keep her voice from shaking.

"He's to come down here with Lenny and work with Terry. They will be on a flight here later this afternoon. After we complete the handover, which will take a couple of days, most of our gang will depart. Bent is to join the BI work, and QuickNick will hook up with the FBI squad back in the States. For the safety we have here, I recommended the rest of us stay to work with Brian and Terry on Noble Firs business. The Chief expects BI's concurrence if only to keep us out of trouble."

"Will this same threat continue to hang over Brian, Moll and Terry?" Ivy asked.

"In answer to your question, Ivy, I stressed the importance of nailing all three members of the Triad. The Intelligence agencies want to do one humongous operation once they round up additional, conclusive evidence. We were thanked for our efforts, of course. The Chief is happy with the result, but our successes irritated certain people in each organization because we unearthed NadirNet when the agents at the FBI, BI and Interpol failed to do so. At least we can value one small satisfaction."

"Our achievements are not small. We made a contribution here that will prove decisive in tracking down these criminals. I suggest we make this a time to celebrate for the team's sake," Ivy said squaring off with Steve. "Our terrific team members need to approach the changeover in a positive way. If you think about what we accomplished here, you might discover this is the perfect new role for you – heading up research projects, finding hidden nuggets and passing them on."

The ice blue in Steve's eyes became more intense as Ivy's words sunk in and Moll feared he might make a forceful rebuttal.

Instead he said, "Moll would you organize an early tea with the housekeeper for three this afternoon? Order the Dom Perignon too. We'll raise a glass with the full team when I brief them. Tell Terry to join us.

"Nicola, they nixed the idea of you training an agent to cuddle up to Arielle. However they do want you and Maxim to go through those photos of international persons of interest. The batch we'll receive will be winnowed down to those suspected of the crimes we talked about – drugs, mob-style criminal activities, bank fraud and information theft. Expect to receive at least three images of each person tomorrow including how they appear today, back-aged five years and back-aged ten years."

Maxim nodded and asked, "Online or paper?"

"Online, along with a tool to approximate various angles of the face from the photo."

Turning around he grabbed the sandwiches Ivy had packed for him, took her hand and together they left the dining room. Moll understood Steve well enough to appreciate he needed time to adjust to the change of circumstances. Through the dining room windows, they saw Steve and Ivy heading out for a walk a few minutes later.

"You going to be all right with Brian coming here?" Maxim asked Nicola.

"I'll need to be."

As he went up to his room, Moll found himself thinking of Terry working over in the ballroom. He had mixed emotions on the day of Terry's arrival. While apprehensive about seeing him every day, they had quickly settled into a routine similar their old working relationship at Noble Firs. Here they overlapped for several hours a day, with Moll working on Noble Firs business from four in the afternoon to ten at night to provide coverage for the remaining employees from the Portland office, checking in with each of them every day at their home or work locations.

Since learning of Terry's love for him, Moll began to regard him from a different perspective, discovering within himself more than feelings of friendship. His body reacted to Terry's presence, making him sit at some distance from him whenever they happened to be in the same room. Was he wrong to run away from Terry? He remained uncertain about owning up to his own homosexual tendencies.

While they never talked about Terry's feelings for him, by inaction did he string him along? Why couldn't he see a clear path to his future? Why did love and sex make life so darn complicated?

Chapter 50
Arielle

"Update on Operation Payback? C." 10:12:45 10/18/2016

Such read the text Arielle had just received from Carlos late in the afternoon her time. She had little to tell them with everyone off the grid. Nonetheless she called Carlos, not wanting him to have any excuse to bully her for a lack of response on her part.

"Carlos? Quick sighting of the Chinchilla at his London apartment with what looked like three agents. One went up with him, one guarded the front door and another stayed by the back of the building. He departed with a suitcase and the three trolls."

"Where to?"

"Town car to a parking lot at British Intelligence in the Vauxhall area of London at what they call the National Crime Agency. My guys waited all day and into the night but no sign of him. I am guessing they loaded him into some other vehicle and took him to a safe house. The facilities at NCA are large and secure. Not a place my guys can just wander into without being questioned."

"What does this agency do?"

"Fights organized crime."

"Which means the Chinchilla is working with them. Fuck these guys. Waste of time trying to find them right now."

"If Tovey is involved with the NCA, they may be working up a case against us," Arielle said.

"Particularly you, sweetheart. You're the one in London and in Western Europe."

"They know you or your father were involved in that first Portland shooting. I'll keep a man in London, but for now we need to cool our activities unless we see our way to a clean capture or bump off."

"How much do these agencies work together, like the FBI and this NCA and whatever you have in France?"

"Interpol shares information and helps coordinate activities between the police forces in its member countries. Of course France, the UK and the US are members. The agencies also deal directly with each other. The FBI keeps what they call legal attachés in most countries to help with local actions and coordinate activities with the in-country intelligence and police forces."

"If the Chinchilla is working with them and we are the targets of their investigation, then we are in deep shit."

"The possibility exists that he is working with them on some investigation totally unrelated to us, but with the disappearance of the Wild Hare and the Rabbit, I suspect you are right."

"Some days I think we should just fold up shop, live off what we have and only run our legit businesses," Carlos said in a tone that let Arielle know how discouraged he felt. "This underworld shit is a lot less fun than I thought it would be."

"We'd leave Kazimír screwed. He has product bought and warehoused."

"Let him dump it and move on. He never wanted to do this anyway. You and me – we always wanted to take over the family operations. Not him. He used to want to be a technology geek and stay completely legit. Maybe he was the smart one."

"Should we have a summit meeting to discuss this?"

"You ready to give it up?" Carlos asked.

Arielle was questioning her role and motives more and more frequently but she had a need to prove herself. "I want to know I can do this, and I feel I owe it to my father. Maybe later I will walk away, but not yet. Let's be careful and see how this plays out week by week."

"That's my Arielle. You always know what you want. You used to love being your Daddy's ray of sunshine. Even though he is dead, you still want to be that for him."

"Very perceptive of you, Carlos," Arielle said, surprised that he understood her.

"Let's get a code going between us for weekly texts. If we want to bail, we will text "Daylight!""

"And if we want to stay the course, we'll say "Keep to the shadows.""

"Take care of yourself, Arielle."

"You too, Carlos. Keep to the shadows."

Arielle hung up the phone and thought about her own plans. She still liked the idea of turning the Chinchilla to work for them. If he were an inside man working with the NCA, he could become a more valuable informant than she originally thought. She would keep her men in London and see if any opportunities turned up to snatch the Chinchilla.

Chapter 51
Brian

Disappointed when Nicola did not come out to meet the helicopter, Brian found she did attend the briefing in the evening with the takeover team. Their two weeks apart had done nothing to heal his anguish over her rejection of him. After dinner and the kickoff transition meeting, Steve posted starting times for the next morning. When the group dispersed, Nicola surprised him by asking him to take a walk with her.

A half-moon lit up the sky on the clear, crisp night. They walked in silence side-by-side out of the house and into the gardens, reaching the far side where Nicola opened a side gate. They headed up a dirt track through the middle of the estate towards an old piggery about half a mile distant. Two-thirds of the way up the hill, Nicola stopped to rest, leaning against a stone wall.

"Nicola ..." Brian said by way of beginning.

"Let me talk. This will not be easy for me."

When Brian reached out to take her hand, her smile flashed out, quick and tenuous.

"You remain ignorant of my secret? Tell me the truth," Nicola said in a soft voice laced with emotion.

He studied this woman he wanted to share his life with. Bundled into an old mac with a wool scarf looped around her neck and her feet jammed into wellies, she attracted him more than ever. "Whatever you are keeping from me, I don't have any idea what your secret might be."

When she spoke again, her words came out in a rush. "I'm pregnant. A doctor in London confirmed what a local doctor told me. I thought you bought the ring because you learned about the baby. Brian, I don't want you trapped into ..."

He gathered her in his arms so fast she didn't finish her sentence, kissed her and scooped her up, spinning her around on the moonlit path.

"A baby," he announced to the world with jubilation ringing out in his voice. "We're having a baby. I'm going to be a father."

As he set her back down, he noticed a change in her expression. Nicola seemed both relieved and surprised by his reaction. He gathered her again in his arms and kissed her. The kiss started softly but soon deepened and he hoped they were moving back towards the loving relationship he thought they had been building. All too soon Nicola pushed back and knowing the he could not press her into intimacy, he suggested they sit down on the old wall.

Side by side in the moonlight, Nicola's temporary spark of love for him seemed to fade. "How long have you known?" he asked.

"Around two weeks. I fainted while out for a walk and Maxim guessed that I could be pregnant."

"How far along are you?"

"We think I will finish eight weeks next Thursday."

Brian started counting backwards and thinking about where they were when. "The last weekend in August when the weather was sunny and hot, the air conditioning at the apartment wasn't working. You treated me to a suite at the Goring Hotel with the balcony overlooking the terrace."

Nicola nodded. "You remember?"

Brian smiled, "How could I forget? We had that romantic view of their back courtyard garden from our room. After we had our intimate couples massage, we went to our suite and slipped into the shower together. We didn't use protection during our lovemaking. The water felt so refreshing, we just enjoyed each other." He closed his eyes and murmured, "We made the baby then. Afterward we sipped that lovely Pouligny Montrachet on the terrace. The night remained warm and you fed me chilled lobster.

"I remember thinking life could not get any better, but it has. Nicola, marry me. I want to marry you because I love you. Do you want to build a life with me?"

"Yes," she whispered, "but not if you feel forced into marriage. It would take this beautiful love we share and sour it."

"With you? Never. I will walk freely into your arms."

Hoping not to be unlucky twice, Brian pulled out the small red box he put in his pocket every morning for the last two weeks. Then he knelt on the damp grass and asked Nicola to marry him. This time she agreed, and he slipped the engagement ring on her finger. Grasping the wall for support, he jumped up and gathered her into his arms for a long, slow kiss. They stood, his hands resting on her shoulders and hers on either side of his face, lost in the joy of their reunion.

"Let's find out how soon we can be married," he said, breaking their silence. "We'll have to figure out the procedure here."

"We don't need to rush."

"But I want to, if you are ready to be Mrs. Tovey."

Nicola smiled, "Is tomorrow too soon? Oh Brian, I do love you. You are a sweet, kind, noble, magnificent man. Are you sure you want me with all my problems?"

"Yes and yes – the first yes is for you and the second is for our baby." Marveling at the happiness his new prospects brought him, Brian began laughing.

"Are you happy or is something funny?"

"More than happy. I'm ecstatic, but I should have realized some change occurred when you ate so much at dinner. You sliced up a whole potato then wolfed every speck down and you ate some of everything else on your plate. And did you actually have the apple crumble when dessert came out?"

"Both doctors told me I must eat more."

"Both doctors?"

"As I mentioned, a local one here and the specialist in the city." Nicola described to him more detail how she had fainted the one day and how Maxim had helped her realize she could be pregnant. "I was thunderstruck by the news and happy, so very happy. But I have been afraid of what my pregnancy might do to the relationship we were building."

Brian pulled her closer. "Never doubt. Never doubt my love of you. I find that I can put my fears aside with you in my life."

They kissed again, slowly at first, and then more passionately. Nicola seemed breathless when she pulled away just a little and said, "Brian, will you make love with me? The doctor indicated intimacy is safe for a while yet and I want to be close to you."

"Let's wander back. No need to hurry. We can anticipate being close for the rest of our lives."

Their lovemaking in Nicola's room progressed with luxurious slowness until they lay replete and slept curled around each other. The gong for breakfast sounded the next morning, but they dallied in bed, enjoying each other once more. Some time later they again lay entwined.

"This is what people mean when they talk about losing themselves in love," Nicola said. "I never thought I would experience the true meaning of the phrase."

When a knock sounded on the door to Nicola's room, Brian jumped up, grabbed a towel to wrap around himself and answered it. Steve was walking away after leaving a tray of coffee and croissants in the hallway with three roses in a vase. He waved without turning around and went down the back stairs. The thought of Steve playing cupid made him laugh.

Nicola needed to work with the decoding team. They would have to eat in a hurry for her to attend her first transition meeting. Turning back into the room, the shower started up. Nicola must have come to the same realization. He set the tray down, poured coffee and began pulling on his clothes, aglow with the knowledge of his engagement and his future fatherhood. As soon as they could find the time to be alone with his friends, he wanted to let them know the great news about their engagement and equally importantly about the baby.

Chapter 52
Brian

The transition took two intense days and then the agents on the telecommunications and encryption teams departed to work in their respective locations. Each person remaining at Snoop Hall carried a sense of incompleteness and wandered around with a hangover of worries about the future. Soon they must reopen the Noble Firs offices and try to resume normal lives in spite of the risks.

Secreted away in a private phone room, Steve received daily updates from the head of the FBI takeover team. Impatient for results as ever, he voiced his frustrations with the slow pace but revealed none of the detail of what he learned.

A little over a week after he arrived at Great Snoop Hall, Brian received a call from a prospect in London inviting him to a preliminary screening meeting in advance of a presentation to their department head. He hurried to the ballroom and called the group together, except for the BI agents still working with Terry. Once assembled in the drawing room, Brian explained the call.

"You must go," Ivy said. "Noble Firs has too many gaps in your marketing efforts over the last few months."

"A group of us should go up to London," Steve said. "I'll arrange for protection for us at the hotel and as we travel around. Brian, Lenny, Moll, Maxim, Nicola, Ivy and me should go. I need to meet with a few of the planners for BI and Interpol. Nicola needs to see her doctor. Brian when did the fellow want to meet?"

"Friday afternoon."

"We'll go up on Thursday and come back here late Friday afternoon. Maxim and Lenny, we will schedule into three groups moving around at one time. One of us with each group. Maxim, we'll pick up firearms for you when we land. We'll also have agents to trail around with us."

Steve paused for a moment before continuing, "Maxim and Nicola, we finalized your addendum. I should receive a signed copy this afternoon. Once your signatures are added, you are welcome back in the United States under your current identities or any new ones we decide upon. I must report your whereabouts each month."

"What if we want to return to our homes in Spain?" Maxim asked.

"Let me know about any travel," Steve said with a frown. "I hoped you might live near Spook Hills."

"Kind of you to say those words. While I will keep my glass studio in Spain, I want to explore options out in Oregon, so I can spend time with my niece or nephew as well as see my friends."

"First learn to say the state name right," Ivy said gently. "Pronounce the state name as Or-Y-Gun, not ORE-E-GONE."

"Gotcha."

"Nicola, what will you and Brian do?" Steve asked.

"We both want the baby to grow up as an American. While we might live abroad sometimes, I think our home will be in Portland. We will look for a house near the city close to Moll. During my short visit some years ago, I liked Portland. It is like Barcelona, small enough to be manageable and yet vibrant with excellent restaurants, decent shopping and worthwhile cultural alternatives. Now I think of comforts more than the glitzy life I used to lead in Miami."

"And your place in Barcelona?"

"We'll use the condo as a bolt hole when the Portland rain becomes too much for any of us."

"I'll book rooms for us in London," Steve said. "Brian, I think you should stay at the hotel with us instead of your apartment, which may still be under surveillance. Easier to protect you if we are clustered together."

Wanting to go to the London office to organize marketing materials for their sales pitch at three, Brian left the hotel with Lenny early Friday afternoon. An agent rode in the front of the town car and he would keep watch at whatever buildings they went into. Moll planned to join Brian for coffee before the meeting to discuss any final tactics.

The afternoon sun amidst the billowy clouds floating over London lit up the city as they stepped into the waiting town car to head to the Noble Firs offices in Whitechapel. Nearing the office building, Brian and Lenny went on high alert, as if their appearance in the vicinity might arouse criminal activity. After about twenty minutes in his office to assemble materials, Brian and Lenny left with the agent, walking back to their waiting town car for the drive to meet up with Moll at a coffee café in the Shard.

Right when they went to get in the car on a side street, six men appeared out of an alley. Two men pulled the agent away from the car, slammed him into the side of the building and dragged him down an alley. Two men attacked Lenny, wrestling him to the ground.

Simultaneously a rough French voice said by his ear, "Not one word," The man smacked a rag smelling of chloroform over Brian's nose and mouth, shoved a pistol into his back and forced him onto the backseat of the car.

Thrashing and trying to break away, Brian used that one moment to take in what was happening around him. The driver was missing. On the other side of the car, the men were struggling to stuff Lenny into the front seat until one man clunked him hard on the head with the butt of a pistol. As Brian slipped away from consciousness from the choloform, rough hands tumbled him to the floor.

Chapter 53

Nicola

Leaving the doctor's suite, Nicola joined Steve and Ivy. As they stood outside the door, Ivy asked her if everything was all right. Nicola was so stunned by what the doctor had told her she had trouble taking it in, much less saying it out loud.

"Nicola?"

"Twins! I'm having twins. They run in the Fuentes family, like Cristo and Cruze, but I never thought ..."

"Boys or girls?"

"Too early to be sure. They will do an ultrasound again in a month."

"Wait till Brian gets this news," Steve said with a grin.

"I will tell him as soon as we are back and safe at Great Snoop Hall," Nicola said.

Right then Steve's phone rang. The three of them clustered around his phone as he tapped the speaker button.

"Something is wrong," Moll said. "Brian isn't here. He's never late for a client. He's not answering his phone. Lenny's not either."

"Might be in a dead spot. You and Maxim handle the appointment. When you finish up, call me."

"Where are you?"

"At the doctor's office in Mayfair with Nicola, Ivy and an agent. I'll do some tracking from here."

A dreadful panic welled up inside of Nicola. The man she loved might be in danger or worse. She could not face the thought of losing Brian. Just when her life had opened up with hope and promise, doors began closing again. Nothing must happen to Brian or to Maxim.

Ivy gave her hand a quick squeeze. "Keep calm. We must stay focused. Can you think of any way to trace him?"

She thought for a moment and gripped Ivy's arm. "His cell phone. He gave me some tracker software."

She took out her iPhone. Her hands shook so badly she had to key her security code in three times before bringing up the right app and selecting Brian's number. The screen displayed a map and showed his phone sitting stationary on a street in the Docklands. She reached over and tapped Steve on the shoulder.

"Here," she shoved the phone at him. "This is the location of Brian's iPhone."

Steve barked the address into the phone and ended with, "Get at least one more agent to meet us at this site."

He turned to Ivy, "Take Nicola back to the hotel in the town car."

"No," Nicola said firmly. "We are going with you. The man I love is in danger."

Ivy glanced around, took her gun out of her purse, slid the small pistol into her jacket pocket and signaled Nicola to do the same.

"Let's go," Steve said turning to the elevator. "Might be better for you two to be where the agent and I can protect you, but you both must stay in the car."

They ran down and jumped into their town car only after Steve checked to ensure the same driver who picked them up at the hotel sat behind the wheel. As they drove down to the Docklands, Steve's phone rang. They listened anxiously to his brief conversation.

"Brian's driver called in. A couple of thugs knocked him out. He woke up next to a dumpster in a little alley behind their offices. The agent with them was still unconscious and slumped down near him."

Their own driver drove as fast as possible through the increasing Friday afternoon traffic, estimating they would not reach the Docklands location until thirty minutes later. Together they sat in the town car regularly checking for texts from Brian or Moll and calling the numbers for Brian and Lenny's cell phones.

Leaning forward in her seat, Nicola willed the car to move faster. What had happened to Brian and Lenny? Why did they let them go off on their own? She should have stepped in to demand the two men received more protection.

When at last they pulled up to the address, they spotted a DHL office occupying the space at the street level of the building. Swearing, Steve told them to stay in the car while he ran in. The agent jumped out and stood on alert by the car.

From the car, they could see the big man bringing out his identification. A woman rushed into the DHL office. She conferred with him and showed her badge. The two of them barged through the counter opening and began sorting through packages which might contain Brian's phone. Tired of waiting, Nicola poised herself to run to help when Ivy laid a restraining hand on her arm.

"Wait a minute. Let me finish this search on my iPad."

"What are you after?" Nicola asked.

"Installing an app. I put the PC version on my laptop the other day. For Christmas I gave Brian and Moll trackers for their keyrings. If by any miracle Brian still carries his keys, we may be able to locate him."

Before Ivy could stop her, Nicola sprinted into the building to advise Steve.

"This box," the female agent said. "Heading to France. Sized right to hold a laptop and cell phones."

Steve tore the package open.

Nicola recognized the silver case on Brian's iPhone. The black one had to be Lenny's. "Oh no. Their phones and Brian's laptop."

"Tell someone to research the address on the package," he told the agent. "Where the hell did they take Brian and Lenny? If they are overnighting the tech gear, they are not likely to be hustling them to France."

Ivy burst into the DHL office. "Brian's keys are east of here, some area off Alfred's Way."

"Moving or stationary?" He asked.

"Stationary."

Moll and Maxim ran in. "The guy canceled on us. Will reschedule next week. What did you discover?"

"Located Brian's keyring. Let's go." Steve yelled and turned to the BI agents giving them the location. "Organize backup for us. Send medical help too."

Not waiting for the agents, the five of them ran out to the town car. Steve jumped in the front seat after Moll and gave the driver the address.

"Dodgy area, sir. You sure you want to go?"

"Two men's lives are in danger. We're on our way to rescue them."

"Are you with the police?" he asked dubiously.

"Federal agent in the United States. These are our operatives. British Intelligence will be right behind us."

The aging driver sat up a little straighter. "On my way, Captain."

He shot out into the street at the first break in the stream of vehicles and gunned the town car. "Used to drive an ambulance during the border campaign in Northern Ireland defending the Crown against the IRA."

Minutes ticked by as they wove between trucks, buses and cars. Over ten minutes later they pulled up in front of a derelict warehouse. They saw no sign of Brian's town car. Ivy rechecked the app which still showed Brian's keys at this location.

"Maxim, you stay here with Ivy and Nicola," Steve said.

"But ..." Ivy began.

Steve cut her off. "Brief the backup team when they arrive. We are going to circle the building."

He and Moll took off running with Moll going right down the sidewalk and Steve heading left. Nicola went to run after them, but Maxim held her back.

"No you don't. Think of the baby!"

She struggled to break away. Maxim gripped her tighter. "We need to stay put. What if they come staggering out the front of the building?"

"All right. I'll stay here."

The agents they left at DHL pulled up in a car. Ivy directed them to the back of the building.

Maxim regarded Nicola fiercely and let go. They stood facing the derelict warehouse, waiting impatiently to hear news from Steve and Moll. From the back of the building, a sudden, huge bang sent debris soaring high into the air. Part of the roof of the building blew off, sending shingles and tar paper flying. As the rubble came back down, a smell of smoke drifted towards them. Sparks shot up and fanned out. A glow of flames began lighting up the back of the warehouse. The smoke blackened with soot.

Nicola gasped in horror. This could not be happening, not to Brian and Lenny. She went to run to help them, but the ground shifted underneath her. As she started falling towards the sidewalk, strong arms clutched her on both sides. Everything went gray and darkened. Even as she fought for consciousness, blackness blocked her vision.

Chapter 54
Moll

At the back of the warehouse, Moll spied Steve heading towards him, skirting around the area where smoke billowed out from the explosion. In the distance behind him, a black town car sped away down the street.

Above the noise of the fire, Moll yelled, "They in the car?"

"Dunno."

"We gotta search the building." Without waiting for a response, Moll turned to race up a short ramp by a trio of loading docks, his pulse pounding in his ears. His friends might be trapped inside this hellhole. He stopped on a narrow walkway by a closed metal door next to three overhead doors. All lacked exterior door handles. Grappling with his fingernails, he tried to pry open the human-sized door but failed to find a purchase.

Maxim ran up and pulled on his arm to stop him. "Better to enter the building through the front. Flames are spreading here in the back."

Right then firetrucks pulled up along with police cars. Firefighters jumped out and prepared to tackle the blaze. The police herded the three men away from the building and left them standing on the sidewalk across the street.

"I can't stand here and do nothing," Moll yelled over the noise.

"Let's see what's happening out front," Steve said.

Sprinting off the way he and Maxim had come, Moll feared for the lives of Brian and Lenny. They needed to enter the building and fast.

"Nicola fainted," Maxim huffed out as they ran. "We laid her on the seat in the back of the car and elevated her feet. Ivy took her gun out for protection and gave Nicola's to the driver."

As they ran up Ivy was just getting into an ambulance with Nicola. Steve ran over to them before the doors were closed. Charging up to the boarded front door of the rundown building, Moll threw himself against the timbers. They gave but only a little. The ambulance started up behind him, putting on its siren and moving away.

"Together on three," Steve said running up just behind him with Maxim. The three men formed a line. "One, two, three."

They hit with such force the door flattened on the wooden floor of the old building. The acrid stench of the burning materials at the rear of the rambling warehouse permeated the air.

Steve regarded each of them sternly, holding them back by their shoulders. "Stay sharp. Use your jacket or sleeve or whatever to filter the air as you move further in. Count your paces and remember your stride. We'll fan out. Maxim go to the right. Moll take the middle. I'm going left. Keep your phones handy. Call if you find any sign of our guys. I'll phone in the info on the departed town car. They might find it on the CCTV cameras."

Heading across the room and towards a doorway, Moll counted ten steps from the front door at a left angle. What appeared to be a single expansive structure from the outside had been split into multiple rooms. Twisting the first door handle and finding the metal cool to the touch told him he should be safe to proceed into the next room. Except for piles of junk near the walls, the room sat empty in front of him. After sprinting across the wooden floor in twenty-six running steps, he reached the far wall where he chose a door on the right. The knob felt warmer, but he needed to keep going. Something told him those thugs had dumped Brian here with Lenny. He pulled up his sleeve towards his nose and mouth, then jerked the door open.

Stacked with old, flattened packing boxes, discarded furniture and pallets, the exposed floor in the next room turned to rough cement. Flames were licking their way up the far wall. Estimating himself as more than halfway into the sprawling building, Moll hustled down the pathway in the room, weaving his way around the junk-laden platforms. Many were stacked with flattened cardboard boxes which would burn fast once ignited. This time with all the zig-zagging, he mentally recorded thirty short walking strides. Again he chose the right-side door. The level of heat on this door increased so much over the last one, he wrapped his hand in his shirtsleeve, turned the handle and pulled.

The room in front of him disappeared in the dense smoke. As he remembered from his FBI training, he dropped to his hands and knees and began crawling along on a diagonal to stay away from the burning walls, recording each of his four-legged paces. After nineteen of the herky-jerky steps, irregular shapes on the floor loomed up about three feet away.

As fast as possible on all fours, Moll scuttled over to find Brian and Lenny sprawled on the grimy cement. Lenny slumped over on his right side with his leg stuck out at an awkward angle. Brian lay collapsed face down to the left of him. Moll pulled Brian upright, horrified by his beaten face. One arm hung crookedly by his side, and his head gushed blood down into his eye. Thick gore from his nose covered his mouth and chin. With his breaths sounding shallow and raspy, Brian remained unconscious. Snatching his phone out of his pocket, Moll dialed Steve.

The room to his left exploded. No answer from Steve. Oh God, had he been trapped in the blast?

With time almost out, Moll went behind Brian, turned around, hoping he faced the way back, and scooped him up into his arms. Lenny came to and struggled to rise, but his cracked knee kept him down. Moll reached for him with one hand and pulled, staggering in place to hang onto Brian.

"Get going, kid. Take Brian. Can't take me too. Be behind you," Lenny said, his breath coming in short gasps. Moll took a step forward and looked back. Grimacing with intense pain, Lenny began to crawl, using his arms and his working leg while dragging the damaged one.

Moll sucked in his gut, searching for strength. Despite his thinness Brian's toned muscles made him heavy in his passed out state. Struggling to keep his bearings, Moll lurched his way back to the door. Right when he started to wrangle sideways through the opening, a loud screech of metal sounded. With no time to investigate, he continued past the doorjamb, protecting Brian's head and broken arm. Dense smoggy air filled the room he entered. He could only hope to be heading for the far door.

Counting his steps but knowing his strides shortened from carrying Brian, he reached twenty when he tripped, banging both shins into a stack of rough lumber. After recovering his footing, he gripped Brian closer and pitched forward another ten short steps until he whacked into what he thought might be the boxes stacked by the far wall. Using his feet to bump along the wooden boards of the bottom platform, he searched for an opening.

The smoke made the air too dense to see. When his right foot found an empty space, he toed his way along until he located the side of the doorjamb, then he backed up a step and turned to shimmy Brian through the doorway into the next room. A third boom sounded. The building behind him collapsed in a roar of smoldering beams, flame and debris.

"Lenny," Moll yelled as he turned towards the blast area.

"Here," Steve said, running up and grabbing Brian.

Moll spun back, pushed Brian into Steve's arms and turned to find a way back through the doomed building. Flames engulfed the far wall. With a huge whoosh the ceiling cascaded down, a beam caught him on the shoulder and pinned him to the floor. He clawed the floor in an effort to free himself, wanting only to rescue Lenny. He scrabbled harder even as the nasty air made him cough and filled his lungs with too little oxygen.

Strong arms grasped him and pulled. His shoulder hurt in a dull cold ache. Stinking, thick air occupied his lungs. He weakly called out, "Lenny."

"Coming with me, old boy." The voice sounded far away.

Another beam fell, thumping him on the side of the head and causing his vision to blur as he pulled away to go back for Lenny.

Moll came to in an ambulance, his memory fuzzy. An oxygen mask covered his face. He wanted to cough. Bleepy sirens sounded all around him. Pulling off the oxygen mask and batting away the medic, he struggled to say, "Lenny. Need to bring Lenny out."

The medic roughly pushed him back down and fastened straps over him. A warmth spread up his arm, the oxygen mask went back over his face, and he faded from consciousness.

When he woke up again Moll found himself in a white and green tiled room. He struggled to sit up but stopped with his head decidedly woozy. A sling bound his right arm to his body. He found himself secured to the bed. His throat burned and his chest hurt. The building, the fire, Brian, Lenny. Oh God, Lenny.

A bulldog of a nurse barreled into the room. "You shouldn't be awake yet," she said by way of greeting.

"Brian? Lenny?"

"Don't you bother now." She bustled out, coming back with a glass of water and a little plastic cup.

"Take these." The woman raised up his bed a little.

"My arm?"

"Dislocated. The doctor put the shoulder back while you were out. You're a bit banged up and suffered a concussion, but you should consider yourself lucky. Now take these."

"What are they?"

"Pain medication and a sleeping pill."

"I must go back."

Ivy entered the room, filling the small space with her presence. The nurse flushed with anger at the sight of her.

"You, Ms. High and Mighty. You do not belong in this room."

Ivy glowered at her with the haughty demeanor of the righteous and went to stand by Moll.

"Brian?" Moll asked

"Came out of surgery. Broken arm reset. Scanned for a concussion too. But materially he will heal."

"His face? A beaten-up mess."

"Cracked his cheekbone and squashed his nose. The doctor splinted the nose to stabilize the cartilage and added packing to staunch the bleeding. Brian is dosed with pain meds and is sleeping. He should heal up without too much of an issue. He'll sport a small scar on his eyebrow from a few stitches."

"Lenny?"

Ivy shook her head. "Steve called in. The warehouse became an inferno. The firemen were working to beat back the flames. Maxim is missing too."

"Maxim! But he ran into the building on the right-hand side. That area was less damaged. I need to go back. I told Lenny I would be back for him. And now Maxim is missing too." With his voice faltering Moll broke into a sob. "Why didn't I find the strength to carry Lenny? His damn broken leg. When he couldn't get up, he crawled. Oh God, he crawled."

Ivy grasped his hand, her expression sad and fearful. "Flames engulfed the dilapidated building when we left. A fourth explosion ..."

"Dammit Ivy. I'm going back with you or without. Where's Nicola?"

"She fainted after the initial detonation. I rode with her in the first ambulance coming here. She just found out she is having twins. The babies are fine, but the doctors want to keep her for a day for observation."

"Twins. I'll never be able to face her if we lost Maxim. What happened to him? Lenny told me to take Brian. Where was my super-human surge of strength? I tried, but I couldn't take both of them. I wanted to. Aw fuck. I fucking wanted to save them both," Moll started crying.

"Take these or I am calling for the doctor," the nurse said in a tone indicating she gave the orders to patients.

Using his uninjured arm, he knocked the pills out of her hand. The nurse marched angrily out of the room.

"What's the time? Where's Steve?"

"A little after midnight. Steve stayed at the site. Three firemen pulled him out of the building after he tried twice to go after Lenny and Maxim," Ivy said. "They threatened to cuff and shackle him to keep him out."

"I need to go back," Moll said again struggling against the restraints on the bed.

"We better put some clothes on you before that sour mug returns. I did my best Ivy-at-her-worst to hustle medical help for each of you, starting with Nicola. No NHS cards."

Ivy unfastened the belts on the bed and snatched Moll's grime-laden clothes from the chair.

"Can you stand?" she asked and helped Moll to his feet, where he half-leaned on the bed. Keeping her eyes averted, she helped Moll into his boxer shorts and trousers before moving him to a chair where she pulled on his socks and wiggled his filthy dress shoes back on his feet, tying them into place. The grubby garments reeked of smoke. One pant leg showed a large v-tear. After gingerly removing the hospital gown, she pulled his shirt over his uninjured shoulder, followed by his suitcoat. Seizing the blanket off the bed, Ivy folded it into a shawl to drape over his shoulders and tucked it in around his sling.

Together they left the room. She guided him away from the nurse's station and down to the reception space in the emergency entrance. Their town car driver dozed in a chair. Steve must have sent him to wait for her.

Leaving Moll to lean on the wall, Ivy shook the man's shoulder. "You awake enough to drive?"

The old trooper stood, shrugging himself awake. "Yes, madam. Learned the art of the quick nap in the war. Where to, love?"

"Back to the same warehouse."

"Dodgy place at night, madam."

"My husband stayed with the fire brigade. We have two men in that hellacious furnace. We must go back."

They walked out to the town car with Moll doing his best to move along on his own. Breathing the air outside restored a little of his vitality especially after the stale air in the hospital. His head ached from whatever had knocked him out, and his lungs and throat continued to burn, but he needed to return. Despite his logic telling him Lenny must be dead, his heart willed him back to the warehouse on the remote chance of finding the grizzled agent and Maxim still alive. Again Moll asked -- why didn't I possess the strength to carry both men? How had Maxim gotten trapped in the building? Maxim should live to experience the joy of Brian and Nicola's twins. How could the babies grow up without their Uncle Maxim?

Chapter 55

Arielle

As she sat sipping a glass of white burgundy in her apartment, Arielle's phone buzzed with a call. Checking her phone she saw it was from one of the men she had in London.

"Louis, what's happening?"

"We finally spotted the Chinchilla and his bodyguard near their office space. Acting fast, we knocked out their driver and some other suit. The suit looked like an agent or something. Moving fast, we left the driver and the suit knocked out in an alley. Then we dropped their cellphones and a laptop for the Chinchilla at DHL to overnight to you and we drove to that warehouse we talked about to interrogate them."

"What did you find out?"

"Nothing. The Chinchilla's id said he's Brian Tovey so we got the right guy. The other guy had a U.S. passport with the name of Lenny Bruckner. Address in Oregon. We got rough with each of them, but they weren't giving us a damn thing.

"Somebody pulled up out front. We lit the charges, just like we planned, then ran for it and drove away. We ditched the Chinchilla's town car and used the tube to get to Paddington and then out to the airport. We split up on different flights. I paid off the four locals helping us."

"How did those guys who pulled up at the warehouse know where you went?"

"One or both of those guys must have had some kind of tracker on them.

We were damn lucky to get away once we lit the fuses. The way we wired that building, what wasn't blown up will be burnt and the bodies with it."

"All right. Text me when you get to Paris and we will meet in the parking lot behind the new Emporium in Marais. You can give me a full debrief."

Arielle ended the call and tried to decide if she should send those two guys out of the country for a few months. They were good men, particularly Louis. She needed to reward loyalty. Perhaps she could have them scout out the market potential in French-speaking Canada, starting in Montreal and Quebec. Liking that idea, she went over to her computer to make up a quick budget of what the Canadian venture might cost for preliminary research.

Chapter 56
Moll

The building smoldered as a wet ruin in front of them. Still filled with the bitter pong of smoke, the surrounding air stung their noses. Firefighters trained hoses on the left front wall which spouted weak fumes in the last gasp of burning. Half of the roof had collapsed in on the building.

Moll stood staring at the wreckage, his stomach doing flip-flops as he thought of Lenny and Maxim. Dry-heaving at the curb and hating himself for lacking the strength to carry Lenny out with Brian, he slumped over, horrified by his own ineptitude. He had left a worthy man to die, and he would never forgive himself.

And Maxim. What had happened to him? Maxim wanted to do his part for his friends. How could he have been wasted by that inferno?

Steve ran over from where he stood with the firefighters. "What are you two doing back here?"

"I told Lenny I would come back for him," Moll said. "I needed to fulfill my promise."

Steve looked puzzled but then he nodded and placed a hand on Moll's good shoulder. "They're preparing to go into the building to conduct a search, provided things are not too hot inside. If you want to go in, we will need to suit you up. Three guys will go in ahead of us. Think you can retrace your path to where you discovered Brian and Lenny?"

Moll nodded. The nightmare of the run into the building and back out until the ceiling collapse knocked him unconscious stayed with him, as the horror of deserting Lenny always would. The worst choice he had ever made -- save one man while sacrificing another. And now Maxim had likely died somewhere in the ill-fated building too.

Their driver came over carrying a tray of tea in paper cups he had hustled up from somewhere. "Drink this. Doused with lots of sugar and milk. Don't have anything stronger."

Moll took the tea shakily, fearing he would heave it right back up. Still he sipped from the cup, needing the comfort of its warmth. Steve donned the heavy fire-retardant gear first. Once he was suited up, Ivy forced a cup into his hand, and he gulped the contents down before helping Moll into the protective gear, working around his arm in the sling.

The firemen started moving spotlights into position. Others already in place were switched back on. Guiding the firefighters in front of him with verbal commands, they crept through the building. Hot charred debris and remains of felled beams slowed their progress. The further in they went, the more debris they encountered.

After the scorched second interior door frame, Moll became disoriented. He stood and wobbled a bit, as he moved his eyes to the right and back to the left. Some fragment of a memory guided him. They moved and stopped. Now he remembered -- by the far wall he had found the two men. Nothing but burnt rubble remained on the cement floor. At his direction a fireman and firewoman moved towards a half standing wall in search of Lenny.

The firefighters began to move pieces of the wreckage, searching for any remains of a body. While Moll stood at the side with Steve, his eyes roved around the burned-out walls and fallen timbers. Over on the right a glint of metal attracted him. He walked forward towards a pile of blackened material to peer around, trying to discover what might lay beyond. Another flicker, another glint of a shiny object.

He let his eyes travel up. The wall here stood blackened but intact. Moving to the left, he spied a floor to ceiling wall running backward about ten feet. Debris blocked his pathway on the right.

"Here," he yelled.

Hopping over struts and litter on the floor, Steve reached his side. The firemen moved over fast behind him.

"Might be a room here. Small but still standing." Moll said, pointing down through the blackened remains of the adjoining wall. "I can spot a little steel, like a door handle."

"Stand back," one fireman ordered. "I'll call more people in here."

For the next two hours, the fire crew moved blackened girders, charred wooden beams, supports and ceiling debris, working in a fast but methodical way to avoid injury. Through the gloom, the outline of a blackened metal door to a room stood in front of them.

"Fireproof safe. Guess they stored sensitive stuff here once," a firefighter said.

Moll could stand still no longer. He wormed his way forward and tugged on the door with his good arm. Nothing moved. "How do we break in?"

"Old mechanism. Move away. We'll try a pry bar."

The firemen worked at the door. The old lock and hinges held fast. They called for a device called a hydra ram. Moll walked up to the door and pressed against the dense metal which felt warm against his hand. Laying his ear against the door, he listened, straining to catch any sounds. Did he imagine a faint tapping or did he pick up a real noise?

He turned to call out, "I think I hear a soft rat-tat-tat. Weak and muffled. Hurry."

The firemen pushed him away and brought up a hefty device. After moving into position, conferring and repositioning the gear, they started working again. When the door continued to resist, they tried a combination of pry bars, sledgehammers and the hydra ram. The old safe door began to give on the hinge side with a screech like the one Moll had heard before. They kept working for the next half hour until they shifted the door enough to shine a light inside.

"Two men are down in here," a fireman shouted.

"Alive?" Steve called out.

"Can't tell. One is clutching a pistol, but he is not moving."

A fireman called for medics. They pried the door open further. The thinnest of the firefighters squeezed into the room.

All went silent as he checked the body of what looked like Lenny.

"Breathing but not conscious. Need oxygen in here. NOW." He moved to Maxim and put a hand on his neck seeking a pulse. "Same here. Wait, he's coming to."

Still holding his gun, Maxim struggled to rise and swore. The fireman pushed him back down. "Stay right where you are. We'll help you out."

Two medics ran up and squeezed into the room. Moll burst forward and slid in after them. The firemen continued to work on widening the passage.

"Need to take them to Hospital, STAT. This one has a shattered knee. Smoke inhalation has likely caused damage to his lungs. Burns on his left side. The other one is a little scorched and will suffer from smoke issues too. They used up almost all the air in here."

Steve stepped forward, pushing his sizeable body through the opening.

"Let me carry each one out. Lift Lenny – this guy -- up into my arms. Careful now. This man is one hell of a fighter."

The door gave way further. Steve slid Lenny out sideways. Two more medics appeared with a stretcher to take him out of the building. Steve turned back to the vault to bring Maxim out. Independent as ever Maxim insisted on walking, although Steve kept a firm grip around his waist to guide him.

Moll pressed forward and gripped Lenny's hand as the medics lifted the stretcher.

"Hang on man. Hang on."

Lenny's eyes fluttered open. He tried to speak.

"Not now. You're on your way to the hospital. Brian will heal up. Nicola is okay. You are our priority now. You're the one who needs help."

Steve pulled Moll back to let the medics take Lenny out. Another stretcher came in for Maxim but he insisted on walking out on his own after sucking up some oxygen in long, thankful breaths. As they carried Lenny away, Steve said to Moll, "What made you think they might be alive? Something told you these men needed your help."

"Blind faith, man. Like radical," Moll spluttered the words out as he began crying again.

Steve slung an arm around his waist and pulled Maxim along behind him, guiding the two men out through the rubble of the building to the front door. Right by the town car, Terry stood with Ivy. When he spied Moll, he let out a whoop and ran to him. Without thinking he wrapped Moll in a hug, holding on to his uninjured side like he would never let go. Moll pulled off his helmet and gripped him back with his good arm, inhaling the minty scent of his hair. For those moments as they stood hugging each other, his mind filled with the warmth and closeness of Terry.

His doubts cleared away like the smoke from the warehouse. Life came at a person with too many uncertainties to be lived alone and without love. They would find their way through. They would still be Moll and Terry. Best buddies. Business partners. Lovers.

He pushed back from Terry and saw the longing and yet hesitation in his face. "I know how your feel about me. Until now I couldn't make my way through the obstacles I put in my brain to prevent myself from being attracted to you. You're my best friend. You're my business partner. Now I know you're a whole lot more."

"You've been through one heck of a lot of trauma," Terry said looking at him worriedly. "Let's get last night behind us. You need to think this through for a few days. I'll be here. Right now, we need to make sure Lenny will pull through."

"He has to, Terry. He just has to."

As they walked over to the town car, Moll heard Ivy ask about Lenny. Steve pulled her close and said,

"I think he might survive, thanks to Moll. One of your angels kept whispering in his ear. Good thing that he fought for coming back here. Maxim must have stumbled over Lenny when he was trying to crawl out. He carried Lenny into a big old document safe and kicked the door shut to keep the fire out. If he hadn't, for sure they would be dead. With the hours they were in there, they almost used up all the oxygen in the room."

"Nicola called twice. I must call her. Then we better get to the hospital to make sure she doesn't try to see Brian or Maxim before she should be up and about."

"Okay but soon all four of us need to get some sleep. You must be exhausted. I know I am.

While Ivy called Nicola, Steve forced Maxim into an ambulance. Once he was loaded up on a stretcher, Steve and Ivy walked away to wait for Moll and Terry by the town car. The driver slumped in sleep at the wheel. Steve woke him up while Terry settled Moll in the front seat before clambering in the back seat.

"Hospital," Steve said.

"Just like the old days. Never thought I'd be making runs to hospital again with the stench of smoke in my nose and the echoes of explosions in my head. My last week of driving before I retire -- this will be one to tell my wife, son and grandkids."

"You're the best," Steve said. "Once you drop us off, you better get yourself home. Would you have the hotel send another car for us in an hour or so?"

"Of course, sir."

Steve moved away to squash himself into the backseat with Terry and Ivy.

Moll sunk down on the front passenger seat, letting the motion of the car relax his stretched nerves while listening to the quiet conversation in the backseat of the car.

"How did you know to come here?" Steve asked Terry.

"While the doctor was shifting Moll's shoulder back in place, Ivy called me. I woke up the groundskeeper to drive me here. Is he an agent or something?" Terry asked. "I thought of him as this kind old retainer, but he drove the Land Rover like he took the wheel of a souped-up assault vehicle."

"Probably is under the hood," Steve said. "Each member of the staff at Great Snoop Hall is a trained agent and sharpshooter. British Intelligence puts pre-retirement agents at the site if they are not ready to be moved entirely out of the game. Not surprised some would be skilled assault vehicle drivers too. Did you know that under the ballroom where your team is working, there is a secured shooting gallery? The staff does target practice down there when no guests are staying."

Moll tilted his head back against the headrest, lulled by the voices around him. For years he had worried he lacked real courage. Tonight with the lives of his friends on the line, some hidden part of him had surfaced to help save those men. The rift in his soul had mended, making him feel complete. As long as Lenny survived, Moll was confident he would remain whole.

His thoughts drifted to the possible chain of events with Maxim. He must have found the safe on his way in and opened the door, making the old metal screech from the unaccustomed movement. Discovering no one inside, he went on, likely tripping over Lenny as he tried to crawl his way out. With the third explosion going off, the safe would have become Maxim's only hope of survival. Even with the blasts, the thick smoke and the fire, Maxim must have moved Lenny to the safe, shutting the door in hopes the fireproof materials would protect the room.

The faint tapping had come from Maxim trying to signal with his pistol. From the thinning levels of oxygen, he must have lacked the strength to pull the trigger or possibly he feared any bullets would ricochet. What stories they would each possess to compare! Moll smiled to himself and drifted to sleep, remembering the warmth and rightness of hugging Terry.

Chapter 57

Terry

In twos they returned to Snoop Hall with Moll and Terry going back first. Once the doctors released Brian five days later, they met him and Nicola at the helipad. Ivy and Steve arrived late the same afternoon. Once the hospital released Lenny, they decided he should remain under guard in London with a mostly recovered Maxim staying on to assist in his recuperation.

Terry could not help but notice how Moll acted differently with him -- chummier and more relaxed than in the prior weeks. Still he hung back, afraid of destroying their friendship by confronting him with his love. On the day after Steve returned, Moll went out for a long walk with him, and Terry went in search of Ivy.

"What did Steve hear about the criminals after us?" Terry asked when he found her taking tea in the library.

"Nothing he is sharing. Progress is slower than he would like or would tolerate if he stayed in charge. The problem with all the layering of the various security forces is the reduction in their ability to be nimble. When the sting does happen, the impact will be massive and involve actions in at least half a dozen countries, perhaps as many as a dozen."

"What do you think Moll and Steve are talking about?" Terry asked as the two men sauntered across the hill behind the library.

"A relationship between you and Moll, I suspect," Ivy said with a small smile. "Can't you tell Moll is reconciled to his feelings about you?"

"Can he possibly be ... ?" Terry asked still afraid to fully believe Moll loved him.

"It is time for you and Moll to sort your relationship out. His experiences in the warehouse changed him. He will never be the same."

"Moll was trying to meet a goal Steve set for him, wasn't he?" The bitter tone of the words revealed the resentment he had over Moll's unwavering commitment to his former boss and continuing mentor.

"If a goal was set, it was done by Moll and he needed to achieve for himself," Ivy answered. "With his difficult upbringing I think inside his head he never measured up. No matter how hard he worked or how much he achieved, feelings of inadequacy haunted him. Now he acts more complete, more content, less needing to hide behind superficial goofiness."

"Too bad -- I like the goofy side of him."

"His amusing ways will always be a part of Moll, but not to mask the way he perceives himself. He wielded the goofiness as a way to attract and deflect attention. If dismissed for acting like a clown, he would never be fully challenged to measure up. His transformation needed to come from inside."

"Moll served with the FBI for goodness sakes – of course he's brave."

"In his mind he always choked. At the warehouse with Brian's and Lenny's lives on the line, he acted. He saved Brian. Refusing to accept that Lenny had died in the last explosion, he fulfilled his promise by coming back for him. Whether Lenny turned out to be dead or alive, Moll needed to deliver on his commitment.

"Terry, Moll never knew his father. Steve has come to serve as his father figure. His mother disappeared into her world of hallucinogens. Although we are still trying to find her, she may be dead. If he needs a parental discussion, Steve is the person he would turn to. As for you and Moll developing a relationship, Keep the Faith."

"KTF," Terry echoed.

Ivy left the library to return to work on Noble Firs analysis, leaving Terry to mull over his conversation with her. A quick knock made him look up. Moll entered the room and closed the door behind him. Terry turned to him, anxious about what his friend might say.

Striding over Moll pulled Terry to his feet and kissed him full on the mouth.

Terry was so surprised that he pulled away from Moll and looked at him questioningly.

"You love me," Moll said. "First twigged your feelings after the shooting in Portland. My fears held me back. I'm attracted to you too, but a part of me was afraid to take what appeared as a gigundo step."

"By moving into my world -- the world of the homosexual. Being gay doesn't have to be a radical departure. The extremes are too much for me. I'm Terry, a man who happens to prefer men."

Moll grabbed his hand. "Whatever. Now you are my man."

"Steve gave his nod of approval?"

"You misjudge him. Sure he's strong, but he isn't narrow. Like Ivy he is accepting. He cares about values such as honesty and loyalty."

"Fidelity, bravery, integrity," Terry said with a scoffing laugh. "I read about the FBI motto."

"Nowhere do the words say you need to be straight. Terry, I want you. A part of me always wanted you. I buried my tendencies my whole life. However with you my predisposition to be inclined towards men surfaced and did not go away."

"Is this about your death-defying experience where you now need another person in your life because you're alone?"

"While I did go through an experience, I came out feeling whole and free to be my own man. Not only do I understand who I am, but I also accept my true self. Under extreme pressure I measured up. Through my ordeal I found the courage to act. Now I am complete enough to be confident of who I am. I envision my future with you – house, marriage, a family."

"Whoa. Let's find out if we are right together first."

"We will be. You'll still be a determined asshole, and I'll continue to be a goofball, but we'll smooth the edges off of each other."

"I should take over the London office from Brian. Give you space to think this through."

"Too much thinking already. If you leave Portland, I'll move to be with you. For chrissakes, Terry, we're in our forties. What are we waiting for?"

A lop-sided grin lit up Moll's face in an endearing way. They would be here at Great Snoop Hall for some time yet. For now in this place of sanctuary, he and Moll might form a connection as more than friends.

"All right, but in front of the staff ..."

"As we did before, we act as business partners," Moll said. "But at times like this when we are alone, we get to be us as a couple."

While remaining concerned that Moll might yet regret his choice, Terry decided he would do his best to secure his love. He wrapped his arms around Moll. Placing one hand behind his head and the other on his lower back, he pulled Moll into their second kiss. This time he did not hold back. As they kissed he felt a growing passion for the goofy yet heroic man he held in his arms. This was their chance to find happiness and Terry intended to take full advantage of it.

When Terry poked his head into the kitchen a couple of nights later, Steve stood by the long stainless steel center island wiping his hands with a dishtowel.

"Hi Terry, Ivy is having a spa night in our room. I got tied up on the phone with the Chief and missed dinner."

"Not looking for Ivy. I came to talk with you."

"Want something to eat?" Steve asked, pointing at the food on the counter. "I make mean sandwiches."

"What's on for tonight? Your great Reubens by any chance?"

"Double Gloucester cheese melts with slices of naturally cured English ham and a smear of chutney, if you want it."

"Yeah, sure."

After opening up the double-wide fridge, Steve pulled out two bottles of ale and grabbed mugs off the shelf. "After the phone time I spent today, I earned this ale."

As soon as he slid the toasties under the broiler, he pulled a couple of plates out and tore lengths of paper towels for each of them. "These English cheeses are great," he said, as he rewrapped the cheese with care and checked the broiler, pulling out the tray with the toasted sandwiches.

They sat down on stools at the center work counter. Around a mouthful Steve asked, "What did you want to talk about?"

"Moll."

"Didn't things work out between you two?"

"They're better than I imagined, but I need your unfiltered perspective."

Steve put his sandwich down and regarded him. "You're worried the day will come when Moll will think he made a mistake."

"Yes."

"Everyone worries when they fall in love and want their heartfelt attachment to last forever, or at least the rest of their lives. I wondered why Ivy would want to marry an oversized, awkward geek like me and I still worry one day she will realize she made a mistake. All I can do is try to make her days with me happy ones and earn her continuing love."

"But this is bigger, different. You didn't make a major lifestyle adjustment with Ivy."

"I left the FBI for her."

"Was Ivy the only reason you took retirement?"

"Lots of reasons. Would I have left only for her? I only knew I didn't want to live without her."

"Moving from straight to homosexual is a hurdle for a guy. I'm worried Moll will regret his choice."

"He told me he perceived his tendencies from the time he was a young teen. The knowledge scared him, making him hide away from his homosexual leanings. More than anything Moll wanted to be accepted."

"In rescuing Brian and Lenny, he went through a sort of mystical experience. The glow may rub off."

"Moll used to freeze in our FBI field operations. Once when he froze in place, I pitched him overboard because the boat we raided was about to explode. The sequence of events in London forced Moll to find the courage inside himself to act. He also realized he possessed the grit to face leaving one man to die in the fire while saving the other one.

"Going back made Moll dig inside himself and face the worst. The change you are witnessing in Moll is confidence. This fundamental shift will stay with him. When challenged to save lives, he found himself more than equal to the task."

"He may love me?"

"Moll is a compassionate man. He would only move forward with you when he became certain. You are too much of a friend to him to risk losing. Terry, no certainties exist in love. Every day you must work at living as a couple. The risks are worth how much fuller your life will become. Why not take the chance and savor what Moll is offering you?"

Ginger-Pinger walked in and poised himself to jump up on Terry's lap. He shifted his stool back and the cat bounded up in a graceful arc. He pulled the reddish-gold ball of fur into his arms to enjoy his warmth and comforting purr. "With Mikael gone, I seem to have become his person-of-choice. Although he deserted me for Lenny last night."

"Animals can be tele-sympathetic. When Mathew was injured late in 2012, every time we went up to Ivy's house, the two corgis sat guard by him. Same with Ivy and me when we were shot the following summer. They sense injury or emotional upsets and try to do what they can."

Terry continued to stroke the purring cat. "Moll wants to be married at your place at Christmas with all the little white lights around us. Trying to put him off – think he is moving too fast."

"Not sure why you would wait, but you two decide. Ivy would have me stringing up all those lights in July if you choose a summer wedding." Steve glanced at Terry's untouched plate. "Let me reheat your sandwiches. They're not as tasty when they cool down."

Rubbing his chin along Ginger-Pinger's head and spine, Terry found the sensation reassuring. He bet Moll would like a puppy for Christmas or as a wedding present. Something silly, yet appealing and with curly hair. An Airedale might suit him. They could put a kennel for the puppy at the office to avoid leaving it alone all day.

Steve returned with the toasties hot once again from the broiler and said, "Accept the realities, Terry. Moll will always follow his own drummer. If he says he wants a relationship with you, believe him. Are you ready to make a commitment to Moll?"

Terry nodded. "You bet I am. Thanks, Steve. You helped me find the answer."

"You understood what you wanted. All I did was help you to become comfortable with your conclusion."

Chapter 58
Arielle

At the chateau in the Loire, Arielle occupied her father's old office which she was transforming with each visit to become more of her own. While he had left her mother a generous trust fund for income and life rights to the chateau, all his other property went directly to herself. The effort of rebuilding, streamlining and changing her father's legitimate and less savory enterprises wearied her. With every step she met resistance from the people in place who expected her to stick to her father's ways. Starting the previous month, she had begun changing the top-level men and women who resisted her authority the most, while rewarding those who shifted their loyalties to her.

Like her father she now traveled with bodyguards. They had arrived at the Loire estate with her and made themselves disappear, one moving into a small gatehouse and the other into an apartment over the garage. Today she needed to check in individually with Kazimír and Carlos, as none of them had time for a full conference call. She dialed Carlos, wanting to undertake the harder conversation first.

"Carlos? Arielle."

"I can't talk for long. Something is going on here."

"What?"

"More undercovers than usual around our ops. Sure they are out as streetpeople, utility van drivers, delivery men and so on, but the increase in numbers is suspicious.

"Alarming. Assume you are taking extra care."

"Call me if your people report anything similar. So you blew the capture of the Chinchilla, huh?"

"We nabbed him, but neither he nor that bodyguard – the Cougar – would talk. After my men had dropped their electronics at DHL, some plain-clothes agents raided the office and seized the package. Out at the old warehouse where my men took the Chinchilla and his protector, those same agents turned up. My guys scarpered right after lighting the explosives they had planted. Some daredevils risked the flames to rescue the Chinchilla and the other guy. They went to a nearby hospital where they stayed under heavy protection. My guys thought they recognized the Wild Hare and Tovey's girlfriend with the agents."

"And now?"

"Disappeared again. One of my men is watching the office and the apartment."

"You ever figure out who that girlfriend is of Tovey's?"

"No. Something about her is familiar, but I haven't figured out her identity yet. Too much else going on."

"What else?"

"Replacing uncooperative people here. You talk with Kazimír lately?"

"He called early yesterday, but we didn't connect. I gotta go. Text me if your people spot anything suspicious going on. Arielle?"

Carlos paused, and she waited to hear his question. When he continued his tone sounded full of despair, "Got a bad feeling about the business. How did all this get so complicated, so fast? Seems like only yesterday we were two kids bumming around Europe together. Daylight. I'm giving Daylight serious thought."

"We kept wanting to take over. Now the world accelerated. Some days I feel I can never get caught up. Let's give it another week to design our bail-out strategies and talk again"

"Watch out for yourself, Arielle. You're … a part of me."

Arielle was stunned by hearing this admission from Carlos, although she acknowledged they shared a close bond.

"You too, Carlos."

Arielle ended the call and stood in her office for a few moments feeling as if a windy vortex had caught her up and the security she used to know could be torn out of her grasp. Should she give it up, dump the illegal business lines and settle into a calmer life with the shops and the legal export channel? Her father had told her early on she was choosing a commitment for life when she wanted to take over all of his businesses. She had only been in control for a few months. Could she still walk away from the operations in the shadows and live safely?

Shaking herself back into action, she texted her two security guys to put them on a higher alert here and began calling her key leaders in Paris who ran the drugs, the three upscale houses of sensual pleasures and logistics. None of them had seen anything out of the ordinary, but each agreed to step up their security sweeps.

When she dialed Kazimír, his line flipped immediately to voice mail. Midway through leaving a message, a car slid to a stop in front of the house. Running to the high window, she peered around the edge of the thick frame. A black Citroen with all its doors open sat below her. From behind the house, she heard two shots. Pounding sounded on the front door.

While she shoved her laptop in her briefcase, Arielle dialed her mother at her art studio in a turreted tower on the east side of the Chateau. "*Maman, gendarmes. Être préparé. Fais attention. Je t'aime.*" Ending the call she grabbed her gun and swung out a bookcase where she opened a hidden door to a narrow staircase secreted into the side of the west tower. Stepping inside, she pulled the set of shelves back in place, took off her shoes and trotted down the curved stairs leading to the wine cellar. Her feet padded noiselessly on the stone steps

She paused and opened a small peephole by the front entry. The new maid stood wringing her hands by the open door. The police must have run by her. Arielle closed the slit and listened. Footsteps sounded above her. Outside another vehicle skidded to a halt. Although distressed at deserting her mother to the interrogations to follow, Arielle needed to escape to safety. Did someone in Paris squawk to save themselves?

Hurrying down to the wine cellar, she stopped but did not enter the vaulted room. Instead she opened a small door to a tunnel leading under the short back driveway to the garage and beyond to an old *fermier calvados* distillery where she kept an armored Peugeot SUV. Closing the door to the turret, she seized a heavy flashlight from the wall and sprinted down the underground alley, stopping to listen as she reached the stairs up to the garage. No noise came from above, but with the shots fired earlier, she couldn't risk surfacing here.

Instead she pressed on and entered an older passageway with a rougher floor made of old cobbles. Each time she visited the estate, she cleaned the walls of cobwebs and refreshed the rodent bait as her father had taught her. Afterward she would run down the full length, the way her father had trained her to do when he first introduced her to the hot side of his business operations. While the villagers might gossip about the old tunnels, no one knew for certain if they existed or where they led.

For nearly a kilometer the channel ran southeast, taking her behind a soft hill blocking the view of the old distillery from the house. The old stones chilled her feet as she ran. She slid her shoes back on, thankful to be dressed in a casual hoodie, jeans and deck shoes. Despite the exertion she shivered from the earthy chill underground. She jogged towards the distillery while trying to determine if she should jump into the SUV, crash through the old doors, and race away across the back of the old vineyard now or wait until nightfall.

Once she reached the end of the passageway, she grabbed her cell phone but found no signal. Should she warn Carlos and Kazimír? She would call them later after she sped safely away from the chateau towards a railway station about 20 kilometers distant. She stopped and listened. The old barn housing the distillery sat quietly above her. Slipping her shoes back off, she crept up the narrow stairs to the trap door in the floor of the old stone building. Once below it, she stopped again to listen. In the distance a tractor droned out in the field, while closer to her a few birds chirped in the apple trees.

Making each movement slow and deliberate, she cracked open the trapdoor and listened again. Hearing nothing more she pushed the heavy wooden door up enough to peer around. The SUV sat in front of her. The keys would be under the dashboard. She decided to bust out now before the gendarmes found the distillery. Squirming under the trapdoor, she slithered out on the floor, rose into a crouch and crept to the driver's door. After another pause to listen, she grabbed the handle, jerked the car door open, sprang up and jumped inside. She pulled the door softly into a shut position, grappled for the keys, found them and jammed them into the ignition.

In one quick motion, she started the Peugeot, threw it into gear and hit the accelerator. With a loud crack the old doors loomed and broke around her as the SUV burst into daylight. Two men with assault rifles jumped into shooting position on her right. She turned the wheel hard to the left just as shots bounced off the bullet-proof windshield. One shot penetrated the glass on the passenger side and hit her in the arm. Although she screamed out Arielle kept the car under control, eased off the gas and skidded on to the farm road. The Peugeot fishtailed and settled. She hit the gas and surged forward.

Additional shots hit the tires. The SUV began rocking. Arielle pressed on, wanting only to escape. The back window shattered as bullets sprayed through from what must be a large caliber sniper rifle. A deep pain exploded in the back of her head. She flew forward in her seat. Her foot jammed on the gas pedal as the trunks of the apple trees jumped towards the SUV. The world went red and then black.

Chapter 59
Brian

Once Maxim returned to Snoop Hall with Lenny during the second week following the inferno in the warehouse, Steve called a meeting in the middle of the afternoon for everyone but the rookie agents still on loan to them. Brian sat with his two partners in a line at the massive library table, with Nicola on his left and Ivy and Maxim sitting opposite them. With his leg elevated in his wheelchair, Lenny parked crosswise to the end of the table while Steve sat at the head ready to speak. Mikael had flown in that afternoon and came in with Steve, bringing his good-natured cheer to an on-edge group. Ivy pulled a chair out of the way so that Mikael could position himself between her and Lenny.

Slipping into the library with Mikael, Ginger-Pinger stalked around the room once before circling the table twice, as if trying to assess which person needed him the most. He stopped between Lenny and Mikael and sprang in a neat leap up to the table where he sat down at the corner, licking a paw. When Steve began to speak, the cat walked over, reached out and tapped Lenny's cast twice, then walked up it, tummy waddling from side to side. He settled on Lenny's lap but kept his eyes on Mikael.

"Here's the situation as of about an hour ago," Steve began without preamble. "Simultaneous actions occurred in Paris, Prague, Philadelphia, Chicago, Los Angeles, Caracas, Bogota, Mexico City, Singapore, Jakarta, Melbourne and Kyoto. They used our findings of the networks, decryption methods and decoding as the basis for collecting sufficient evidence to make arrests.

"In total fifteen gang leaders are either dead or incarcerated. Intelligence services acting with police units rounded up hundreds of goons, dealers, pushers, and technical staff. This is the largest international action in history, and it is the direct result of the breakthrough work accomplished here by all of you, Nick and the assigned agents. Each of us should be proud."

"What about the three after us – the so-called Norway sphere?" Moll asked.

"In Philadelphia Carlos Ochoa, the man behind the two hits out in Portland, was wounded. When out of the hospital, he will join his father in prison. He should be away for a long time.

"The French police killed Arielle Moreau, the woman after Nicola and Brian, earlier this afternoon. They nailed her when she tried to escape from her mother's home in the Loire Valley. Her father had been taken out in the arrest attempt last spring.

"The third one, Kazimír Horak, is more notable."

"What do you mean?"

"Kazimír called me here just over a month ago."

"You didn't tell us?" Moll asked.

"Apologies to each of you for not keeping you informed, but the situation was too delicate. Kazimír offered to make a deal, not unlike the one we made with those two rascals, the Fuentes cousins." Steve shifted his gaze to Nicola and Maxim and smiled. "Your deal inspired him. From my perspective your arrangement worked out well, except for Maxim's recent injuries."

"What about this Czech?" Maxim asked.

"Smart man, Kazimír. Although he never wanted to become involved, his father strong-armed him into learning about his business interests last winter. The paternal bully threatened the safety of Kazimír's wife and baby daughter to make him cooperate. His father was a real prick."

"How did he figure out he should call you?"

"Bit of a story. Kazimír wanted out, but he thought he needed to collect enough information about this New Age group of gangsters to bargain for the safety of his family. Turns out Kazimír penetrated the network sphere of the Nucleus and gathered all sorts of info on the operations out in Asia. He also stole into Arielle's London hotel room the day Brian spotted her tailing him. Once there he hacked into her laptop.

"On Arielle's laptop, he found photographs she had snapped of Nicola and Brian in Barcelona, and he thought he recognized you, Nicola. Using the snapshots from Arielle, he ran photo comparisons and figured out you might be Julio. That find led him to carefully study the history of the Fuentes case, starting with the shootout in the Albuquerque cemetery with the staged deaths of Julio and Cruze and working his way backward. Next he examined the raid resulting in the deaths of the brothers, Cristo and Eduardo. Then he went back further in time to the first staged death of Cruze in the op I did with Mathew down in Mexico City.

"Kazimír feared eventually Arielle would figure out who Nicola is, so he needed to act. Finding my name associated with the bust in the first staged death of Cruze, he began assembling the pieces and reconfirming facts. This information ultimately led to the call to me. Since Kazimír had reckoned that I engineered the deaths and witness protection program for at least one and possibly two Fuentes, he thought he might succeed in convincing me to help him make a pact with Interpol.

"After talking about Kazimír's proposal with the Chief, I took Brian into my confidence. Once Lenny arrived to guard him, he flew to Schiphol airport in Amsterdam for a clandestine meeting with Kazimír. Lenny understood only his role as Brian's protector."

All eyes moved over to Lenny and then to Brian.

"Nicola, your refusal to marry Brian and the whole kerfuffle with the baby helped us. While we were worried about any secret plans by Arielle to take out Brian, we needed him in London to negotiate with Interpol and British Intelligence."

"Brian, you put yourself in worse danger than I thought." Nicola said and reached across to grip his uninjured hand. "Once more you protected me. My sweet, noble man."

Brian colored at her compliment. "I wanted to safeguard you and keep us all safe. This offer from Kazimír added to the evidence we started accumulating. Since he gathered a spectrum of facts and insights used towards engineering the giant bust just accomplished, Interpol arranged for him and his family to be flown out of Prague yesterday. They are now in a Witness Protection Program, and they will live outside their native country under new identities.

"Kazimír agreed to serve as a roving operative with Interpol wherever he is needed doing a desk job in technology. He claims a high-tech career is all he ever wanted, but his father and his shady business dealings derailed him."

"What about us?" Maxim asked, pointing to Nicola and himself. "This Kazimír Horak discovered we are still alive and he likely learned the names we go under."

"Likewise you have equivalent knowledge of him and his family. They are recorded killed in an auto accident while fleeing Prague when the raids started. I would recommend that you assume new identities when you return to the United States."

"But he can find us if we are associated with you."

"I don't believe Kazimír will sell you out, if you are afraid he might," Brian said. "Steve and I will receive the new names and locations for him and his family. Like in your agreement, Interpol is demanding certain obligations including harming no one engaged in this action. One false step and he will be hunted down."

"My assessment of him says he is a decent man. If you go back through the transcripts of calls and other communications, never does he agree to any concrete action against any of us. While he listened, he did not support killing us. In fact he tried to refocus the other two on converting me to serve as their tool in money laundering."

"Leaves me kind of flat," Moll said. "Like what did we really accomplish here if some of us are still in danger?"

Lenny struggled up a little straighter in his wheelchair and let his gaze rove over each person. "We should not dwell on the negatives. Many, many perpetrators are no longer selling drugs, stealing data, enslaving teenagers, laundering money, whatever. Focus on our achievements. Our direct enemies – the Triad -- are neutralized."

While his eyes remained fierce after his rare outburst, Lenny settled back in his wheelchair.

Chastised, Moll asked, "When's the champagne?"

"Toast before dinner," Steve said. "The best in the cellar. I hope Nicola will risk one of her tiny sips. Nicola and Maxim, first the Chief personally extended his appreciation to you two. The inputs you gave on the photographs of suspected underworld figures contributed to the mounting cases against the criminals rounded up. Your new identity packets arrived this morning," Steve said and handed over two envelopes. "From this moment forward with what we hope will be a last name change, you will be known as Caroline and Charles or Charlie. Last names of Martin and Barton respectively."

Brian reached over and touched the envelope held by Nicola or Caroline as he corrected himself, pleased that she could disappear once more and hoping this was her last change of name but one – she would take his name of Tovey in a few weeks.

Maxim slid a hand over his envelope and gave a deep sigh.

Mikael reached out held up his hand for a hi-five. "Way to go, Charlie!" he said.

After returning the hi-five, Charlie said, "Thank you, Steve. Having the freedom to go back to the United States means more than either I or Caroline can say."

"You each earned it," Steve said. "We'll wrap up here in the next few days, but first, I want to share another bit of news with Brian, Moll, Terry and Mikael." Steve said. He studied the three men sitting in a row together at the long library table and then flicked his glance over to Mikael.

"What's the news?" Brian asked.

"Provided you are interested, this Friday you are scheduled for back-to-back presentations of your Noble Firs software and analysis methods to British Intelligence and Interpol. On Monday you will do the same for a group at the FBI in D.C.

"Mikael, they would like you to team up with these three to provide consultation on how banking transactions might be altered in transit, such as by the Oblivious Ram method you mentioned. That is if all four of you are comfortable working together.

"While too early to be certain, I think each organization wants to license the Noble Firs software and put all four of you on a retainer for training and consulting services. You will need to negotiate the terms, but I would say you could be awarded three multi-million dollar contracts."

The four men exchanged glances in disbelief, like they did not trust their windfall.

"Fucking A," Moll shouted.

"Double Fucking A," Terry echoed.

"I third – Triple Fucking A." Brian said jubilantly but as a thought occurred to him, his smile turned into a frown. "How will this impact our work for the banks?"

"What do you want the change to mean for your clients?" Steve asked.

"I'm damn tired of being shot at, fearing for my life, taken off to warehouses, whatever. I'll soon need to consider my family." Brian grasped Nicola's hand again.

"Me too," Moll said, gripping Terry's hand and holding their joined hands up. "If I'm lucky."

"After we talk this over, perhaps we can lay out a way to allow the banks to license the software for a nominal fee from the government organizations," Brian said, looking at his two partners.

"You mean give up our consulting work?" Moll asked.

"We would do training and audit the results, but the findings will be from the governments or the banks themselves. We would be out of the dangerous part. This is me brainstorming. The three of us will meet, come up with a plan and present our proposals to our board. I don't want to be in the line of fire anymore."

"None of us do," Moll said.

Ivy leaned forward, her green eyes aglow in the way they became when finding something of interest to her. When she spoke she fell back on her business voice. "Think about retaining the rights to the Noble Firs software for use with other types of analysis, such as compliance or billing or whatever. That would give you different areas to consult in, without the high risks of unearthing money laundering operations. You might be able to give your company and your employees a safe and profitable future. I can help you to think that through if you like."

"We'll need something to do besides enjoy our millions." Terry said. "Our idle brains would drive us all crazy. But we haven't heard from Mikael. What do you say to hooking up with us on this?"

Mikael pounded the table in the way he did in celebration. "I say quadruple Fucking A."

"Thanks Steve," Brian said. "When I say how much we appreciate this opportunity, I think I speak for each of us. You are opening up new channels of distribution -- ones we never considered. Now we need to decide how to best capitalize on this potential business and what the future of Noble Firs will be."

Charlie nodded and smiled at them. "If anyone can figure this out, you four can. Remember to save time to savor life."

Pushing back his chair, Steve rose. "Terry, if you can spare us from Noble Firs work, Ivy and I will break away for a few days starting tomorrow to go where we will be away from money laundering, criminals and friends getting shot. That will give you time on your own to talk these opportunities through and to make the pitches in London – I'll email you the logistics.

"We'll see you all back here late Saturday. Departures on Sunday. With Maxim's insightful advice to savor the joys of living, let's hit the champagne around six tonight."

Looking somewhat tired, Steve helped Ivy scoot her chair back and together they left the room. Even so Brian could tell that given a couple of good nights of sleep, Steve would reflect with satisfaction their achievements.

"Caroline, Charlie," Lenny said as he backed up his wheelchair slowly to keep Ginger-Pinger steady in his lap, "I think we should leave these entrepreneurs to talk about the future of their Noble Firs Company and how they and Mikael will work together."

After Caroline, Charlie and Lenny departed, the four men sat still, letting the news of the opportunities they were offered sink in. Moll spoke first.

"Brian, since you kicked off the brainstorming, how about we start recording uncensored ideas as fast as we think them by keying them into a laptop? We have about an hour before the fizz-biz. Terry, you and I will take turns keying as we talk. For right now no idea is too wild or too risky. The only stupid notion is the one you don't bring up."

Terry grabbed Moll's laptop, connected the projector, opened a new document and started keying. The text on the screen was entitled, *The Four Fucking A List,* and included Brian's initial ideas first, added Ivy's on new business lines and then Terry listed an item with a question mark, *Need a Telecom Expert -- Fourth Noble Fir for Future Endeavors?* Each of his partners nodded, and Mikael again pounded the table.

Over the last five months, each of their lives had changed and would continue to evolve. Brian, Moll and Terry loved and they would marry. They would move from entrepreneurs to established businessmen, and they would grow into their new lives. Each of them could embrace the changes because they had each other to rely on.

As different as they were from each other, they shared common values, goals and attributes of character. Together they would move forward, work hard and thrive. Adding Mikael to their team would only strengthen their company as they changed their logo to show a fourth Noble Fir.

Epilogue
Callie, Ivy, Mathew, Charlie & Steve
Holiday Season, December 2016

To Caroline/Brian & Terry/Moll – On Your Marriages

As you begin your journeys into your new lives, may you look back in this photo album to savor the memories of your joint weddings and a few key moments before. Now that you have found the loves of your lives, you will begin to live afresh. Take a time each day to show your life partner your love, respect and joy. Little times can mean as much and sometimes more as significant events. Savor each one.

Our lives have become so intertwined with each other, none of us can imagine moving forward without the others. We have raised numerous glasses of champagne, pinot noir and ale together in celebration, in satisfaction and in solace. Often we have shared our concerns, woes, secrets and wishes over cups of tea, mugs of coffee and sometimes demitasses of steaming hot chocolate. Always we seem to be relishing a delicious meal or tasty snack together.

Now we all stand at a time of transformation. For the four of you, the changes will come as you settle into your new lives in your homes above Portland. Our hearts are warmed by keeping Ivy's house in the family with Moll and Terry living there and with Caroline and Brian settling nearby in Portland Heights.

Brian and Caroline's lives will change dramatically with the arrival of their twins. For Mathew and Callie the changes will come a month or so later when their son is born at the beginning of June. Moll and Terry will begin to search for surrogate mothers to pass their creative minds on to their children.

For Ivy and Steve this will be a time of growing affections both now and when your families expand. As Charlie joins our merry band, we look forward to seeing the house he plans to build up on the drier side of the Cascades. We each hope he has a couple of comfy guest rooms where we can escape the dreary rains of winter. Likewise we hope to entice Mikael, the fourth Noble Fir, to spend more time with us.

May you enjoy this compendium of memories from your wedding day and from the unforgettable times leading up to them. Ivy snapped the surprise on Terry's face when his father had a last-minute change of heart and offered to walk him up the aisle. Steve snuck around and took shots of a sedately raucous bachelor gathering and a merry laugh-fest of a bachelorette party.

Who would have thought we would see Charlie strike the pose of a matador? Lenny play an air guitar in a wheelchair? Or Mikael slide down a banister? Did we imagine Brian's mother leading us in a Congo line? We are all thankful that the bunny-hop did not make an appearance, but our sweet Susannah did get us up for the hokey-pokey. When was the last time we laughed that hard?

These were our third and fourth weddings here at Spook Hills, and we hope to host more celebrations as the years pass, with summer events at Callie and Mathew's house and winter ones at Ivy and Steve's. Life has its down times, and our lives have known danger. Even so we are skilled at healing and at moving forward. A bit of the hedonistic pagan lives in each of us to lead us from gloom to celebrate joys, victories, accomplishments and life's milestones.

When you return from your honeymoons, Ivy and Steve will be off on a revitalizing walking and photography winter adventure in Japan. Soon after Mathew, Callie and Susannah will be exploring the wonders of Hawaii from coasts to mountains to volcanoes to waterfalls.

All of us will look forward to the renewal of spring and the upcoming years of growth in our lives, our families, our vineyards and our business interests. Always we have each other in a growing circle of friendship. The bonds we share will forever keep us together in our hearts, our minds and our souls.

May your lives resonate with laughter and love!

The End

49394480R00179

Made in the USA
Middletown, DE
15 October 2017